Praise for *Some Boys*

"A bold and necessary look at an important, and very real, topic. Everyone should read this book."
—Jennifer Brown, author of *Thousand Words* and *Hate List*

"Blount hits home with this novel… *Some Boys* belongs in every YA collection."
—*School Library Journal*

"A largely sensitive treatment of an emotionally complex topic."
—*Kirkus Reviews*

Praise for *Nothing Left to Burn*

"An authentic, fast-paced romance with emotional intensity to burn."
—Huntley Fitzpatrick, author of
The Boy Most Likely To and *My Life Next Door*

"A heartbreaking novel—real and full of hope."
—Miranda Kenneally, author of
Coming Up for Air and *Defending Taylor*

Praise for *Send*

"Blount's debut novel combines authentic voice with compelling moral dilemmas…raise[s] important questions about honesty, forgiveness, the ease of cyberbullying, and the obligation to help others."

—*VOYA*

"A morality play about releasing the past and seizing the present…the ethical debates raised will engage readers."

—*Publishers Weekly*

Praise for *TMI*

"Blount has a good handle on teen culture, especially the importance of social media…realistically expressed…[and] honestly portrayed."

—*School Library Journal*

"[A] tech-driven cautionary tale… Blount addresses the potential perils of online relationships and the sometimes destructive power of social media without proselytizing."

—*Publishers Weekly*

ALSO BY PATTY BLOUNT

Send
TMI
Some Boys
Nothing Left to Burn

THE WAY IT HURTS

THE WAY IT HURTS

THE WAY IT HURTS

THE WAY IT HURTS

THE WAY IT HURTS

THE WAY IT HURTS

THE WAY IT HURTS

PATTY BLOUNT

sourcebooks
fire

Published by Sourcebooks Fire, an imprint of Sourcebooks, Inc.
P.O. Box 4410, Naperville, Illinois 60567-4410
(630) 961-3900
Fax: (630) 961-2168
www.sourcebooks.com

Library of Congress Cataloging-in-Publication data is on file with the publisher.

Printed and bound in the United States of America.
VP 10 9 8 7 6 5 4 3 2 1

For Kimberly Sabatini, a gifted author in her own right,
who inspired and helped me explore
the idea that became this story.

ELIJAH

Ride Out
@ride_out

862 FANS

@Ride_On747: Hey, gr8 cover of Simple Man. You guys rock!

@BroadwayBaby17: OMG, these lyrics are so incredibly sexist! Girls aren't really impressed by your "pogo sticks"! *barfs*

@Ride_On747: Beotch, go back to drama club and leave metal to the boyz! These guys rock!

2 LIKES 4 SHARES

A crash followed by a scream sent a shiver of worry down my spine—a sharp high C that totally fractured the new melody stuck in my head, scattering the chord progression I was just about to lay down. I was on my feet out of pure instinct, laptop sliding to my bed, guitar following with a *thunk*. The screen shifted to my band's listing on the Beat, a website that did nothing but taunt me with its pathetic statistics.

New Fans: 2

Yay. Now we had 862.

I flew down the stairs where I found Anna wrestling with Dad over the splintered remains of the cookie jar.

"No!" she cried and kept trying to break free, hands grabbing for the cookies scattered among the shards of pottery. Dad's face was red from the effort, and his graying hair stood out on end. Anna was strong when she was in a mood like this.

I grabbed an ice pop from the freezer and held it near her face. "Anna! Anna, chill out—look. Look what I have for you." I pitched my voice higher than her wails but kept up a singsong cadence to calm her down. Anna adored music.

Like me.

"Want this?"

"Want!"

"Okay, be calm, and you can have it, okay?" I met Dad's blue eyes over Anna's head. She'd inherited the same eyes. Mine were brown, like Mom's. He jerked his head toward the family room, and I nodded. I walked backward, dangling the ice pop at her. Dad didn't let go until she was safely in the middle of the room, well away from the broken jar. I let Anna have the treat, and he blew out a loud sigh, stretching his arms up over his head until things cracked and popped.

"You okay?"

"Yeah," he said on a grunt. "Just a cramp. She's so damn strong."

I nodded. I still had a bruise from a similar tantrum last week. Anna was thirteen now, almost as tall as me and definitely as strong. I left him in charge of Anna and her ice pop and returned to the scene of the crime. I picked up the largest pieces of pottery and tossed them into a bag. Where was Linda? She was supposed to be here until four thirty, and that wasn't for twenty more minutes.

"Oh no!"

I lifted my head and found Mom in the door from the garage, clutching a pair of grocery sacks, hair half falling out of the clip on top of her head. She had sunglasses on, but I could see the pucker on her forehead behind them. She loved that stupid pig cookie jar. She'd had it as long as I could remember.

"Where is she?"

"Family room with Dad. I gave her an ice pop."

"Oh, God. I just cleaned in that room!"

"Mom, I didn't know how else to distract her. She was standing in the middle of the broken pieces."

The lines around Mom's lips deepened, but she nodded and tried to smile. "It's okay. I'll get her into the tub."

I studied her face for clues about what she was really thinking because she didn't sound like it was okay at all. Mom did stuff like that a lot... said one thing, but meant something else. She put the groceries on the counter and stared at the scene of the crime, sighing loudly. She took off her sunglasses, folded them, put them inside their case, zippered them into her pocketbook, and then hung that on a hook inside the broom closet. You had to do things like that to Anna-proof stuff.

Mom looked…old. The lines on her face were etched deep, and she wore no makeup to hide them. Her hair was grayer than Dad's now, even though she was three years younger than he was. With a start, I realized I didn't know how old that was. I was seventeen. I think she was twenty-eight when I was born. So Mom was forty-five and Dad was forty-eight.

That wasn't that old, was it?

She disappeared into the family room. Ten seconds later, the arguing started, and I fell back against a cabinet with a sigh.

"What the hell do you want me to do?" Dad said.

"Watch her, Nathan. I want you to watch her—like I do."

"I *was* watching her, Steph."

"Not very well, or she wouldn't have broken the damn cookie jar!"

I clenched my jaw and grabbed the broom and dustpan, swept up the rest of the mess, and scooped it into the trash bag. I was going over the floor with a damp cloth, hoping to pick up whatever small shards still remained, when Dad stalked back into the kitchen.

"I got this. Go."

"But I—"

"Elijah! I said I got it."

Fine. I hoped he was planning to deal with the groceries too, because that was what I was about to tell him. The family room was empty, except for the bright red stain on the coffee table. Guess Mom was already strip-ping Anna out of her clothes and getting her cleaned up. I headed back to my room, where the laptop on my bed called to me.

Music was peace to me—sanity in all the chaos Anna caused. Aw, hell, that wasn't fair. Anna couldn't help it and I knew that. I tried so damn hard not to hold it against her, but with Mom and Dad fighting so much, it wasn't easy. Whenever I had the chance, I escaped with a guitar and a computer or my headphones.

I tapped my email program, hoping to find a few replies to the messages I'd sent trying to secure some gigs for the band. Any gigs would work, but paying ones would be even better. Dad kept pushing and nagging me to visit colleges and whatnot, but I figured if Ride Out hit big, I wouldn't need college, and then I'd be around to help my parents with Anna.

I scrolled through my inbox. Not a single reply.

Damn.

With a sigh, I raked both hands through my hair. I clicked over to our website and checked stats. Views were up today—that was good news. The YouTube channel also had some traffic. The latest cover we'd posted was generating some clicks—always a good thing. I logged into the Beat, a network for musicians like me, and crawled through the comments.

Ride Out was hard rock, not pop. So, yeah, we didn't attract mainstream fans, but the fans we did have were vocal and loyal. I grinned when I saw the latest comment from some chick calling herself BroadwayBaby17. She *hated* our stuff. Said our sound was just noise and what words she could make out in our lyrics were misogynistic and disrespectful. Like we gave a fuck. I didn't know why she bothered to click any of it, but she did and then tried to give us shit about it that she claimed was *feedback*. I had to admit, she knew technique, but if her scene was Broadway, there was no way she'd *ever* get what Nick, Sam, and I were trying to do with Ride Out. I mean, anyone who went to a Metallica show expecting Michael Bublé was bound to be disappointed, right?

And vice versa.

Sure enough, BroadwayBaby17 wiped the floor with our latest cover.

BroadwayBaby17: Someone explain to me why growling into a microphone is considered talent 'cause I'm just not seeing it. (Can't hear anything right now either. LOL.)

> **BroadwayBaby17:** OMG, these lyrics are so incredibly sexist! Someone tell these guys girls aren't really impressed by your "pogo sticks" *barfs*

> **BroadwayBaby17:** Boom, boom, boom. That's all this band does is play percussion like it's sex. *sighs* Sex and drums, drums and sex. BORING.

Another user named Ride_On747 crawled up BroadwayBaby17's ass: Beotch, go back to drama club and leave metal to the boyz! These guys rock!

6

Thank you, Ride_On747! He was a huge fan of ours. Neither user had a photograph in their profile, so I didn't know if they were male or female. It was kind of obvious that BroadwayBaby17 was a girl because of the way she always harped on us. Our lyrics were sexist, our beat was too primal, and our sound was too noisy.

Whatever.

But Ride_On747 was always there to take BroadwayBaby17 down a peg. I grinned and sent the brother a mental high five. Don't like us; don't listen. Easy.

I logged in using my personal account FretGuy99. This was mine; I didn't post band stuff from that account. The band's account was Ride_Out. I liked keeping them separate. We all had the password, but it was usually Sam or me doing most of the band's postings.

Looked like he'd just posted.

Ride_Out: Hey, BB! You ever shredded a guitar? You ever cut loose with a metal scream? You ever play any original stuff at all? Until you can say yes to any of those questions, you got no right telling us we suck so _|_.

Oh, crap! He'd given her the Internet version of the middle finger.

> **BroadwayBaby17:** OMG, so mature. If you can't take criticism, get off the forums. This is a place for serious artists.

Okay, time for me to make an appearance.

FretGuy99: BroadwayBaby17, you only think people like you are artists. You're elitist. You can't respect anyone who takes a different view.

> **BroadwayBaby17:** Not elitist. Just telling it like it is. Dude, don't suck up to Ride_Out. Take my advice and study classical guitar before you ruin your chances of being original.

My phone buzzed. Dude, I am going to rip this chick a new one for the trash she's talking about us.

I texted back. Relax. Let her dig her own grave.

FretGuy99: I have studied classical guitar. I can play lead or rhythm. I can strum chords, and I'm hella good at fingerpicking. I can play it all, baby. Just because I want to play metal doesn't mean I have no talent. So shut up about shit you don't know anything about and go shopping or something.

> **BroadwayBaby17:** And there's the sexism! I didn't say anything about you having no talent. I just don't like Ride Out.

> **FretGuy99:** Then why the hell are you here on a heavy metal forum? Go back to the show tunes forum!

My phone buzzed. The shopping bit was clutch, dude. LMAO!

8

I shrugged. She had it coming.

Sam changed the subject. Nick wants us 2C North's play tonight. Said we'd B there. 7 PM.

Hell. I raked my hair off my face. Sitting through some boring school play for a school I didn't even attend was just about the worst way to spend a Friday night. But it was for Nick, so yeah—I'd go. Nick and Sam were more than just guys in the band. They were my brothers. Not a lot I wouldn't do for either of them.

I used to believe it was only a matter of time before our band took off. But years had gone by, and we were still begging for birthday parties and sidewalk fair gigs. It hadn't happened—despite YouTube and the Beat and our website, despite our outrageous sound, we still hadn't broken out. We needed something provocative, something that could put us on the map *today*. A knot swelled, rose up in my throat while I swiped through the screens, trying to think of that something—

What the hell was this? I clicked a link in my news feed and found an ad for the county summer festival. I skimmed the text, and my heart took off like a snare drum when I saw the sponsors: Island Sound and WLIS FM radio. *Looking for musical acts with style, substance, and that certain unique X factor.*

I frowned and thought it over for a couple of minutes. Festivals like this wanted feel-good music, and that's not what Ride Out was about. We weren't pop rock. We were head-banging heavy metal hard rock, and people didn't want to take their preschoolers to hear bands like us. Then again...yeah. There were songs we could cover that would get festivalgoers of all ages clapping along. It just wouldn't be *our* stuff. Seeger. Lynyrd Skynyrd. Mellencamp. Maybe some classic Zeppelin.

But if it worked, if it got us a gig and that led to another, maybe record labels like Island Sound would call us.

A splash and a shout from the bathroom pulled me away from my texts. I put my gadgets down and headed across the hall. Anna loved water. For some reason, water play soothed her and made her laugh. Ms. Meyer, my guidance counselor, said that some children with my sister's sort of issues are terrified by their surroundings because they don't have the capacity to understand them. Water play, she says, allows Anna to relax her often-tense body, plus it helps teach her about the world. We didn't have a pool, but there was a huge sunken bathtub in my parents' bathroom. Mom let Anna sit in it until she pruned.

Some days, it was the only way to get her to stop screaming.

I opened the door, peeked around it, and found my sister already in her favorite red bathing suit, up to her armpits in water.

"Eli." She held out both arms and let them drop, all but drowning Mom in the process.

Anna's verbal skills were pretty low, but she could say my nickname clear as a bell. I grinned. "Hey, Anna Banana. Hey, Mom."

"Elijah. Can you take over? I've got to get dinner going."

"Sure." I sat on the marble edge of the tub built into the corner of the room. Mom smiled, ran a towel over her face, and left before Anna could notice. "Are you better now?"

Anna smiled up at me but didn't answer. She didn't like talking to people, but when I talked to her, she seemed to like it. It was hard to tell how much she actually understood though, because she didn't usually respond, except to smile. So I kept talking. "I hope so."

She splashed me and smiled again.

I grabbed two cups from the sink and showed her how to pour water from one to the other. This always fascinated her. She tried to grab the water and giggled when it poured through her fingers. From experience I knew this could just as easily piss her off, but for now, she was happy, her huge blue eyes soft and wide with wonder. She handed me a cup of water. Slowly, I tipped it over and let it spill over her hand. She laughed and splashed me and then held out her arms.

"Eli."

"Do you want to get out and dry off?"

Her forehead puckered. "Eli." She grabbed the cup out of my hand and threw it into the water. "Eli."

Crap. She wanted me in the tub with her. Mom hated this. Said it wasn't right for teenage siblings to take baths together. Since Anna was wearing a bathing suit, I didn't consider it *taking a bath*. I glanced at the door. *Fuck it.* I emptied my pockets onto the sink, kicked off my shoes, and peeled off my shirt. When I lifted one leg over the edge of the tub, Anna clapped.

The water was warm, and the spa's bubble jets were off—they scared Anna. I sat opposite Anna and grabbed the cup she'd tossed. She found the other and tried to drink from it.

"No, Anna. Look at me." I poured the water over my hand and tried to catch the stream. Then I poured water from my cup into hers, watching her bright eyes follow every drop. I swallowed hard. It was tough watching her try to process simple physics like this. It was like part of her *wanted* to learn, was desperate to know what was happening in the world around her, but another part of her jealously guarded the first part, growling and barking at everything that tried to get by. The two sides of her mind were at war. I always thought that was why she sometimes exploded.

I wasn't a doctor though. I only knew what she liked. And the frown between her eyebrows said she was tired of cups of water. I took one of the cups, flipped it upside down, and put it against my leg. I started tapping out a beat on the bottom of the cup, amplified by my wet jeans. Anna watched the movement. This was something she could do—something she liked to do. I waited until she copied me with the other cup.

Tap. Tap. Tap.

Ever since my first guitar lesson when I was about seven years old, I'd been hearing how special I was, how much talent I had. I think it must be in our genes because I sure as hell wasn't the only musician in the family. Anna not only had impeccable timing, she had an ear for the musical scale. She couldn't always manage the words, but she could hit the notes. She tapped out a strong, steady rhythm, I added in the downbeat, and then I started to sing Van Morrison's "Brown Eyed Girl." Anna watched my lips, smiling when I got to her favorite part. I hoped she'd sing with me. It was a good song for her because it was in her range. So I sang it to her every day.

It was our thing.

"La la la."

I grinned. There it was. Perfect pitch, baby. "High five, Anna." I held up a palm, and she hit it with a happy shriek.

The bathroom door opened. "Elijah! What have I told you about bathing with your sister? People think it's weird."

"Mom, she's dressed. I'm dressed. What's the big deal?" I rolled my eyes. "People won't know if we don't tell them. Besides, it calms her." I subtly pulled the tub's plug so Anna wouldn't notice and stood up.

"Oh, Eli, those jeans are going to take forever to dry." Mom took a towel off the rack and handed it to me. Anna noticed the water draining and started her protest.

I ran the towel over my body and kept singing our song. Anna stopped her complaints and obediently stood up when I held out my arms to her. I wrapped her in a towel and dried her fast. She liked when I did that.

"Okay, okay, out you go. Say bye to Eli, Anna. Time to put clothes on."

"Bye."

I laughed, grabbed my stuff, and headed to my room, anxious to peel off the wet denim, grab some dinner, and then get my guitar. Nick and Sam were counting on me to come up with a new arrangement for our next post, and so far, I had nothing.

"Yes…uh-huh…that's right. She's thirteen."

Dad was on the phone.

"No. No, there hasn't been any improvement, and that's one of the reasons I called you. Definitely… A big problem."

The door to my parents' room was open. I hovered in the hall, listening to him talk to some faceless person on the phone about my sister…about his *daughter*…as a problem. Who the hell was it? One of Anna's doctors?

"Oh. Yes. That would be good… From a list of referrals. Yes, that's right… Well, we're looking at several facilities, but yours was the most highly recommended. Great… Let's set that up as soon as possible… I honestly don't think we can take care of her much longer."

A shiver ran up my back, and even though I'd made a puddle on the thick carpet in the hallway, I stayed rooted exactly where I was, Dad's words repeating in my head.

Facilities.

A big problem.

Take care of her.

The bathroom doorknob twisted, startling me out of my daze. I bolted to my room and locked the door, shivering in my wet clothes while Anna sang "La, la, la" in her room across the hall.

"Goddamn it, Eli! You've left a puddle out here!" Mom pounded on my door.

I opened my mouth but couldn't squeeze any words out. I just slid to the floor on my side of the door, pressing the soaking wet towel to my mouth to hide the sobs.

2

KRISTEN

Kristen Cartwright
@kristencartwright

Tweets	Following	Followers
6,894	**735**	**1,198**

@kristencartwright
Ugh. Stupid email. Why won't it come?

I clicked through the website that showed smiling faces of successful students, and my mouth watered… It literally watered. This summer, I'd be spending four weeks, four incredible weeks in New York City, studying drama, voice, dance—oooh, maybe even production. I'd be living on campus, studying with the greats, seeing Broadway performances, and going to museums.

I checked my email again—still nothing.

When were they going to let me know?

Sighing heavily, I checked the calendar again. All it said was sometime this week. I crossed my arms and blew hair out of my eyes. Didn't they know how *important* this was? Didn't they understand entire *lives* were getting planned around this decision?

Oh, God!

I sounded just like Etta. And then I rolled my eyes because Etta would raise one eyebrow and demand to know just what was so wrong about a girl sounding like her favorite grandmother?

Groaning, I shut down the computer. I couldn't keep watching the inbox for news. I had a show to prepare for. I decided to change clothes, grabbing some yoga pants and a top from the pile of clean laundry on my dresser. Yeah, I had to put all that stuff away before Dad had a cow.

Later.

Headphones. *Check.*

Towel. *Check.*

Water. *Check.*

Mirror. *Check.*

I jogged downstairs to the basement, carefully holding the full-length mirror that usually hung on the inside of my closet door. I set it up horizontally, leaning it against the washer and dryer, then took a few steps back to gauge the visibility.

Yeah, it worked.

I tied my hair up, plugged in earbuds, and let the soundtrack from *Cats* fill me up. Tonight was opening night. I let the tingles wash over me for a moment. God, I loved that feeling! I was Victoria—the White Cat. Well, kitten, really. Victoria was young and immature, which I was using as my motivation.

I performed Victoria's solo once, twice, a third time—each time, making sure I nailed every mark and every emotion. Etta always says the mark of a gifted performer isn't what she shows, but what she makes you *feel*. I wanted the audience to feel the show. I wanted them crying.

Ninety minutes later, I was dripping sweat and so hungry, my belly sounded louder than my singing voice. I couldn't really eat though. Not yet. I chugged some more water and headed back upstairs, carefully rehanging the mirror on its hooks.

Don't break. Please don't break. Not tonight.

Okay. Phew! I grabbed fresh clothes and headed for the shower. Then I stopped. I turned back and studied my laptop. There was an email in there. I could just feel it. *Tingles.* Okay. Breathe. You're in. Of course you're in. I booted up, waited, and opened the inbox.

There it was.

The Tisch summer program.

More tingles. I opened the message, wondering when I'd get to meet my new roommate and—

Oh my God.

I read the message again.

The tingles faded to nausea.

Dear Kristen, We regret to inform you that…

Oh my God. Oh my God! I…I'd been rejected.

I fell onto my bed, both hands pressed to my mouth to muffle the sobs. I didn't get in. Not special enough, the message said. *Not special enough.*

Tears dripped through my fingers onto the pillow. I sobbed for minutes—hours? I didn't keep track—while those words drilled all the way into my heart. Not special enough? Seriously? I sing, dance, and act—a triple threat according to Etta.

Footsteps coming up the stairs had me cringing. *Oh, please don't be Mom. Don't be Mom.* The feet stopped at my door, and I grabbed tissues, quickly blotting and blowing and wiping away all traces of tears.

"Kristen?"

I swallowed and pitched my voice to its usual speaking cadence. "Not dressed!"

"Oh. Well, hurry up! You don't have much time before the curtain goes up." The footsteps faded away back down the stairs, and I sagged in relief. How was I going to tell them? Mom, Dad. Etta. My brothers? Tisch's summer program was supposed to be the shining spot on my applications to Julliard, Berklee, Peabody, and the Boston Conservatory, and without it—

"Kristen! Hurry up!"

I wanted to crawl into my bed and pull the covers over my face. I wanted to turn back time and repeat my application. But I had a show to do tonight. Even though I was *not special enough*, that show had to go on. I scrubbed both hands over my face, pulled myself to the bathroom, splashed water over my face, and changed my clothes. By the time I got downstairs, I'd found my motivation…I just wouldn't tell them. There had to be some other way to impress the college admissions people.

I had to find it.

I had to.

3

ELIJAH

Ride Out
@ride_out

862 FANS

Ride_Out: Hey, @Ride_On747, thanks, man! Glad you liked it.

The darkness hummed, and the audience held its breath. A circle of light found the figure on the stage, and beside me, Nick leaned forward, lips parted, eyes forward.

I shifted my gaze and tried to see what was so friggin' special about Leah Russo and shrugged in the dark. Okay, yeah, she was hot under the rags of her theater costume, but so were a dozen other girls on the stage tonight. Hotter still were the girls who came to hear our band play. As far as I was concerned, no girl was worth the time away from our music—except Anna. But, like I said…this was for Nick, so it didn't matter what I thought. We were here, wasting a Friday night numbing our asses on crappy auditorium seats for him. Hope he at least gets laid after this.

I shifted in my broken seat, wondering how many more minutes of the hell that was Bear River High School North's production of *Cats* I'd have to endure. My fingers itched for my guitar and notepad. Melodies played in my head, begging to be put down on paper, and there were a dozen other things we should have been doing to promote Ride Out so we could get the band some notice.

I gulped back panic when I thought of us…the future. I hadn't told the guys yet about my dad's plans to put Anna in a home. I hadn't even told them about the festival or my plan for our band to go mainstream so we could guarantee ourselves a spot on the ticket.

The music rose. Beside me, Nick sucked in a breath. I didn't know Leah. Nick met her at a concert a few months back, and they'd been hanging out whenever they could because, Nick claimed, Leah was the One.

I hid half a laugh and shook my head. I didn't get the whole concept of the One, but I'd help Nick get what he wanted.

Leah raised her face. When she opened her mouth, I sat up a little straighter. Her voice… Jesus, it was astounding. Clear. Strong. Powerful but sweet. I watched and listened, the audience around me fading away.

21

Her voice swelled, and she attacked the high notes without hesitating, making goose bumps jump out of my skin. What was the top note of her range? She glided across the stage; she never struggled or stumbled. The audience waited for the crescendo, and when she reached it, holy God, it was like a…a promise kept. She blew me away. The notes faded out, and the rest of the production was a blur. I had no idea Leah could sing like that and couldn't take my eyes off—

My best friend's girl. *Shit.*

I glanced at Nick sitting next to me, but he didn't look pissed off. He looked…confused.

"Dude!" Sam reached over me and punched Nick's arm. "Why the hell didn't you tell us your girl could sing like that?"

Nick just stared at Leah and shook his head. "I…I didn't know."

The lights came up, and everybody got to their feet, applauding like mad. Nick held up this lame poster board sign he'd made. I used that time to get my hormones under control and put Leah and her amazing voice out of my head. The rest of the cast assembled on the stage for their curtain call, and I locked eyes with one of the actors— the White Cat. She was incredibly hot—a solid body with an impressive rack. Her solo dance was the best part of the show up until Leah's song. She looked amazing in that white cat suit. So freakin' hot.

"Ladies and gentlemen, a moment please." A teacher walked to the right of the stage and waved her hands. "Thank you all for attending our opening night performance! I am so proud of these kids. They made all their own costumes and designed the set themselves. And tonight, I want to share with you an amazing last-minute change-up to our program. Grizabella, played by Leah Russo, is ill and was unable to sing this evening. Her songs were actually sung by our White Cat, played by Kristen Cartwright."

The teacher's hand swung to my favorite cat, and my mouth fell open. That awesome voice was *hers*? Whoa. I stuck two fingers in my mouth and let loose with a shrill whistle while the audience roared their approval. The white cat's eyes met mine, and I started to picture her in different clothes…maybe some black leather, studded bands on her wrists, hair long and wild down her back, strutting across a stage while I shredded the hell out of the guitar. If she could sing Broadway songs without breaking a sweat, what could she do with a hard metal rock track? I wondered—again—what her range was. Could she get low with some Halestorm or full-on mean with a Slipknot metal scream? I should put her in Ride Out right now. I grinned like a maniac because I knew that would really twist BroadwayBaby17 into a knot.

A brilliant idea struck. I pulled out my phone, snapped a photo of the white cat, and from the band's Twitter account, posted this:

@Ride_Out
This cat's HAWT! And damn, can she sing.

It needed a hashtag. I tapped out "#CatCall." Oh, this was awesome. My phone buzzed a minute later with a reply from a fan calling himself JJStix88.

> @JJStix88
>
> Sweet! Get her to meow. #CatCall

I tapped out another post.

> @Ride_Out
>
> Meow? Gonna make her purr! Gonna invite her to jam with us. #CatCall

> @JJStix88
>
> Make her arch that back! #CatCall

> @Ride_Out
>
> Wanna hear her scream! #CatCall

Sam elbowed me. "White cat's awesome, right?"

I nodded, but *awesome* didn't even come close to describing this girl. I couldn't tear my eyes off her rockin' body, and then to learn that voice—the most incredible sound I'd ever heard—had come from her and not Leah? I dragged both hands over my face and shivered.

Sam laughed. "Jesus, dude, close your mouth before a puddle forms."

I didn't notice it was still open. I closed it, swallowing hard. I had to find this girl, talk to her, and beg her to sing with us. She could be what we needed to finally break out. With her up front in some cleavage-revealing outfit, she wouldn't just *get* attention—she'd damn near *compel* it.

Sam flung an arm around my neck. "Okay, man, spill. What are you thinking?"

I grinned wide and turned to face him. I wanted that girl in our band like I wanted my next breath. "Her, Sam." I jabbed a finger toward the stage. "I want her."

"I'll bet you do." Sam's smile turned into a knowing leer. "So go get her."

My face burned. I meant I wanted her in our band, but for Sam, everything always came back to sex. I could have corrected his perception, but he wouldn't have believed me anyway. I turned back to watch the white cat work the room and pose for pictures like a pro. My hyperactive imagination stuck a mic in her hand, and suddenly, I was thinking of a hell of a lot more than the music too.

Sam ran his eyes up and down my favorite cat's body. A sudden urge to rip out his throat gripped me. He folded his arms and angled his head. "She's got it all, bro."

Damn, did she ever. A smokin' hot body and roof-raising voice? We'd be unstoppable. Before I could think again, I shoved past Sam and climbed over a row of seats.

I was a man on a mission.

4

KRISTEN

Kristen Cartwright
@kristencartwright

Tweets	Following	Followers
6,903	**735**	**1,201**

@kristencartwright

Opening night! #tingles Can't wait! #Cats

#BearRiverHSNorth

6 FAVORITES

@ToniOnStage

@kristencartwright Break a leg!

@Gina6x

@kristencartwright You'll do gr8! Have fun!

The sound of applause thundered in my ears and galloped in my chest. My fingers tingled, and all the muscles in my legs quivered. *Actor's high.* It was the best feeling on earth.

I'd practiced Victoria the White Cat's solo dance for so many hours, I often woke up with my legs in pose. But tonight? I hadn't just nailed it—I'd *owned* it. I could see Mrs. Dixon's smile from here. The audience was still applauding wildly. The lights came up, and people jumped to their feet, cheering and smiling. I scanned the audience, row after row, and finally found my family and waved. Mom and Dad looked a little stunned.

Oops. I kind of forgot to mention the White Cat's costume was nothing more than a unitard and a wig.

My little brother waved, my older brother applauded. Gordie hated losing video game time, and Dylan commuted to a local college, and seeing them in the audience caused a blush to warm my face. Etta pressed both hands to her heart, teeth blinding me behind her trademark bright red lips.

My God, I wished I could bottle these feelings and preserve them forever—like the canned peaches my other grandma used to make. They were so sweet, your whole body would hum in anticipation.

That's what actor's high felt like. I was a child's balloon, filled with helium, rising higher and higher—

"Did you get your acceptance letter yet?"

Pop.

My own stage smile froze on my face. Leah Russo's hoarse croak behind her bright stage smile killed my actor's high. I'd just provided the vocals to her solo so she could still be onstage, even though she'd had to lip-synch, but Leah would never think to thank you when she could stab you.

I didn't want to think about that letter.

Not special enough. God!

I didn't answer her. I would not answer her.

And then, I forgot all about her when my attention was snagged by a really hot guy near the pit orchestra. His dark hair was long enough to touch his shoulders, and there was a bit of scruff on his face—really cute, but that's not why I noticed him.

No, I noticed him because he had the most incredible eyes I'd ever seen. I couldn't tell what color they were from the stage, but they were so freakin' *intense*, I couldn't look away. Etta always said the eyes told you all you ever needed to know about a person. Anybody who couldn't make eye contact with you wasn't worth your time. Most boys' eyes never made it past my chest, but this boy's eyes were pinned on *mine,* and that impressed me.

Mrs. Dixon walked onstage with a mic and asked everyone to settle down.

"Ladies and gentlemen, thank you all for attending our opening night performance! I am so proud of these kids. They made all their own costumes and designed the set themselves. And tonight, I want to share with you an amazing last-minute change-up to our program. Grizabella, played by Leah Russo, is ill and couldn't sing this evening, but she soldiered on and went onstage anyway. Her songs were actually sung by Victoria the White Cat, played by Kristen Cartwright."

Leah smiled brightly and applauded me, then grabbed my hand for an extra bow to another standing ovation. My cheeks ached from smiling through the compulsive need to push her into the orchestra pit.

The boy with the intense eyes stuck two fingers in his mouth and let out a piercing whistle, then pointed at me with a wide grin. Beside him, another guy held up a sign that said, "Break a Leg, Leah!"

"Do you know him?" I asked her.

"That's Nick. My boyfriend," she croaked. Her voice was shot, but her face unfortunately still spoke volumes. The glare she shot me said very clearly to stay the hell away from Nick. Too bad, since he was cute. He had short, almost buzzed hair with a little fuzz lining his jaw all the way to his ears.

"How about the guy next to him?"

"The blond is Sam, and the dark-haired one is Elijah. Don't even bother, Kristen. You're totally not his type." She dropped my hand as soon as the applause died down.

Oh, really? We'll just see about that.

We were shuttled off the stage, and Mrs. Dixon was almost crying, she was so happy. The entire cast high-fived and hugged each other, but I kept one eye on the crowd, anxious to find my family. Finally, I spotted familiar red hair. "Etta!"

My grandmother spun around, clutching my mother's arm. Mom opened her eyes wide. "Oh, Kristen, you were fantastic. I didn't know you were singing tonight." Mom wrapped me in a huge hug and rocked side to side.

"I didn't know either, not until the last minute."

"You were amazing!"

"Kristen Elise, could you go please put some clothes on?" Dad tried to shield me with his body.

"Da-a-a-d." I rolled my eyes.

Etta gave him a playful tap on the arm. "Richard, don't *embarrass* the girl."

My grandmother used to act back in the day and still talked as if she were delivering lines, punching certain words with unnecessary emphasis and dynamics. Drove Mom nuts, but I loved it. She wrapped me in a hug and a cloud of Chanel. "I am so *proud* of my little star. How about we all go out for ice cream to celebrate Kristen's *smashing* opening night?" Etta raised her arms in a grand gesture, earning cheers from my brothers. "Oh, darling, you have a *public* to greet. Go, go!" She shooed me toward a group of little girls standing behind me, bouncing on their toes with their programs clutched in their hands.

Etta was my first acting coach. Taught me everything I knew. I turned with a huge stage smile to greet the trio of eight-year-olds, whose moms asked me to pose for some pictures. I extended a cat claw, and they happily snapped a bunch of pictures and thanked me when I signed their programs with a tiny paw drawing. I turned to head backstage for my stuff and collided with a body.

Hands grabbed me by my elbows. "Sorry."

"It's okay." Holy crap, it was him. Intense Eyes Guy. Elijah, one of Nick's band buddies.

"Hey. You were awesome." Those eyes were dark brown and glittered when he grinned at me, revealing a dimple on the right side of his mouth.

My face burst into flames. "Oh. Um. Thanks."

"No. Seriously. I have *never* heard a voice like yours. Blew me away."

Oh, he liked the song, not my dance? Slowly, my lips curled. "Thanks."

We stared at each other for a long moment. He still had that wide-eyed look of amazement, and I was sure I was still smiling a dopey smile. Suddenly, he thrust out his hand. "I'm Elijah Hamilton. Eli."

"Elijah. Cool. I'm Kristen Cartwright."

"Really great meeting you," he said, shaking my hand. His hands had calluses.

His eyes drifted lower, and I felt my face burn hotter. I was very much aware that I had a big chest—my dad could be a real pain about it—well, *them*. And in this costume, they were *right there*. I glanced at my family. Mom was watching Dad. Etta was waving a hand under her chin—a reminder that I should stand up straight. Dad was scowling at Elijah.

Uh-oh.

"I should, um, you know." I waved a hand in the vague direction of backstage where normal clothes waited for me.

"Oh. Yeah. Right." His cheeks turned red. When I turned to go, he suddenly asked, "Do you sing anything besides all this Broadway stuff?"

I frowned at the way his nose wrinkled when he said that. "Like what?"

He shrugged. "Anything. Rock, pop, country—whatever."

I shrugged too. "Yeah, I guess. Why?"

His smiled brightened. "I have a band. We do—what?"

Crap. He'd seen the look on my face when he revealed he had a band. His smile melted away. Was he a member of the Beat too? One of the faceless, nameless masses who loved to shoot me down because I had the confidence in my own abilities to point out the flaws in theirs? I knew my stuff inside out and backward. The whole point of the Beat was to exchange our wisdom. I didn't take it personally; I figured most of these immature morons couldn't stand getting schooled by a girl. This boy seemed so nice. I hope he wasn't one of them. "Nothing," I lied. "Go on. What were you gonna say?"

He angled his head and nodded. "Um, sure. We do hard rock mostly. But we do covers of almost all kinds of stuff. You'd be amazing on classic stuff from Joan Jett, Heart, or Fleetwood Mac. Hell, you could do new stuff like Halestorm, I bet."

I didn't know what kind of band hailstorm was, but suddenly, I really wanted to cover it. "Oh. Um, well. I don't—"

"Shoot me a friend request. I'd really love it if you could jam with us some time."

Jam? I frowned. Those jerks on the Beat thought their crappy music was over my head—out of my range, and now, a guy with his own rock band was inviting me to jam. I should record it, just so I could post it. *In your face, FretGuy99.*

"Um. I don't know. Maybe."

Those incredible dark eyes of his dimmed a bit, and his lips lost the smile. "Think about it. If you're as good as I think you are, you could sing some duets with me, Nick, and Sam." He jerked a thumb over his shoulder at his friends. Nick stood with Leah, and the other boy was tall, blond, and beautiful.

Right. Rock band. Boy, did they look the part.

"Duets. Okay. Yeah. Sure." Jesus, get a grip, moron! Like Dad would ever allow that to happen.

Elijah took a step closer. "Yeah. Duets. I'm not ready to give you center stage. Yet." He grinned, full wattage, and my heart almost stopped. Jesus, who was this guy?

"Kristen, it's getting late." Dad tapped the watch on his wrist, but his glare was aimed at Elijah. Elijah just kept grinning—like a dare or something.

"If you can shake off your entourage, message me. I'm anxious to see what else you got." He ran his eyes over me from wig to bare feet, and then he walked over to Leah and his friends. I watched them all—but couldn't tear my eyes off Elijah. He was dressed all in black— black jeans, black band T-shirt, leather cuff on one wrist. My fingers itched to touch the stubble around his lips. I didn't see any tattoos or piercings, but I could picture him with both. Total bad boy. If I told my family I was invited to jam with Elijah's rock band, Etta would frown and ask me if I was sure singing in a rock band would look good on my conservatory application, Mom would wonder how I could possibly find the time, and Dad? Well, he would have a cow.

Suddenly I wanted Elijah Hamilton the way I'd wanted a puppy when I was six.

———————

"Who was that boy, Kristen?" Dad asked when I'd changed and caught up with everyone out by the minivan.

"His name is Elijah."

"Elijah. How very *Old Testament*," Etta announced.

"Is he a friend of yours?"

"No, he doesn't go to my school." Nick didn't go to our school either. Leah met him over the summer. I figured Elijah and Sam went to his school.

"He goes to South," Dylan piped in, and I wondered how he knew. "And he's a player, Kris. Stay away from him."

"A *player*? What do you *mean*? What does he *mean*, Richard?" Etta demanded.

And starring as the Worried Grandmother, Henrietta Cartwright. I managed to halt the eye roll that accompanied that thought just in the nick of time.

"Mother, relax." Dad put up a hand to halt Etta's dramatic interpretation of the worried grandmother role. Etta straightened her shoulders and inclined her head, a regal little motion she used to refocus and find her center.

I shot a glare at Dylan, sitting beside me in the third row of the minivan. He leaned over and quietly explained. "I know him, Kris. He's a heartbreaker. Doesn't date, just hooks up with random girls at the shows his band plays."

I rolled my eyes. "Come on, Dylan. He's what, eighteen?"

"Come on, Kris," he shot back. "It's not the age. It's the attitude. Girls throw themselves at Elijah Hamilton because he's got that whole *dangerous* vibe thing going on. They don't get it—he doesn't care about any of them. The only thing he cares about is music."

"I don't see how you could *possibly* have time for boys, Kristen," Etta said, her waving hands visible even in the dark car. "You've got conservatories to apply to—oh! Wouldn't it be *grand* if you were accepted to Peabody?"

Peabody. It was an option. Of course, Mom and Dad wanted Julliard. Not that anyone asked me, but I wanted Berklee because their emphasis was on contemporary sound rather than classic.

I was spared having to reply when Dad pulled into the parking lot behind the Main Street Creamery. Minutes later, we were digging into huge sundaes—dainty cups for Mom and Etta. "You never mentioned you'd be onstage in that…that…" Dad waved his hands in the general direction of my waistline.

"Unitard, Dad."

"Right. Very revealing, don't you think?" He turned to Mom, who shrugged.

"Relax, Richard. The entire cast wore the same thing. Didn't you see that one boy with his genitalia bulging?"

"Mom!" Gordon clapped his hands over his adolescent ears, but she only rolled her eyes.

Dad wasn't soothed by that argument. "How many more performances are there?"

"Uh, five more." Two on Saturday and Sunday and one on Monday for the school, and then all the weeks of practice and rehearsal and designing would come to an end. I tried not to think about it. Gordon changed the subject—thank God.

"Hey, I forgot to tell you guys I'm going to pitch in tomorrow's game."

Etta's perfectly penciled eyebrows arched. "You *guys*? Am I to understand that I have achieved *guy* status, at long last?" She flexed her biceps, the rings and bright red nail polish on her fingers at odds with the motion. "I knew all that *lifting* would eventually pay off."

"Sorry, Etta," Gordie said, chocolate sauce outlining his sheepish smile.

"I should hope so." Etta smoothed her already smooth hair behind her ears. "I take great pains to *assure* I am never *mistaken* for just one of the guys."

"Yes, Mother, we know." Dad rolled his eyes. "The hair, the makeup, the clothes—I'm shocked your stylist hasn't already seen Gordie's comment on Twitter yet so he can scurry over here to touch up your *ensemble*." He delivered that last line with the same inflection Etta put on her words. Mom hid a smile behind a spoonful of ice cream, but Etta's carefully made-up eyes narrowed at Dad.

"You know, Richard, sarcasm is the lowest form of wit."

"Of course, Mother. I was merely catering to my audience, as you taught me."

Gordon and Dylan cracked up at this. Even Mom laughed silently. But Etta was glaring at Dad so ferociously, I was worried she'd pop a blood vessel or something.

"Oh, come on, Mother. You know we adore you and your biceps." Dad pressed a noisy kiss to her cheek, and her lips twitched. With his arm still around Etta, he swiped the cherry off Gordie's sundae.

"Um, excuse me."

We looked up to find some old man standing beside our table, a hopeful expression on his face.

"I'm sorry to interrupt, but are you Henrietta Cartwright?"

Etta's spine straightened a bit more. "I *am*," she admitted with another incline of her head, and the man's face lit up like Broadway.

"I knew it!" He clapped his hands and wagged a finger at her. "I saw you at the Helen Hayes Theater many years ago in *Prelude to a Kiss*. You were brilliant!"

"Oh, that's so kind. Thank you." Etta flashed a huge smile. The man was willing to leave at that, but Etta insisted on posing for a few pictures with him and signing both a menu and a place mat—one for the man and one for the restaurant.

Mom and Dad exchanged a look that so obviously said, "Let her have her fun," so we sat back and waited for Etta to do her thing. Fifteen minutes later, Dad looked at my brother and asked, "What's this about pitching tomorrow?"

Gordie beamed at the proof Dad hadn't forgotten his big news. I had to admit it—Dad was brilliant at handling the extra-large egos in our family, and Etta's was definitely the largest. Of course, Etta would call it *caprice*.

"Coach says I'm really good now—most improved player, and he wants to give me a shot at pitching an inning. A whole inning!"

"That's really great…"

Gordon was eleven and had only one gear—baseball. Now that the spring season had begun, it would be all he'd talk about until June. Baseball wasn't my thing, so I glanced out the window, letting the conversation fade into the background. A swing of long, dark hair captured my attention. There was Elijah Hamilton, accepting three small dishes with covers from the server at the window that opened to the parking lot. A girl approached him, pretty in jeans and a school hoodie. I watched him stop to chat, flip his hair back, and smirk. My stomach lurched when the girl laughed and twirled a lock of hair around her finger. When he leaned in to whisper something into her ear that had her landing a flirty smack on his arm, I almost looked away.

But if I had, I'd have missed it.

He walked to the passenger seat of a white Chevy, the smirk and swagger gone—dropped, like some director had just shouted, "Cut!" He didn't even look back. My brother had called him a *player*. But I didn't think that was accurate. No, I think Elijah Hamilton was a *performer* playing to his audience—like Etta. Like me. And now I had to know what Elijah Hamilton was *really* like.

I tossed my hair over my shoulder and tuned back into the table conversation. We were apparently done with baseball and had moved on to Dylan's on-campus job. My oldest brother was twenty years old and in his last semester of college. He commuted to a state school here on Long Island—SUNY Old Westbury, where he majored in business. Dad was psyched about that because he owned a bar on the west side of our town and was looking forward to having Dylan become his partner.

"…and might even get a promotion out of it," Dylan finished.

Etta turned to me and, with a knowing smile, took the conversation right back where I didn't want it. "So that *boy* who seemed so interested in you. The *player* with the adorable ass. What exactly did he want?"

"Etta!" I scanned the table, but luckily, Dad and Gordie were still talking stats. I shrugged. "He said he liked my voice. He's in a rock band. Thought it might be cool if I sing with them."

Etta's proud nose went a little higher into the air. "Sing in a rock band? Is he *mad*? Doesn't he understand that you're not just some part-time karaoke fan but a career *performer*?"

"Well, no, Etta, I never had a chance to tell him all that. He asked and—"

"You said no, of course," Dad interrupted.

"I didn't have a chance to tell him that, either." Jeez, it's not like he asked me to marry him or anything. It was just singing. It sounded kind of fun. And it was super flattering. How many drama club cast members got invited to jam in rock bands? Wish I could tell that jerk on the Beat that I *do* know some shit about metal.

"Kristen, I don't like the look in your eye." Dad narrowed his eyes at me.

"Oh, Rick, stop. She spoke to the boy for five minutes." Mom dipped her finger in whipped cream and dotted it on Dad's nose, which he promptly wrinkled and rubbed against hers. My heart sighed. Pretty much all of my friends had parents who despised each other, and even though my parents were so sweet it was sickening, I secretly cherished that about them.

On paper, they shouldn't work. Dad was a dedicated businessman, the son of Etta, a former stage actress who had more ex-husbands than she had kids. And Mom was a free spirit artistic type who liked to wear long, flowy dresses and no shoes. He loved watching sports, while she preferred documentaries on the History channel. She loved to cook with organic food, while Dad was happy with chain restaurant half-price appetizers. I couldn't believe they ever got together in the first place, let alone made it work all these years.

A little sniffle from Etta caught my attention. She stared at Mom and Dad and caught a tear at the corner of one eye with her napkin. Etta had been married four times. Four! I wasn't sure which of the four husbands was Dad's father—I'd never asked—because he and Aunt Debra called them all *Dad*. Etta was still on friendly terms with all four of the dads, who'd remarried and started other families. Dad and Aunt Deb had dozens of half and stepsiblings, so now, our family gatherings needed bracket charts to keep track of everyone. It was loud and weird and fun and unconventional, just like Etta, and I absolutely adored us.

"I think you should avoid that boy. You have to focus on your summer program arrangement. Have you chosen a piece yet?" Etta asked.

I shook my head. "Not yet." Oh, God. I had to tell them.

"Well." She leaned closer, her exotically painted eyes twinkling with secrets. "I suggest 'Fever.' It's a *classic,* darling. So *hot* and *sultry* and certainly within your *range.*"

That was the problem—"Fever" was in everyone's range. It wasn't a technically difficult song to perform. Besides, I'd already been rejected, so what was the point? I leaned over and murmured that news to Etta while the boys were chatting baseball and jobs and stuff.

Etta made a tiny O with her mouth. "Oh, darling, I am *so* sorry. I know you had your heart set on Tisch, but there's still time."

"Not really." I shook my head. "Summer programs are already full. The best I could hope for is the wait list."

The tiny O-shaped mouth slowly morphed into a calculating smile. "What you *need*, darling, is an edge. And you've already been presented with the means to get it."

I blinked at her. "What, the rock band? No. Absolutely not."

Etta patted my hand. "Well, if you don't think you can *do* it, that's fine, of course."

Couldn't do it? Please. I peered at her through narrowed eyes. "I know what you're doing, and that's not gonna work on me."

She gave one of her elegant little shrugs—patent pending—and just smiled. "I just think this band would showcase your *brilliant* flexibility." She clapped her hands when a new thought struck. "Oh, and

41

you might consider recording an original composition. That *always* impresses conservatory people."

My conservatory applications were a real BFD in our house. Ever since I'd taken my first voice lesson, when it was clear I had talent, my parents had been planning and saving for this. Me? Not so much. Truth was, I didn't know what I wanted. I loved performing—of that, I was absolutely certain. But I loved dancing and acting as much as I love singing and didn't want to study only classical music.

The conversation stopped, and everybody stared at Etta, who lifted her shoulders in another elegant shrug. "Well, it could," she insisted. "At the very least, it will give you notoriety."

"Mother, I'm not sure Pam and I want our daughter to be notorious."

"Nonsense, Richard." Etta waved off his concern. "First rule of performing—there's no such thing as bad press. If Kristen sings in this band, she'll be famous locally, and the conservatories will fight to *scoop* her up."

Fight for me? I doubted it. I'd be one of thousands trying out.

"I don't get it. Why bother applying if she gets famous?" Gordon asked. "I mean, at that point, she'll have all the success there is."

Dad shook his head. "It's not just about things like record sales or screaming fans, Gordie. It's about getting to work with masters, rising out of anonymity to earn the respect of leaders in the industry."

Etta and I both cringed at Dad's mention of the A word. *Anonymity* was the very worst thing that could happen to a performer. That was why Etta was wearing her diamonds to the ice-cream parlor. She wanted to be noticed and remembered for the work she'd done back in the day. I saw the way pure joy beamed out of her like light when that man recognized her. I wanted that. Oh, not just for the money and the perks. I wanted my talent to be admired and have little kids look up to me. I wanted to be *remembered*.

To matter.

If I could find a way to impress the admissions committees with something fresh and daring, I'd have a shot. Etta was right. Tisch may have rejected me, but their summer program wasn't the only way to impress the Berklee admissions people. Maybe this rock band idea wasn't so bad after all.

I glanced out the window again. Elijah Hamilton was gone, but I smiled into the bottom of my ice-cream bowl and decided to send him a friend request. I'd give his rock band a shot.

It could be just what I needed.

5

ELIJAH

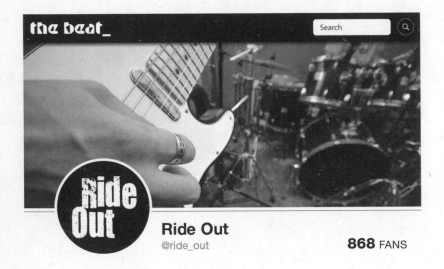

the beat_

Search 🔍

Ride Out
@ride_out

868 FANS

Ride_On747: Nice riff on the video! Keep 'em coming!

1 LIKE

"I thought you wanted to hook up with Kristen Cartwright," Sam said, shaking his head. "But all you want is for her to sing in our band with us? Why? Things are fine the way they are." He sat with his arms crossed and face scowling on a stool in my garage, where amplifiers and Nick's drum kit lined the back wall. Against a sidewall, on a cheap plastic banquet table, we had our soundboard, which was essentially an iPad and an old, trusty Mac. In boxes stacked on a ceiling-high shelf unit, we stored speakers, mics, and other gear we needed for shows—when we could book them. We typically played restaurants, cafes, and sometimes private parties. On Saturday mornings when my parents took Anna for her therapy appointments, we rehearsed. Except today. All we'd done was debate about Kristen.

I hadn't told the guys about Anna. About what my parents were planning to do.

It sucked hard enough already. Telling them, risk having them feel all sorry for me and shit? They'd do whatever I asked, and if that was adding Kristen to our band, they'd do it. They'd hate it, but because I asked, they'd do it.

Fuck it. I had to be honest with them. Wincing, I pulled in a deep breath. Time to come clean. "Things *are* great. But we're not going anywhere, guys. We had a plan to hit it big, and that has to happen for us like *right now.* Otherwise, I'm going to have to pull out."

Sam shot off his stool, sending it crashing to the concrete floor. "Pull out? What the hell, Elijah? We made a promise!"

"Chill out, Sam." Nick shot to his feet and put a restraining hand on Sam's shoulder. It took a lot to rile up Nick, and for that, I was grateful. "Elijah, what's going on with you? You've been acting kind of—" He circled his hand a few times.

I looked at Sam, still breathing fire, and at Nick, who studied me with his head to the side, eyes full of concern. My throat closed up.

Aw, fuck.

I couldn't look at them, but I had to finish what I hadn't been able to tell them last night. "It's Anna, guys. She just… She's getting worse. Harder to handle. She's thirteen and hormonal and just…well…my dad—" To my extreme embarrassment, my voice cracked. "He, um… They want to put her in a home." Just the thought of that made me clench my hands into fists.

"Maybe that's not such a bad thing," Sam said quietly.

The blood in my veins went icy. I straightened up and got to my feet. "Say what?"

"Chill." He put up both hands. "Just listen. You said she's getting worse. If we do this thing with Kristen and suddenly take off, how are you gonna take care of Anna and still make Ride Out work?"

"That's the whole point, Sam!" I spread out my arms. "If we can get Ride Out to the next level—get this gig, get the next one, maybe land a recording contract—I could afford a whole team of caregivers for her. She'd be in her own home instead of some prison cell with a bunch of other kids with disabilities."

He looked down at his feet. "And you really think Kristen Cartwright can help?"

"You heard her last night. That voice is like a superpower. With her aboard doing duets, we'll bring an audience to its fucking knees."

Sam looked from me to Nick and then down at his feet, jaw clenched. He shook his head and finally flung up his hands. "Okay, fine. You want to give her a try, we'll do it. But I'm not doing any chick shit pop music songs just to showcase *her* voice. We're a metal band,

and she needs to sing metal. No 'Over the Rainbow' crap." Sam slashed his hands through the air. "Why can't she just sing backup in some leather outfit, and show off her tits and ass?"

The thought of Kristen in a skintight leather outfit had my jeans tightening to the point of pain. I grabbed my guitar to hide it from the guys.

Brothers or not, some things were just private.

"Christ, Elijah, is that what this is about?" Sam asked with a smirk. "You want in that girl's pants? Why don't you just take her out? Why dangle our band under her nose?"

"I want her voice."

"I'm calling it." Sam raised one hand, like a referee. "Bullshit." Nick laughed and shook his head while my face burned.

"Okay, she's hot! I admit it. Hottest chick I've ever seen—no offense, Nick. But that's not what this is about. It's about the music. She brought the house down last night with that song."

Sam laughed once. "She brought the house down because she had a hella nice rack in that cat costume."

I stood up and walked away so I wouldn't knock his teeth in. Yeah, Kristen rocked the cat suit. Yeah, she had nice boobs. Didn't mean that was the only reason I wanted her in the band. I wasn't a tool. I respected girls, which was why I didn't date. You shouldn't make a girl promises you can't keep. Dad taught me that.

"Okay, my vote is she sings with us—duets, maybe even lead on some songs. But I like the idea of hot outfits to show off her body," Nick cut in. "The lead singer of In This Moment got voted hottest chick in metal. That could be *us*."

"I agree." Sam crossed his arms. "Two against one, Elijah." When I remained stone-faced, he flung his hands in the air. "What is the problem with this?"

"Because it should be about the *music*."

"Come off it, Eli. You said we needed a push. A shot of adrenaline. You think she's it. What's the big deal about using her looks, too? I do it. I have fucking highlights in my hair because chicks dig it." He waved a hand over his long, flowy blond locks that looked like something out of a shampoo commercial.

"The girls love that whole Brad Pitt/Zac Efron thing," Nick added with an eyebrow wiggle. "So why not give the guys some eye candy?"

Sam flipped him off but added, "Exactly."

"Okay, so you'll sing backup in a tight outfit? That could be interesting." I smirked when Sam shot me a glare. It suddenly hit me that this was the real problem. Sam hated sharing the spotlight.

I needed to make him see that this was for the good of the band. If Ride Out had a future, we had to take some risks. With a long, loud sigh, I grabbed a stool, tapped my tablet, and brought up the county festival website.

"According to the sign-up FAQs, the county plans to start picking acts for the festival later this month. Every teen idol and pop star wannabe probably applied by now. But how many heavy metal bands do you think did? And how many of those can brag about not one but two powerhouse voices?" Yeah, I knew that was arrogant as hell.

It was also the truth, and the guys knew it.

Sam pressed his lips together but didn't say anything, so I figured I'd scored a point. He sat down on a stool, arms crossed, face flushed. Finally, he dragged both hands through his hair and shrugged. "It was supposed to be the three of us. All the way to the top. I wanted this to stay ours—just ours, you know?"

I knew. I just didn't think that was going to happen before I was thirty, and I couldn't wait that long.

He stood up and put a hand on my shoulder. "Okay. You want her, you got her. But I swear to God, Eli, if you're just doing this only to get laid, tell me now. I don't want her being our Yoko. You guys are my brothers. Nothing comes between us."

"Bros before hos, man." Nick put out a fist.

I bumped his and then Sam's. "Deal."

I could totally keep my hands off Kristen Cartwright.

No problem.

———————

An hour later, the question of asking Kristen to join our band settled, we were sitting on stools, huddled around the ancient Mac, listening to a track from a new band. Cymbals clashed, drums raged, and the final notes of the outro faded, leaving their echo in my head. I sat back and swiveled to face Sam and Nick.

"Well?" Nick asked, a smug smile curving his lips.

"Okay, okay, it's got potential. Happy now?" I rolled my eyes.

Nick didn't answer me. He just exchanged high fives with Sam, who grabbed my iPad and started tapping. I looked over his shoulder.

"Common Kiss?" I raised my brows. "Lame name. But yeah, okay. The lyrics were decent."

"Yes!" Nick raised both arms. "We're unanimous. This band is our next cover."

Frowning, I put up a hand. I knew Nick was trying to make up for the time we'd lost by watching the play last night, but this was a stretch for us. "Hold up, guys. I only heard one song off that album. There's no way I can play any of this."

"Yeah, especially if you don't stop checking your phone every ten seconds for texts from Kristen the White Cat."

I flipped Nick off while Sam sighed and scrolled through the songs. Common Kiss was a new pop rock band—FM radio stations would play them like they were the second coming of Nickelback. But their sound wasn't special.

Special... The word made me think about Kristen—oh, she was special—beyond special. I couldn't get her or her amazing voice out of my head. I'd already spent hours imagining what she would sound like singing death metal...and had to take a cold shower when I was done.

"Look, with everything going on right now, I don't think I can make the time to learn this."

"Got that covered, bro." Sam took back the tablet and tapped a bunch of keys, head-banging as he typed, long blond hair flowing to the beat from the last track that seemed to drip from the air. Finally, he looked up. "What if we only cover one song from the album, but do a video review of the whole thing?"

Nodding his head, Nick took the tablet. "I like it. Kind of a *Wayne's World* thing?"

"No, seriously review it. We're musicians, *and* we're fans. It's fine if we don't eviscerate them—not like that bitch on the Beat does."

I laughed. BroadwayBaby17 was a pain in all our asses. I took the tablet from Nick, glanced at the guitar tabs Sam had found, and then back at the website so I could skim some of the lyrics. There was a real storytelling skill here…kind of folksy, kind of Bob Seger. We'd reviewed songs before but never a whole album. Our reviews were a big hit with our fans. In fact, I was convinced our online reviews were why we had fans in the first place. We were good and called ourselves Ride Out because we figured we'd hit it big one day, and then we could just sit back to ride out our fame for however long it lasted. Sam on lead guitar, Nick on percussion, and me on bass guitar. I was our front man too. I could switch from a gas-gargling howl for our aggressive death metal tracks to a powerful sound for crowd-pleasing power ballads, and even manage the husky texture needed for those rootsy songs from our heartland playlists—and could do it all in the same set.

I'd worked my ass off to be able to do that. I took a talent I was born with and developed it into something real and strong and—if all went according to plan—marketable.

Sam was the same way with his guitar. He made the strings sing. Then there was Nick. His drumming was nothing short of brilliant. People always assume it's easy to beat a skin, and Nick would just smile, hand over his sticks, and let them flounder for a couple of minutes. Then he'd take the sticks back and cut loose until jaws dropped. I didn't know anybody who could make the time between beats really *groove* the way he did.

We weren't just good; we knew what we were talking about and had the chops to back it up. I took a closer look at the guitar tabs Sam found and nodded. "Yeah," I said, already liking the Common Kiss plan.

"Okay," Nick joined in. "Where do we start?"

Sam booted up the Mac. "How about a comparison? We start with their band members—who they are and how they met, where they came from, who influenced their sound, and compare that to our own situation."

"Excellent," Nick said, and I agreed. "You do that. Elijah and I will listen to the whole album and start taking some notes."

I grabbed a splitter, stuck one end into the jack, and waited for Nick to do the same. Pens ready, I tapped Play and shut my eyes.

Music was all about the feelings. A teacher once told us that music affects our brains kind of like sex, food, or drugs. He rattled off things like *dopamine* and other scientific and biological crap that just took all the fun out of it for me. I didn't care why we liked music, how it affected us, or why it was so important. I knew only that it mattered. Some days, the music was *all* that mattered. I shut my eyes and just let the sound in, tuning everything else out. I liked to feel music with my whole body. My pulse synched up to the percussion, and I could taste the lyrics on my tongue—bitter and angry. And the smell? Leather and sweat. My pen flew over the page, recording observations and feelings while the music filled me up.

It took twenty minutes or so to play through the album. Despite the terrible name, Common Kiss was actually good. I put a question mark next to that name in my book; I needed to find out what the hell it meant. I switched focus to the lead singer. His voice was unusual; he had an impressive extended range that almost *forced* you to listen, and he didn't just hit the high notes—he put them into comas. But yet, he only did that for the high notes. I don't know… It felt like he was holding back, like he was afraid to cut loose on the rest of his range. Common Kiss could be *uncommon* if their front man would take a few risks.

Risks.

Hmm. I kind of liked the idea of doing something risky with this song. The lyrics were edgy; they just needed a voice with the guts to punch them. I jotted down a note and turned to lead guitar next. Sure, every other guy can play a decent guitar these days, but finding a solid axeman whose technical ability and creative potential were *both* excellent was like finding the fucking Holy Grail. This guy wasn't bad, but he wasn't great, either. The riffs were cool, the sound was sturdy, but I kept hearing the same couple of chords repeated. The nicest thing I could say about him was he was…competent.

"Eli, what's your favorite track?"

I glanced over at Sam. "Uh, I guess 'Shout from the Roof' and maybe 'Lie Like You Mean It.'"

"Yeah. 'Lie Like You Mean It' is good," Nick agreed.

Sam nodded. "Okay, what do you guys think of amping up the power?"

My eyebrows shot up. "Lie Like You Mean It" wasn't death or thrash; it was just a little rougher than radio rock, and that, I figured, was their goal. Common Kiss was straddling the line between mainstream and hard rock. If we amped up the power, that could add in the element of risk I was just thinking about. "Give it some head-banging potential? It'll never get air time."

Sam grinned. "True, but it *will* get attention."

And by *attention*, Sam meant clicks for us. I nodded. Maybe this would be the one that went viral. "Okay. You work on the melody, and I'll do something with the lyrics." I did some fast calculations. We usually put up a blog post on the last Friday of the month. That gave us a couple of weeks for the cover song arrangement and the review. We'd post it to our website and to YouTube and hope the resulting Internet traffic would impress the county festival planners before they made their final decision.

My cell phone buzzed with a Facebook notification. "Shit. It's a friend request."

"Your white cat?" Nick grinned, but Sam just looked away.

"What?" I demanded.

Sam shook his head. "We're busy right now. Can you not drop everything just for some chick?"

It took every ounce of strength I had to shove the phone back in my pocket and be cool.

KRISTEN

Kristen Cartwright
@kristencartwright

Tweets	Following	Followers
6,909	**737**	**1,212**

@CalaLilly22

OMG just saw the best show evah off Broadway! #Cats #BearRiverHSNorth White Cat = Awesome!

9 RETWEETS 4 FAVORITES

> @MikeyT
>
> Damn, the White Cat is fine! #Cats #CatCall
> #BearRiverHSNorth
>
> 12 RETWEETS 8 FAVORITES

> @Abby99x
>
> U seen this @kristencartwright? RT Ride_Out: Wanna hear
> her scream! #CatCall
>
> 49 RETWEETS 78 FAVORITES

I woke up Saturday morning to the sound of my phone buzzing on the nightstand. Smiling, I swiped at it, wondering how many reviews and congratulatory notes awaited me. I scrolled through the list, happy to see so many. Rachel, my best friend, sent me this: **Hey, Kris! Check out Twitter! You're trending. #CatCall**

Oooh. I grabbed my laptop, logged into Twitter, and did a quick search. Sure enough, the #CatCall hashtag had been really busy since last night. There were over a hundred tweets. Oh my God, how cool! With my heart thundering and my stomach flipping, I started reading them one at a time.

> @KitKatKar
>
> @kristencartwright Excellent technique, Victoria #CatCall

> **@Luv2Dance**
>
> Impressive solo dance @kristencartwright #Cats
> #BearRiverHSNorth #CatCall

> **@BeAStar**
>
> OMG just saw the best show evah off Broadway! #Cats
> #BearRiverHSNorth White Cat = Awesome!

> **@everKool**
>
> Damn, the White Cat is fine! #Cats #CatCall
> #BearRiverHSNorth

Okay. This was good. I smiled wide and was about to get out of bed when I saw this one.

> **@Like2HaveFun**
>
> Whoa, the tits on the White Cat are niiiiiice. #CatCall

I glanced at the bra I'd tossed on the floor and wished—not for the first time—that it was a dainty A cup.

Please God, make sure Dad never sees this stream.

Like a terrible accident you can't turn away from, I kept looking. Oh, the posts weren't all about my chest. Some were just generically mean.

> **@LaceWing**
>
> I hate when high schools attempt Broadway shows.
> They're never good. #CatCall #BearRiverHSNorth

> **@JaneAir**
>
> OMG, who played Victoria? Amazed she didn't topple over!
> LOL! #CatCall

Okay. That one *was* about my boobs.

> **@SewWhat**
>
> Wow, costumes look like leftovers from some teenager's
> Halloween party. #CatCall #BearRiverHSNorth

I closed my laptop with a sigh. Why did I read the reviews? I knew better. I had to be onstage in a few hours! And I had to figure out a new plan for my conservatory applications now that my summer program wasn't going to happen. Now all I was going to be thinking about was how big my boobs looked. I needed a distraction.

Like magic, a name danced through my mind.

Elijah.

I grabbed my computer, went to Facebook, and searched for Elijah Hamilton.

What a great name for a guy in a band. I said it out loud a few times, loving the way it felt rolling off my tongue. I scrolled through a couple of profiles before I found him. He played bass guitar—which explained the calluses—and was the lead singer for a band called Ride Out.

Oh my God.

Quickly, I opened my browser and logged onto the Beat's metal forum, scrolling through all those insulting posts directed toward me.

It was the same band.

Damn it, damn it, *damn it*. I liked this guy. A lot. I wasn't just flattered he wanted to sing with me, I was honored, and now I discover he's the same jerk posting these insulting comments? Well, he could just drop dead. I won't ruin my vocal chords for him trying to scream and growl the way he did in those sample files he always posted.

> Metal singing takes a lot of skill, BroadwayBaby17. Stick to Bieber! Leave the hard stuff to us.

That was the last post on the Beat from some jerk called FretGuy99. Whoever he was, he was an even bigger ass than Elijah Hamilton. He had no respect for music outside his own genre, like I did. Pop, rock, country, opera—I respected it all and understood it took different skill sets to deliver different performances. I had no doubt I could handle the dark heavy metal that FretGuy99 seemed to worship so much—if I were into it. I wasn't into it.

But I was into Elijah Hamilton.

I scrolled through the stuff on his wall I was allowed to see (until we were officially friends according to Facebook) and found an image of Elijah curled over a notebook, pen between his teeth and guitar on his lap. His hair was tied back in a ponytail, and he had this look of intensity, but it wasn't frustration.

It was happiness.

Wow. The only time I was happy, truly happy, with my work was when I was onstage. The problem was that was the *end* of the process—the delivery. Everything that led to that moment—the rehearsing and practicing, the studying, all that theory and technique—well, it was starting to bore me now.

I had at least four more years of that grueling work ahead of me at whatever conservatory finally accepted me.

I stared at that image for a long while and then clicked the link to send *Elijah of the Intense Eyes* a friend request.

Okay, so what if he was the jerk in Ride Out who posted mean replies to me? He was also hot. And he didn't know I was BroadwayBaby17. So maybe, if I sang in his band, he could teach me that kind of happiness.

―――――

The days passed. The show was over. I just wanted to pull the blankets over my head and stay in my bed.

I *hated* this part of theater. Tearing down sets, putting away the costumes. Was it good? Was *I* good? People in the corridors at school shouted compliments and even applauded, but that would fade away too. Life would move on. Things would go back to normal.

Normal.

God, I *hated* that word. It was a lot like *not that special*. Who the hell wanted to be normal when you could be extraordinary and legendary? That's what I wanted. Etta always said a life worth living is a life lived. When people met Henrietta Cartwright, they became immediate friends. She was this force, this magnetic field everyone else just revolved around—you couldn't help it. I learned how to work an audience from my grandmother. She *hated* her name, but she worked it into a legend. She'd pound guys on their backs and tell them, "Call me Hank." And when she met refined young ladies, she'd sit up straight and say, "I'm Henri. I'm very pleased to meet you." Except she pronounced it *Ahn-ree*. And if she really, really liked you, she'd let you call her Etta. I loved calling her that, even though it pissed off Mom. She thought it was disrespectful, but Dad just shrugged.

Sighing loudly, I dropped into my seat in my first-period class. Rachel raised her eyebrows.

"What's wrong with you?"

I shut my eyes and slouched low in my seat. "Everything."

Rachel laughed. "Kristen, the show is over. I know how depressed you get, but seriously, it's time to get over that. Everyone thought you killed it. Poor Leah can't escape it."

I opened my eyes at this ray of sunlight peeking through darkness. "Leah's upset?"

"Oh, yeah." Rachel leaned in, blue eyes sparkling with unshared gossip. "I heard her in the first-floor bathroom telling Lorna that it was all her idea that you provide the voice for her role."

My back snapped up straight. *Her* idea? That troll!

61

And then I slunk back down in my seat. I didn't care as much as I thought.

Rachel's eyebrows knitted together. "Wow, you're *really* upset. What's up?"

I blew out a long, loud sigh. "I haven't heard from that guy from the show yet. He still hasn't accepted my friend request."

"Maybe he hasn't seen it." Rachel shrugged.

I thought about that for a moment. Could be. But he'd seemed so into me. Like he couldn't wait to hang out. Maybe I waited too long. Maybe he moved on. I took a deep, steadying breath and found my center. Okay. It wasn't like Dad was going to let me go out with Elijah anyway, so maybe it was just as well he hadn't accepted my friendship.

Less temptation.

The bell rang, and I opened my notebook, but the teacher's lecture on George Orwell quickly faded into white noise. I couldn't get Elijah Hamilton out of my head, and it really pissed me off that I wasn't in his. I thought I'd made an impression. By the time class ended, I was past *pissed off* and into *furious*. If I ever saw Elijah Hamilton again, I'd tell him to just drop dead and go to hell.

It was lunch when I next caught up to Rachel. "Hey!" I smiled wide.

She blinked at me. "You're happy now. What happened?"

I batted my lashes. "Nothing. I just decided to snap out of it."

"Yeah, right. Come on, Kris. Spill."

I sat down and unwrapped my sandwich. "I decided that Elijah Hamilton isn't worth a second of my time, that's what."

"The boy from the show? The one with the intense eyes?" Rachel stared at me.

"Yeah. What? What's wrong?"

Slowly she shook her head. "Uh, nothing. You just never mentioned his name is Elijah Hamilton."

"You know him?"

Again, she shook her head. "No. But I've heard of him. He's bad news, okay? You should stay away from him." She crumbled up her napkin, grabbed her tray, and left me there, wondering what the hell was so terrible about a guy who clearly liked me.

I watched her dark head blend in with the dozens of others roaming the school and sighed. Rachel was my best friend, but she actually liked *normal*. I didn't get it. Why be normal when being extraordinary was so much more fun? Etta was never part of the crowd. The crowd followed *her*. She once picked me up from school wearing a royal blue turban with a diamond pin in the center. Everyone laughed. But a week later, Beth Sullivan's mom wore a pink one, so you know what that taught me? Everyone wanted to be noticed. Everyone wanted to be admired.

I glanced down at the scarlet leather boots on my feet. I wore those because Etta gave them to me, but I loved how nobody else owned anything like them. They were like my trademark now. Maybe I should do more, something to make me completely unique? I ran a hand along my own hair. It was blond, and it looked just like all the other blond girls at school. I should cut it. A nice pixie style—or maybe that totally awesome chic bob that Etta wears. Dad tells me all the time how much

I look like her, so maybe I should play that up more? Wear bold red lips and the dramatic eyeliner Etta wears. Or I could do something even more daring than Etta, like—I gasped and smiled as a sudden inspiration struck me: hair color. I could pick up a box after school. Something bold and unexpected like a blue or a purple.

I finished my lunch, but Rachel's words kept bouncing around my brain. I snuck my phone out of my bag, made sure no teachers with grabby hands were in confiscating distance, and logged onto Twitter. I searched for the #CatCall hashtag and found the same list of crap I'd already read. But there were more of them now.

A lot more.

Don't read the comments, I told myself. But I did because I was weak and lived for the adoration of my public—such as it was. And then I found something horrifying.

Elijah Hamilton was the one who started that stupid #CatCall tag.

The entire thread just got worse. They wanted me to meow, to scream, to howl. I thought he liked me. I really thought he…

It didn't matter what I thought. Elijah Hamilton was just another jerk. God, I hated when Dylan was right.

"Miss Cartwright, are you ill?" The assistant principal suddenly loomed over me.

"No, Mrs. Powell."

"I'll pretend I don't see what's clutched in your hand and allow you to get to your class."

"Oh, right. Thanks." I stuffed the phone in my bag and left the cafeteria, battling tears.

"How could he *do* that, Etta?" I sobbed.

"Hush, darling, hush." She stroked my hair. "Are you absolutely *certain* he—what is it again?"

"Twitter. And yes. I am. He posted a picture of me." I lifted my head from her shoulder and curled my legs under me. Etta handed me the box of tissues from the table beside the sofa, where a framed photo of Etta and Dad sat. I blew my nose loudly and sniffled a few times. "I thought he liked me, Etta. Really liked me."

"He *does*, darling. I saw the boy's face, and I'm an *excellent* judge of character, remember?"

Despite the knife twisting deep in my soul, I laughed. I couldn't help it. Etta could always make me laugh no matter how crappy I felt. That was why I came straight here, instead of running up to my room and hiding under the covers. "Maybe he's just a good actor."

Etta raised both eyebrows over her teacup at that. "Nobody's *that* good, darling." She studied me for a long moment. She wasn't fully dressed today—no red lips or outlandish eye makeup, but she still looked amazing to me. "Come with me. I have just the thing to cheer you up."

I followed her into the kitchen—a tiny room at the back of the apartment my parents built for her. The apartment was just large enough for Etta's acting souvenirs and her. She had a tiny sofa and a flat-screen TV on the wall. Every spot of wall space boasted autographed pictures of Etta and her leading men, Playbills, or reviews of her performances—the good ones, that is. Knowing Etta as well as he did, Dad provided only a basic kitchen. Etta didn't cook. Not even a little. Her refrigerator held leftovers from the meals Mom cooked or the meals Etta ordered in. I watched while she opened the door to the tiny fridge, rooted around inside for a moment, and surfaced bearing a foil-wrapped package.

"Sit, sit." She waved me over to the small bistro table in the corner. I sat on a high stool while she opened the cabinet in the hall, took out one of her fancy plates, the kind rimmed in gold, and brought it to the counter near the fridge. A moment later, she put it down in front of me.

I gasped.

Six chocolate-covered strawberries circled the plate, on top of a lace doily. Fresh tears choked me. Etta wrapped her arms around me and squeezed. "Oh, hush now. No boy is *ever* worth your tears, darling. I should know. I married four."

"You never cried over a boy, Etta?"

She pulled out a chair and sat opposite me, studied the plate, and chose a strawberry. She bit into it, closing her eyes with a moan. "Not since I was thirteen years old and Harold Fine decided that Rose DeLuro had nicer...*assets*...than I did." She looked pointedly at her chest—noticeably flatter than mine.

I took after Mom's side of the family in that department.

"What about the Four? Didn't you love them?"

She slowly chewed her berry, licked her fingers, and shrugged. "I certainly thought I did at the time."

"And now?"

She smiled brightly. "And now I know I am far too self-absorbed to love any man more than I love myself."

"Uh." I blinked. I had no idea how to respond to that. I grabbed a strawberry of my own, took a bite, and felt immediately better. "Where did you get these? They're amazing."

"The chocolate shop off Main Street, near the theater. Wonderful, aren't they?"

Wonderful didn't come close.

"If you were a tad bit older, I'd pour you a shot of whiskey in that tea."

I stared at her. "I won't tell if you won't."

She smiled and gave me the nice-try look. "Now then. Tell me from the beginning everything that happened."

So I did. We drank our tea, finished the strawberries, and I told her everything: the band and the Beat and all the crappy insults and put-downs I'd had to deal with just because I posted my opinions.

"And these insults…you're certain they were from Elijah?"

"Um, well, no. Only the one about making me scream. Oh, Etta!" I buried my face in my hands and sobbed. "I really thought he was great. But he's just—he's just—"

"A man. The question is, how will you *use* this information?"

I lifted my head and stared at her through my tears. "I don't know what you mean."

"Kristen, my darling, whether this Elijah is great or not is *not* the question you should be asking. You now know something about him—how can that something help you get what you need?"

"I don't know what I need!"

"Of course you do." She repeated with a subtle eye roll. "You were heartbroken about your summer program rejection. What if you created your own summer program? What if you accepted Mr. Hamilton's *indecent* proposal?" She leaned in closer. "And what if *screaming* in his rock band is *just* the sort of unexpected something *extra* that you need on your conservatory applications?"

I rocked back in my seat. Could I do that? Could I hide the crack in my heart and pretend this is just my next role? Yeah. Yeah, I decided, I could. "I guess I could call him."

Etta gasped. "Oh, no, you will *not*. You will wait for young Mr. Hamilton to come to you, begging. When he does, and he *will*, you'll agree to sing in his band and then you will *capture* all of his fans with one simple technique that has *endured* through the ages. It's called sexual competition, darling."

I choked and then quickly looked around to make sure Mom and Dad hadn't possibly heard that.

Etta patted my back. "It's not what you think," she said, waving a hand. "The concept is quite simple, really. Despite it being the twenty-first century and all, it's just that people—especially *men*—cannot believe women can do anything as well or, heaven forbid, *better* than they can. You turn this into a competition like that, and people who don't even *like* this sort of music will fill seats just to see who wins."

My eyes widened. If I did this, I could *really* give Elijah Hamilton's fans something to talk about—and maybe, with a little luck, that something might involve revenge of all sorts of unspeakable agony.

A slow grin spread across my face. I raised my teacup, and Etta clinked it, a matching grin on her face.

7

ELIJAH

the beat_   Search

Ride Out
@ride_out   **1,024** FANS

@BryceG: WTF @Ride_Out? You got BroadwayBitch on her back? Sweet. #CatCall

> **@Ride_Out:** @BryceG: On her back? Hell, gonna have her on her knees. Wait and see. #CatCall

SHARES: 6 LIKES: 22

Shit. I seriously messed things up.

Today was Thursday. I didn't get around to accepting Kristen's friend request until yesterday, and she'd sent it on Saturday.

And I hadn't heard a word from her.

I didn't know much about girls. But I knew this: you don't keep them waiting. And I damn well couldn't tell Kristen *why* I'd kept her waiting. I laughed, imagining that conversation. *Oh, yeah. Sorry about not getting back to you. My friend, Sam, was acting like a total girl, and I had to reassure him that he was still number one in my life. You know how it is.*

So after school on Thursday, I cut my last class and booked it across town to Bear River High School North. When the bell rang, I waited—not patiently—for Kristen Cartwright to appear at the main exit so I could convince her to give me—give *us*—a shot.

A couple of freshmen gave me the eye as they went by, and I realized I was still laughing. I quickly shuttered my face and tried to look like Elijah Hamilton, Rock God. I thrust my thumbs in my belt and leaned casually against a rail, hip cocked like I was too cool for school. I worked hard on my rock god rep so nobody could see the sweat rolling down my back.

Students walked out the main exit and down the stairs to waiting buses. I studied faces and skidded to a sudden stop. What the hell did Kristen Cartwright look like out of her cat costume? Was she a blond or a brunette? Was her hair long or short? The only things I remembered about her were those kissable lips and that seriously awesome rack—

Whoa.

Speak of the devils.

The same awesome rack just walked out the exit. She was with some other girl, whose eyes practically exploded out of her face when she got a look at me.

I tensed up and waited for Kristen to spot me. When she did, I could tell I was definitely in some deep trouble by the way her spine snapped up straight. She was a blond, and her hair fell past her shoulders in a silky curtain. She wore bright red boots with jeans and a North sweatshirt.

Kristen Cartwright liked to be noticed. Why else would anyone wear red boots?

She met my eyes and then walked down the steps and right on by, her friend glued to her side.

I laughed. Okay. Game on. Let the chase begin. I pushed off the rail and caught up to her in a couple of strides. "Hey."

She made a sound of some sort, halfway between "Hi!" and "Drop dead."

Thinking fast, I blurted out, "I have a present for you." I didn't. Not really. Shit. Now I had to improvise.

Another sound, this one louder. "Would you like me to tell you what you can do with this present?" Witnesses to our game laughed, and I suddenly found myself losing patience.

"Look, you're pissed off, and I get that. But I meant what I said at the show last weekend. I want you to sing in my band."

She stopped walking and turned to face me, her hair lifted by the breeze. Ignoring her friend and the rest of our audience, she curled her lip in a sneer that told me just what she thought of my band. "Oh, really? Because I heard all you wanna do is *make me purr and scream*."

My jaw dropped. What in the actual fuck was she talking about? "Uh—"

Her hand shot up. "Don't even." She tugged out her cell, tapped some buttons, and shoved it in my face while her friend skewered me with a disgusted look. I jerked when I saw the #CatCall tweet stream, starting with my *wanna hear her scream* post.

Oh, crap. Yeah. I'd seriously fucked up.

She stuffed the phone back in her pocket and started walking away. No. What she was thinking was wrong. I'm not that much of a dick. "I said *hear*, not *make*!" I called after her.

She halted, turned around, and shot out a hip. "Big deal."

"It *is* a big deal." I caught up to her. "I was talking about heavy metal screaming. It's a kind of singing style?"

A tiny crease formed over her brow, but she hadn't run away, so maybe, just maybe, I still had a shot.

"I know what it is."

I had a feeling that was a lie, but I let it go.

"I think you'd be able to do a great metal scream."

"So…you're saying you didn't mean that tweet in the pervy, sick, misogynistic way it sounded?"

Uh, misogynistic? Holy shit. I held up both hands. "No!"

"Then why did you post my picture?"

I was so busted. "Okay. Yeah. I posted your picture because you're like…well, *hot*. And I kind of wanted to—"

"Exploit me," she finished for me.

Aw, hell. "Yeah. I guess so." I hung my head. "I didn't really think about that. But I didn't *lie* to you. I still think you have the most amazing voice I've ever heard. I just really want to hear you sing in my band."

She smirked. "No offense, but I hate rock."

"Yeah, and I hate show tunes. Doesn't change anything."

While her friend kept making impatient sounds, Kristen crossed her arms and studied me, her head angled like she was trying to get a glimpse of the real me through my nostrils, open mouth, or ears. "Why?"

I opened my mouth then closed it. "Why what?" Hadn't we just covered this?

"Why me?"

"I told you. Your voice completely blew me away. I really want to see what you can do with hard songs."

Blue eyes narrowed to tiny pinpricks. "Hard songs? You don't think 'Memory' is a hard song?"

"Kristen, the bus is gonna leave without us." Her friend tried again to get her moving.

Aw, hell…were girls always this much work? I renewed my commitment to not date and tried to explain. "Hard *rock* songs. The genre," I clarified, praying for patience. It worked. Her eyes went back to their normal size, and she waved a hand.

"Okay. So you want to hear me sing hard rock so badly, it takes you a week to accept my friend request?"

Sam *so* owes me for this. I should have responded the second she sent her request, but I didn't want him to think I was whipped. And then, Anna had a meltdown that sucked me into the vortex, and I just forgot. "I had some stuff going on. Doesn't mean I changed my mind about you."

She sucked in a cheek and rolled her eyes. "Oh, right. *Stuff*. Of course." She turned and started walking again. In a few more yards, she'd reach the bus that idled in the parking lot, and I'd lose this opportunity.

"My sister is... She has special needs," I blurted out. Shit. I hadn't planned to tell her that. It just...I just...*fuck*! What was it about Kristen Cartwright that made me forget all my moves? Girls usually bought whatever line I sold them but not her.

She halted in the middle of the parking lot, ignoring a horn that honked at her. With wide eyes, she stared at me, lips parted in an O of shock. "Seriously?"

"Kristen, come on!"

Impatient, she waved at her friend. The girl growled in frustration, spun on her heel, and climbed aboard the bus, leaving Kristen and me alone. Finally.

My face burned, but I nodded. "Uh, well, yeah. Kind of messes up the family dynamic, you know?" Of course she didn't know. Why the hell did I say that? My face burst into flames, and I decided now would be a very good time to retreat. "Uh, fuck. You know what? This was a bad idea. You should just stick to your show tunes, and I'll head back to the wrong side of the tracks you obviously think I come from, and we'll just forget the whole thing." I turned to go, panic rising like the tide. I wasn't sure how the hell we'd get the county festival gig without Kristen to appeal to the general public but whatever. I'd find a way to make it happen without her because there was no way I could look at this girl and just take it when she looked back at me with such an expression of disgust on her face.

"What about my present?" That powerhouse voice shouted after me, freezing me where I stood.

Slowly, I turned, trying like hell to force my face back into its rock god sneer. I went with the first thing that came to me. "I was writing you a song." Okay. Yeah. This could work. I could rhyme on the fly. But then, both of her eyebrows shot up, and a goofy smile spread across her face. Uh-oh. Rewind! Rewind! "Not a song *to* you, like a dedication or something. Just one for you to sing. With us."

The smile dimmed back to a normal level, and I breathed easy again. Didn't want her getting the wrong idea. She was off-limits.

No matter how amazing she looked when she smiled.

Or how good she looked in those jeans.

"Okay, let me see it."

"What?" I blinked.

"This song. Let me see it." She snapped her fingers at me and held out a hand.

I laughed at her. "Can you read sheet music?" She gave me the side eye, but before she could retort with some other sarcastic dig, I held up both hands. "I'm just asking."

"Fine. Yes, I can read sheet music."

"Okay." I took out my phone and showed her a melody I'd been working on. I watched the emotions and reactions play over her face.

Her lips twitched, and her breath caught. A moment later, I swear her lips moved. She was humming silently to herself.

I almost pumped my fist in victory.

"Wanna hear it, done hard?"

She let out a sigh and handed back the phone. "I guess so."

I tapped some buttons, and my guitar strumming played out, tinny and thin. The parking lot was almost empty now that the buses had pulled out, but I'd have sung for her even it was packed. I sucked in a deep breath and prayed I didn't fuck this up.

> *Born on the stage with mics in our hands.*
> *You and me.*
> *Strangers in the same land.*

Kristen bopped her head to the beat, so I took that as a sign to keep going. I sang her the chorus.

> *We can make this work.*
> *Heads. Tails.*
> *Passing. Fail.*
> *Two sides of the same damn coin.*
> *Sing. Play.*
> *Writing. Pray.*
> *Baby, let's get our forces joined.*
> *We can make this work.*

The guitar riff ended, and I shoved the phone in the pocket of my jeans, my face burning. "Okay, so it's not my best work." Still it wasn't bad for spur of the moment.

"Is that it?"

She wants more! Yes! Inside, I was cheering. But outside, all I did was flash her my best wicked smile. "I always leave 'em wanting more."

To my total surprise, her face went red, but she didn't back down. "Spare me the TMI on your sex life and stick to music, okay?"

I almost choked on my own spit when she said *sex*. "Fine. What did you think?"

She shifted her bag to the other shoulder, and I hid my smile. The bag had a *Cats* logo on it. That was pretty damn dedicated. Then again, maybe that wasn't a bad idea. I could have Ride Out bags printed to hand out at our shows.

If we ever got any more, of course.

She nibbled a fingernail painted blue and looked up at me from under her lashes. Damn, those lips were hot. "Okay. It was good. Really good."

A distinctly shocked note was entirely audible in that response. I crossed my arms and got ready for battle. "Awesome. Next question… why are you so surprised? I told you I was in a band."

Amazing lips parted in a laugh that was ten times better than the smile—or worse, depending on your perspective. "Yeah, you did. It's just when you said hard rock, I expected pentagrams and black candles and howls."

"We do that kind of stuff too. The howls, I mean," I quickly added when her jaw dropped. "Not the pentagrams and black candles."

She looked a bit reassured to hear that but then shook her head. "I can't do that."

"No problem. I can teach you."

She smiled at me like I was a four-year-old who'd just learned to tie his own shoes. "Let me rephrase. I meant I *won't* do that. I won't ruin my throat for your band."

Her hand crept up to her throat and rested there, and my eyes settled on the pulse I could see beating just under her fingertips. I licked my lips and nodded. "So noted. But just so you know, metal screams and death growls won't ruin your throat when they're done right. There's a technique to it, just like learning any other extended vocal technique. Plus, not every song needs a metal scream."

Her eyebrows shot up, obviously surprised at my knowledge. Silence extended between us, and just when it got awkward, she asked, "So do you, um, write your own music?"

"Oh, sure. We have a ton of fresh stuff now. We'd love to cut a record, but for that, we need interest."

She flashed me a wide smile, full teeth, and my brain went dead for a second. "And that's why you need me."

I tried not to kink up at that. "I *want* you, Kristen. Never said I *needed* you." Let her take that however she wanted to. That sexy little flush was crawling back up her neck and into her cheeks. Damn, this was *fun*.

"Oh, you need me, Guitar Hero. You just don't know how much." She took off, leaving me standing there with my mouth open. She'd walked a few yards away and then called out over her shoulder.

"I'll give you a chance. Message me details. I guess you want me to rehearse?"

"You know what they say." I had to have the last word. She rewarded me by walking backward, waiting for me to tell her what the mysterious *they* say. "Try before you buy." She laughed and turned back, giving me a most excellent view of a most excellent ass striding away on bloodred boots.

I watched that ass sway and suddenly remembered my manners. "Hey!" I called after her. "Can I take you home? I mean, I made you miss the bus and all."

She spun around and shook her head. "Don't push your luck. I'll just grab the late bus."

And with that, she turned and strode back inside the school, leaving me alone in the parking lot with this urge to finish writing that lame-ass song I just made up.

————

Early Saturday morning, Mom and Dad took Anna to her therapy appointment, so I dragged my ass out of bed to open the garage for Nick and Sam. I hadn't heard from Kristen Cartwright.

Would she show?

A girl like her probably had a dozen guys chasing after her. Then again, she seemed like the type who wouldn't turn down a good challenge.

I tossed down a bowl of soggy cereal, brushed my teeth, tied my hair back, and returned to the garage. The warm red hoodie I tugged over my head kind of reminded me of Kristen's boots. It was spring, and even though I wasn't a fashion designer, I did notice that the flip-flops hit the scene as soon as the snow season ended. And yet, Kristen still wore her boots. There was a story around those boots, I was sure of it. I should write a song. Hmm. Maybe something like this:

> *The girl wearin' hot red boots*
> *Pointed at me and said, "Hey."*
> *I stared at those end to end curves,*
> *Pointed right back, and said, "'K."*

Not bad. I jotted it down so I wouldn't forget it. It was a start and might spark some more ideas later. I played around with the riffs I'd started for Kristen's song. I'd sent it to Sam and Nick, but only Nick had replied so far and said he liked it. Guess Sam was going to make an issue out of everything with Kristen. I shook my head, put in my earphones, and got lost in the sound.

I almost didn't hear Kristen come up the driveway. I looked up just in time to see her take a bicycle helmet off her head and shake out her blond hair. She was wearing tight jeans with the bottoms tucked into those same bright red boots. I didn't even realize I was staring until she shot me one of her looks. I just grinned and made no apologies. She angled her head, frowning at me.

I squirmed. "What?"

"Nothing." She shrugged. "Just trying to figure you out."

I grinned. "Keep trying, baby. I'm an enigma." When she rolled her eyes, I swallowed the groan I'd nearly let out. *An enigma?*

Kristen let it go and stepped inside. "Where's Sam and Nick?"

"Not here yet." Which was cool by me because I'd get more time alone with my white cat. I stared at her for a long moment…until she shifted her weight to one leg and crossed her arms, clearly bugged. Yeah. So we should get down to work. "Have a seat." I led her to a stool and grabbed my iPad. "Do you listen to any music that's not from Broadway?"

"Uh, yeah," she said with a distinct tone of *duh* in her voice. "Of course I do."

I doubted it. "Well, who do you like?"

"Let's see. I like Taylor Swift and One Direction and—"

"Please don't say Bieber."

"Why not?"

I shuddered and changed the subject, fast. "What about rock music?"

"I like a lot of oldies. Led Zeppelin, Bon Jovi, Aerosmith."

My eyebrows lifted. Hope flared, and I put up a hand. "Okay, that's a start. Any newer stuff?" When she shrugged, I tapped my tablet and played a song from Avenged Sevenfold's latest album. We listened to the heavy beat, but she didn't seem impressed, so I played Thousand Foot Krutch. She did some head bopping, so I figured she liked that band a bit, but there was no real appreciation. Hmmm. Converting a theater girl to a hard rocker was going to be a lot tougher than I'd expected. "Have you ever heard of Halestorm?"

"Nope." Kristen shook her head. "Well, except for you. You mentioned them after my show. It is a *them*, right?"

"Yeah." I laughed. "Female lead singer. Amazing." I played "I Miss the Misery" for her, and when it was over, searched her face. "What do you think?"

She wrinkled her nose. "It's all…so noisy."

I stared at her for a minute and then cracked up. "That's the point," I said when I could breathe. "Rock music is all about the decibels, baby. Rebellious. Defiant." I lifted a fist, and Kristen's eyes lit up.

"Defiant?"

"Sure. Rock was born in the fifties…maybe even the forties, depending on where you look. Some experts believe it was born in the South, a fusion of jazz and gospel."

"What do you believe?" She leaned forward and cupped her chin in her hands, and I had to fight the urge to stare at her chest, which was suddenly *right there*.

"Me? I believe rock and roll was born in 1948."

"Exactly in 1948." She raised her eyebrows. "Why? What happened?"

Slowly, I smiled and pulled over the second stool. "I'm so glad you asked." I tapped the tablet's screen, brought up a web browser, and showed her. "*This* was born."

Kristen took the tablet and examined the picture I'd pulled up. "A guitar."

"The electric guitar. The *first* guitar whose sound could be amplified. This was a game changer. But that's not all." I swiped at the screen and brought up another image. "This also happened in the same year."

"The record?"

"The LP record, which established the *album* as a musical showcase." Jesus, did she not know anything?

"Cool," she said.

"Not done yet." I grinned at her comment. "There was one more thing invented around this time that spread rock and roll to every corner of the country." I swiped, tapped, and gave her back the tablet.

She squinted at the image. "What the hell is that?"

"That's a transistor."

Nodding, she slowly smiled. "Oh, I get it. Radios."

"Yep," I said, popping the *p*. "Wanna take a guess why this matters?"

"Easy." She lifted her shoulders. "Radios got small and portable, which extended your rebellion, your defiance."

Impressed, I leaned closer. "You learn fast." She smelled really good. I just sat there, letting that scent wrap me up. It was oranges, I think. Something citrusy, and it was making me dizzy.

"So…um….what next?"

I jerked. *Stop smelling the girl and get to work, you idiot.* I cleared my throat and asked, "Want to give one a try?"

Her eyes snapped back to mine and popped wide. "Wait, just you and me? I thought you wanted me in your band."

"Oh, I do. I just thought we could try a few on our own." *So I can keep you to myself.*

She angled her head and studied me. "So I'm *really* here for my voice. Nothing else?"

Warning! Danger! Danger! "Um." I paused, cleared my throat. "Look, Kristen. If the only thing I wanted was a hot babe in black leather, I could have held tryouts after cheerleading practice. I want *you*, Kristen. Your voice. Your skills. You."

She lowered her eyes and murmured, "You sounded good the other day. I don't see why you need me."

Good? Huh. I was shooting for awesome. Abruptly embarrassed, I queued up a Seether song called "Words As Weapons." "Can you howl?"

Kristen's mouth fell open. "Sorry, what?"

"Howl. Like a wolf."

"First you want me to purr and scream, and now you want me to howl? Can't we just sing like normal people?"

"It's really just an *ooh* and an *aah*. No big deal." She lifted one eyebrow in a classic *yeah, right* look, and I squirmed on my stool. "Okay, I'm going with no howling." I tapped the tablet screen and brought up the lyrics to the song. "You sing this part. I'll do the rest," I said, indicating the chorus.

"Okay, I've got the notes." She met my eyes and nodded. "Yeah. I can sing this."

Of that, I had absolutely no doubt. I stood up, found my camera, and set it up. I didn't even ask first. I didn't want to make her more uncomfortable than she already was and give her time to reconsider. The camera would help me convince her that she was good at this because I had a feeling she was gonna keep fighting me on it.

"Okay. When you're ready, sing. I'll follow with the strings and the rest of the lyrics." I gave her a count off, and she took a breath and sang the first line in a tone that was so pure, I almost missed my cue. I added the guitar track and then took over the lyrics, hoping like hell I could impress this girl. When I got to the *ooh* and *aah* howl, she grinned and joined me, making me flub my strumming. Her voice, God… It was the most flawless sound I'd ever heard, and just like I'd hoped, once she got started, she took over and sang the rest of it, even the parts that were mine.

I was more than willing to give it up for her.

We plowed through "Words As Weapons" again and then switched things up. I took her through some Evanescence, Stone Sour's "Do Me a Favor," and Avenged Sevenfold's "Hail to the King," which she knocked out of the fucking park. Kristen had a good ear and an even better eye. All I did was show her the sheet music, and she knew exactly when to time her delivery, punching her vocals with a little whine. People walking their dogs stopped to listen, and by the time Sam and Nick got there, we were dripping sweat and guzzling down bottles of water.

"Hey, guys."

Nick held up a hand for a high five while Sam shook out his mane. I took a moment to redo the tail keeping my own too-long hair off my face. Full disclosure? I hated long hair, but it went with the rock god image.

"Kristen, this is Sam and Nick."

"I met Nick before. Hey, Sam." She nodded to the guys and held the cold bottle of water against her head.

"Damn, that was sick!" Nick said, emphasizing the last word with a wave of both hands. "We heard you guys before we got out of the car and—whoa!" He pointed to the amplifier setting. "You're not even jacked up. That is some serious skill."

Kristen smiled and looked away, maybe a little embarrassed, but definitely pleased.

"So what do you think?" Sam asked. "Jamming with a metal band's more fun than a night on Broadway, right?"

She angled her head and narrowed her eyes, pretending to think about that for a moment. "It's...um, different."

"Oh, come on!" I protested. "You were definitely into it."

Kristen didn't answer, but I saw the way her blue eyes sparkled behind a smile she couldn't totally hide. Sam dropped a paper bag on the table that I knew held bagels—I could smell them—grabbed his guitar, and jacked in. The speakers whined out a bit of feedback, and Kristen clapped her hands to her ears.

"Let's get on with it." Sam took his position. "How much time have we got, Eli?"

Shit. Anna. I glanced at my phone. "Couple hours, at least."

Nick grabbed his drumsticks and sat down behind the kit my dad let him keep here. "What are you in the mood for?"

"Let's do one of our own," Sam said, and I nodded.

"Uh, hold up a minute." Kristen put up a hand. "I'm not singing anything that disses girls or is pure sex. And I'm most definitely not screaming, growling, howling, or meowing."

"Here we go," Sam muttered, but I shot up a hand to cut him off.

"Wait." I frowned. "Why do you think we dis girls?"

"Never mind. Let's just do this. Nick?" Sam spun his hand in the air, and Nick counted us off, and we performed our crowd-pleasing hit, "Let You In." I wrote it about two years ago. Every time we performed it, we got the crowd on their feet.

Okay, so *crowd* was a bit of an exaggeration.

It was more like the twenty or thirty people who just wanted to sit down for a while after spending all afternoon wandering through the street fairs and malls we usually played, which is exactly why I considered it a hit. If we could get *them* on their feet, we must be good. It began with a mellow beat that morphed into a violent chorus of screaming metal and heavy vocals that I loved. I couldn't stop watching Kristen chair-dance.

You're looking at me with those big soft eyes.
Everything in your heart is undisguised.
I can see all of your hopes and dreams.
Pinned on some words and a diamond ring.

You don't know, you can't ever understand.
For all that to happen,
I gotta open wide and let you in.

Inside my head,
Inside my soul,
Inside my heart,
Where there's still a hole.
I can't let that happen.
I can't go back there again.
I'm broken in pieces,
I can never let you in.

When I hit the chorus, I caught Kristen's eye and waved her over. She joined in, ad-libbing her own lyrics.

"*Inside my head,*" I screamed.

"*Baby, let me in,*" Kristen sang, coming in just as I finished the line. She was soft and tentative, and Sam rolled his eyes. *Come on! Cut loose!* I mentally begged. This song was harsh—that was its point. A soft mood just didn't cut it.

"*Inside my soul.*"

"*Baby, let me in,*" she repeated, holding the last note.

"*Inside my heart, where there's still a hole.*"

Sam dropped off, and I knew he was about to call for a do-over when Kristen took off like she was born to sing this song. "*Baby, let me in, 'cause I'm not her. I can make it better, make you whole. Let me love you, let me be the one, let me, baby, oh, let me in.*"

I always thought the growling vocals and the hot guitars fully conveyed the song's theme—a guy afraid of commitment. But Kristen's sweet voice added an element I never knew was missing until now. The song was *also* about a girl who refused to give up on this scarred and scared guy. I nodded and grinned because Christ, it was so damn perfect, I wanted to hop in the car and head straight for the nearest record label. We played the last notes, and when Nick ended with one last clash of his cymbals, all hands went up in a cheer.

"Yeah!"

"Woo!"

"That was fucking awesome!"

"Kristen, that was insane." I grabbed her in a hug and felt those luscious curves melt against my edges.

"I know, right? You guys are incredibly good. I had no idea! You should play at my school. They're looking for a band for a rally next month."

Nick rolled his eyes. "They would never let us. We're too hard-core."

"That's just wrong," she decided. "You guys wrote that song? It was fabulous. Seriously."

Fabulous? I laughed. Who says that? Everything about Kristen was big and bold and over the top, and I couldn't wipe the dumb-ass grin off my face. "Kristen, tell me you didn't enjoy the hell out of that."

She laughed and shook her head. "I totally loved it."

"Enough to do more with us?" I looked to Sam and Nick for confirmation. Nick nodded with enthusiasm. Sam just shrugged. I'd have to deal with him later. "We have a YouTube channel and a website. Every month, we review a new band and post a song cover. We want you in." When she didn't say anything, I shifted gears. "Check this out." I tapped a few buttons on the tablet, and Common Kiss's website opened. "This is the band we're review-ing this month. They're called Common Kiss. It's Shakespeare, or something."

"No." Kristen shook her head. "I think it's Elizabeth Barrett Browning."

"Who the hell's that?" Sam asked.

"She's a poet. I think it's from *Sonnets from the Portuguese.*"

He flung up a hand. "I don't actually care."

"Sam, will you just chill, please?" I turned back to Kristen. "Anyhow, we're gonna cover their song, 'Lie Like You Mean It.' I've been working on new arrangements, and we've played around, recording bits of it."

"Can I hear it?"

I swiped at the tablet and queued it up for her. "It's still raw," I said with a shrug, abruptly anxious for her to love it. A second or two went by, and then my vocals slashed through the air.

> *You said you don't love me,*
> *Said you don't need me,*
> *Said you don't wanna see me anymore.*
> *You told me things you couldn't possibly mean.*
> *I refused to listen. Baby, I'm wounded to the core.*
> *Tears in your eyes, so why can't you admit*
> *You're just lying like you really mean it.*

And without any preparation, without any thought, Kristen just opened her mouth and added her own touch.

"I don't love you anymore. I don't wanna fight this war. I'm not lying. I really mean it."

Her voice had an Adele tone that added cool depth to the biting pain my lyrics gave the song. Her face was incredibly expressive as she sang, and as far as I was concerned, that was just the cherry on top.

I tapped the Stop button and opened the camera. "Sing it again, just like that."

Kristen rolled her eyes but sang the lines again—better this time. I shot some video of her, then grabbed a mic and plugged it into my laptop. "One more time, Kris. Same way."

Her eyebrows went up at the nickname. Oops. She sang it a third time, just her, and I recorded it to the sound editing software installed on the computer. "Kristen, this is so fucking amazing. Thanks for hanging with us."

"Yeah. Thanks, Kristen. You were seriously awesome." Nick held up a hand for a high five. "I wasn't sure at first, but you were clutch."

Kristen grinned.

"Not bad." Sam jerked his head in something thinly resembling a nod.

"Go ahead. Admit it. This was awesome, right?" I grinned at her, and she rolled her eyes but nodded.

"Yeah, it totally was. I wasn't sure I would like it. I mean, I see what you guys and your fans post on the Beat and figured it would just be noise and some obscene lyrics, you know?"

My stomach clenched when she mentioned the Beat. The only person who ever said we were obscene was BroadwayBaby17. "Aw, fuck." Nick looked at me sharply, but Sam was biting back a smile. He got it.

"What? What's the matter?" She circled her hands. "Come on, I know you know that site. There's a Ride Out account being used."

No. Please, no. I shut my eyes and waited for all of my plans to pop like one of Anna's soap bubbles.

Sam's grin spread slow and wide. "Of course we're on it. We're just stunned someone like you is."

Kristen turned to face Sam, shot out a hip, and narrowed her eyes. "Like me? What the hell does that mean?"

"Nothing, nothing. Untwist your panties."

"Jesus, Sam! Will you knock that shit off?" Nick slapped the back of Sam's head. Sam just laughed and pulled out his phone.

"Okay, okay. So what's your user name?" he asked Kristen, and I wanted to stuff my fingers in my ears so I wouldn't have to hear her say it. *Don't say it. Please don't say it.*

"BroadwayBaby17."

My shoulders sagged. *Fuck me.*

Sam let out a holler. "Christ on a bike, this is fucking hilarious!" He waved an arm at Kristen and turned to Nick. "This is the girl he said doesn't know shit about singing. The one who couldn't tell radio rock from thrash metal if it hit her on the head with a guitar. The one who said our lyrics are sexist and whose ass Eli said he'd like to kick all the way to Broadway so she'd just shut the fuck up." He doubled over, laughing.

Nick stared at me and then looked at Kristen. "Sam, shut up, man!"

Nice effort, but it was too late. Kristen's huge blue eyes filled with fury, and her face went red. "So…you're FretGuy99?" She never waited for me to answer. "God…was this…this really was all some kind of setup." She stared at me, huge blue eyes swimming with tears, and I wanted to throw myself at her knees. "It's bad enough dealing with the crap Ride Out posts but *FretGuy*?" She stared at me, eyes watery, and then she snapped straight up, lips narrowing. "What the hell is your deal? You just lurk online, waiting for someone to criticize Ride Out, and then you swoop in, hiding your identity behind a different account? I cannot believe this. You're a troll… You totally suck." She grabbed her stuff and stalked out of my garage, out of my plan, out of my life.

Damage control. I had to do damage control right fucking now before she blabbed to the entire Internet that FretGuy99 was part of Ride Out. I worked hard to keep those two accounts completely separate, and I wanted them to stay that way. If this got out, I'd get nothing but newbies asking me to offer free advice or listen to their demo tapes.

I grabbed my phone, only to discover that Sam had beaten me to it.

Ride_Out: So we let BroadwayBaby17 jam with us today. #CatCall

One step, two steps, and I had Sam's shirt bunch in my fist. "Sam, what the hell did you do?"

8

KRISTEN

Kristen Cartwright
@kristencartwright

Tweets	Following	Followers
6,917	**740**	**1,228**

@Ride_Out

Check it! @kristencartwright rockin' out with us. Amazing sound. #CatCall

@DTMilo

@Ride_Out should change name to Ride Her! #CatCall #lemmebefirst

@Ride_On747

@Ride_Out Wait @kristencartwright is BroadwayBaby17? OMG #CatCall

@Ride_On747

@Ride_Out @kristencartwright Stick to the stage and leave metal to the men. #CatCall

@Mikey_T

@Ride_Out @kristencartwright Nice! Post pics of those tits! #CatCall

@kristencartwright

That's right! I'm singing with @Ride_Out. Somebody's gotta show the boys how it's done. #CatCall

@kristencartwright

@elijahhamilton will be on his knees screaming for ME. #CatCall

> **@Mikey_T**
>
> @Ride_Out @kristencartwright @elijahhamilton oooh, it's #KrisVsEli! #CatCall
>
> RETWEETS 38 FAVORITES 102

> **@Mikey_T**
>
> @kristencartwright Did you scream yet? RT @Ride_Out: Wanna hear her scream! #CatCall
>
> RETWEETS 33 FAVORITES 212

"It was a bad idea, Rachel. I shouldn't have listened."

Stretched across her purple bedspread, Rachel looked up from this month's issue of *People* magazine and popped another nacho chip into her mouth. "Yeah, well, Etta's kind of hard to say no to."

"Exactly!" I flung out my hands and paced around her room. "And now, Elijah's got video footage of me rehearsing with his band that he could post all over the Internet, tell the whole world how bad I suck, how much of a sellout I am."

Rachel's hand froze halfway to her mouth, the nacho chip clasped between her fingers. "And that would be a bad thing, why again?"

I rolled my eyes. "Because he knows I'm BroadwayBaby17 on the Beat. I take enough crap from the guys on that site. If everybody found out my real name, it would never stop."

Rachel went back to page-flipping. "You're making too big a deal out of this. Okay, he knows your name. But you know *his* real name too. You could post crap right back if he did. Ooooh, he is so gorgeous," she said on a gusty sigh when the magazine opened to a two-page spread of her favorite actor.

I angled my head and appreciated the eye candy, but I couldn't stop worrying. Elijah Hamilton—hiding behind his FretGuy99 account—was one of the chief slingers of insults online. Etta kept asking me why I didn't just stay offline if the abuse bothered me so much, but that always struck me as running away. I wasn't doing anything wrong and shouldn't have to hide myself because a few oversensitive jerks couldn't deal with criticism. They hid behind their little keyboards, safe in their little cocoons, free to say any vile, disgusting thing they'd never have the guts to say to my face.

And just in case they *did*, I never posted on the Beat under my real name.

I'd joined the Beat about a year ago. The site was organized by genre, but you can follow anyone you want. At first, I followed other drama club people—actors, musical theater performers, dancers. I don't remember exactly how I found Ride Out. I probably followed someone's link. I listened to a few of their tracks and it was…raw. I thought I could help them refine their sound. That was the site's mission—artists helping artists. You post snips of songs, riffs, a little video—and you ask for help. *Am I hitting the right mark? Is this the right emotion?* Stuff like that. Your followers can vote on your posts, share them, or reply back. I had a few thousand followers on the Beat now who requested my opinions and feedback and respected me—mostly. But there was this whole hard rock contingent that did nothing but antagonize me. I ignored most of their crap, blocked the truly nasty ones, and just tried to do my thing. My stomach clenched into a knot every time I thought about Elijah of the Intense Eyes as one of those jerks.

My phone buzzed. I swiped at the screen and read a message, and my heart thudded against my ribs. "Oh, no."

Rachel looked up from her celebrity crush. "What?"

I showed her my phone. He'd done it. He'd posted video of me with my real name.

> @Ride_Out
>
> Check it! @kristencartwright rockin' out with us. Amazing sound. bit.ly/Pmm2nxps #CatCall

The link attached to the post on the Beat led to a video of my first attempt at rock music.

Rachel clicked the link, and a second later, the sounds of Elijah's guitar played out of the tinny speaker. It was only about thirty seconds of raw footage. Elijah was an incredible vocalist—not that I'd ever admit that in public. His sound was edgy, brutal in one verse, sweet and soulful in the next. I wasn't sure how he changed up his sound like that. My voice was impressive too, but I wasn't sure I could do that—not that it mattered. I wouldn't be singing with these guys again, which would clearly make Sam happy. The video made it painfully clear that he hated me. He made faces, shot meaningful looks at Elijah, who ignored him, and nearly dropped the mic at one point. Jesus, I just had to get warmed up. And I did. It was rehearsal! It wasn't supposed to go public.

I could *kill* Elijah for this.

I took the phone and played it a second time, and this time, I focused on me. I remembered getting sucked into the sound, dancing in place, and then jumping in because I just couldn't help it. I was in the zone…skin tingling, body tuned, and it showed.

"Oh my God, Kristen! This is so cool." Rachel forgot about her chips and her magazine and grinned at my phone. "Sam is seriously hot."

I scoffed. "If you like guys who have better hair than you do, I guess so."

"Hey, be nice." Rachel flipped her own long, dark hair. She grabbed another chip. "You're making too big a deal out of this. This gives you publicity, right? I thought you loved publicity."

I do. Or I did. "Etta always says there's no such thing as bad publicity." I sat down on the corner of Rachel's bed and folded over my middle. "Now, I'm not so sure."

"Why not?"

I handed her my phone. "Read the comments. They're actually scary."

Rachel frowned at the screen. "Wow. *Ride Out should be Ride Her.* Um, here's another. *Stick to the stage, BroadwayBaby and leave metal to the men.*" And then she gasped. "Oh, ick. *Nice! Post pics of those tits!*" Rachel tossed the phone to the bed in disgust. "I see what you mean. So what are you going to do?"

"I don't know. Etta thought this could be a good thing. Singing in a hard rock band might give me an edge for conservatory apps."

Rachel pursed her lips and picked at the label on her magazine. "I don't know, Kristen. Etta's great and all, but she doesn't know *today*."

Rachel's words pissed me off, but I took a deep breath and let them go right by because she had a point. Etta didn't know anything about Twitter or the Beat. She didn't deal with the kind of sexism and insults I put up with. On the other hand, I had a great time singing with Elijah, Sam, and Nick, even though Sam hated me. And yeah, I really did want to write my own rock song.

A sudden idea struck me so hard, I gasped.

"What?" Alarmed, Rachel sat up straight and examined me for signs of bodily injury.

Could I do it? Could I be that bold? I mulled it over for a moment and decided Etta would totally do it if it were her. She took crap from nobody. So why should I?

"What, Kristen? Jesus, will you say something?" Rachel grabbed my shoulders and shook me.

Slowly, I grinned at her. "I have the most amazing idea."

She blew her bangs out of her eyes and bounced back to the bed while I tapped out a tweet. When I showed her the screen, a matching smile formed. "You sure about this?"

No. "Yes."

"You realize this is a volley, right?"

I nodded. "I do. But I have almost as many followers as the band does and definitely more followers than his personal account does."

"Okaaaay," Rachel said with a wince. "But I don't think this is one of those situations where there's safety in numbers."

Oh, I disagreed. That was exactly why I was doing this. Elijah thought he was such a player? Time to prove I could play too. This would shut them up.

I clicked Send, flopped back on Rachel's bed, and met her palm in a high five.

9

ELIJAH

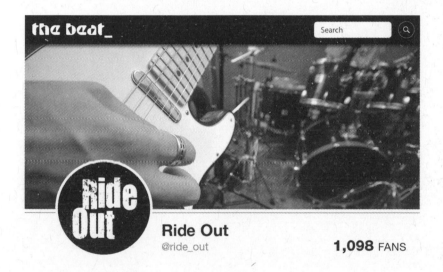

the beat_ Search

Ride Out
@ride_out   **1,098** FANS

Ride_Out: BroadwayBaby's got metal pipes! #CatCall

> **Ride_On747:** She's hot, but metal? #jurystillout

> **JJStix88:** More! More @BroadwayBaby17!

I sat for ages, trying like hell not to pitch my guitar across the garage.

I had her! Damn it, I had her hooked, and now she'd never talk to any of us again. Behind me, I was totally aware of Nick and Sam watching me.

Waiting.

We'd tried to practice after Kristen took off, but nobody was into it. Nick was tense and kept looking from me to Sam, but I knew he would not step in the middle of that unless blood was about to be shed.

"Well," Sam finally said. "It's been real."

I raised my head to see him buckle his guitar into its case.

Chest heaving from the effort not to tear his fucking head off, I said, "Sam, you are a colossal dick."

"Not just him, Eli. You acted all caveman," Nick added, stepping between us.

"I…you're—" I couldn't even think straight.

"That's because he wants—" Sam pumped his fist in front of his mouth, and I lunged for him, but Nick held me off.

"You see? An hour. That's all it took. A fucking hour before Yoko Cartwright came between us."

"So *that's* why you antagonized her? You did everything but call her a hypocrite!" I jabbed a finger at him.

He straightened up, gave me another one of those casual shrugs, and shook the hair from his face. "That's exactly what she *is*. All that bullshit about a sound that's all sex and drums and lyrics that disrespect women? Underneath it all, she wants to be just like us, bro. Everybody wants that! They want to be in a rock band—even repressed Miss Drama Queen."

I sneered. He just couldn't face it that somebody could be better than him. "That why you couldn't wait to tell everybody she jammed with us?" Beside me, I heard Nick pull in a sharp breath before he pulled out his phone to see for himself.

"Oh, Christ! What the hell did you do, Sam?"

Sam studied Nick for a minute and rolled his eyes with a curse. "I called her out on her bullshit so we can go back to doing what we do best."

"Sam," Nick said, shaking his head. "You posted video nobody had a chance to even review. That makes *us* look like shit."

I managed to get a hand twisted in Sam's shirt again before Nick tore us apart. "You're an asshole, Gowan!" I shouted. "Look at these alerts." I waved a hand at the tablet that was pinging a couple of times a minute. "You posted video that makes us look worse than the garage band we are. How the fuck are we supposed to book gigs?"

Sam crossed his arms until I finished my rant. "Hamilton, you can't see past the hard-on you have for this chick. Are you reading those alerts? It's working! We're generating buzz, just like you wanted. All I did was spin things a little. So don't get pissed at me because it's working." Sam grabbed his guitar case and strode out of my garage without another word.

I watched him go but didn't stop him.

Behind me, Nick shuffled. "Uh, Eli. He's right. This tweet's getting a lot of traction. I mean, that's what we wanted, right?"

Some publicity, some controversy. Yeah. That's what we wanted.

Okay. I sucked in a deep breath, trying to think.

Okay, this could still be salvaged. Kristen was a pro; she would understand Sam's lame-ass attempt at generating buzz.

Right?

I raked both hands through my hair and checked the comments online.

WTF @Ride_Out? You got BroadwayBitch17 on her back? Sweet. #CatCall

Yeah, it was sweet. Oh, not the comment, but having Kristen jam with us. She was every bit as good as I imagined…maybe better. I had to get her back. I *had* to.

I thought about it for a long while. We'd spent days learning new riffs and recording song covers and gotten maybe a dozen views at most. Our stats on the Beat followed a pattern—they spiked after we posted some other band's cover and then dropped the rest of the month. Kristen could break us out of that pattern. She was fresh, she was sick on the mic, and she was fearless. After one session, *bam!* Kristen had those numbers rising. But I wanted them to stay up. So now, everything inside me was begging to give them more. And still more after that. I thought about what else I could say, what else I could post, and it suddenly came to me, something that was sure to get this whole thing trending in our favor. Kristen wouldn't like it, but I knew it would work.

The answer was *drama*.

People ate that shit up. I remembered hearing somewhere that the conflict among the Beatles instigated by Yoko and Linda McCartney translated directly into record sales. And hadn't Sam just said he didn't want Kristen to be our Yoko? Well, okay then. It was time to plant exactly that seed. Once we got the numbers and the recording deal, then I could rein it all in and refocus everyone back on the music. But until then…

I grabbed the tablet and tapped out a post:

@Ride_Out
@BryceG: On her back? Hell, gonna have her on her knees. Wait and see. #CatCall

This would work. I was sure of it.

———

In silence, Nick and I dug through the bagels Sam left behind, both of us afraid to talk about what had happened. Kristen's voice still echoed in my mind—it was that amazing. But Sam's words replayed too.

Okay, so I liked Kristen. Who wouldn't? She had a hot body, truck-loads of talent, and was funny when she wasn't pissed off at me. If I were being totally honest with myself, I'd have been putting moves on her already if not for the band.

I stopped because the band meant more to me than scoring. I played out half a dozen scenarios in my mind, devoured two bagels, and still had no clear idea how to make this right.

A throat cleared, jerking me out of my thoughts.

I looked at Nick, sitting by his drum kit, looking like a brick just hit his head, which was pretty much how I felt. "What?"

"So…are we…we're not over, are we? Tell me this isn't it for us."

Sam and I frequently had loud, volatile disagreements, but Nick?

Nick was always so…so easy. He had a Teflon coating that nothing ever stuck to long enough to get beneath. So when I looked over at him and saw the vein pulsing on his temple, I almost bolted. Instead, I waved a hand and tried to look unconcerned. "Nah. Sam's a diva. He'll be back." And then I heard the words that I'd just said. Sam really was a diva.

Sam Gowan was jealous.

He didn't like sharing a stage with anybody else and that included Nick and me. But he dealt with us because we respected his guitar skills. But sharing a spotlight with someone who didn't—or couldn't—appreciate his talent? No matter how successful the band might become because of Kristen, Sam would only see her as…well, as Yoko.

Shit.

I grabbed the tablet and checked the stats. It hadn't been long since Sam posted the raw, unedited video with Kristen's actual name. The tweet had been shared close to three dozen times and favorited more than a hundred. It also had a long list of replies.

That was when I saw it.

> @kristencartwright
> That's right! I'm singing with @Ride_Out. Somebody's gotta show the boys how it's done. #CatCall

> @kristencartwright
> @elijahhamilton will be on his knees screaming for ME. #CatCall

I let out a whoop. "Holy shit, Nick. Check this out."

I handed him the screen, and his eyes went wide. Then he laughed and nodded. "Did *not* see that coming. The girl's pretty cool."

Yeah. She was. For the first time since she left my garage, I could breathe easy. She got it. She understood the game.

"So what do we do now?" Nick stood up, stretched his arms over his head, and then poked his head into the bag of bagels. "I guess Kristen'll be back. She doesn't seem too pissed off anymore. But Sam? I don't know, man. He was definitely pissed off." He tore a cinnamon raisin bagel in half and bit into it dry.

I shoved my hands in the pockets of my jeans and looked around the garage. "I guess we move on. Let's take a look at the rest of the stuff we recorded before." We moved to the table where the old Mac sat, Nick dropping bagel crumbs on the keyboard. I clicked a few buttons and opened my GarageBand software.

Nick glanced down the driveway, but it was still empty. Sam was long gone. "Okay, I know this could just make everything a hundred times worse, but what if we forget about the whole plan to amp up that Common Kiss song and just use what we recorded today? Maybe splice together a kind of music video…one that tells a story, you know?"

"A story? What kind of story?"

"We could create an *I'm sorry* story." Nick laughed and shook his head. "But I'm pretty sure it wouldn't make a dent in the egos that just stalked out of here."

Wait. *Egos.* I grinned. "Nick, you're a genius."

Thick eyebrows shot up to his buzzed hairline. "Uh. Sure. We'll go with that."

"Seriously. I thought I could get Sam to put the band's needs ahead of his own, but I forgot about his ego. What?" I demanded when Nick's eyebrows shot up in a mocking look.

He shook his head. "Nothing. Forget it. Go on."

If it was nothing, he wouldn't have looked like that. But I let it go. "Um, yeah. Okay. So, we need to feed it."

"Uh. Sure," Nick repeated.

I laughed, encouraged by the idea. "Come on. I'll show you." I started uploading bits of footage from the video we recorded and then switched to the old computer. "Here. This is good." I marked frames where I found raised eyebrows, mocking smiles, a pair of crossed arms, and an open mouth. I separated the sound from the video so I could play the song straight through as a background track. Then I started laying down the elements. "See?"

"But this is all out of context," Nick protested.

"Yeah. Exactly. I'm creating a *new* context, and it's a bitter rivalry between Kristen and us." I jabbed a finger at the monitor.

"It's a...contest?"

"Got it in one." I slapped his back. "Kristen is *pure*, Nick. Her voice is... God! It's how heaven would sound. But Sam can't see that. In his mind, every time I tell him how great Kristen is, he hears how bad he is."

"But he's not bad. He's amazing. Besides, he doesn't sing!"

"I know that. But it's how he's thinking. So I'm going to show him how much better he is *with her*."

"He won't listen to you."

"You're right. But he'll listen to *them*." I angled the Mac's screen toward us and took another look at the stats from our earlier posts. "Look at the traction this little Twitter war is getting. I've been trying for months to get this to happen, and Sam did it with one shot."

"Kristen shot back," Nick reminded me.

I laughed once. "She sure did." Damn, I *loved* it that she did.

Nick scratched his head and thought about that for a moment. "So are you hot for Kristen? Are you doing this just to get laid?" When he waved a hand toward the driveway, I knew he was trying to confirm what Sam had accused me of.

I crossed my arms and stared at him hard. "Don't you have a girlfriend, one whose play you dragged me to? How is this different?"

"Because I'm not hanging Ride Out's success on Leah singing with us."

I made a sound of frustration. "Okay, look. Do I think Kristen Cartwright's hot? Absolutely. What's the big deal if I hit that?"

Nick rolled his eyes and ran a hand over his buzzed hair. "Eli, you're a good guy, most of the time—"

"Most of—what the fuck, Nick?"

He shot up both hands. "Most of the time. Just…not with girls."

I opened my mouth to defend myself. I didn't date. I devoted every minute to taking this band all the way to the top. "What the fuck are you talking about?"

Nick shut his eyes with a long, loud sigh. "Jesus, Eli, you're completely oblivious. Girls are like background singers to you. Most of the time, you don't notice them, and if you do, you hurt their feelings when they get too close. Remember that girl at the spring concert we did at the park? Jenna. She took two buses to hear you sing, and you never even posed for a fucking picture with her."

I cleared my throat. "Dude, she was…an emotional basket case. I didn't want to encourage her."

"Bullshit. You didn't want to be stuck with her." He sneered at me and shook his head. "Look, man, I like Kristen Cartwright. I don't want you to hurt her like that, and I especially don't want you to hurt her like that if she *does* become the secret to our success."

I met his eyes and tried not to show how deep his assessment of me cut. "Okay. So you're siding with Sam on this. Hands off Kristen."

He shrugged. "Yeah, I guess I am." He stared at me for a long moment and then tapped the screen. "Let's just get back to this, okay?"

Yeah. Sure. Fine. Whatever.

I clicked through screens on the Mac. I dragged, dropped, and shuffled, and twenty minutes later, clicked Play. The final version of the song—now connected to good speakers—filled the garage. The first scene was an extreme close-up of Sam's fingers on his guitar. Slowly, I pulled it back to frame Sam, whose face was tight and pained while he watched something to his right. I added a split-screen effect and, in the second half, showed Kristen bopping her head to the beat.

"Oh, okay, Eli. I see what you're doing," Nick said. "Move this one here." He pointed to footage of Kristen making a disgusted face and slapping her hands to her ears. In context, she'd been reacting to feedback from one of the speakers. Out of context, it would look like she was not impressed with my scream. But my performance was gold, just like always, so it would ratchet up that sense of competition between us—and hopefully, the comments we were seeing online. It hadn't taken long to cut the whole song this way.

"Okay. What do you think?"

Nick let out a low whistle. "This could blow up in our faces."

I rocked my head side to side. "Yeah, it's a risk. But you wait. Sam'll be back just to play to this crowd. I'm betting Kristen's the same way." I clicked a few more buttons, and Nick's hand shot out to stop me.

"You sure about this, man?"

"Absolutely. This is it, Nick. This is our ticket all the way to the top." Big egos like Sam's and Kristen's fed off their audience like sharks on a shipwreck. All I was doing was dropping a little chum. He let go of my hand, and I clicked the Upload button and watched the video spool to our YouTube channel. "All we have to do is ride it out." I grinned and held up my hand for a high five.

After a moment's hesitation, he slapped my palm.

———

At school on Monday, I'd just tossed my math textbook into my locker when I got shoved from behind. I whipped around, fists ready, to find Sam's Clairol locks practically standing up like a lion's mane. Crimson-faced, he stared me down but said nothing.

"What the hell, Sam?"

"Yeah. That's my question, Eli."

I shifted my weight to one leg. "You saw the video."

"I saw the video," he mimicked me. "Payback? Is that what that was?"

"No, shithead, it's not payback. It's damage control. It's an attempt to get you to see how stupid you're acting. This isn't all about you."

"Yeah. It's all about *you*."

Like talking to a fucking wall. I ground my teeth together and counted to ten. "Kristen is the turbocharge the band needs. Admit it, you just don't want to share your stage."

"That's right, I don't—especially not for a girl who'll be gone the second you nail her."

My arm twitched, and suddenly, I had Sam shoved up against my locker. Everyone in the corridor suddenly shut up to watch the floor show. "You want me to swear on a stack of bibles that I won't touch her? Done. Now can you get your shit together?"

"Fuck that." He broke my hold and shoved me back a step. "And fuck you too."

The students watching the show all hissed and gave me pathetic looks of fake sympathy when Sam stalked away from me for the second time in three days.

The rest of the day crawled by in inches and centimeters. I had to find a way to fix this—all of this. I needed Sam to be cool, but I wanted Kristen, and I was sure if I could get the two of them focused on the music instead of each other, this would work. By the time lunch rolled around, I was ready to sneak out the side exit so I could be sure to see Kristen as soon as she left her school. But instead, I took out my cell, scrolled through messages, and nearly choked on my own spit.

Oh my God. Holy hell. There was a message from our local mall. They wanted us to play the food court this weekend. This couldn't be on the level.

Could it?

I read it once. Twice. Three times, just to be sure. Then I forwarded it to Nick and Sam because if there's one thing I knew for sure about Sam, he'd be all over this no matter how pissed off he was. In seconds, I got their replies back:

Nick: WTF? In cafeteria.

Sam: Is this 4 real?

I headed for the cafeteria and found Sam sitting with Nick at an empty table. I took out my phone and showed them the email again. "I think it's real."

"No way. What would *the mall* want with our band?" Nick asked.

"Probably saw the video with Kristen and thought it kicked ass," I suggested, but Sam rolled his eyes and flipped me off.

"Maybe the person running this account's been following us since the beginning. Maybe he's one of the fans on the Beat," Sam added. "Maybe this has nothing to do with what's-her-name, and everything to do with us."

I was about to fire back when Nick waved his hands. "Give it a rest, Sam."

Before anybody could say anything, the phone buzzed. I glanced at the screen. It was another email. My knees bounced under the table as I read it.

"Read it, Hamilton." Sam ordered.

I cleared my throat. *"I'm the event planner here at the mall. I saw your tweet, watched the video, and loved the battle of the sexes thing that your band has going on. Blew me away. Let us know if Ride Out is available to play the food court Friday night from 7:00 p.m. until close. We've already secured cover rights to the songs listed below. Know it's short notice, so we'll pay five hundred dollars."*

Beside me, Nick choked. "Five hundred actual dollars? Hell yeah, I'm in."

We both turned to Sam. "Um. Sam. It's pretty clear he wants us because of Kristen."

"Yeah. I heard that part." Sam was busy peeling the label off a water bottle. "Guess you'd better go sell what's left of your soul to get her back."

I let that one go by me. "And what about you? Are you in?"

He was silent for so long, I was sure he was going to leave, but he nodded. "I've been in this since the beginning. I'm not walking away because of some girl, no matter how impressive her tits are."

Nick's hand suddenly clamped down on my shoulder, and I realized I'd risen half out of my chair. Sam took his bottle and left.

"Eli. This is never gonna work with you and Sam fighting over every little thing. You know that, right?"

"So I'll fix it." I *had* to.

An hour later, I'd successfully sneaked off campus and was waiting outside North for Kristen. I had to convince her to come back. I stood at the tree line for decades, waiting for the damn bell to ring. The buses lined up in the parking lot, so I knew it would be soon. Finally, it rang, and a few minutes later, students began pouring out of the exit like the building was burning. I skimmed every female form that went by but Kristen's wasn't among them. Cursing, I shoved off the tree I'd been leaning against and tugged at the leather cuff on my wrist. Where the hell was she?

My heart lurched when I caught sight of her friend—the one who had tried to separate us the last time I was here. I jogged up to her. "Hey. You're Kristen's friend, right? She here?"

The girl twisted away from the hand I'd put on her arm and sneered at me. "What makes you think she wants to see you after what you did?"

Oh, boy. "It was a misunderstanding. That's why I'm here. To straighten it all out. Is she here or not?"

The friend pressed her lips together in a blatant show of solidarity that I'd ordinarily respect—under different circumstances. But right now, I needed to find Kristen and beg her to come back. I dropped my alter ego of the bad-boy rock star and went with honesty, straight up. "Look. I fucked up and want to apologize."

The girl put both hands to her mouth and let out a squeal.

Huh. Honesty works.

"Okay. You just missed her."

I cursed under my breath, but the friend leaned in. "You didn't hear this from me, but Kristen has lessons after school today. You'll find her at the studio over on Kinnear. She has an acting coach there."

"Thanks." I smiled and grabbed the friend in a hug. "Hey!" I called her back when she turned to go. "What's your name?"

She looked at the ground. "Rachel."

"Rachel. You're the best. Thanks again."

I left her blushing and smiling.

Since I was on foot, it took me until well past four to get to Kinnear Street and find the performing arts center. I tiptoed inside, found a seat in the rear of the theater, and waited for Kristen's acting class to wrap up. I watched her standing just behind another girl, who was doing a scene with some dude. It looked like he was about to propose to her. Sure enough, he dropped to one knee and pretended to open a box. The girl's face lit up with love and adoration, and as she opened her mouth to deliver her lines, Kristen tapped her shoulder. The dude froze in place, still on one knee, still smiling his *I've won the best prize ever* smile. The girl exchanged places with Kristen, who arranged her features into the same expression of love and adoration…and something else.

"Yes! Yes, of course I'll marry you," Kristen said, pulling the imaginary diamond onto her finger and admiring it. When the dude went to kiss her, Kristen put a finger across his lips and added, "But I have a few concerns. First, where are your bank accounts? And second, you should know that I know." At that line, her expression turned almost evil.

I leaned forward, suddenly extremely interested.

The smile dripped off the guy's face, and he stood up. "You know *what*?"

Kristen moved toward him, about to kiss him. "I *know*." She emphasized. "About the silk and lace fetish you enjoy at night, when you think no one's watching." She grabbed at his belt. "Are you wearing them right now?"

When he leaped back, the second guy tapped him. The two guys exchanged places, and guy number two slipped into the same position and then slapped her hand. "Okay. So you know I enjoy wearing women's underwear. But I assure you, it won't be an issue when we're married."

"No, of course it won't. Provided you also develop a similar fetish for diamonds and gold."

The second guy grinned. "Diamonds. Gold. Cars. Trips. Oh, I think this is going to be a very successful marriage. But there's one more thing I need from you."

Kristen stepped into the second guy's arms, and the first girl tapped her shoulder. They exchanged places, and I watched, mesmerized. Kristen was so...so immoral, and it was the hottest thing I'd ever seen.

When the scene was over, I approached the stage and waited while she said her good-byes.

"Ah. You must be Elijah."

I spun and found an old lady sitting in the front row. I knew her. I saw her at Kristen's *Cats* performance. Kristen's grandmother. "Yes, ma'am. Elijah Hamilton."

"Ah, here she is. You were marvelous, darling!" The old woman stood up, and when I turned, I found Kristen walking down the stage steps, shooting me with laser glares.

"Thanks, Etta."

"Kristen, I'll leave you to find your own way home so this young man can accomplish his goal of groveling without an audience."

Groveling? Jesus.

"Etta, I don't—"

"Of *course*, you do, darling. Run along now. I'll see you at home." She kissed Kristen on both cheeks and, with one last laughing look at me, walked out the rear of the auditorium. She didn't look a thing like any other grandmother I knew. She had perfectly smooth blond hair and wore the kind of makeup my mom wore to go to someone's wedding. She was dressed in a whole matching outfit, right down to her purse. All I could think was *Wow*.

Behind me, Kristen cleared her throat. I turned, and we stared at each other for a long moment. I had so many things to say to her. But I couldn't seem to find one. Finally, I settled on the most boring one I could find. "I'm sorry."

Kristen folded her arms and angled her head. "Sorry you have to grovel, you mean? Save it. I'm not interested." She took off in her grandmother's wake, and I jogged to catch up.

"No. Sorry for the tweets. For everything, Kristen. Come on. Let me buy you a burger and explain."

Her eyebrows rose, and she pressed her lips together, and it made me think about stuff I shouldn't be thinking about. "Fine."

We walked in silence down Kinnear and over to Main to the diner, where we snagged a booth in the corner. We ordered some food—a loaded burger for me, and a soup and salad combo for her. When the server walked away with our orders, she waved a hand. "I believe I was promised there'd be groveling?"

I snorted out a laugh. "I never promised that. I did say I'd explain."

"Right. An explanation for setting me up."

My eyes snapped to hers. "I didn't set you up. I never lied to you, Kris. Your voice is beautiful." *And God, so are you.* Sam's mocking face popped into my brain, and I cursed. I had to keep this just business. I pulled in a long, slow breath, really hating my best friend right now. "I've been friends with Sam Gowan for years. He's so good, he's practically gifted, and just because he prefers to play metal does not mean he can't play classical, pop, show tunes, or even jazz. Trust me. He can do it all."

She held up her hands and applauded quietly. "Good for Sam. So why do you need me?"

"I think you can do it all too, if you give it a chance." She wasn't buying it. Frustrated, I rushed on. "Kris, you're new, exciting, and bring something we don't have with just my voice. Did you see the video I posted to YouTube?"

She flinched and then nodded. "I saw the video. You know what else I saw? A tweet about getting me on my knees. I can't believe you posted that." She turned big blue eyes on me that were so filled with hurt, I wanted to shrivel up. "I...well, I thought you liked me."

"I *do* like you. And I know that comment was wrong."

She rolled her eyes, and it was clear she didn't believe me. So I took control of the conversation and steered it back to where I wanted it to go. "And I know that video wasn't flattering."

She let out a snort. "Got that right."

"It wasn't meant to flatter any of us. I thought you understood that, since you posted a tweet of your own. The comment, the video—it's all just a way to create controversy and competition. You know...a means to an end."

"Oh. An end," she mimicked. "Let me guess. How to lose a girl without really trying?"

Aw, hell. "No. To whip online fans into a frenzy."

She took out her phone and tapped a few buttons. A minute later, she nodded. "Okay, so you have tons of views, likes, and shares. Impressive."

"It *is* impressive. I know social networks. That's my contribution to the band—that and my songwriting. When we hit, it won't be about the music. It'll be about drama and popularity and likability. And it's already happening. We got a gig, Kris. The mall wants us to play at the food court on Friday night."

"So you're saying you sold me out for a gig?"

The server arrived with our food. I waited—not patiently—for her to move along. As soon as she did, Kristen poured crackers into her soup, scooped up a spoonful, and blew on it.

My heart stopped when I watched those lips pucker.

"Elijah?"

"Oh. Yeah. Sorry." I shook my head to clear all those inappropriate thoughts that had suddenly descended and took a bite of my burger.

"You didn't answer my question."

Right. What the hell was it? "Um. I don't look at it as selling out. I look at it as exploiting opportunities."

"Oh, really." She said it in such a tight-ass way, her eyebrow arching, I shot up both hands before she could argue...or bolt.

"I get how it looks, but I swear, I'm just trying to get some buzz going. The video and your tweet about getting *me* on *my* knees? That was awesome! There's nothing the Internet loves more than a good argument, Kris. They'll fight about it, take sides. They'll share, like, tweet, comment, and drive our numbers even higher, maybe even go viral—and take the band with them."

Her eyes snapped to mine, and her spoon froze halfway to her mouth. "You're gaming the system. Manipulating them."

I shifted and looked away. She made it sound so bad, and it wasn't. Not really. "I'm just using every tool, Broadway. Trying to give the public what they want. You're a performer, right? I watched you, on that stage just now. You were brilliant. Made it all so real, I actually believed you were willing to provide that slimeball with ladies' undergarments."

I got the double eyebrow arch that time.

"And you understood the exercise?"

I blinked. Did she really think I was stupid? "Uh, yeah. You were playing alter egos, right? An improv exercise, right? I've heard of them."

"Close enough. I was playing an evil twin." She sipped more of her soup. Chicken noodle. When she sucked up a noodle, I nearly face-planted on the table between us. I could watch her mouth for the rest of my life.

"I'm playing an evil twin too."

Her eyebrows shot up so I elaborated. "The bad boy rock god." I popped a fry into my mouth as her lips curled and she scooped up more soup.

"So you're saying offstage, you're a choir boy who loves to read to the elderly?"

I choked on my food. "No, not exactly. But I'm not the asshole everyone thinks I am, either."

She shot me the side-eye, so maybe I was a better actor than I thought.

"So what do you want, Elijah?" Kristen demanded while I tried to stop coughing.

You. I want you. But I couldn't have her now. "I want you to come back to the band. Give it a try. See if I'm right." I swiped the napkin over my face.

"What if you are? What if Sam gets pissed off that I'm getting all the fans and takes off?"

I shook my head. "Sam's a pro. Just like you. He doesn't like you here, but he is willing to concede the point."

She smiled. "Which is?"

Okay. She *was* gonna make me work for it. "That we wouldn't have this gig without you."

"And?"

"And that you're a hell of a talented singer, no matter what music genre."

She looked back at her soup bowl and swallowed a few more bites. "What about all that crap you said about me online?"

And there it was. We finally reached the point in our program with the giant elephant on the stage. I squirmed. "Okay, look. BroadwayBaby17 said a lot of shit about Ride Out that pissed me off, shit that makes it pretty damn clear she knows nothing about metal."

"So FretGuy99 said shit to get even." She dropped her spoon and sneered at me.

"No. Not to get even. To correct perceptions." I threw my burger back to the plate and leaned over. "Look, do you put in a ton of practice time on your performances? Spend all your money on gear you don't need because you think it'll give you an edge?" When she didn't say anything, I figured I'd scored the point. "I spend every minute I can on my music. I took piano lessons for five years, taught myself how to play guitar, and devoted hours to raking leaves, shoveling snow, washing cars, and any other work I could get to scrape together enough money to buy that soundboard in my garage. I took voice lessons to learn breath control, build up my range, and yes—master the metal scream you once said online sounds like a cat in labor."

This time, she squirmed on her side of the booth.

"I'm not into show tunes, Kristen. I don't really like rap music, and I'm so over radio rock, but I *can* appreciate them as art forms in their own right. You *won't*, and that's why you'll probably never get on any stage besides North's."

She jerked like I'd just stabbed her with my steak knife.

"You assume everyone who doesn't do what you do or like what you like isn't *good*. So that's why I called you out."

She stared at the ice cubes melting in her glass and shook her head. "That's not what I was doing at all."

"Oh, really." My eyebrows shot up. I sat back, crossed my arms. This should be good.

10

KRISTEN

Kristen Cartwright
@kristencartwright

Tweets	Following	Followers
6,920	**744**	**1,488**

@Rawr4Fems

@kristencartwright Uncool that you let @Ride_Out exploit you. What is this #CatCall nonsense?

@Mikey_T

RT @Ride_Out: Wanna hear her scream! #CatCall

RETWEETS 431 FAVORITES 239

I opened my mouth and shook my head, watched the waitress refill a few coffee cups. I couldn't decide which words would make him stop looking at me like the hypocrite he'd just called me. Tears burned behind my eyes because he had hurt me. I liked this boy. Really liked him. But it was clear he didn't think I was all that special despite all of his attempts to say otherwise. Etta said all the time that actions speak far louder than words. I opened my mouth and shut it. How was I supposed to find the right words so I didn't sound like the pathetic loser he obviously thought I was?

He watched and waited. Finally, I decided to follow his lead and just correct the perception. I shoved away my food and leaned in. "I'm lucky, Elijah. I'm lucky, and I know it. I've had the full support of my family since I was a baby, and because my grandmother was in the business, I had lots of help." I couldn't help the grin that spread when I thought about Etta buying my first pair of dance shoes. I adored those ballet slippers.

I still had them.

"She was the one who got me hooked on the spotlight. There were dance lessons, voice lessons, acting lessons. I studied classical as well as contemporary techniques, and I've worked with some of the best names in the business—cross-genre. I know you don't believe me, but all I was doing was trying share my knowledge with people who didn't get my opportunities—offer them critiques, educate them on the mistakes they probably don't know they're making."

He stared at me for a minute and then burst into laughter that only got louder when I crossed my arms and seethed.

"You really have no idea how stuck up that sounds, do you?" he finally asked.

I blinked at him, wounded. "Stuck up? Is that what you think?"

"*Share? Critique?*" Elijah's mouth curled when he mimicked my words. "Oh, baby, you can't critique anything without a pedigree, and BroadwayBaby17 hasn't got one of those."

"Excuse me?" I glared at him.

"A pedigree," he clarified. "If your profile said you studied with Rodgers and Hammerstein, then yeah, sure! Critique all you want, but the truth is, BroadwayBaby17 is just another faceless account who has more guts when she's behind her keyboard than in real life. Would you walk straight up to Sam or Nick and tell them face-to-face that their notes were flat or their timing too slow?"

I squirmed and put up my hands. "Well, no. But you're mixing metaphors. If someone asked me for feedback, I'd give it—"

"Nobody asked."

"Yes." I smacked a hand on the table. "They did. The Beat is a virtual version of my acting class. You stand up, give it your best shot, and prepare for feedback—good and bad. That's how you learn. If you're on that site, then you're implicitly inviting that feedback."

Elijah rocked his head from side to side, considering my words. "Okay. But you'd still be nicer about delivering that feedback in person than you are online." He gestured with a fry from his plate. "Look, the truth is, your opinions don't have any more clout than anybody else's online."

"Again." I was shaking my head before he finished talking. "The entire point of the Beat is to exchange ideas and encourage artistic exploration. If I'm not nice when I point out someone's mistakes, it's usually because they drew first blood."

"Okay, you want to point out mistakes? Stick to your own genre. Nobody gives a shit about your opinions of genres you know nothing about, can't sing, and admit you don't even like."

"I could sing hard rock if I wanted to. I choose not to."

Elijah's grin spread wider. "Riiiiight. You *choose* to make it your mission to insult every damn member of the site."

I blew a hair out of my eyes and flung myself back against the back of the booth. "I only started saying things about noise and primitive beats because you guys started harassing me about *my* work."

He sat forward and aimed a finger at me. "That's bullshit. I never harassed you. I never even replied to you until you called us sexist and misogynistic."

"Well, you are." I shrugged. He shook his head, obviously frustrated. But damn it, so was I. "I'm serious. You absolutely are," I pressed my point. "What the hell is that pogo stick lyric anyway?"

"You really need me to explain that?" He looked at me with another of those stupid smirks I supposed he thought were sexy, and I flung up my arms.

"See? That's just what I'm talking about. Everything is always sex with you." A sharp look from an old couple sitting opposite us made me remember where we were. "Admit it. The only reason you want me in this band is because I have boobs," I finished on a furious whisper.

Elijah sucked in a breath when I said *boobs* and blinked several times. I knew he was doing his best not to look at my chest. I arched an eyebrow and held his gaze, daring him to tell me I was wrong, but we both knew he couldn't.

"Look, Drama Queen, I've told you a dozen times now that you have an amazing voice. I think your voice in my band will shoot us both up the charts. What more do you want?" He leaned back and tossed an arm across the back of the seat.

I propped my chin in my hands. "What if I'm not interested in the charts?"

Both eyebrows shot up at that, and then he frowned. "Why wouldn't you be?"

"Because I want a conservatory slot. I have plans of my own. I need to develop an original piece of music, something only I can perform. Help me write one, and maybe I'll sing in your band."

He opened his mouth to respond, but I stopped him with a raised hand.

"Hold on. There's one more thing. The song has to have wide appeal."

His dark eyes narrowed, and his lips thinned. "Stab in the dark here, but I'm gonna go ahead and guess that means no pogo stick lyrics. Would you like me to compose a concerto in harp for you?"

I tossed a napkin at him. "No offense, Guitar Hero, but the heavy metal strings you pluck won't impress my admissions board much."

"No, but the classical piano I also play might."

My jaw almost smacked my dinner plate.

Elijah continued laughing and then reached out one long, callused finger to shut my mouth. I slapped it away. "Ha ha. So you really play piano? You're not just shoveling more bullshit at me?"

He shook his head and tossed his dark hair out of those intense eyes that had so hypnotized me the night of my performance. I narrowed my own and studied him closely. He was hot—there was absolutely no denying that. Long hair, the expression he typically wore—all smooth and confident and said, *Yeah, I know*, no matter what the question was. Even his dark, edgy clothes—it all made him look like he was born into the role he was playing.

"Fine. You want fucking proof?" He shifted on his side of the booth, pulled out his cell to tap and swipe at the screen, then slid it across the table. "Tap Play."

I did. It was a video shot a few years ago, judging by his hair. He wasn't wearing his Rock God clothes. He had on a dark suit and sat at a baby grand piano, smiling at someone out of the camera's range. A second later, he nodded and then put his hands to the keys. He played "Carol of the Bells," one of the fastest and most technically challenging pieces that existed. Even through the cheap basic speaker on his iPhone, I could tell this was special.

He didn't miss a note.

"How was that, Anna?"

"Who's Anna?"

He snatched the phone out of my hands, his face suddenly tight.

"No one *you* know."

I flinched like he'd kicked me. "I was just asking." I shoved away my plate, no longer hungry. The waitress dropped the bill on our table, and he lunged for it. I just sat there. Frozen.

He finally looked at me and sighed. "Anna's my sister. She loves that song—and she loves the stuff you say is nothing but primitive beats."

"So she's musical too?"

Half a smile played on his face and then blurred. "Yeah. She is."

"Then why don't you parade *her* onstage in your band instead of me?"

Elijah's eyes slipped shut, and a muscle in his jaw pulsed. "I can't."

I rolled my eyes. "Oh, you can't? You mean you won't exploit your sister the way you will me."

"Were you not listening when I told you Anna is disabled?"

I looked away. I'd heard what he said about his sister. I just wasn't sure I believed him yet.

His phone buzzed. He glanced at it, stood up, and tossed a few bills to the table. "I gotta go."

"Wait!"

He was already at the door by the time I grabbed my books and caught up to him. "Okay. You win. I'll do it. I'll sing for you."

I expected one of those hot grins of his. But he just stared at me. Finally, he shook his head. "No. You'll sing for *them*." He wiggled his phone at me.

———

The week passed quickly. After school on Friday, I got a message from Elijah telling me to be ready by five.

Be ready? I looked down at my outfit. I had on my red leather boots, dark blue skinny jeans, and a long, flowy black top. With an eye roll, I knew my outfit would not make Elijah happy. That was the point. I wasn't putting on my *Cats* unitard for his band. He kept insisting his interest in me was about my singing talents.

Time to test that claim.

"Going out?"

I turned from the mirror over my dresser and found Dylan standing in my doorway. "Yeah. Heading to the mall." I conveniently left out the part where I'd be singing in a rock band.

Dylan's narrow face tilted as he studied me, a frown wrinkling his forehead. "You look weird. What's up with you?"

"Nothing. Just stuff on my mind."

"Yeah? Anything I can help with?"

I sat on my bed and thought about that for minute. "You heard I got rejected from Tisch."

My brother made a sympathetic sound and sat beside me on the bed. "Yeah. I did. I'm sorry." He nudged me with a shoulder. "But you'll bounce back. You always do."

I managed half a smile. "Working on it."

Dylan smiled, and it was like looking at Dad through some kind of time vortex. "I love when I'm right. So what are you planning?"

"I—" Abruptly, I clamped my mouth shut. I didn't want to tell him about Elijah's band. "Well…Etta thinks I need to do something unique. Edgy. Something that puts me ahead of the competition."

"You mean for the conservatories."

I nodded. "It's kind of too late for a summer program. Plus, there are only so many slots."

"I get that," he said, scratching the back of his neck. "It's just... well, I don't see you studying the old masters."

"Me neither!" I laughed. "I really want to go to Berklee, Dylan. I love stage, and I love dance. I want to study it all."

"Then do it."

I sighed long and loud. "It's not that easy. Berklee is super competitive, and I don't have a lot of cutting edge stuff in my repertoire." My phone buzzed, and when I saw the time, I cursed. "I'm late. Gotta go."

"Kris. Don't do anything...you know, desperate, okay?"

Desperate. Right. "Sure, Dyl." I grabbed my jacket and bag and took off, pangs of guilt stabbing me in the back as I headed downstairs.

———

An hour later, we were gathered at the food court, surrounded by a ton of music gear. I had no idea Elijah and his friends had so much stuff. Speakers, microphones, amplifiers, miles of cable... I stood off to one side with Rachel while the guys connected things to each other.

"Oh, groan! Look who's here."

I followed Rachel's gaze and cursed. Leah Russo was walking toward us, flanked by her friends Brooke Greco and Addison Rhodes.

I liked Addie very much, but Brooke and Leah together were practically toxic.

"Heard you're singing with the boys now, Kristen?" Leah ran her eyes over my outfit and did that lip curl thing, the one that made it clear something stank.

"Yep." I tucked my hands into my back pockets.

Leah exchanged a look with Brooke that broadcasted exactly how they felt about this. But before Leah could take another verbal swipe at me, Elijah called out. "Hey, Cartwright! Give us a hand."

Gladly. I joined Elijah on the makeshift stage. "Can you connect the mics?" He handed me a box of wireless microphones and a package of batteries. I inserted the batteries in five microphones, flipped them on, and gave them a tap, happy to hear the sound picked up by the speakers erected to the side of the stage. When that was done, Elijah handed me a few sheets of paper.

"These are set lists. Could you tape them to the floor? One here, here, and here?" He indicated the placements he wanted. "I have one for you too. Just have to decide where you want it."

I glanced at the list of songs, happy to recognize most of them as ones we'd practiced last weekend in Elijah's garage. "So, what do you want me to do?" I waved the list.

He grinned down at me. With his hair tied back in a tail and wearing his usual black garb, he looked kind of like a pirate, and the image made me smile back. "What you do best, Broadway. I want you to fill in for now. At some point, I'll want you to lead a couple songs, but not sure which ones yet, so maybe we'll skip that tonight."

"This one. I want to do this one." I indicated the set list.

"'Going Under'? Tonight?"

"Why not? Gotta start somewhere."

His cocky grin faded a bit when he glanced at Sam, who was busy setting up a mic stand by Nick's drum kit. "Yeah. Okay. Let's do it." He smiled again, his eyes lingering on my body, but he never said a word about the way I was dressed.

"Elijah?" The mall's event planner waved him over.

"Coming!" he called back. "Break a leg, Broadway." He flashed the killer smile and strode off to confer with the mall guy.

Rachel was at my side in a heartbeat. "Wow. What were you two talking about? I could feel the sizzle from all the way over there." I glanced over her shoulder and saw Leah, Brooke, and Addie staring at me. I straightened my shoulders and decided it was time to pull out some enthusiasm. I grabbed Rachel's shoulders and shrieked, "Oh my God! He's letting me lead a song!"

Rachel could always tell when I was acting and when I was real and knew exactly when to put on her own performance. She squealed back, adding in a little bounce and a hug. She was good, too. Wish I could convince her to give drama club a shot, but Rachel was a member of that strange species who liked blending in. Nick joined us, which made Leah's face turn an interesting shade of purple.

"Hey, Kris! What's this about leading?"

Oh, shit. Elijah hadn't had time to tell them. "Oh, well, Elijah said I could sing 'Going Under' tonight."

He shut his eyes, hands beating a rhythm only he could hear, and nodded. "Yeah. Yeah, I think you'll rock it!" His smile faded when he saw Leah's face. "Oh, um, I'd better go say 'hey' to my girl before she gets too pissed off at me to wish us luck."

Rachel and I watched him jog over to Leah, grab her in a bear hug, and spin her in a dramatic kiss. "Wow. That was uh…"

"Yeah." I nodded. There were no words. Nick was awesome, but Leah? She was a troll. Troll or not, her face lost its pinched look, and she seemed genuinely dazzled by Nick's PDA. It was sweet and reminded me of my parents. I snuck a glance at Elijah and noticed at least half a dozen other girls gathered around the food court checking him out too.

The rest were glued on Sam. In fact, one brave girl already got him to autograph her chest and pose for a selfie or two. I couldn't take my eyes off Sam, either. He worked the room, knew there were eyes on him, made sure he tossed his blond mane around, bent over a lot to showcase his butt, and swigged a lot of water. It was a performance, just like any other stage show, and you know what? I could completely respect that.

I did my vocal warm-ups, felt the butterflies in my stomach starting to dance, and went over the set list again. The stage area was all set up—Nick's drum kit in the back, Elijah's lead singer mic up front, Sam's lead guitar on the right. I squared my shoulders, grabbed the tape, and stuck my copy of the set list to the floor beside Elijah's. I grabbed the last mic stand and put it right there.

That's where I'd be.

Suddenly it was time. Elijah grabbed his guitar and slung it over his shoulder. "Is your family here?" I asked him, but he went stiff and shook his head.

"No. They have to stay with my sister."

"Oh."

"Yours?"

I shook my head. I hadn't told them what I was doing. "No, but that's my best friend, Rachel, over there."

He followed my gaze and waved. "Oh, yeah. Rachel. I remember her."

"You do?"

"Oh, um. Yeah. Don't be mad. She told me where to find you."

"Oh, right. My acting class. I'm not mad," I admitted. "Anymore."

His eyes snapped to mine when I added that last word, but before he could say anything, the event planner guy was back with a mic of his own.

"Good evening, Bear River Mall shoppers! Tonight, the mall is proud to give you a local band, whose mix of hard rock and potent vocals will get you up and dancing along." He waved his hand at Elijah, who took over with ease.

"Hello, Bear River! I'm Elijah. These are Nick, Sam, and Kristen. We are Ride Out!" He stuck a hand in the air, and the few people in the food court applauded. "We've got a sound all our own, but we thought we'd kick things off tonight with something familiar." He turned back and gave Sam a signal. Sam started strumming the intro to the Rolling Stones song "Satisfaction." A second later, Nick joined in with the beat. "If you know the words, sing along. We don't mind!"

And with that, he plucked at his bass and launched into the song's famous opening line. I just stood there at first, kind of bopping and dancing, but added background vocals when Nick and Sam did. I didn't want to do it, but I couldn't help it—Elijah was impossible not to admire. His stage presence was huge, and I had to admit it; a shiver of doubt that I could keep up ran down my back.

He worked that small crowd into a larger one. People leaving stores stopped to listen. The girl whose chest Sam signed was dancing right in front of us. And yes, a number of people started singing along. Elijah held out his mic to them, encouraging more. At the end of the song, he faced me to deliver one of the lyrics, so I put on a little show, holding up a hand, turning my back, pretending not to be interested. Our audience roared its delight, and cell phones came out.

Shoppers forgot about their food trays as we moved to the next song on the set list, another oldie, the Who's "Won't Get Fooled Again." We played for forty minutes, the crowd growing with each song. People who stopped to listen stayed to listen more, recording us with cell phone cameras, singing along, and cheering us when we finished.

Elijah put the mic in its stand. "How's everyone doing tonight? Do you want more?"

There were a few hundred people watching us now, standing on the upper floors as well as filling the food court. When they shouted, "More! More! More!" it shook the floor and vibrated deep inside my belly. My skin tingled from hair tips to toenails. Oh my God, this was better than drama club.

"This next song is original, written by us. It's called 'Let You In.' If you like it, let us hear you!" He tossed his wild mane of hair over his shoulders, turned to Nick and Sam, and counted off. "One, two, three!"

We did it just like we'd practiced in Elijah's garage. Soft intro, rising emotion leading to an explosive climax when I took my mic out of its stand and joined Elijah at center stage. I added more than my voice to his. I made it look like I was madly in love with the big jerk. Sam wasn't happy about sharing his stage, but he hid it well. He kept crowding Elijah and me. I was pretty sure only the first row of spectators could see the sneer on his lips and probably figured it was part of his style. The song ended, and Elijah applauded me.

"Kristen Cartwright, everybody!"

Nick stood up and applauded for me too. Sam had no choice but to make it look good for the crowd. He grabbed me in a hug, and when he stepped back, kissed my hand. Our audience cheered more. Elijah held up his hands and quieted the crowd.

"Okay, we're gonna slow things down a bit and give you more of Kristen. This is an old song from Evanescence. It's called 'Going Under.'"

"Don't mess up," Sam said loud enough for only me to hear when he handed me his mic and moved to take my place on the side. My smile melted at the edges for a second, but then Elijah stepped forward, guitar over his shoulder, and started strumming the bass. I lifted the mic and sang directly to him. The audience ate it up, whistling and shouting, "Woo!" While I sang, Elijah ad-libbed some stage directions to engage our new fans. "Come on, make me feel it, baby."

I took a breath between verses. "I'm not screaming, growling, howling, or roaring for you, Elijah." I tossed my hair back, and he grinned when the crowd totally lost it.

I'd been singing this song for years. I knew all the words, knew where the strong parts were and the soft ones. But Etta taught me a long time ago not to imitate anybody. So I didn't deliver another Amy Lee imitation. I delivered *my* version. When I reached the chorus, I poured extra emotion into it, and the entire audience joined in. I slid the mic back into its stand and let the music fill me and got the crowd swaying. The food court was lit by the blue glow of a couple of hundred cell phones all aimed at us. When the song was over and I'd sung the last note, Elijah held up his hands, quieting the cheering crowd. Nick came out from behind his drum set, and we stood in a line at the center of our stage. "That's it for us, everybody! Thanks for hanging with us. I'm Elijah. This is Sam and Nick and Kristen. We are Ride Out! Good night!"

Some girl shouted out, "I love you, Nick!" I applauded for Nick along with most of the crowd. Leah was distinctly *not* amused, and that made me a bit happier. Then, a guy shouted out, "Marry me, Kristen!" I blew him a kiss, and this time, Elijah was the one who wasn't amused.

It was the best night of my entire life.

———

It took about an hour to break down all the equipment. The mall was closing, and a few people remained inside. Sam signed a bunch of autographs. Nick and Elijah did too, but not as many.

Even I signed one—it was for the guy who proposed. And he asked me out on a date. His name was Glenn, and he was a college sophomore.

"Kristen, did you say yes?" Rachel ran up to me as soon as we left the stage.

I shook my head. "Are you kidding? My dad would freak so far the hell out, it would effectively end my social life as I know it." Out of the corner of my eye, I watched a tall girl with straight, dark hair long enough to reach her waist chatting up Elijah.

"Aw." Rachel's shoulders sagged. "He was cute. And really nice. I talked to him for a while."

"I didn't get a really good look at him." But I *was* getting a good look at this skank, twirling her hair, smiling at Elijah. He was coiling up cable, packing it into plastic bins, and making it look super heavy.

It wasn't.

I'd carried that bin earlier.

"Kris, you signed an autograph for him."

"Oh. Right." Now *he* was twirling a lock of her hair.

"Kristen, what is the matter with you? Didn't you have fun?"

"Oh, um. Yeah. It was amazing." I rolled my shoulders and deliberately turned my back on Elijah.

Sam was making out with some girl in the gated entry to GameStop. Oh my God! They were taunting me. It was like some kind of band initiation, right?

"Uh, excuse me?"

I glanced around and found Marriage Proposal guy behind me again. A tiny shiver danced down my spine, and I took a step back.

"Oh, sorry. I didn't mean to scare you." He held up both hands and smiled shyly. "Actually, that's why I came back. You know, so you *wouldn't* be scared. I wanted to make sure you had a ride home."

I exchanged a look with Rachel, and she nudged me with a shoulder. "Oh, um. Yeah. We're good. Thanks."

"Kristen, you were…amazing." He actually blushed and looked down at his feet, hair flopping in front of his eyes.

They were so blue.

"Thanks."

"You guys been together long?"

I shook my head. "No, tonight was my first gig with the band."

Glenn laughed once. "No, I meant you and him." He jerked his chin toward Elijah.

"Oh, we're not together like that."

"No?" Glenn smiled. He had dimples—one high, one low. He was sweet, in a puppy dog sort of way.

So why didn't I feel a single tingle? I glanced at Elijah and his brown-haired Barbie doll. He had an arm slung over her shoulder. Both of them had their phones out, and it absolutely did not bother me one bit.

"So, um, can I walk you to your car?"

Why not? It wasn't like anybody here would notice. "Sure. Hold on a second, though." I looked for Rachel, who was next to me a second ago and now sat at an empty table over by Leah, Brooke, and Addie. "Rachel, is it okay if Glenn walks us to your car?"

"Ooooh, first names? Did you get his digits?" She leaned forward and patted the table. Before I could reply, Leah sniffed.

"Jeez, Kristen. Elijah *and* this guy? Kind of cheap."

My face burned, but Addie shot Leah down. "Oh, shut up, Leah. You know Kris and Eli are just singing. I mean, look at him putting the moves on that girl. Why is it okay for him, but not Kristen? I say go for it." She grinned at me.

"Okay, let's go." Rachel jumped up. "Bye!"

"Bye." Addie held up a hand. "Kris, you were seriously awesome."

"Whatever." Leah examined her French-tipped manicure.

Whatever was right. Rachel and I walked back to Glenn, who smiled like a kid on Christmas morning. "I drove here with Rachel."

"No problem. I'll walk you to your car since the guys seem to be busy."

I managed to laugh once. Nick had just grabbed Leah in a hug, Elijah was making out with the brown-haired Barbie, and Sam hadn't even looked at me. "Let's just go."

"Lead the way."

Rachel took out her keys. "This is so nice of you."

"No problem," Glenn said. "So your band rocks. You guys were sick."

I shrugged. "It's not my band. But thanks."

"You seemed so into it."

I *was* into it. The rush was outrageously cool. But now I felt totally let down and all deflated. I just wanted to go home and climb into bed with a container of ice cream.

"Oh, she's always like that onstage," Rachel explained.

"Wait, I thought tonight was your first time?"

"With the band," Rachel clarified. "Kristen does a lot of theater work—acting, dancing, singing."

"Cool, cool." Glenn nodded, and I could tell he didn't really mean that, but it was sweet how hard he was trying to impress.

"This is me." Rachel aimed the key chain at her mom's Toyota, and the headlights flashed once. She climbed behind the wheel so Glenn walked me around to the passenger side and opened the door.

"It was great to meet you," he said. "Maybe I'll see you at Ride Out's next gig."

"Cool." I tried to muster some enthusiasm, but even I wasn't that good an actor.

"Can I like, text you or friend you?"

I almost said no. "Sure."

He lit up like a Christmas tree and stepped back so I could shut the door. Rachel started the car, and Glenn waved as we drove off.

"Kristen, he's adorable!" she squealed.

Yeah. Adorable. Glenn was tall, had spiky blond hair and blue eyes. But they weren't intense like Elijah's, and he probably would never write me a song. I slouched in the passenger seat and stopped fighting my tears.

11

ELIJAH

Ride Out
@ride_out   **1,254** FANS

Rr_32Blue: Yo! @Ride_Out in da house at #BearRiverMall! Awesome! Check it out!

8Note_NY: @Rr_32Blue Thanks for video, bro! Who's new chick? Great tits!

Ride_On747: Can't believe I missed this! Thx for video link. @BroadwayBaby17 is HAWT and can sing!

> **Rr_32Blue:** @Ride_On747 HAWT? She is off the f*cking charts!

> **45ConnorLI:** @Ride_Out @Ride_On747 @Rr_32Blue: Who cares if she can sing? Post more pics.
>
> SHARES: 64 LIKES: 99

"Glad you liked the show," I said with my eyes on Kaylie's—or was it Kylie's?—chest. It was a hell of a great view. Her friend Michaela was currently wrapped around Sam, but Kaylie or Kylie was seriously into me.

I wiped the lip gloss she'd left on my mouth after she'd kissed me and…was that…ketchup? Ugh. I peeled her off me, wishing desperately for some mouthwash. I might have been into this chick if I hadn't met Kristen. Now, *she* was all I could think about. I looked around but didn't see her anywhere.

A phone was suddenly thrust in my face, and once again, Kaylie/Kylie grabbed me, mugging for the camera. I angled my face away from hers, flashed rock fingers, and broke away from her as soon as the flash lit up. We had to get all the gear packed up and loaded up so we had time for our celebration—half-price apps at the local family chain place. I took a good look around, and saw Nick talking with Leah and her friends, but where the hell was Kristen?

I scanned the entire food court once more and caught a glimpse of that fine butt leaving through the main exit, her friend Rachel and her surfer-looking boyfriend beside her. With a curse, I realized I never told Kristen the half-price apps tradition. "Hey, Kristen!" I called after her, but she didn't turn around. California Boy smiled at her, and that's when it hit me—the dude wasn't with Rachel at all, and I suddenly wanted to pitch my guitar through a store window.

"Elijah," Kaylie/Kylie said in that annoying pouty voice girls all seem to think guys actually like. But I ignored her and watched Kristen until she disappeared from view.

"Hey." She put a hand on my chest, and I stepped back, repulsed.

"Sorry. I gotta get moving."

"I want to send you the pictures I took." She held out her phone to show me.

"I really need to—"

"Elijah? Need to lock up." The event planner walked over and handed me another form to sign. "That was really cool. The crowd enjoyed you guys. Would you consider coming back?"

I forgot all about Kaylie/Kylie. My eyes went wide. Hell, yeah! "Definitely. Thanks for having us." I shook his hand, pried Sam off Michaela, and started getting gear onto the hand truck we'd picked up at a garage sale. "Hey, Nick! Can you go get the van?"

Nick waved his acknowledgment and took off with Leah and her entourage, leaving through the same exit Kristen had just disappeared through. I kept watching the door, hoping she'd come back, but no.

Brett Shields, the event planner, pulled out a brochure from the folder he always seemed to carry. "We're hoping to book talent on this date and this one," he said, pointing to squares on the calendar. "If you're interested, and I hope you are, go to this website and fill out the form. We're booking on a first-come basis."

"Very cool. I'll do that. Thanks again."

"You bet. Let me give you a hand with your gear."

New gigs. Holy hell, it was happening. It was really happening. I wanted to grab Kristen Cartwright and spin her around like those wimps in chick flicks because no matter what Sam thought, this would *not* be happening without her. I glanced at the exit door again, and my stomach tightened the way it always did when I thought about her. There was something about her that was so incredibly hot, and when she sang…when she got lost in the music, it was—*she* was—the most beautiful thing I'd ever seen.

And now she was off with some other guy. My stomach cramped, and I really wanted to punch Sam in his perfect teeth.

"Let me grab those dates, Eli." Sam took out his phone to record the calendar.

"Here. Take it." I shoved the paper into his hands.

Hard.

"What the fuck is your problem?" he demanded.

I whipped around on him. "You. You're the problem. Kristen was fucking amazing tonight. You couldn't say one nice thing? She left here all pissed off—"

"And you immediately figure that's *my* fault?"

Staring daggers through him, I nodded. "Yeah, it's your fault. You can't stand sharing the stage."

149

"Look, asshole, I'm not the one she was watching with big, sad eyes before she left. That's on you."

Me?

Sam jerked his chin toward what's-her-name twirling her hair beside her friend, eyeing me up and down like a cake in a bakery display. Aw, hell.

Is *that* why Kristen walked out of here with Surfer Dude?

I pulled out my phone and tapped out a quick text.

Elijah: Kristen, u were awesome tonight! We're going for half-price apps—meet us?

I stared at my phone, but it insisted on remaining stubbornly silent.

"Yo, Hamilton, how 'bout some help?"

Sighing, I grabbed the hand truck and shoved some gear through the doors. Nick left the van idling at the curb, so I started piling equipment into the back. It was just about all packed up when my phone buzzed.

Kristen: No, thx

Jeez, this wasn't good. I considered possible strategies and decided to go with nonchalant.

Elijah: OK. Meet tom my place 4 rehearsal. Mall wants 2 more gigs! Also, need 2 start working on ur song.

There was no reply. I shut the doors and tried to figure out a way to fix this.

———

The next morning, tension crackled around the garage like static through speakers. We'd skipped our half-apps thing last night. Sam was pissed at me, and Nick was pissed because Sam was pissed—it was a clusterfuck.

I hadn't been able to sleep, so I got up before my parents did to check the band's email and social network feeds. There was one message from Brett at the mall, asking if I could meet him to go over show details. I shut my eyes and tried to remember what I had going on. Shouldn't be a problem. Last night's show was a success in my eyes and in his too—given that he'd invited us back for two more. I switched over to Instagram and found pictures from Kaylie, who'd tagged them with the band's name.

Excellent.

The Beat was buzzing about our mall gig too. My friend Ride On747 had some cool shit to say. And then I checked Twitter. My eyes popped open, and my jaw dropped.

> @kristencartwright
> First gig with @Ride_Out so cool! But I def did better than the guys. Check it! #KrisVsEli #CatCall bit.ly/vdpil87xs

She'd attached a video from last night's gig that Rachel must have shot. The crowd definitely seemed more engaged in *her* singing than the rest of the show. Holy hell! I couldn't help grinning. Kristen had some seriously big balls, and Sam was going to lose his shit, and wasn't *that* gonna be fun to see? I raked both hands through my hair, thinking about damage control just in case it wasn't fun, when my dad opened the door to my room.

"Oh, good. You're up. How was the show?"

"Good. Um, really good. We got invited back to do two more."

"Great," he said with the kind of smile you tack on because it's expected. But I knew my dad and wasn't exactly sure why he felt like he had to pretend around me.

"What's wrong?"

Dad's dark eyes rounded. "Nothing's wrong."

He was lying. I knew it. Pretty sure he knew I knew it. But still, he pretended. I waited—not patiently—for him to get around to his point. I figured he was here to finally tell me it was a done deal; Anna would be moving out.

I put my tablet aside and swung my legs to the floor. "Dad, look. I'm not a baby anymore. Spill."

He lifted shocked eyes to mine, eyes with lines around them and those purple circles from lack of sleep. A quick grin that was gone before it could leave any evidence. He sat down on the bed next to me, shaking his head. "When did you grow up? I swear it was yesterday when there was a crib in this spot."

I shot him a look. "I know what you're doing, and it won't work. Spill," I said again.

This time, he laughed. "Always were too smart for me. Okay, I'll tell you." He paused, and the laugh evaporated. "I have a favor I need. I need you to come with us to a few…um, facilities. For Anna."

My stomach clenched. There it was. "Facilities," I echoed.

They were still going through with it. They were still planning to give Anna away.

"Elijah, please."

His tone held so much desperation, and I wanted to grab him by the shoulders and demand he tell me why the fuck he wanted to give her away if this was hard. But instead, I turned to face him. He looked lost and scared, and aw, hell—I'd just told him I was eighteen now. Not a baby anymore. So I swallowed hard and nodded.

"Okay. I'll come."

His shoulders fell a few inches, and I knew he was relieved. That was something, I guess. He stood up and thumped me on the back a few times. "You guys practicing today?"

"Yep."

"Okay, do me a favor and keep the door shut. Got a few complaints from neighbors."

I rolled my eyes. Neighbors obviously didn't appreciate good music.

After my parents left with Anna for therapy, I tugged on some jeans, a heavy sweatshirt, and a knit hat. I went downstairs to sit in the garage by myself, strum my ancient acoustic, and scribble some lyrics on a pad. Even though Kristen hadn't texted back, I figured I'd get started on her original song.

"Hey, Eli."

I looked up and found Nick walking up the drive. "Hey, man."

He grabbed my pad. "What's this?"

"Some notes for Kristen. She wants to compose something original for her entrance applications."

"Oh, yeah. I know. She asked me to help her. We were gonna meet up later, actually—or not," he added quickly with his palms up after my eyes shot to his.

"No, it's fine." I grabbed the printout of the set list to try to hide my spiking temper.

She'd asked Nick for help after I—forget it. It was probably better this way.

Sam strode in just then, carrying a paper bag. "Brought bagels. I don't have a lot of time today. You got the set list?"

Swallowing back the need to curse him out because I knew Nick was already upset, I handed him the printout in my hand.

"'Simple Man'?"

"Yeah. It's a classic. It's also a favorite of yours, so what's the problem?"

He shrugged. "Bored."

What a diva.

"Where's Lady Cartwright? Sleeping in?" he asked with a grin.

"I'm right here, and don't even try to tell me you were waiting long for me because I saw you pass right by me on the road."

I whipped around when I heard Kristen's voice. She wore yoga pants today with those hot red boots and a long sweater that hung off her shoulders. My mouth dried up. "Hey." I grinned.

She didn't smile back. She just pulled her sleeves over her hands and burrowed in. "So what are we doing today?"

"First, new business. The mall guy wants us back for two more gigs. One is next weekend, and the other is on Wednesday night."

"Can't do it," Sam said.

I crossed my arms and glared at Sam. "Why not? I gave you the dates last night, and you never said a word."

"Got a date. Michaela from last night. Her friend Kaylie is really hot for you. We could double."

Kristen flinched.

"No. Change your date. The band comes first."

Sam laughed once. "Does it, Eli?"

"Can we just play, please?" Nick grabbed his sticks and sat behind the drum kit I'd spent an hour unpacking for him last night, not that anybody had noticed.

Sam shrugged. "Sure. What do you want to sing, Kris?"

Kristen put a hand to her chest. "Me? I get an actual vote?"

"If you want."

She bit her lip. "Fine. Whatever."

What the hell was wrong now? Fuck it. "Great. Everybody's happy." I grabbed my guitar and waited for the count off.

"Count off, Sam."

"Count this." He shot up a finger.

"Jeez, guys, can we just get on with it?" Nick demanded.

"Don't ask me!" Sam shot back. "I'm not the one with his dick in a knot."

"Me and my dick are fine," I shot back.

"Yeah? Doesn't look like that from where I stand," Sam taunted. He took an exaggerated look at the watch on his wrist. "Didn't take long for exactly what I said would happen to actually happen." He turned to glare at Kristen.

She jerked like he'd just kicked her in the teeth. "Okay, that's it. I'm outta here." She took off down the driveway.

No! Jesus, she couldn't leave. Not now. Not when we were so close. "Sam, you realize none of these gigs happen if Kristen's not with us, right?"

"Hey, I asked her what she wanted to play." He flung up both hands. "Not my fault she's on her period or whatever."

Kristen heard that and whipped around so fast I felt the damn breeze.

"You're an ass, you know that?" She shouted from the middle of my driveway. I took the guitar off my shoulders and went after her.

"Kris! Please. Just…just hold up."

She gave me a furious look and stalked the rest of the way down the driveway. I chased her, snagged a hand, and tugged her around. "Please. Just wait a minute."

"No! I've had enough of his bullshit."

One look at her face and I felt like crawling into the sewer at the curb next to us. "Oh, God, Kristen, don't cry. I'm sorry."

She looked horrified and hid her face for a second, wiping the tears with her fingertips, and twisted her lips into a sneer. "Yeah. Sure."

"Seriously. I am sorry."

She snapped to a stop and confronted me. "Why am I here, Elijah?"

I blinked down at her. "I told you. I—"

"Yeah, yeah, amazing voice, blah blah blah. I heard that song before. I mean why am I really here? Sam can't stand the sight of me, Nick's tiptoeing around me like I might detonate at any second, and you! You're the worst!"

I looked at her sideways. "Me?"

"One minute, you're telling me how great my voice is, and the next, you totally forget I'm in the room," she said with a disgusted expression. "You're a player, Elijah. A collector. I can't figure out who's the better actor—me or you. So I repeat, why am I here?"

Because I want you.

I shoved my hands in my pockets and looked at the ground. I couldn't tell her that. Even though Sam was acting like a total tool, I wouldn't make a move on Kristen because I owed him. But that didn't mean I liked hearing her opinion of me. I opened my mouth only to close it. Anything I confided in Kristen Cartwright could end up online. Risky. But necessary if we had any hope of working together. "Remember the video I showed you? Of me playing piano?"

She crossed her arms and shot out a hip. "'Carol of the Bells.' Yeah." The April breeze kept blowing her hair into her eyes.

"I told you my sister is—" I broke off and gulped loudly.

"Developmentally disabled." A tiny frown creased her forehead.

"I…" Hell. Anna was a good reason—the best of reasons for working so hard to put Ride Out on the charts, but how was I supposed to tell Kristen I was exploiting her talent to keep Anna home? "Christ. Okay. My parents are struggling to take care of Anna. And now, they think it would be better if we moved Anna to a facility." My voice cracked. "I can't—I *won't* let them do that to her."

Kristen's eyes went wide.

"Ride Out is all I have, Kristen. I'm not a great student, and I don't give a crap about college. All I want is for this band to make it. And if there's a chance, the slimmest chance of that happening right now, I'm gonna do all I can to grab it."

She was quiet for a long moment and then blew out a loud sigh. "I don't want to see another disgusting comment online like the one you posted about getting me to purr, scream, or on my knees."

"That was just—"

She shot up a hand. "I don't care what *you* think it was. I'm telling you *I* think it was disgusting."

I blew out a loud sigh. "Okay."

"I still want your help with my song, but maybe I'll work with Nick too. I think it's better that way."

"Oh. Sure. Okay." It *wasn't*. Not by a long shot. But I'd give her whatever she wanted.

"Okay." She nodded and turned away. "I think it's best if I don't come to any more practices. I don't need these sessions."

My eyebrows shot up at the sheer conceit in that statement, but I didn't say a word.

"Just send me your set lists, and I'll look up the songs you're planning. I'll add my spin. If you want me to sing bigger parts, let me know and I'll practice them on my own."

This was never going to work. Not a prayer. "Yeah. Okay. Is there anything else?"

She thought about that for a minute. "Just one thing. I want my song to start out soft and slow, like a ballad. And then I want you guys to add in all that anger and punch."

I could work with that. "Is that the mood you're going for—anger?"

"Yeah. Your music makes me angry. And anger's what I'm feeling now."

I flinched at that but nodded. "I'll work on some melodies for you."

She nodded. "I'll start on lyrics."

I didn't tell her I'd already started those too. I got the feeling she wouldn't appreciate it a bit.

A gust of wind blew her hair forward again. I brushed it out of her eyes, and she immediately pulled away, blue eyes cold and full of suspicion. I let my hand drop. I worked hard to earn my Bad Boy of Rock reputation, to give the band's lead singer the right image, the one people expected. Maybe even admired.

I never expected it to hurt *me*.

KRISTEN

Kristen Cartwright
@kristencartwright

Tweets	Following	Followers
6,928	**748**	**1,512**

@Mikey_T

RT @Ride_Out: Wanna hear her scream! #CatCall

RETWEETS 644 FAVORITES 313

@Tomtom

Whoa, baby! Rock out! #CatCall #KrisVsEli

@djJiggs

@Ride_Out @kristencartwright That voice is better than Evanescence! #KrisVsEli #CatCall

@Rosebud

@Ride_Out @kristencartwright Go Kristen! School that boy! Rock girlz rule. #KrisVsEli #CatCall

@Rawr4Fems

@Ride_Out @kristencartwright Who's raising these boys to be so disrespectful? #entitlement #CatCall Why do you put up with it?

@Mikey_T

I made @kristencartwright scream! #CatCall #KrisVsEliVsMikey3way bit.ly/2IDS6Lxtr

@Rawr4Fems

Are you serious right now, @Mikey_T? Do you not get how disgustingly insulting this is? That's a person! #KrisVsEli #CatCall

@MadisonKellyLI

Is #CatCall and #KrisVsEli just boys being boys or indicative of the pervasiveness of #rapeculture?

Um. Yeah. Wow.

I stared at the image some troll named Mikey T probably spent hours photoshopping just so he could feel like one of the cool kids on Twitter. It was one of me in my *Cats* costume. I'm on my knees at Elijah's feet while he holds a mic out to face a crowd, smirking his lead singer smirk. There is a wet spot on his jeans…right by my face.

I blocked the little turd on Twitter, shoved aside the plate of blueberry muffins Mom had just put in front of me, and tried to remember Etta's favorite saying—*there's no such thing as bad publicity.*

"Not hungry?" Mom raised both eyebrows over the rim of her favorite World's Best Mom coffee cup.

I shook my head, unable to think up a convincing lie, and kept scrolling through Twitter. My stats weren't just up—they were hitting the stratosphere now. Too bad half the tweets were gross—full of photoshopped images like that one…images of me in my *Cats* costume with exaggerated breasts, images of me with my mouth open, and images of me in various poses—most of which are on my knees. The other half of my tweets were from outraged feminists wondering why I wasn't fighting back.

How the hell was I supposed to do that? Everybody knows if you feed the trolls, they just multiply. So how was I supposed to express my outrage without giving all these trolls the attention they feed off of? I thought about blocking and reporting them, but there were so many, and I'm just one person. I should put Elijah to work. It was his fault the trolls even found me.

"Got plans today?" Mom asked, putting one of the muffins in front of me in a not-so-subtle suggestion to eat something.

162

"Yeah. Think I'll go for a bike ride. Now that the show is over, I feel like I'm going to lose all the muscle tone in my legs if I don't do something." I didn't want my parents or my brothers to know about Ride Out. Mom would consider it beneath me. Dad would obsess over me hanging out with three guys. Dylan and Gordon would go all Neanderthal and try to protect me from Elijah's bad boy rep. I frowned at my muffin. Since I didn't have long, glossy, dark hair like what's-her-face from last night, it was clear I wouldn't need brotherly protection.

"So I was giving your summer some thought," Mom began, pausing to take another sip of coffee. "I think you should consider volunteering. You could call the music chairperson at the two high schools and maybe even the middle schools, offer to run your own summer theater program."

I stopped chewing, my mouth full of blueberry muffin I hardly remembered biting into, and thought about that for a moment. It was a good idea. Actually, it was a totally amazing idea. I could contact Mrs. Reynolds from middle school and see if she had any interest in working with me. "That could look even better on my applications than Tisch." And possibly, singing in a rock band. Then I could put Elijah and his stupid brunette Barbie doll groupie, these disgusting tweets, and the feminist cops out of my mind.

Mom smiled. "Exactly. Do you want me to help?"

I shook my head, getting excited about the idea. "No. I'll email my middle school teacher and see what she says." I grabbed my muffin, popped another bite into my mouth, and kissed Mom's cheek. "Thanks, Mom."

Upstairs in my room, I typed out a fast email to Mrs. Reynolds and noticed my inbox was full of auto-generated messages from the Beat.

I'd gotten so pissed off about Twitter, I'd never even checked the Beat. I squared my shoulders and braced myself, gasping out loud when I saw the list. Oh my God, this was insane! Dozens and dozens of comments on my mall debut with Ride Out. Even better, they were all relatively positive, if you didn't count the ones about my breast size, my clothes, or my hair. The tweets weren't all bad. Some were pretty flattering.

This one liked my voice. And one loved the "banter" between Elijah and me.

Just then, my cell phone buzzed.

Glenn: Hi! Busy today? Wanna grab some breakfast?

I frowned. I should never have given him my number, and I'm not sure why I did. That stupid groupie just pissed me off. Elijah had been clear—our arrangement was just about the music, so he was free to tangle tongues with anybody he wanted.

But did he have to want *that*?

Glenn wasn't bad. He was cute, he was nice, and he obviously liked me. Shouldn't I want that?

"Ugh!" I curled my hands into fists and pounded my bed. Then I called Rachel.

"Hey. Glenn texted me," I informed her when she answered. "He wants to go out. What do I do?"

"Forget Glenn. Did you see Twitter?" Rachel's voice was a whole octave higher. "This is so totally amazing! Half the Internet is watching your whole battle of the sexes thing! Even if they don't actually care about music, they're following the hashtag because they're pissed off about Elijah's comments. There's even one here from Madison Kelly from

164

Channel Twelve's morning show. She said, *Is #CatCall just boys being boys or indicative of the pervasiveness of #rapeculture?* You need to reply, like, *immediately*. Oooh, maybe she'll do some kind of report on you or interview you."

"Yeah, right." I rolled my eyes.

"What? If she's tweeting about you, she sees a story. You should totally tweet her back or at least favorite the tweet."

"I guess." Looked like Etta was right. The bad publicity was leading decent publicity my way. "I do want to keep the Kris versus Eli thing going."

"Okay, so what are you gonna tweet?"

I gave that some thought. The Internet was the biggest stage there was, and on that stage, two shows were performing at the same time. One was Elijah's stupid "catcall" thing, starting with that disgusting comment about making me scream. The other was the "Kris versus Eli" battle of the sexes thing, as Rachel called it. I just wanted to sit back and watch them play out. "Sam was pretty pissed last night. I don't want to make things uncomfortable for Nick or Elijah."

"You *have* to, Kristen! You have to keep this going. It's Sam's problem if he can't handle it. People want to know what's next. What *is* next anyway?"

What's next? I thought about that for a moment. I'd really hoped Elijah and me could... Well, no sense obsessing over the not-in-this-lifetime stuff. "We have two more mall gigs. They liked us so much, they invited us back."

"That's what you need to tweet. Let it be known that the band's success is from you."

That's just what Etta would say.

And that is why Elijah invited me to sing with them in the first place—to give his band the edge they hadn't been able to find by themselves. Rachel was right—too bad, so sad.

"Okay, I'll do it." I typed out a tweet, added all of the trending hashtags, and posted it with an exaggerated flair of my fingers. "There. Done." It was my way of flipping off Sam, who I hoped would freak out when he saw it. If he couldn't deal with it, not my problem. Elijah, though… Well, I hoped Sam wouldn't give him a hard time over this.

"So, a lot of these pictures are really vulgar."

I tightened my jaw. "I can handle it." If it led to more press, I'd have to put up with it.

"Oh my God, Kristen! The tweet you just sent has been favorited six times so far and retweeted thirteen times."

I'd been watching it. "I know. I'm looking now to see who's sharing it. Huh. Elijah shared it."

"This is good, right?"

Was it good? "Yeah, I guess he's not mad at me." I couldn't be sure with him. Those intense eyes of his guarded much of what he thought… unless he was thinking of girls. Then, they got all dark and swirly, and his lips curled into that smirk, and everyone in a thirty-foot radius could tell exactly what he was thinking. I fanned my face for a moment.

"Soooo, about Glenn," Rachel said, changing the subject. "Maybe you should give him a try."

My mouth fell open. "Jeez, Rachel. He's not a pair of jeans. You can't just try on a guy."

"No, not like that!" She giggled. "I mean give him a chance. Maybe, when you get to know him a little better, the sparks will start to fly."

Actually, that wasn't a bad suggestion. "Okay. I'll call him now. Thanks."

"No problem. I'll see you later. We're still going shopping, right?"

Crap, I totally forgot. "Oh, um, sure. Pick me up whenever."

"I'll text you."

I stared at my phone for a long moment after Rachel and I ended our call. Finally, I tapped Glenn's number.

"Hey!" he said, picking up after the first ring. "What's up?"

"Nothing much."

Awkward silence.

"So, um, last night was seriously awesome. I've never heard anybody sing like you."

Yeah, well, maybe that was because I actually sang instead of wailed into a mic like the guys did. "Yeah, I get that a lot. My teachers always say my voice is unique because I can cover four octaves."

"Oh, right! That's like Mariah Carey, right?"

"I wish! No, she can do more. I can't hit the same high notes she can, but I get close."

"Yeah? What's your highest?"

"Um, let's see. I can go as high as C-five or maybe six but not consistently." I shrugged and then remembered he couldn't see me. "I'm working on it with my voice coach."

"You have a coach? That's so cool. How does it work?"

"What, voice lessons? Um, well, it takes practice. Lots of practice."

"Yeah, but that's only if you can sing to begin with."

"It's technique. Like any other technique, practice refines it."

"Wow. Okay, I'll take your word for it. So, what are you doing now?" His voice shook a bit, like he was nervous.

"Uh, just catching up on my social networks."

"I guess that's a lot of work for your band."

"Not really. Elijah takes care of most of that," I admitted.

"Oh." His voice went flat. "Are you sure you're not into him? Elijah, I mean."

I sighed heavily. "Yeah, I'm sure."

"Great!" The life returned to his voice. "Wanna do something? Maybe we could hang out?"

Yeah, sure. Why not? "Okay. Let's meet back at the mall."

"Okay. I'll leave right now. See you soon."

He ended the call before I could reply. I stared at the silent phone, hating myself for making Glenn feel exactly how Elijah made me feel.

———————

Thirty minutes later, I'd made it to the mall, Rachel in tow. "Thanks for driving, Rach."

"No problem. So do you want me to hang out, just in case?"

I shook my head. "I'll text you if I need you."

"Okay. I'm heading to Forever 21. Have fun!" she said with a grin and a sassy wave of her hand.

I laughed once and scanned the food court. Tables were now covering the spot where we'd performed last night. I found Glenn sitting alone at one of the tables right where my mic had been. He hadn't noticed me yet, so I hung back and just watched.

He was taller than I was—taller than Elijah too. He was kind of dressed up today with dark blue jeans and a plaid button-down open over a T-shirt, and his blond hair was gelled into place. He had a soft drink in his hand and, on the table in front of him, a bottle of water. He'd shaved too. My stomach clenched. He was a nice boy—a genuinely nice boy who deserved someone who completely appreciated him.

Pressing my lips together in a tight smile, I walked across the food court, dodging shoppers and parents with strollers. "Hey."

His eyes lifted, and his face split into this huge grin. He stood up and pecked me on the cheek, and I forced myself not to pull away. "You made it!"

"Yep. Made it."

Awkward moment number thirty-four, or was it forty-three? I'd lost count.

"Oh, um, this is for you. I wasn't sure if you liked soda, lemonade, iced tea, or whatever, so I just played it safe." He slid the bottle of water toward me, and I clutched it, grateful for something to do with my hands. I cracked the seal on the cap and swallowed a cool gulp.

"So you liked the show last night?"

"Oh, yeah. You guys rocked. I liked your version of 'Going Under' a lot."

"Cool. Thanks."

A shout and laughter from the next table diverted my attention, saving me from awkward moment forty-four.

"How did you meet Ride Out? Are you guys all good friends or something?"

A snort fell out of my mouth before I could stop it. "Definitely not. In fact, those guys can hardly stand me."

Glenn's eyebrows shot up, and his eyes popped. "Why the hell not?"

I lifted my hands and let them fall. "Because I'm good, and it kills them to know I might actually be better at their genre than they are."

"Their genre? What do you mean?"

I shifted on my metal mesh seat. "Rock's not really my thing. I'm more into musical theater and dance. Elijah—that's the lead singer— saw me in *Cats* a few weeks ago and begged me to sing with his band. It sounded fun, so…" I trailed off with another shrug.

"Smart guy." Glenn leaned forward with a wide grin. Then he got serious again. "So…you're like…you know, single?"

Uh. Whoa. "Yeah. I'm single." My face flamed.

Glenn frowned. "I couldn't be sure. You seemed really into him, and he seemed totally into you, and then he was huddled up laughing with that guy in the suspenders, and after that, it was that girl with the dark hair." Abruptly, Glenn shook his head, a warm flush crawling up his neck. "Hard to tell."

Hard to tell. Glenn's words hit me hard. It shouldn't be hard to tell at all. And the truth was, I wanted to like Glenn. I really did.

"Glenn, how do you feel about chocolate-covered strawberries?"

His eyes went wide. "I adore them!"

"Me too. Come on. I'll buy."

ELIJAH

the beat_

Search 🔍

Ride Out
@ride_out

1,874 FANS

Ride_On747: Saw the mall show. Am now #TeamKristen #KrisVsEli

SHARES: 106 LIKES: 212

"Where you going?" Dad shot me an annoyed look when I walked out the front door and found him trimming hedges in the front yard.

"Mall. I've got a meeting with Brett, the event planner."

Dad's eyebrows rose. "A meeting?"

"Uh, the mall wants us to play two more gigs—one's midweek and one's on a weekend."

He blew out a loud sigh. "Fine. Just don't take my car."

Shit. "Mom said I couldn't take hers."

"Why not? Where the hell's she going today?"

I lifted my shoulders and bit back a smart-ass comment that would have gotten the car keys confiscated while Dad stomped indoors. "Steph! Where are you going that you need a car?"

I couldn't hear Mom's response. "I can't stay with her. I've got to head over to the garden store and pick up fertilizer. Yes, I did! I told you three times…"

The rest of his tirade faded away when he walked farther into the house. I glanced at his car parked on the street. I could just take it. I'd probably be back before they stopped arguing. Before I could take a step, the storm door opened. Dad forgot to the shut the front door, and Anna stepped outside.

"Eli. Music."

I hurried toward her before she could take off. "Yes, we'll play more music later. I have to go in the car now."

"Me too."

Christ. "Not this time, Anna Banana."

"Yes. Shoes." She held out a foot, and I laughed.

"Yep, you did remember your shoes this time." I angled my head and studied Anna closely. She was dressed and clean and was in a calm state of mind today. Plus, I wouldn't be that long. "Okay. Let's go."

Anna beamed her brilliant smile and headed straight for Dad's car. I got her buckled into the seat belt, grabbed my phone, and shot Mom and Dad a quick text message to let them know I was taking Anna to the mall with me. Predictably, both of them immediately replied with the usual warnings and reminders. I assured them I knew the routine, started the car, and took off. I turned on the radio and let Anna pick the music. She enjoyed drumming her hands on her legs to the beat.

When I'd parked, I pulled out a notepad and pen from the center console and wrote out the usual instructions and tucked them into Anna's pocket. "You stay close to me, Anna. If you get lost and can't see me, do you remember what to do?"

She stared up at me, her blue eyes huge and a bit scared. Then she smiled and pulled the slip of paper from her pocket. "Help."

"That's right." I smiled back and put the paper back in her pocket. It showed my name, her name, my cell phone number, and her favorite song, to help calm her.

Just in case.

"Stay in your seat until I walk around the car, okay?"

I got out, walked around to her door, and helped free her from the seat belt. I took her hand and led her toward the main entrance, dodging drivers looking for places to park and clusters of people carrying bags. The closer we got, the slower she walked. She clung to me with both hands.

"It's okay. You hungry? Want a snack?"

Mom would flip out if she heard me bribe Anna with food, but luckily, the only witness to my rule violation couldn't testify against me. Conscious of the stares aimed my sister's way, I rolled my shoulders and walked tall, daring them all to say out loud what I knew they were thinking.

No one had the guts.

I led Anna to the cinnamon bun counter and ordered two, plus a couple of drinks. She behaved, standing calmly at my side while I paid for the food and found us an empty table. I dragged my chair around the table so I could sit next to her and cut up her bun. Anna was usually a messy eater, so I'd use one bottle of water for clean up. While she chewed happily, I looked around for Brett.

"Eli. Music."

I pointed to the ceiling. "There's music. Can you hear it?"

Anna shut her eyes to find the melody. "No! No! No!" She sang loudly, causing more than a few heads to turn. I grinned and tapped my fingers on the table, trying to ignore that pit in my stomach that seemed to grow whenever she sang. She had pure talent that would never have the chance to develop. How many minds like Anna's were there? Minds that could play piano concertos, sing arias, or solve that Hodge conjecture one of my teachers told us about if they weren't trapped in this endless inward focus, while their siblings lived normal lives? There were flashes—no more than seconds long—of Anna's brilliance.

And then they were cut off.

"La, la, la." I tried to subtly change her tune so people nearby didn't think I'd abducted her or something. Luckily, Anna picked up on it, mimicking me and stopping only long enough for bites of her cinnamon bun.

"Elijah. Thanks for coming down." Brett Shields strode toward our table, his ever-present folder tucked under one arm.

I stood up and shook his hand. "Hey, Mr. Shields. This is my sister, Anna." I touched her shoulder. "Anna, can you say hi to my friend?"

"Hi." She smiled but wouldn't meet his eyes.

"Anna my friend's name is Brett. Can you say that?"

Anna kept smiling.

"Oooh, you have cinnamon buns? Yum." Brett tried to engage her.

Anna gave him the side-eye, and I laughed. "It's okay, Anna. He has his own snacks." Reassured that her cinnamon bun was safe from poachers, she went back to singing. "Sorry, Mr. Shields. She kind of freaked when I left the house, so it was easier to just bring her along."

"Elijah, it's fine. Really. I'm happy to meet her."

Okay. I breathed a bit easier. I sat back down, and Anna resumed her attack on her bun, adding in a few lalalas whenever the music moved her. Brett opened his folder and showed me some paperwork. "There are two events I have your band in mind for. The first is Saturday. You won't be in the food court, though. We'll be setting up on the first level, at the elevators."

I nodded, hoping like hell he couldn't see the way my stomach just flipped over. The elevators in the mall were open glass that covered three floors near a water fountain feature. It was actually a bigger space than the food court, which meant—bigger audience. Holy shit.

"We'd need you here first thing in the morning for setup and sound check, and you'll play three sets throughout the day, each one an hour long. We'd prefer you did covers, but if you want to perform original music, that's okay too, as long as there's no profanity."

I nodded. That was a fairly common request, especially for metal bands like Ride Out.

"The second date is the following Wednesday. There's a fall fashion show we're hosting. We'll have a runway set up over there." He indicated the south section of the food court. "We want Ride Out to play the accompaniment for the models."

Fall fashion in April? Okay then.

"So we'll be in the background?"

"Exactly. Not much adoring audience for you that night, but still—it's exposure."

I thought it over for a minute. Background accompaniment might mean Sam could potentially have a problem with it. Nick wouldn't mind one way or the other.

"Oh, and there's one more thing. We'd like Kristen to model a few of the outfits."

"La!" Anna sang. I just blinked. Kristen…strutting down a runway? Something told me she'd love that. Which meant Sam would claim that this was exactly what he was worried about when I first invited Kristen to join us. He'd wanted our band to be about just the music not about Kristen's good looks. Sam was wrong—Ride Out had to be about business too. And we had to have commercial appeal.

Sam was a chick magnet, no doubt about it. He'd appeal to the girls in any audience. The musical talent was definitely a big factor for any hard-core experts. And then there was Kristen—she appealed to a much wider audience than the three of us put together. She'd bring in the younger girls, who were traditionally a pop music market.

Kristen had mass market appeal in great big truckloads. I could see her strutting around onstage, wearing some hot little dress with her red leather boots. I just wasn't sure I liked the idea of everybody seeing her that way—especially if they had her wearing bras and panties.

I narrowed my eyes. "What kind of outfits?"

Brett laughed. "Don't worry—nothing from Victoria's Secret."

Okay. That was good. "I'd have to check with Kristen about that part, but the band is definitely happy to return."

"Can you ask her now? She's right over there."

I swung my eyes in the direction Brett indicated, and every person in that food court faded into the background, no more than white noise. My stomach coiled, and breathing started to hurt. There was a burst of power deep inside me, and the second my eyes landed on Kristen sitting with the surfer dude from last night, that power inside me converged into a single laser point: *mine*.

But she wasn't mine.

I tried to tell myself that, but it did no good. I had no right to interfere. I had no right at all, but I was on my feet and stalking across the food court anyway.

"Eli!"

Anna's panicked voice suddenly brought the entire food court back into focus, jolting me out of my hormone rage.

"Oh, God. Sorry." I hurried back to my sister. "Come on, Anna. Let's say hi to Kristen. You can bring your bun."

"No," she said with an emphatic shake of her head, and my frustration shot to red line levels.

"Elijah, I'll sit with Anna if you'd like."

I glanced at Brett. "Two minutes. I'll be right back."

I strode across the court and watched Kristen laugh and take that dude's hand. I fought down the urge—the *need*—to rip his hand from his body and beat him with it. They turned and saw me, freezing where they stood.

"Elijah." She sounded strangled.

"Kristen." I jerked my head in greeting.

"Oh, um, this is Glenn."

I jerked my head again in some lame impersonation of giving a shit, but I didn't so much as spare the dude a glance. "Can I talk to you for a minute?"

She looked at Glenn for permission or something. He smiled and nodded, giving her hand an extra squeeze, and I wasn't entirely sure, but I may have growled or something because Kristen shot me this glare of pure outrage. She walked about ten feet away, and I was right on her heels.

"What the hell is your problem, Elijah?"

"No problem," I lied easily. "I'm here meeting with Brett Shields. He's the event planner."

"Oh, right." She nodded, her face smoothing back into its normal look.

"He's offered us two more gigs. One of them is a fashion show. He wants us to play the background music while models strut their outfits up and down the runway."

"Okay."

"He wants you on the runway."

"Me?" Her eyes popped wide. "Modeling what?"

"Not sure what, except that it won't be Victoria's Secret." The coil in my gut tightened even more when the thought of Kristen in lingerie slithered through my mind. I'd already entertained way too many fantasies along those lines. "You in?"

She wrinkled her face and shrugged. "I don't know. I'm supposed to be singing with your band, not letting you exploit me."

Exploit? "Whoa, whoa, back up." I held out both hands. "It's fall fashion. That's it. If you think you can walk and sing at the same time, we'll work that in so you can do both."

Her eyes narrowed to slits. "Walk and sing. At the same time? Are you for real?"

I sighed heavily. Here we go. "Look, it's not easy to play guitar and sing at the same time. You admitted you don't play any instruments. All I meant was that strutting down a runway and trying to sing—"

"ELI!"

My stomach crashed to my feet when I recognized the tone in Anna's shriek. Full-out terror. She was about to explode. I shoved by Kristen and ran back to Anna. Her cinnamon bun was splattered on the floor beside her.

"Anna, Anna, don't cry, I'm here. I'm right here." I crouched to her level, took her hands, and rubbed them gently.

"Bun."

"Elijah, I'm sorry. She dropped it, and I was afraid to leave her alone to buy her another one."

"It's okay, Mr. Shields. She'll be fine. She has trouble processing stuff." I lowered my voice and softened the cadence. "Anna, do you want to go home now?"

She shook her head, great big tears falling from her eyes, and my heart cracked. "Bun." She wrapped her arms around me and cried. I grabbed the empty chair next to her, sat down, and just rocked her while she sobbed, stroking her hair and trying to sing the "la, la, la" part of her favorite song.

"Anna, Anna, look! Look what I have for you." I slid my own untouched bun across the table with the one hand I had free.

"Eli." She buried her face in my shoulder, oblivious to all the disapproving looks getting shot at us.

Two more hands appeared to take the carton from me.

Shit! Kristen.

I made some noise of protest, but Kristen just shook her head and sliced a chunk off the bun. "Hi, Anna." Interested by the new voice calling her name, Anna looked up. "Do you want some?" Kristen held out a forkful of cinnamon bun. Her new guy hovered just behind her, shrinking under one exceptionally nasty look from a woman with three kids. Kristen cocked her head and glared right back, which made the witch turn purple and hustle her brood away.

Anna's grip on me tightened painfully. Aw, fuck. "Anna, Anna, look at me. Look at Eli. Kristen sings. Kristen likes music, just like you. Music, Anna."

She shook her head frantically back and forth, and panic surged through me. If she started screaming, someone was sure to call security, maybe even the police. I'd promised my parents I'd take care of her. Shit, I'd totally fucked this up. Mr. Shields looked like he wanted to bolt and forget he ever met me, the dirty looks were turning uglier, and Kristen's new boyfriend kept staring at me like I'd just hatched out of a pod.

Kristen slapped my arm. "Take out your phone."

What the hell? I stared at her blankly. She stood up, and in a clear, high soprano I'd never heard from her before, sang the first verse of "Carol of the Bells." Stunned, I just gaped until she rolled her hands. Quickly, I grabbed my phone and cued up my piano version of the same song. Kristen started over again. People started exchanging confused glances and whipping out cell phones to record the spectacle. I added a few *ding-dongs* in tenor as background, knowing Anna would soothe faster if I sang too. Mr. Shields joined in and so did Surfer Boy.

Anna lifted her head, fixed her eyes on Kristen, and started to sway to the rhythm. It was working. I swayed with her and pounded a hand on the table to add a little more focus, just as Kristen hit the chorus.

Then a dozen people added their voices. It was fucking April, and we were singing a Christmas carol in the middle of the mall. I looked around, saw teenagers, an elderly couple, and a bunch of parents with kids stand up to sing, smiling at us. Holy hell.

"Ding dong, ding dong." Anna sang, and my limbs shook in relief. Kristen hit the last note, and applause broke out across the food court. Even Anna clapped. My eyes met Kristen's across the table, and that tight coil in my stomach seemed to snap, then slam into my heart, and suddenly, I didn't give a shit about the promise I made to Sam or the band or getting famous or even Anna. All I cared about, all I saw, all that mattered—was Kristen. I took her hand and pulled her toward me. She was there, right there, staring up at me with big blue eyes, and for a second, I forgot she hated me.

"Kristen Cartwright and Elijah Hamilton from the band Ride Out, everybody! They'll be playing right here on Saturday."

Brett's off-the-cuff announcement got more applause from the crowd. Kristen gave them a theatrical wave and tiny bow. I scooped Anna up, grabbed the rest of the cinnamon bun, and hustled her to the exit, a single thought playing on a loop in my head.

Damn. That was close.

The thing was, I wasn't entirely sure I meant Anna's meltdown.

KRISTEN

Kristen Cartwright
@kristencartwright

Tweets	Following	Followers
6,933	**752**	**1,604**

@Rosebud
#TeamKristen!! #KrisVsEli

@KyleHarmon
When @kristencartwright can write like @elijahhamilton,
we'll talk. #KrisVsEli

@Tomtom

@KyleHarmon Hey, she can sing and she looks amazing. #TeamKristen #KrisVsEli

@KyleHarmon

@Tomtom I can make that cat scream if Hamilton can't. RT @Mikey_T I made @kristencartwright scream! #CatCall #KrisVsEliVsMikey3way bit.ly/2IDS6Lxtr

I stood by helplessly as Elijah practically dragged his sister out of the mall, his face pale and lips tight. I wasn't sure he was even aware how touched he'd been by that small audience's display of solidarity. Etta would have said he'd been *overcome by emotion*. That was her favorite phrase. I'd always thought it was hyperbole, but yeah… Elijah had been overcome. It was an amazing thing to witness. It felt oddly intimate, like a kiss with your eyes open.

I turned to Glenn. "I should go. Give him a hand or something."

He nodded. "Yeah. You should. Rain check on the treats, okay?"

"You bet." Impulsively, I stood on my toes and kissed his cheek. "Thanks, Glenn."

He blushed to his blond roots and waved a hand. "Didn't do anything, except maybe push Mr. Hamilton's buttons. That boy wants you *bad*."

A slow burn crawled up my neck. "No. He's all music, all the time."

"I know. Trust me." Glenn looked weirdly sad for a moment.

"Um…it kind of sounds like you have some experience in this area."

Glenn laughed once. "Oh, yeah." He glanced around, and when he was sure nobody could hear him, he leaned closer. "My ex was totally into somebody else and wasn't honest about it. I took her at her word. She kept denying, but I still kept getting a vibe that something was wrong...and it was. I get that same vibe from you two."

I felt the blush spread heat from my neck to my face. Was Glenn right? Then why hadn't Elijah made a move on me? Was it really all about the music or was something else happening?

And why the hell did I care so much?

"I'm so sorry," I told Glenn.

"I'll survive."

He smiled and left, and I felt like a jerk. He was a great guy! Why couldn't I like him the way he liked me?

Because he wasn't Elijah. Stupid, lead-singing jerk.

I watched Glenn walk away and then typed out a quick text message to Rachel as I skirted around clots of shoppers at the entrance trying to inhale one last cigarette before entering the mall. I searched frantically up and down the parking lot, but I didn't see Elijah and his sister anywhere.

"Ding dong, ding dong!"

I followed Anna's bell-like voice to my left. As I got closer, Elijah's deeper voice asking Anna questions made a warm tingle form in my chest.

"Wow, how high can you go? La, la, la." He sang each note progressively higher, and she mimicked him, going even higher than he could. "Oh, good girl!" He praised her, and it tugged at my heart. "See, all better now. Kristen sang you a pretty song, right?"

I stopped where I was, one aisle over and just watched. Everyone told me Elijah Hamilton was a player, a guy with no heart who collected girls to use and toss away when he was done. But the boy in front of me singing to his sister while he oh-so carefully buckled her seat belt showed me a totally different side to the rock god—a side I really wanted to know.

I took a step forward and felt my phone buzz.

It was like a bucket of ice water over my face.

Elijah and his sister made a pretty picture—so pretty, it was easy to forget he was the same jerk who made those stupid sexist comments about making me scream—stirring the primordial ooze out of which dozens of online trolls now crawled. That girl at the ice cream store after my show…the one he'd smiled for and spoke to—making her think—making her believe—he was totally into her. When he turned his back and walked away, she was forgotten—she wasn't even a memory.

Insignificant.

Nothing.

I didn't want to be his latest *in-this-moment* girl. I rolled my eyes when I remembered that In This Moment was the name of one of the bands he'd made me listen to. Music was all that was real to him. And his sister. I'd seen the panic in his eyes when she'd called his name. That kind of terror wasn't fake. And the love I could see, even from here, was the real deal.

Was there room in his life for me? Was I real to him or just another voice through the speakers?

I rolled my shoulders and stepped forward. I had to know. One way or the other, I had to *know*.

"Elijah."

He jolted upright, banging his head on the car's doorframe. One hand clapped to his head, and he cut loose with a stream of curses. "What do you want, Kristen?"

I flinched at his tone but ignored his question and reached a hand up into all that dark hair to assess the damage. His eyes closed, his mouth fell open, and his hands gripped my arms.

Hard.

"I don't feel any lumps, and there's no blood. Does it still hurt?"

"What?" His eyes opened at half-mast. He looked a bit like…well, like a guy who'd just been hit on the head.

"Your head. Does it still hurt? Do you need me to drive?"

"Which head?" He smirked.

I was seriously tempted to smack him on the head. Maybe I would have if I didn't still see the worry and flat-out terror in his eyes. "Be serious."

"You're right. I shouldn't tease you like that. I'm sorry."

His subtle emphasis on the word *you* made me take a very definite step back. He leaned on the open rear door, one hand pressed to his head. His hair was tied back in a low ponytail, leather cuff strapped around his right wrist. He looked every inch the dark and dangerous rebel until you looked closer and saw the little girl behind him. I much preferred Elijah Hamilton's sweet side. I smiled at the thought. God, he'd *hate* that if I told him.

He pulled his hand away and checked it for blood. "What?"

I started to shake my head, but then decided to risk it. "You're very sweet."

His face went red, and his eyes darted around the parking lot like I'd just revealed military secrets. He shifted his weight and shoved his hands into his pockets. "Fuck, Kristen. I'm not sweet." He made a face.

I sighed loudly. "Don't you know any other words?"

A smile teased his lips, but he wouldn't give in. "I like it. It's a multipurpose word."

"A verbal Swiss Army knife?" I asked, considering. "Don't you worry that, uh—" I broke off, looking pointedly at his sister, singing away in the backseat.

"Oh, um. Nah, she's in her zone." He turned, checked on her, and then turned back. "Thanks. For what you did back there. It helped."

God, there it was again. Now that I'd seen that hint of sweetness hiding under his angry lyrics and punishing beats, I really wanted to throw out my No Way In Hell decision. "No problem. That was fun. Did you see how many people were watching?"

Dark eyes rolled to the sky. "Yeah. Kind of hard to miss when they're all glaring at you."

"They weren't *glaring*. Just that one witch with the chubby kids."

He laughed. "You shot her down."

I winced. "Saw that, huh?"

"Pretty sure you drew blood. You do have looks that could kill." His smile faded. "So, um, where's what's-his-face?"

"Glenn? He's in the mall."

"And don't you think he'd mind his girlfriend hanging out with Ride Out's lead singer?"

"I'm not *his* girlfriend. He took one look at you and backed off."

Elijah's eyebrows went up, and a very definite spark of joy lit up those dark eyes.

I was sure of it.

"At me? I don't get it." He shifted and leaned closer.

I ignored his question. "What about you? Looked like you made a good impression on that dark-haired girl last night."

"Kaylie. No, Kylie. No, wait—"

Pop went all my wishful thoughts. "Oh my God, you seriously don't even know her name? You had your tongue in her mouth!"

"No. *She* kissed *me*. I was trying to escape."

I gave him the side-eye. "Come on. You didn't look the least bit uncomfortable."

"I may not have looked it, but I was miserable. I need the fans. I can't be rude to them. You're a performer. You know the routine, Kris."

I bit my lip. I *did* know the routine. I just couldn't be sure if I was part of it or not.

He squirmed under my gaze. "Truth? The whole time we played last night, I couldn't stop thinking about kissing you." He grabbed my hand, and my temperature spiked, and the really odd thing was that his hand shook. It actually *shook*. But he still didn't move closer.

"Just kiss?" I asked and clapped a hand to my mouth. Oh my God! I didn't mean that the way it sounded.

The smirk returned. "Say the word, Broadway, and I'll make your—"

"Don't say it!" I gave him a push, but he just laughed. "I meant the music, you jerk. You know," I prodded when he just blinked at me. "Our song?"

"Right." He shifted, sighed, shut the door, and took out a set of keys from his pocket. "Get in. We can work on it at my place. Unless you have your own car?"

I shook my head. "I came with Rachel. Elijah, Sam already hates me. I don't want to make things worse. If working on my song pisses him off…"

A muscle ticked in his jaw. "I can handle Sam. You coming?" He walked around to the driver's side, got in, and started the car.

After a moment's consideration, I got in too.

But I still didn't know if this was real life or just a fantasy.

ELIJAH

the beat_

Search

Ride Out
@ride_out

2,209 FANS

BryceG: Purr for us, @BroadwayBaby17

SHARES: 207 LIKES: 433

I cursed my best friend for the first mile of the drive home.

Sam was an asshole, making me promise I'd keep things professional, dooming me to be this close to Kristen Cartwright but never be able to touch her.

Kristen gave me a sharp look so I opened the center console, took out sunglasses, and slipped them on. She could never know how close I'd come to kissing her.

Damn it, why didn't I? Everything we always wanted, everything we'd been working for…it was right here. Two more paying gigs, plus the huge county festival—we should get news on that any day now. Our online presence was climbing like a rocket, and I even had a whole bunch of ideas for new songs.

It was happening.

And the really weird thing? I wasn't sure I cared anymore. Mom and Dad were still fighting like toddlers over every damn thing, Anna's behavior was still getting worse instead of better, and—and maybe the guys were right. Maybe Anna would be better in a different environment. But was I saying that—thinking that for Anna or for me?

Because here's the truth—raw and unplugged: I wanted Kristen.

I slowed for a stop sign. Anna had been singing those damn *ding dongs* for twenty freaking minutes, and I was about to lose my shit. I flipped on the radio, scanned through the stations until I found "Shake It Off," which was better—though not by much in my eyes. "Taylor Swift, Anna."

"Shake, shake, shake!" She sang and bopped in the backseat. The only time Anna was truly verbal was for songs she really liked. I checked my mirrors, but that was really just a handy way to sneak a look at Kristen. She was staring straight ahead, one red-tipped finger slowly rubbing her top lip.

Didn't mean anything.

Maybe she was just itchy. Or thirsty or something.

It absolutely did not mean she wanted to kiss me.

Ten more silent and uncomfortable minutes later, I parked in the driveway and busied myself getting Anna settled. Mom's car was gone, but I found Mom reading a book in the living room. "Hey, Mom. We're home." I led Anna into the living room, Kristen trailing behind us.

"Mama."

"Hi, you guys. Did you have fun at the mall?" She carefully marked her place in the book, closed it, and took off her glasses.

Anna shook her head. "Bun."

Mom sent an exasperated look my way. "Oh, Eli, you didn't."

"Yeah, I did. Come on, Mom, lighten up. When you go to the mall, you buy a cinnamon bun. It's what people do." I handed her the box that held the remaining cinnamon bun. Anna eyed it with anticipation, sat on the floor beside the coffee table, and opened her mouth like a baby bird.

Laughing, I waved toward Kristen. "This is Kristen Cartwright. She's singing in the band."

Mom's mouth fell open. "Oh! Hi, Kristen. I'm Stephanie Hamilton." She stood up and held out a hand.

Kristen crossed the room and took Mom's hand. "Nice to meet you, Mrs. Hamilton."

Mom's eyes met mine, and I knew exactly what she was thinking. *Should I book the church?* I'd never brought a girl home before.

193

I shot her a *be cool* look and took Kristen's hand. "We'll be in the garage, practicing."

"Okay. Say bye, Anna."

Anna waved. "Bye bye."

"Bye, Anna."

"Ding dong, ding dong, ding dong."

Kristen laughed and applauded. Mom looked confused.

"What on earth is that about?"

"Oh, um," I hesitated, smoothing my hair back. "Anna dropped her bun and nearly flipped out." I snapped up both hands when a dark cloud crossed Mom's face. "Kristen starting singing 'Carol of the Bells' and got half the food court singing along. Anna loved it. She's been singing the chorus ever since."

Mom smiled at Kristen. "That was smart thinking. Thank you."

Kristen shrugged. "I knew she liked the song, so I figured, why not sing it in April in front of a few hundred strangers? At least they'll remember my name."

Mom let out a loud laugh and winked at me. "Keep her around, Eli. She's great."

Yeah. She was.

Which was exactly why I wasn't going to touch her. No matter how much I tingled and burned.

I led Kristen through the kitchen and into the garage. "Have a seat. Want anything? Water or a soft drink or something?"

"No, I'm good."

She grabbed a stool near the sound table and shook the hair back from her face. She had on dark blue jeans with rhinestones on the rear pockets, a hoodie, and those hot red boots again.

I'd had dreams about Kristen and those boots. They'd been all she was wearing. I cleared my throat and grabbed my tablet and guitar. "I started playing around with some song ideas for you. Just to get a feel for what you want."

"Cool." She smoothed her hands down her thighs, and there were those fucking tingles—running up my thighs like she'd touched them instead of her own.

I shifted the guitar to hide my groin, cursing Sam Gowan to hell and back, and while I was at it, I added in all his descendants too. "Tap the three newest files in GarageBand."

Kristen tapped the screen and nodded as she read my drafts. "Oooh, I like this: *I want the fame. I need the glory. There's another side to this story.* That's good. That captures me, you know?"

"That's what I do." I grinned. "I was thinking you'd want to stick with your basic love gone bad song."

"Oh, right. Because I asked you for anger."

"It's called 'The Way It Hurts,' but we can always change that if you want." I really hoped she'd keep the title. Not that anyone would believe it, but it was slowly killing me to be this close to Kristen Cartwright and not do anything about it. I tried to write lyrics that she might use, but they were mostly me. About me, for me.

Because I was falling hard for this girl and couldn't ever tell her.

"*I watch you battle your way through the night, every little thing puttin' up a fight. I'll be there next to you, just for you, for the rest of my life.*" She looked up. "Elijah, that's really beautiful. Was that…were you writing for Anna?"

"Yeah," I lied. "Just words I figure you could put a lot of emotion into. Want to hear a few melodies?" I took the iPad from her, tapped a few buttons, and played the files I'd made. Kristen shut her eyes and swayed to the beat.

"Oh, that's really cool." She covered my hand when I played the second file. Her touch, no matter how innocent, was just more fuel on a raging fire. Never should have imagined kissing her. Now it was the only thing I wanted to do.

I repositioned the guitar in my lap, grabbed a pick, and started strumming. "Give the first version a try."

Kristen angled her head, frowning at the tablet. "How? I don't know the key, the timing, or the scale."

"That's because we haven't decided them yet. Right now, anything goes. Just pick."

She blew the hair out of her eyes and shook her head, but gave it a shot. She hit the first line with a high clear D, which sent more tingles down my spine. I hadn't written the song for that range, but damn if she didn't nail it. She extended the lyrics, holding some words for an extra beat while softening others. Words have their own rhythm and have to fit their music. Kristen was instinctively aligning those sounds on the fly, and it rocked me down to my bones. Who knew BroadwayBaby17 really did know her shit?

I fumbled a chord. I'd really been an ass to her.

"What?" She broke off, shooting me an embarrassed look.

I quickly shook my head. "Nothing. Don't stop."

She picked it up from the top, and I adjusted my strumming. "Try it at a slower tempo this time," I suggested.

We went through the first version three times, trying out different tempos, different moods. "Oh, that feels good," I murmured, tapping a note into the tablet. "Start soft and slow, build the cadence, build the emotion, and then belt out—"

"Oh, yeah." She nodded, catching on. "Right here?"

"Or here." I guided the finger she drew along the screen to a different line.

"Can we try it out?" She waved a hand at the equipment.

I stood up and got the camera and the mics set up. "Keep the mic about here," I reminded her, holding it about six inches from her mouth.

Her mouth. God.

She took the mic and regarded me with a cautious look in her eyes. Obviously, I wasn't hiding my feelings very well. I turned my back on her, trying like hell to get myself under control. I fiddled with dials and switches and counted off. "Two, three, four…" I opened with the first chord and played a short intro, and Kristen took a deep breath.

I held mine.

She sang just like we discussed…soft and slow, her voice warm and delicate. She told the story…her voice, her facial expressions, and her gestures all instruments of her craft. The guitar hummed under my fingers, but it wasn't me—it was her, all her, just bringing me along for the ride. She sang the first verse and hit the chorus like an explosion, and the blood vibrated in my veins. This song could be an overnight success, it was that good, but still—something wasn't right.

Something was missing.

I slowed the tempo and faded out, waited a beat, and said, "Check." I'd edit that out later.

"You're making a frowny face."

I looked up with a laugh. "A frowny face? What are you, six?"

She rolled her hands, ignoring my taunt. "Whatever. Spill it. What was wrong with that?"

Slowly, I shook my head. "I don't know. Something feels like it's missing."

She nibbled on one of those red nails. "Can we hear it back?"

I handed her a headset, grabbed one for me, and jacked in. A few keystrokes and the sound filled our heads. It was acoustic and needed percussion. We could try it again with a computerized drum beat. Maybe that would help. I shook my head again. That wasn't it. Kristen's voice was beautiful as always, but…but what?

"You know what this needs?" she asked.

"More cowbell?" I shot back.

She slapped my arm. "Yeah, yeah. Be serious. I was going to say I think it needs two voices. Sing it with me?"

Two voices. Yeah. Yeah, that could be it. Kris versus Eli. The missing piece was that emotional battle we could practically trademark, we did it so well. But it was *her* song.

I sighed and knew this wasn't going to be easy on me.

When she looked up at me, blue eyes huge and pleading, I'd have agreed to pretty much anything she wanted. I reset the equipment, and we took our places. I counted us off again.

"I want the fame, I need the glory, but there's another side to this story." Kristen started off slow and easy, just like before.

I added in a new line. *"Baby, I'm yours, but this is too tough. Why am I never enough?"*

Kristen turned and sang *to* me, and damn if that didn't amp up the song's punch. When we finished, she was grinning ear to ear. "That felt good. Really good!"

It did. And it *didn't*. "Let's hear it back."

Sitting by the computer, headphones on, there was this feeling in my gut—the same feeling you get before the first dip on a roller coaster. This wasn't just good—it was perfect. I shut my eyes and let the song flow over me, through me, imagining the four of us performing it live, an audience swaying to our beat. Kristen would be dancing, hair flowing back, every guy in the crowd wishing he was the guy she took home. We'd be invited on to every late night talk show to perform—it would be a hit single on a critically acclaimed album.

"Let me post this online, Kris."

She looked at me sharply. "What? No! You can't. This is for my conservatory applications."

"I know. But if it's as good as I think it is, we should collect feedback and tweak it, make it even better. Make it a number one hit. Wait until we add bass and percussion—I'm telling you, this song will get airplay."

She lowered her eyes and said nothing for a long while. "But I thought this was mine, Elijah."

"It is." I waved a hand. "But why can't the band use it too?"

"Because it's supposed to be original, remember?"

"And it is." I wasn't seeing the problem here. The song was dynamite, and her voice brought it to life in ways I couldn't even imagine when I'd started writing it.

"You wrote the lyrics. You wrote the music. All I did was sing."

"So change them. Come up with a few verses on your own. Now that you know how all the elements work together, you can add to it easily."

She slid off the stool and tossed her headset to the table, refusing to meet my gaze. "Got a USB drive or something?"

"Uh, yeah. Sure." I rummaged around and found a drive on a lanyard I could clean off.

"Plug it in and transfer everything. Every note. Every word. Every frame of that video," she ordered and stepped back.

The breath clogged in my lungs. "You don't trust me." It wasn't a question.

"Why should I? You already posted a lot of shit about me online."

I blew out a sigh. "Kris, that was just trash talk, you know? It didn't mean anything. It's just a way to get people engaged in the band."

"Elijah, I'm not the band. I'm a person. Our deal was I sing for you, you help me develop something original for my applications. I get that you want to use this, but you can't."

"But this is the one, Kris! This is the song that'll break us out."

"I don't want to break out! I can't deal with the fame we already have." She took her phone out of her pocket, swiped at it, and thrust it in my face. "See this? See what your comments did?"

I glanced at her phone and saw her Twitter feed. "Shit, you have that many Twitter followers?" I'd been trying to get Ride Out's count to break the same mark for months now.

Kristen cursed. "Not the followers, you jerk. Their posts. Do you see what they say about me? I spend more time blocking people than I do talking to anybody."

Oh. I scrolled through her feed and read a few posts that I couldn't disagree with. Things like, *"You're so f*cking HAWT!"* or *"<3 this girl's voice and her body!"* And yes! Somebody recorded our Christmas carol at the mall event. "Check it out. The Christmas carol got posted."

She snatched the phone out of my hands. "That's the only thing you see?"

What the hell more was there? Things were finally happening. "Kris, they're *talking* about us. About you. This is a good thing. The more they talk, the more opportunities open for all of us. Trust me."

She cocked her head to the side and raised both eyebrows. To prove my point, I grabbed the tablet and opened my email app. "Here, look at how much mail we're getting now. Almost a hundred messages today. A month ago, I was happy to see—" Abruptly, I stopped talking and clicked a message from the county council. "Dear Mr. Hamilton, the committee is happy to inform you—holy fuck, we're in! We got accepted for the county fair!" I grabbed Kristen off her feet and swung her around.

She wriggled out of my grasp as soon as I put her down, her face tight and red.

I sighed loud and long. "Kris, do you not get what this means for us?"

"Yeah, Elijah, I get it. Congratulations."

Bull. "Oh, you get it," I echoed. "Then why aren't you happy?"

She held up both hands and shook her head. "Oh my God, are you serious right now? You really need me to explain?" Before I could even think about replying, she barreled on. "This isn't my thing! I'm not even in this band… Your friends barely tolerate my presence, you can't stop looking at my chest for longer than two minutes at a time, and when I show you the kind of crap I have to put up with online, you hold up your hand for a high five."

I opened my mouth to protest, but she shot out a hand.

"Oh, don't even!" She stomped her red-booted foot. "I was speaking figuratively."

Yeah. Sure. "Hey, look, when you're online, you have to expect a certain amount of hazing. You think I don't deal with the same shit? Girls hit on me all the time."

She pressed her lips together and shook her head. "Not the same thing."

"Oh, come on! How is it not?"

"Because you're a guy. Nobody threatens you."

I straightened my spine. "Threatens you? Who threatened you? All I saw were people tweeting that you're hot and have a great voice."

With a groan, she buried her face in her hands. "Yeah. That is all you'd see. Elijah, I can't even log on to the Beat anymore without a dozen people asking me if I've screamed for Elijah Hamilton yet."

I laughed, and Kristen's phone buzzed. "I wish you'd just try one tiny metal scream. I'm telling you, you'd be amazing." She didn't answer. "Kris?"

Her face lost all its color, and she kind of swayed on her feet. I leaped up, guided her down to the stool, and took her hand, rubbing it between both of mine. She was ice cold and shaking.

"What happened? What's wrong?"

She shook her head slowly, eyes blurred by tears.

Scared now, I grabbed her shoulders and gave her a little shake. "Kristen! Look at me. What happened?"

Her mouth opened, but her voice was just a squeak. She said one word, but it was said on the edge of a gasp filled with so much agony, I hurt for her.

"Etta."

KRISTEN

Kristen Cartwright
@kristencartwright

Tweets	Following	Followers
6,941	**756**	**1,687**

@Rosebud

@kristencartwright <3 the Christmas carols at the mall! 2 cool! #TeamKristen #KrisVsEli

@Ride_On747

Check out this vid of @Ride_Out's pre-Christmas concert
at the mall! #CatCall #KrisVsEli

@DTMilo

WTF is wrong with that chick? #KrisVsEli #CatCall

@Ride_On747

@DTMilo: Dude, back off. She's got autism. Can't help it.

@Rosebud

oooh, @elijahhamilton is a god! I'd scream for him!!
#TeamEli #sorryKristen #KrisVsEli

@DTMilo

RT @Mikey_T: I made @kristencartwright scream! #CatCall
#KrisVsEliVsMikey3way bit.ly/2IDS6Lxtr

RETWEETS 445 FAVORITES 1513

I sat in a butt-busting plastic chair in a waiting room near the ICU,
barely holding myself together.

ICU. Intensive Care Unit.

Gordon slept across two chairs, long legs dangling off the edge
while the rest of him was curled into a comma. Dylan sat with Mom,
one arm around her shoulders. Dad was... Dad was in with Etta and
her doctor.

Shivering, I breathed through my mouth, trying like hell to ignore the smell of medications and sickness and bad food and…and…oh, God, death.

She'll be fine. She'll be fine. She'll be fine. "Of *course*, I'll be fine, Kristen. I'm Henrietta Cartwright! I don't *do* deathbed scenes." I could hear her voice in my brain—in my heart. Etta's a legend. She couldn't die. She just couldn't.

She'll be fine. She'll be fine. She'll be fine. No matter how many times I repeated the words, I still didn't believe them.

A hand covered mine and squeezed. I looked up and found Elijah Hamilton beside me. Since the night we'd met, Elijah's eyes had glinted with humor when he teased me or sexual interest when he stared at my chest. Now they were filled with worry and sympathy and a whole bunch of other things that should *not* be there and meant one thing— this was bad. Seriously *bad*. I pulled my hand away and wrapped my arms around my middle.

"Go home, Elijah," I managed to squeeze out.

A brief flash of pain crossed his face, and then it was gone, replaced with that same steely determination I'd only seen him display for his sister. Lips firmly set, he shook his head and took my hand again. "Not leaving you, Kris."

I didn't argue. Finding words was just too much effort. He didn't do serious. He didn't do relationships. He didn't do anything but the music. But right now, I needed to pretend he did because I could feel myself coming apart at the seams. I stared down at the hand holding mine, absorbing its warmth and feeling all the calluses. This was a hand capable of producing the most beautiful sounds—with a piano, a guitar, or even words. I didn't know why he was still sitting next to me. He didn't even like me… Not like I liked him.

Suddenly, a foot appeared in front of me. I looked up into Dylan's scowling face.

"What the hell is this?" He waved his own hand at mine, still swallowed in Elijah's.

Neither of us answered, and an angry red flush crawled up Dylan's face.

After a moment, Elijah cleared his throat and extended his other hand. "I'm Elijah Hamilton."

Dylan ignored the friendly gesture. "I know who you are. Why are you here? With my sister."

Elijah looked at me, eyebrows raised, and something inside me, buried under layers and layers of cotton, reminded me that my family didn't know I was singing with Elijah's band, and for the life of me, I couldn't remember why I hadn't told them.

"Elijah's a friend, Dyl. I sing in his band."

Dylan's blue eyes seemed to get darker right before my eyes. "You sing in his—are you crazy?"

I shifted on my ass-numbing seat. Crazy? No. Determined and industrious. "It was Etta's plan—" I revealed and then abruptly shut up when some invisible fist squeezed all of the oxygen out of my lungs. How would I do this without her guiding me, cheering me on?

I wasn't sure I'd even want to if she…

No. No! Do not go there. She'll be fine.

We sat in our numb little stupors for a while, but time had long since stopped mattering to me. Instead of seconds, I wanted to count heartbeats.

Breaths.

But they wouldn't let us in to see Etta.

A throat cleared from the doorway, and I looked up to see Teddy, glasses perched on his forehead, salt-and-pepper hair in its usual state of disgrace—according to Etta. A completely inappropriate giggle threatened to explode when the thought struck me—is this why she divorced him? Because he didn't share her sense of style?

"Grandpa Teddy." I stood up and wrapped my arms around him, and he hugged me tight.

"Kristen, sweet girl, look at you." He held me at arm's length. "Etta tells me you brought the house down with your *Cats* show. I'm so sorry I couldn't come."

I waved that away. I totally understood the competing demands on his time with all of our various blended families. Mom hugged him next.

"So glad you called me, sweetheart."

"Of course," she murmured.

"Have you heard from the others?"

Mom nodded. "Everyone's on their way." And then her face just crumbled. "It's Etta. Of course everybody's coming."

I think I must have been about four when Teddy and Etta split up. I remember sitting on his broad shoulders, holding on to all that hair like it was horse's reins. When I thought about all of the horror stories kids at school told about their parents' divorces, that ridiculous urge to giggle rose up again. Only Etta could remain such good friends with all of her ex-husbands. She was that special.

Is. Is that special. Oh, God.

Elijah's hand was suddenly on mine, squeezing hard. I looked at him sharply, but his eyes held the most unbearable tenderness, and instead of giggling, I suddenly wanted to dissolve into tiny pieces and have Elijah toss them into the wind and then write a song about it.

The door opened, and a doctor in scrubs and a lab coat hurried out, Dad following at a slow zombie shuffle. His face was bloodless, and lines showed around his mouth, stopping my heart. He fell into a chair next to Mom, and Dylan rushed to his other side. Even Gordon woke up.

"She had a stroke."

His voice was a scrape of sandpaper.

"They think they've treated her in time, but there is damage. We won't know how extensive it is until tomorrow. Maybe the next day."

A stroke.

"A stroke! How perfectly marvelous! Do you know how difficult it is for an actor to learn to droop?" Etta had played a character recuperating from a stroke when I was in seventh grade at the local theater. I squeezed my eyes shut because the irony was just too damn much.

"She'll live, right?" Gordie asked, his voice a squeak of air.

Mom sent Dad one of those looks that telepathically said Gordie was still a little boy and should be lied to so he's not scared. Or something.

"She's strong, Gordie. We'll just keep praying."

That wasn't an answer. I watched Dad for the look he sent Mom—the one that said, "I'm scared too."

Mom's hand came up and cupped Dad's cheek, and he pressed his face into her touch, shutting his eyes. There it was. So I was right. This was a lot worse than either of them were admitting. I searched in my pocket for money and pulled out a twenty-dollar bill. "Hey, Gordie. Why don't you take this downstairs to the cafeteria, bring us back some sugar? I could really use a doughnut right now."

Gordon took the money and glanced back at Mom to make sure it was okay. "I'll go with him," Dylan offered, and Mom nodded.

They left the waiting room. I gave him another minute to be sure and then pounced.

"Tell us the truth now. How bad is this?"

Dad let out a long sigh and slumped in his chair. "We don't know the extent of the damage, but she's showing left side paralysis and she can't talk. They're going to try food soon to see if she can still swallow."

"If she can't?" Teddy whispered, and Dad looked at him, only just realizing he was there. Dad held out a hand that Teddy grabbed, but he never answered the question.

"Dad? What if she can't?" I prodded.

He pulled in a deep breath, and when he spoke, his voice was thick and full of pain. "She may not be able to come home, honey. We'll have to look at places—"

I surged to my feet. "No. Just...just no." I snapped up both hands—like two pieces of flesh could stop any of this from happening.

"Kristen, honey, we're getting ahead of ourselves. We don't know for sure how extensive her needs will be yet. Right now, it's about treatment. We'll deal with care later, okay?" Mom's hand went to Dad's shoulder and tugged him into her arms. He buried his face against her neck and started to cry.

I ran.

———

I ran through doors and down corridors, unable to shake the feeling that the building was closing in on me and I needed to escape before it did. I burst through the exit into the night, gulping in air like I'd been starved of it. My shaking legs collapsed, and I fell onto a bench right near the exit, no longer able to hold in the desperate worry that just kept growing and growing. I was cold, so cold, I was sure I'd never be warm again. Gasps turned into loud sobs, and I couldn't control them, couldn't do anything but let them have me.

Warm hands touched me, guiding me against a solid wall I was only dimly aware was Elijah's chest. "I got you, Kris," he murmured. "I got you."

I got you. His words penetrated the chaos inside me, giving me something to hold on to, so I clung to him and cried until I was empty.

"You're shaking. You cold?" he asked when I finally took a breath.

"Freezing."

He shifted, holding me away from him. I shivered, missing his warmth. He shrugged out of his sweatshirt and wrapped it around my shoulders, resettling me in the crook of his arm.

"Thanks," I said with a sniffle.

He shifted again and tucked a couple of folded-up tissues into my hand. I managed a tiny laugh. "Boy Scout?"

I felt him shake his head. "Nah. Anna's brother." He said it with a sigh that made me picture him rolling his eyes too.

I blew my nose, mopped up my face, and tried to get myself back under control.

"Feel any better?"

Actually, I did. "I'm scared. Really scared. I mean, Etta's old, but I just never—you don't expect—"

"No. You never do." He nodded, his chin against the top of my head. "Your parents are scared too."

I squirmed. "Yeah. I know. I don't know how to make it better."

"Suggestion?"

Puzzled by his tone, I pulled away from the comfortable warm circle he'd given me, searching his face. After a moment, I finally understood he was asking for permission before offering his opinions or advice. About to say no, I suddenly realized I wanted to hear what he thought—desperately. "Yes."

Elijah lifted his hand and ran a thumb under each of my eyes, and the gesture almost made me cry more. "Don't make them worry about you too. If you need to freak out or lose your shit, don't do it in front of them. Do that with me. Anytime you need to talk or cry or whatever, I'm right here."

Or whatever. Seriously? My grandmother just had a stroke and Elijah's hitting on me? I shoved him away. "You're unbelievable."

Shocked, maybe a little hurt, he stared at me. "What?"

"I cannot believe you're still trying to hit on me in a freakin' hospital!"

He shoved his hands in his pockets and looked down at his feet with a scowl. "I was not hitting on you. I happen to know a few things about worried parents and thought you could use a friend. So call Rachel and I'll get the hell out of here."

Rachel. It never occurred to me to call her. She's not really good in situations like these. She tends to cry and mope, and *you* end up taking care of *her*.

"I'm sorry," I offered quietly once I'd thought things over. "In my defense, you have to admit you have a track record where girls are concerned." I'd intended to tease him and make him smile.

Instead, a dark flush crawled up his neck. He shifted, scratched his neck, and cleared his throat a few times. When he finally lifted his eyes to mine, I saw he wasn't amused at all. He looked kind of pissed off.

"Kristen." He lifted a hand and then jerked it away. "I know what my reputation is. I work pretty damn hard on it. But a pretty significant portion of the stuff you've heard about me is entirely made up."

"Really." I drew the word out, lifting both eyebrows. "Sex in the bathroom over at the restaurant where my brother works?"

"Never happened."

"Sex at the homecoming game last year?"

"Never happened."

"What about what's-her-name from the mall? You nearly swallowed her."

He laughed once. "She kissed me. I only made sure people saw it. That's how I build my rock star reputation. But I don't let it go further than that."

I let that sink in for a minute or two. "So why tell me?"

A car door slammed in the parking lot, and Elijah's head snapped to the sound. He watched the driver hurry to the entrance and then shrugged. "Because my friends know me. I want us to be friends and figure that can't happen until you know me."

My head felt like it was stuffed with blankets. "Okay. I'm sorry for what I said. Tell me what you meant by the 'whatever' part."

A slow smile spread across his face. "When I'm really upset over shit, I do things to blow off the steam, you know?"

No. No, I didn't know. "What things?"

"Nick, Sam, and I head to the beach, get drunk. Sometimes, we camp out."

"I can't get drunk with you guys." Dad would send me to a freakin' convent.

He waved a hand. "It doesn't matter what we do. The point is everybody does something when they need to cut loose."

My eyes filled again. "Yeah. Etta and I always eat lots of chocolate and cry together."

His lips twitched. "If you need to eat tons of chocolate or shop out entire stores or go get a facial or something, I'm there."

A giggle exploded. I wasn't sure I'd ever laugh again, but the thought of Elijah Hamilton with his hair in a messy bun and mud all over his face was hard to resist. "Thanks." And then that moment of hilarity ended when I remembered Etta's condition. "I really don't know what I'll do if she…"

"Stop. Don't do that *what-if* shit."

"I can't help it!" I flung out both hands and let them fall. "Etta's all I can think about now."

"If you need to step back, skip the mall gigs to be with your Etta. I'll figure it out somehow. Don't worry."

That's exactly what I wanted. I wanted to go home, find the air mattress, set it upright next to Etta's bed, and never leave her side. I wanted to forget all about concerts and the stupid fashion show and my conservatory applications because none of that stuff mattered. All that mattered was Etta.

Are you mad, darling? A true professional never lets anything prevent her from taking the stage.

I sighed. "No." I shook my head. "Etta would hate it if I used her as an excuse to cancel an appearance."

Elijah laughed. "The show must go on?"

"Exactly."

"Okay." He shifted on the bench and fiddled with the leather cuff on his wrist. "Here. Take this."

"What? No!" That leather cuff was one of the first things I'd noticed about Elijah. I thought it was cool.

"Yes. We all have one of these." He buckled it around my wrist. "Now you're officially in the band."

Slowly, I ran a thumb over the embossed design, Ride Out's logo. I was still wearing his sweatshirt. Oh my God, had I fallen into some parallel universe? A couple of weeks ago, Elijah Hamilton was just one of the many obnoxious people insulting me online, and today, he was holding my hand, drying my tears, and helping me make a dream come true. "Why?"

"Huh?"

"Why?" I looked up at him, into those amazing eyes. "You don't even like me."

"Don't *like* you?" he echoed, looking at me sideways. "You really think I write songs for every girl I meet? Or invite them to sing in my band?" He surged to his feet and paced a few feet away, like he didn't trust himself to be near me. "Or consider breaking a promise to my best friend for?"

I stared at him, mouth hanging open. "What promise?"

He didn't answer my question. "Come on. It's cold. Let's find the cafeteria." As I followed him back through the main entrance, it occurred to me that he'd never answered me. I still had no clue why Elijah was being so damn nice to me.

And I wished—almost as much as I wanted Etta better—for him to never stop.

ELIJAH

the beat_   Search   🔍

Ride Out
@ride_out   **3,002** FANS

BryceG: Wanna motorboat dat rack @BroadwayBaby17 Girl, u rock!

SHARES: 288 LIKES: 449

A stroke. Jesus.

Only a couple of hours ago, I'd been jazzed over Kristen's decision to keep singing with us. The fashion show at the mall would be excellent exposure for the band, and now that the county had green-lighted our appearance at the festival this summer, I was certain bookings would fill up the calendar.

And then, like the snap of a finger, things changed.

A sigh from Kristen compelled me to steal a glance at her. She looked like shit. Her face was too pale, and there was no twinkle in her blue eyes. Her lips were cracked, and there were tear tracks on her cheeks. One look and all I wanted to do was wrap my arms around her and sing in her ear until she smiled again.

But I couldn't do that.

I cursed Sam—again—and flung open the cafeteria door a bit too hard. She looked at me sharply but walked ahead without a word. On a Sunday night, the place was hopping. Doctors and nurses in various colored scrubs sat in clusters around the big room, and others were by themselves, huddled over files or textbooks. Here and there, a few people hunched over cups of muddy coffee for the heat, not the taste, if the looks of disgust were a good indication.

I scanned a critical eye over our choices and decided packaged stuff was a safe bet. I grabbed a couple of cellophane-wrapped snack cakes, a bottle of water, and watched Kristen head for hot chocolate. I snagged us a table far from the joking and flirting going on at the group table, then grabbed a pile of napkins when Kristen jostled her cup.

"Thanks," she murmured softly.

I shrugged. Her eyes still held suspicion. Expectation. Like she was waiting for me to fuck up. I opened my mouth, about to blurt out that I freakin' loved her—and fuck Sam if he said a word about it—because it was suddenly critical that she stop looking at me like she had me all figured out, but her eyes filled with more tears before I could.

"What? What happened?"

She shook her head and waved her hand. "Nothing. I just can't stop thinking the worst, you know?"

I *did* know. And it really sucked. "Yeah. You have zero control over it. Any of it."

Her lips twitched. "Stick to music, Guitar Hero. Leave the God stuff to God."

I propped my elbows on the table and rested my chin on one hand. "You believe that?"

Her eyes met mine over her cup. "What, God?" Then she lifted one shoulder. "I don't know. I guess. We're not especially devout or anything." She stared into her cup like it was going to reveal the secrets of the universe. "What about you? Do you believe?"

I shook my head. "Not since Anna was born, no."

Her eyebrows drew together, and she angled her head, waiting for me to explain, and even though I hated talking about this, about Anna's issues, I suddenly was. "I can't even count how many people told us crap like *God has a plan* or *God only gives us what we can handle.* That's just bullshit. Any God who thinks it's cool to…to doom a kid to live with the kind of shit Anna lives with every day doesn't deserve worship."

Kristen made a sound of commiseration so I kept going. "Do you know what's wrong with Anna?"

Her eyes shot to mine. "Autism, I figured."

I shook my head. "Yeah, but that's not all. It's genetic. She has an extra chromosome and—" Abruptly, I shut up and shrugged. "I'll spare you all the gory details, but the point is it's genetic. It's in me too."

She gaped at me, her eyes falling to my stomach like it was about to burst open from some *Alien* movie creature or something, which might have been hysterical under other circumstances. But she didn't pull away. I looked at her head-on and dropped all my shields. "I love Anna, and there is *literally* nothing I wouldn't do for her, but if there'd been any kind of choice… Nobody gets it, Kris. Nobody really understands." I had to stop when my voice cracked, and I shook my head hard to stop the tears that were suddenly right there, salty on my tongue. "It's hard. It's so fucking hard to watch her struggle. She can't be left alone—ever. She can hardly dress herself. She needs help in the bathroom, and she can't understand why she bleeds every month, and she loves music and will never, *ever* be able to process anything without around-the-clock help, and watching her go through that struggle every damn day is—" The dam burst, and I turned away. I dropped my hand on the table hard enough to make the plastic utensils jump and bit my lips together because for the first time, I got how fucking scared my parents must be.

I scrubbed both hands over my face, ripped the elastic out of my hair, and twisted it around my fingers just for something to look at because I couldn't look at Kristen right now. "It's hard, too fucking hard to pray to a God that doomed a kid to a life that's no life at all."

I looked up in time to see Kristen's eyes slip shut, and she shrank deeper into her seat and farther away from me. "I'm sorry," she said, spreading out her hands with a sad smile. "I knew your sister had some challenges, but I didn't know how…" She trailed off, waved a hand around, and just gave up trying to find the right words.

I changed the subject before I started bawling like a toddler. "I didn't meet Sam and Nick until eighth-grade music class. Sam wanted to start a band. It sounded like fun, so I said yes." I laughed and rolled my eyes. "You should have seen him! In eighth grade, Sam was hilarious. He wore his hair short and spiky and so full of gel, it could draw blood if you touched it. His guitar playing was decent, but nothing like it was now. Nick was…just Nick. The same serious and loyal dude he is today. Rock steady and really cool dealing with the diva personality we had in Sam. Sam wanted to play lead guitar, he wanted to sing, he wanted to write the songs, and he wanted to name the band. The only problem was he sucked at half of those things. I listened to him drone on and on about the hot new song he'd written, and when he showed it to us, I ended up rewriting the whole thing. He complained and protested at first, but when Nick pointed out how my changes worked *with* our talents instead of against them, he listened. It didn't take long for the three of us to mesh."

I broke off, the smile fading. Kristen listened, her eyes pinned to me.

"They saved me," I whispered. "Sam and Nick. They have no idea, but they saved me. Gave me something that I could be good at, something I could be that wasn't *Anna's brother*, and even I didn't know how much I needed that until it was there." I took her hand, felt her quick jerk back, and tightened my grip. "Since eighth grade, it's been the three of us. We made a pact. We'd never let a girl go Yoko on us and break up the band. Sam and Nick showed me how to keep things cool and casual when girls started sniffing around us. How to tell which girls understood I don't do the boyfriend thing and which ones would always want more." Kristen squirmed a little, and I suddenly remembered that she'd heard all about my various hookups, and for the first time since we'd started the band, I was embarrassed.

"Everything worked really well—until now. Nick met Leah, and that nearly split us up until he promised he'd never let her interfere with the band. And she hasn't."

Again, her hand jerked in mine, but I wouldn't let her go. I couldn't now. "Then one night, I had to tell them I might need to quit the band. Unless we could find a way to hit big and hit fast, I wasn't sure I'd be able to give them my all. Instead of letting me quit, Sam and Nick promised they'd do whatever they had to do to keep me. *Whatever they had to do* turned out to be you. As soon as I saw you, it was like, *bam*!" I finished with an explosive hand gesture. "I couldn't take my eyes off you in that white suit thing you were wearing, and then that voice, finding out that voice come from the same body—" I was rambling so I clamped my teeth together before any more embarrassing shit leaked out of my mouth. "Kristen, you could make it happen. You could make it all happen for us, but if you tell me now you want out, you want to be with Etta, I'll understand, I swear it."

Her chin wobbled, and her eyes filled. Her other hand covered the one I was using to hold hers. Squeezed. I breathed a little easier then.

"Elijah," she began. "You're an ass most of the time, but right now, I could kiss you."

"Could you?" I smirked.

"Shut up."

God, I loved rattling Kristen Cartwright. She even managed a tiny smile.

"I'll stay with the band because of what I said before. Etta would *kill* me if I canceled a performance because of her. She was the one who thought this would be a good idea. She wants me to knock those stuffy conservatory admissions committees on their asses. I have to do this…for her." She sat up straight and rolled her shoulders. "I'll do the rock chick thing for you. I'll even put up with Sam's dickish behavior as long as you stop acting that way too." She stuck out a hand, and I grinned.

"Deal."

———

It was well past midnight by the time I got home. The house was dark, except for the single light my parents always kept on in the kitchen. I tiptoed inside, locked up behind me, followed the light into the kitchen, and hung Mom's car keys on the hook near the garage door. The room had been viciously cleaned and smelled like lemons.

I wondered what Anna had done this time.

"Where the *hell* have you been?"

I whipped around and pressed a hand to my pounding heart. "Dad. You scared the crap out of me." He sat at the kitchen table, a glass of water in front of him.

"Good. Now you know how I feel."

Guilt prickled up and down my skin. "I told Mom I was taking Kristen to the hospital."

"Elijah, that was damn near five hours ago."

I spread out my hands. "I couldn't just leave her there, Dad."

Dad opened his mouth, then shut it. He leaned over the table, propped his elbows on it, and rubbed his hands over his face. I got a good look at him then. His face was the color of the tile on the floor… an ashy gray, his eyes were bloodshot, and his hair stood up in places.

"How is her grandmother?" he finally asked.

I shook my head. "They don't know yet. She had a stroke. They think they got her treated fast, but they won't know if there's any permanent damage for a few days yet."

"A stroke?" He sat back and shook his head with a frown. "Jesus, that's got to be rough."

I pulled out a chair and sat opposite him. "Kristen's a mess. She's really tight with Etta—that's what she calls her grandmother. I only met Etta one time, but, Dad, she's not at all your typical granny, you know?"

Dad's lips twitched. "No? So what *is* she like?"

What's she like? That was like trying to describe the sun. "You know that saying, *a force of nature*? That's what she is. I met her after Kristen's acting class. She was dressed up like she was going to a party. Makeup, fancy clothes, and all these accessories that matched. And the way she talks! She has one of those fake accents and emphasizes words with big gestures." I flapped my hands around to demonstrate. "Kristen says she taught her everything she knows."

Dad nodded. "She sounds like an interesting character."

She was. Like I said, I'd only met her once, but I was sure I'd never forget her.

"And how's Kristen holding up?"

My chest tightened. I hated leaving her, but she'd had enough of me. I lifted a shoulder. "I don't know. She was crying her eyes out at first, but I got her to calm down—"

"*You* did? Where was her family?"

"They were all upset, and she was kind of lost, you know? She needed someone…"

"Elijah, what are you doing?"

I blinked at my father. It was late, and I was tired, and there were half a dozen ways to answer that question. I could only stare at him and wait for him to elaborate.

"You've never brought a girl home before, and now this Kristen is singing in your band, going to the mall with you and your sister, and you're sitting in hospitals with her. It sounds pretty serious to me, and I need to make sure you're being safe."

My face exploded into flames. Fuck me. "Jesus, Dad, it's not like that." No matter how much I wished it were. "Kristen's in the band, which means she's off-limits. The guys and I promised we would keep things professional."

Dad stretched out his legs, bare feet sticking out of pajama pants, and angled his head to study me. "So you're saying there's nothing romantic going on?"

"Exactly," I replied with a sigh of relief that this conversation was over.

"But you want it, don't you?"

I said nothing, and Dad smiled.

"Come on, Eli. You think I don't know your heart?"

Awesome. My dad was a freakin' psychic now. "Look, it doesn't matter what I want. We have to do what's right for the band. Kristen's broadening our fan base, getting us noticed. She's got a huge following online, and a lot of them are now following us. We just got three new gigs—including the county festival this summer."

Dad's eyes shot to mine, wide with surprise. "Oh. Wow. That's… um…really great news."

I nodded. It was. So why wasn't he excited?

He waved a hand. "I'm sorry. It *is* really good news. It's just… I'm…oh, hell." He scratched at the back of his neck. "We found two residential programs for your sister, and we're wait-listed. We expect to get calls this week from one of them because they think they'll have space."

His words were like a punch to my gut, and the breath left my lungs in a whoosh. I knew exactly how hard it was to take care of Anna—I was here, wasn't I? But this just felt… Fuck it! We were abandoning her.

"Eli." Dad grabbed my hand. "I know how you feel about this, but please…don't make this harder than it is."

I raised both eyebrows, but before I could snap back with something sarcastic, he squeezed the hand he held. "Come on, son! Why the hell do you think I'm sitting here in the dark instead of sleeping?"

I closed my mouth and bit the inside of my cheek. He was

right. This was hard. On all of us, not just me. It sucked—loudly—and it was killing me that we were so close to breaking out, when I'd be able to afford twenty-four-hour care for Anna. I just needed a little more time.

I fell back against my chair and thought of Kristen. I wished I could call her. Talk to her.

Kiss her.

The clock in the hall chimed 1:00 a.m., and Dad laughed once. "Guess I should go to sleep so I can wake up in four hours for those visits."

I jerked. Shit! "I forgot."

He nodded. "Yeah. I figured."

Another punch to my gut, but this time, I was ready and didn't flinch.

"Good night, Elijah."

"Night."

Dad's bare feet slapped on the tile as he left the room. I sat in the dark kitchen for the rest of the night, listening to the house creak and the clock chime and the battle raging inside my head and felt like the biggest piece of shit on the planet.

KRISTEN

Kristen Cartwright
@kristencartwright

Tweets	Following	Followers
6,949	**759**	**2,195**

@Shopaholic
@kristencartwright Gr8 mall flash mob! <3 #CatCall #KrisVsEli

@joshL
@kristencartwright Damn! Missed u scream at the mall? U are so HAWT. #CatCall #KrisVsEli

@mslake

@kristencartwright Tweet me. You think you're too cool
to tweet me? You're not, you bitch! Scream! I'll make you
scream. #CatCall #KrisVsEli

The night ticked on, crawling its way to dawn. I stopped looking at
Twitter after I blocked a bunch of new jerks. Dylan took Gordon home,
but I refused to leave. If we went home and something happened—I
shoved the thought into a dark corner.

"You have school, Kristen."

"Not going, Mom."

She sighed. "You have to. This is an important year. Don't ruin it
for—"

I looked up at her sharply, and she pressed her lips into a line.
There was really no way to finish that sentence without pissing me off,
and she knew it. Mom and Etta didn't always get along; we all knew
it. But there'd always been a quiet respect between them, a division of
territories. Mom understood that Dad and his sister had always been
Etta's biggest achievements, and Etta understood that my brothers and
I were Mom's. Except for one thing—my interest in performing. That
was all Etta's influence, and sometimes, I wondered if Mom didn't
secretly wish I'd abandon the stage and take up gardening or pottery
or something.

We sat huddled in one of the cafeteria booths, butts completely
numb even though these molded particle board seats were a tiny step
up from the molded plastic ones in the waiting area upstairs. The place

was bustling now as the shifts changed and exhausted interns shuffled in behind fresh nurses and doctors grabbing coffee. Trays of scrambled eggs and bacon steamed from the self-serve bar and made my stomach growl, though eating was the last thing I wanted to do. Dad's eyes were red and puffy, and I wondered when he'd cried. I hadn't seen that, and suddenly, I felt like I shouldn't be here. I should have gone home with my brothers so my parents could fall apart without having to worry about me, like Elijah said.

Elijah.

Thinking about him tugged on my heart. Driving me to the hospital was one thing, but Elijah had stayed with me, held me, comforted me—this was the same boy who said sexist stuff about me?

Maybe Elijah played evil twins better than I did.

This guy was two completely different people. I thought— hoped—this meant he liked me. Then I thought it meant only that he needed me in the band. But tonight—last night—he'd have just escaped the first minute he could if sex was all he wanted from me.

Wouldn't he?

"Mom's right, sweetheart." Dad's rough voice startled me out of my thoughts. "You need to go to school."

Yeah, like that was even possible now. I shook my head. "No. I can't leave her. Not…just no."

"Kristen," Dad began in that voice reserved usually for occasions when I'm about to be grounded. "I know you're worried. I get that. But I'm worried too. Right now, Etta needs me."

She needed all of us! I opened my mouth, but closed it when

everything Elijah said suddenly replayed in my sleep-deprived brain. Instead, I nodded. "You're right. Okay. I'll go. But I have to see her before I leave, okay?"

Mom and Dad exchanged one of those telepathic looks they shared. I supposed it was from being married for so long; they knew each other's moods and faces so well, they could speak without saying a word. I wanted that. I wanted someone who could look at me and know without asking just what I needed, and for about five freakin' minutes last night, I'd had it. Elijah had given me that. But was that a limited-time-only deal or a lifetime supply?

I had no idea.

Maybe it was time to find out. I pulled in a deep breath and left the booth, ducking into a ladies' room just outside the hospital cafeteria. I tugged out my phone and sent Elijah a message.

Did u mean what u said last nite? Parents want me to leave hospital.

A few moments later, he replied. I'm ditching school. Pick u up in 10. We can hang here with Anna.

That was fine by me. I texted back a *yes* and put my phone away.

"Kristen, you okay?" Mom's heels clicked softly on the gleaming floor.

"Yeah. Sorry." I met her at the sink. She put a hand on my shoulder and gave it a squeeze.

"Honey, she'll be okay. Try not to worry."

I nodded even though that simply wasn't possible. I followed my parents into the elevator and back to the ICU and to Etta's bedside.

Dad went right to her side and took her hand. Etta was asleep—or unconscious—with dozens of wires attached to her. A monitor over her bed tracked various signs of life. The only one I cared about was her heart. It still beat—a slow but steady rhythm that made me think of songs and lyrics and mood and tone. Slowly, I approached her bed and took her hand and almost gasped out loud. They'd stripped her nail polish off, leaving red stains surrounding her nails. Her face was bare of the dramatic eyeliner and drawn-on eyebrows and bold red lips that I'd come to think of as purely Etta, leaving behind a shell. *Oh, God.* "Can she hear us, Mom?" I whispered.

"I don't know, honey. But I don't think it'll hurt to try." She nudged me with an elbow, and Dad smiled at her.

"Hey, Etta," I said in an extra loud voice, stroking the hand I held. It was cold and so tragically still. Etta's hands were never still. I had to stop myself from grabbing her by the shoulders to shake her, force her awake, and urge her to make one of those grand gestures. I patted her hand. "Oh, Etta, you need a manicure! As soon as you're feeling better, we'll get manis and pedis."

There was nothing. Just the relentless beep of the machines.

"And the food! Etta, as soon as you taste it, I have no doubt you'll fling aside these tubes and wires, glide down the hall, and say to the head nurse, 'This *substance* is to food what supermarket tabloids are to literature.'" I flung up my arms in a perfect capture of Etta's signature move and heard Dad quietly applaud.

There was still nothing, and my heart simply fell.

"Okay. I have to get to school. And, Etta, the band—well,

my band—we're playing at the mall and at the county festival this summer, and you'll be there, of course, because I'm your favorite granddaughter, right?"

That was our joke—I was her only granddaughter. Tears dripped down my face, falling onto Etta's arm. She didn't even twitch. Mom's arm came around my shoulders and gently pushed me away from the bed. "Come on, honey." She led me out to the main corridor. "We'll call your brother to come pick you up."

I shook my head. "No, it's okay. I called Elijah."

Mom's blue eyes darted to mine. "Elijah. Anything going on there?"

Shrugging, I hit the button to call the elevator. "Maybe. I don't know."

"Well, he brought you here, stayed with you most of the night. I'd say that's a pretty good sign."

My phone buzzed. "He's here. Call me if anything—"

"I will. Of course I will." Mom gave me a hug and a wave as the doors to the elevator slid shut.

Elijah leaned against the passenger door of a different car than the one he used yesterday, opening it for me when I walked through the exit. "Hey."

"Thanks for this."

He shook his head. "I meant what I said. When you need me, I'll be there." He shut the door before he could see the stupid tears fill my eyes. We were silent on the way back to his house, listening to the radio play. I ached head to toe, my eyes felt like they'd been sandblasted, my throat was raw, and my vision kept blurring.

"Did you eat?"

I jerked in my seat and discovered we were parked in front of Elijah's house. "Oh, um, yeah, I think so."

He left the car, came around to my side, and took my hand, leading me through the garage and its music equipment to the kitchen. He pulled out a chair for me, the scrape it made against the tile floor sounding like the roar of an earthquake to my exhausted ears. He left me there and opened the refrigerator, removed an armful of stuff, and started beating eggs in a bowl while butter sizzled in a skillet. I started to tell him I wasn't hungry, that he shouldn't bother, but when he pulled out not one but *four* plates, I let him do what he had to do.

Elijah was nice to watch. He wore blue jeans today instead of his usual black and a plain white T-shirt under a button-down flannel. He diced onions, tossed them into the pan, and shook it, and my face burned when I realized he knew more about cooking than I did. He toasted half a dozen slices of bread and buttered them while the eggs cooked and then scooped a portion of hot, sizzling eggs onto each plate, surrounded the eggs with toast halves, and carried all four plates to the table—at the same time—without dropping them.

"Dig in." He waved a hand at the table in front of me and then disappeared into the hallway off the kitchen. I looked down and discovered a napkin and utensils had been set for me. When the hell had he done that? I picked up the fork, took a bite, and almost cried. It was so good. By the time he came back, followed by his sister and a woman I'd never met, I was done with my eggs and nibbling the toast.

"Ding, dong, ding, dong!" Anna clapped her hands when she saw me, singing the chorus to the Christmas carol I'd sang for her in the mall.

Elijah laughed. "I think that should be your nickname."

"Great," I replied with a smile I couldn't help.

Elijah helped his sister into a chair and spread a huge plastic sheet around it.

"Kris, this is Linda, Anna's aide."

I nodded, smiled weakly, and ate every last crumb in front of me.

"Hey, Ding Dong. Want some juice?"

I shot Elijah a death glare. "I said it was cute when your sister calls me that, not you."

He raised both hands. "Sorry. Couldn't resist." And then he flashed me a wicked grin. "You're fun to mess with."

I blinked at the empty kitchen. "Where's your sister?"

Elijah turned from the dishwasher and jerked a thumb toward the second floor. "Linda took her upstairs to hose her down. Anna's table manners are deplorable."

A giggle burst out of me. *"Deplorable?* What, is there a vocabulary test with breakfast at the Hamilton residence?"

He laughed, but I noted the slow crawl of red making its way up his neck and onto his cheeks, so I backed off. It was fun to mess with him too. He slid the last plate into the dishwasher and closed the door. I watched him reach into a cabinet, find a couple of glasses, and pour orange juice into them. He slid one of the glasses across the table toward me and sat down. "Here you go."

I sipped the juice, watching him over the rim. His hair was loose today, spilling around his shoulders in a dark curtain, glints of red and gold showing up whenever sunlight from the window caught it in just the right way. He shut his eyes and tilted his head. "God, that feels really good."

I jerked when I discovered my hand was on his head. I didn't realize I'd been running my hand through his hair. "Sorry. I…I'm so tired. I don't even know what I'm doing. I'm—"

Abruptly, I shut my mouth and shook my head. Instinct, I suppose. The need to avoid saying something out loud for fear that will make it true. It was a potent terror—that someone I love might die.

"It's okay. I like it."

I tucked both hands into my lap and suddenly blurted out a question burning at the back of my brain. "If there were a way to live forever, would you take it?"

Dark eyes popped wide over the juice glass. He put it down and angled his head, considering. "If it were science, yes. But no vampire stuff."

I waved my hand. "No, no, not fiction. I mean legitimate immortality. Like doctors find some way to cure all the diseases. I mean, you could still die from injuries and what not, but not diseases."

He rubbed a finger slowly over his lips. "Yeah. Yeah, I would."

I nodded. "Me too." I couldn't get a song out of my head, one of the first ones he'd played for me. "Ah oooh. Ah oooh," I sang softly.

His lips twitched. "'Words As Weapons'?"

"It's been in my head since…since Etta. It's like…well, it's like the song is all about her. That line about the broken mind?"

"*Keep me locked up in your broken mind,*" Elijah sang.

"Yeah. That one. And there's another line about being paralyzed."

"*Keep me dumb, keep me paralyzed.*"

"I keep thinking this could be her, this could be her life now. Paralyzed, unable to talk, trapped inside her own mind."

Elijah winced. "Oh. The chorus. Is that what's bothering you?"

Bothering me? I thought about that for a minute and decided that was the most monumental understatement ever. It freakin' *gutted* me. "*All I really want is something beautiful to say. To never fade away. I wanna live forever,*" I sang, and it was like a prayer. And the scary part was I wasn't sure if I was praying for Etta or me. "Etta would *despise* that. Fading away, I mean." Everything she'd shown me, taught me, it was always about making an impression, making sure my audience not only knew my name but would never be able to forget it. That's what she'd done throughout her career, and now she was in a hospital bed while the world kept right on turning. She was fading away. Tears dripped down my face, and suddenly, Elijah was right there, pulling me against him.

"Shhh. You're worrying about stuff that hasn't happened and may not happen."

"It *will*. Etta's old, Elijah. I never thought of her that way before until this morning, when I saw all those tubes and wires and machines. She won't be here too much longer even if she *does* recover."

His arms tightened around me. "Yeah."

He could have lied to me and said everything would be fine. Or he could have said something lame about the circle of life. He didn't say anything else, and in a weird way, that made me feel better.

He shifted his hands to my shoulders and gently held me away from him. "Kris, maybe this is what your song should be about."

I thought about that for a moment and then shook my head. "No. I'd never be able to sing it without choking up."

He started a slow, steady beat of hands against the table. "*It can't get worse; this is the way it hurts.*" Same words. Different tempo, different mood.

"I like that."

A flash of teeth. "What else do you like?"

You, I almost blurted. Instead, I just shook my head and shrugged, trying not to cry all over again.

"Come on." He tugged me to my feet, put our juice glasses in the sink, and led me out of the kitchen to the stairs.

Upstairs, I could hear Anna still singing the ding-dongs from the song I'd sung for her. The latest Disney movie played in the background, and occasionally, Anna would shift gears and sing to that before switching back to her Christmas song. Elijah led me to a room at the end of the hall, opened the door, and turned on the light.

"Have a seat." He waved his hand toward the full-size bed tucked into a sleek black wall unit filled with music.

I ran my hand over the neat black comforter. "You made your bed?" My brothers never made their beds. I was convinced boys just lacked the bed-making gene in their DNA.

He just shrugged and rolled his eyes. "It's a really big deal to my mom, so uh…yeah."

That was beyond sweet.

He pulled out a chair from under his desk, so I sat on the side of the bed facing him. The room was pretty big. Besides the wall unit around his bed and the desk against the wall, there was a tall dresser in one corner and a closet by the door. The closet was open and amidst the sea of black clothes, I saw a set of dumbbells, an electronic keyboard, and a video game console. Hanging on the wall, he had four different guitars.

"Why do you need four?" I asked, jerking my head toward the instruments.

His brows shot up. "They're all different and produce entirely different sounds. Here. Check it out."

He handed me earbuds, plugged them into his phone, and tapped a few icons. The sound of fast-paced, angry guitar playing filled my ears. I think he'd called that *shredding* once. I must have cringed because he tapped the Skip button, and the next sound to play was completely different. I nodded. "Oh, I like this." Elijah pointed to the first guitar on the wall, a battered Martin, according to the logo. I shifted on Elijah's bed, leaning back against the pillows. This was beautiful, a soft strum, kind of lonely, almost harplike. I was sure I could hear every string, every note whispering to me that Etta was going to be fine, and even though I knew that was impossible, I believed it and felt… I don't know. Safe, maybe.

Yes, that was it.

Safe.

ELIJAH

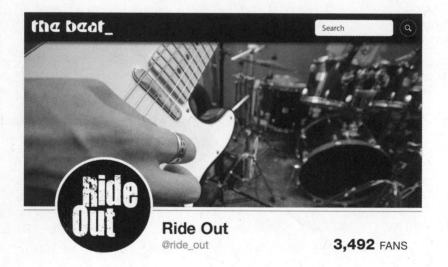

the beat_

Search 🔍

Ride Out
@ride_out

3,492 FANS

MicInHand12: @Ride_Out You guys are da bomb but @kristencartwright is f*cking awesome!

> **Cruisin:** @Ride_Out Latest riff is off the charts! Post more #CatCall vids.

SHARES: 248 LIKES: 445

Kristen fell asleep.

On my bed.

With a start, I jerked myself out of the kind of thoughts I should *not* be having and remembered she'd been awake for damn near twenty-four hours now. She was scared to the bone for Etta, and I got that. I was scared for Anna living with a bunch of strangers. I glanced at my phone to check the time. Mom and Dad had to be done visiting those two facilities by now. But the phone was silent—no texts from Mom or from Sam and Nick. Maybe they hadn't noticed I wasn't in school today.

I shoved the phone back in my pocket and watched Kristen sleep, lips slightly parted, chest rising with each breath. Her arms were folded over her middle and her hands tucked inside her sleeves. Jeez, she was probably cold. I grabbed a blanket and carefully covered her up to her chin, and for a second, I considered stretching out next to her, but the landline rang downstairs. I quietly hurried to my parents' room to pick up their extension.

"Hello, may I speak with Nathan Hamilton, please?" asked a professional voice on the other end.

"Sorry, he's out right now. I'll take a message if you'd like."

"Yes. This is Elizabeth Nicholls from the Avalon Avenue Home."

My heart twisted inside my ribs. A third facility. *Great.*

"We have an opening and are reviewing our waiting list. I need to know if there's still interest in our facility for Anna Hamilton."

I tightened my grip on the phone to stop myself from pitching it against the wall. *No!* I squeezed my eyes shut when my brain decided now would be a really great time to project images of mentally ill teens strapped to their beds, drool dripping out of the corners of their mouths and eyes glazed. My hands fisted tighter when I imagined sleazy staff copping a feel…or worse. *No, there's no fucking interest!*

"Hello?"

My eyes snapped open, and my gaze fell to the table next to Dad's side of the bed, on the jumble of papers—printouts from the Internet, brochures on residential programs for disabled teens, and…and what the fuck was this? I picked it up and stared at it in hands that shook.

"Yeah," I finally said. "Yes, there's interest."

When the woman hung up, I sat on my parents' bed, still clutching the phone, staring at my father's last will and testament and trying really hard not to puke all over it.

Anna was watching a Disney movie in her room; I could hear her singing with the princess. Would they allow her to watch her favorite movies? Play music for her and let her sing? What about water play? Who'd climb in the tub with her?

I put the phone down, scrubbed both hands over my head, and stood up. I needed answers. I tiptoed back into my room, where Kristen had curled into a cat shape on my bed. I thought about leaving her in peace but worried she'd freak out and wonder where the hell she was when she woke up.

Okay, I really just liked watching her sleep.

Jesus. When the hell did I turn in to Edward friggin' Cullen?

I grabbed my tablet and started checking out the Avalon Avenue

Home. Forty minutes later, I learned it had a heated pool, *a vibrant community*—whatever the hell that meant—and a music therapy program, and it allowed family members to visit whenever they wanted. They claimed that music therapy with severely disabled kids like Anna could improve their social, communication, and focus skills. Yeah, well, I could do that myself. Didn't need to send her away for that. I shut my eyes, let my head fall back against the chair, and tried to keep my mind open.

A thud followed by a shriek had me on my feet. I burst into Anna's room just as the tears started. Linda had her arms wrapped around Anna from behind—one of the most effective ways to control her and keep her from hurting herself when she spiraled out of control like this. On the floor was a mess of epic proportions. Anna's box of movies had fallen over—DVDs were strewn all over the place, and at least one was broken in half.

"Hey, Anna Banana." I kept my voice soothing and low-pitched. Sometimes, that helped Anna to calm down, if she wanted to hear what people were saying.

"Eli," she said on a sob, pointing to her beloved movie collection.

"It's okay. They just fell down. They're not hurt." I quickly hid the broken one from her sight. "Let's fix them, okay? Look, Anna. Watch Eli." I picked up one and put it back in the box. "Want to help Eli, Anna?"

Linda gave me a wary look. "I don't know, Elijah. She may stomp all over them."

"Give her a minute. She's coming down."

And she was. Maybe she was learning—finding a way to break

through the limits on her brain. She didn't need some fucking residential program. I kept picking up DVDs, putting them back in the big box we kept them in, and hoping it would provide some order to the chaos inside her.

"Help."

"Okay, Anna can help." I nodded to Linda, and she released my sister, hovering close in case Anna tried again to hurt herself—or one of us. Still sniffling, Anna fell to her knees on the floor and picked up a disc. "Mine."

"Yes, Anna. Yours."

"Mine. Mine. Mine." She chanted as she handed me discs. Soon, they were all back in the box except for the broken one that I'd hidden.

Anna's scream made me realize—too late—that Anna had her own way of keeping track of all her movies and *knew* one was missing. Her face contorted in a mixture of rage and grief for her beloved movie. She couldn't understand that it was her fault it was broken—all she knew was the end state, not the cause, her heart mourning its loss like someone's death, even if she didn't know which movie it was.

Beauty and the Beast.

I'd bought it for her a few years ago with money I made raking leaves.

Linda tried to soothe her, but Anna shoved her away. I didn't move fast enough, and Anna swung at me, hitting me with one of the movie cases still in her hand. The blow landed on my cheek. Rage and pain filled her face, and I cursed. We'd had her! We'd had her calmed down, and I fucked it up.

Anna in a rage was difficult to stop—she frequently needed to just exhaust herself. Singing never helped in these situations; in fact, it made things worse, adding another thing for her to process on top of all the other things she was unable to handle. And once the flow of adrenaline and other crap started inside her body, it just completely took over.

Her eyes swung to the box of movies we'd just cleaned up, and I knew she meant to upend them again. Before she could, I moved the box out of her reach. Bad move. She lost all control, lashing out at me and then at Linda. Restraining her was the only thing we could do at this point. I tried to hold her flailing arms, but damn, she was strong when she was like this. She tried to kick Linda, and I knew we had to stop her before she drew blood. I managed to get her off balance and onto the floor, sitting in front of me. I wrapped myself around her, but she bucked, twisted, and smashed her head against my chin. While the circle of fucking stars faded from my sight, I adjusted my hold to make sure she couldn't do that again. She raked my arms with her nails, and when she started kicking, I pinned her legs with mine. There was nothing else I could do.

Linda moved in front of us. "Anna. Anna, look at me. Look at Linda." She tried to catch her flailing hands.

"Turn off the TV, Linda."

Linda grabbed the remote we kept on a high shelf and powered down the TV. That got Anna's attention fast but made her scream louder. Linda took the box and headed for the door.

The only thing we could do now was make sure Anna didn't hurt anybody or herself. That meant time-out. Her room was completely safe with bars on the windows, and there was nothing breakable, except for the TV, but that was suspended from her ceiling. Her bed was low to the floor. There was no dresser—her fingers could get caught in the drawers—and no door on her closet, and no mirrors. I nodded to Linda and released Anna, who rolled around on the floor, still screaming. We left the room, locking the door behind us, while Anna screamed.

"Elijah, let me look at your face."

I waved her off. "No, it's fine. Did you grab the monitor?"

"Yes." Linda took the small video baby monitor from the box of discs and handed it to me. The transmitter was also mounted high by the TV in Anna's room. I powered it on so I could keep an eye on my sister from outside in the hall. She was now standing in the center of her room, staring at the locked door, screaming "Mine!" over and over again. She ran to the door and beat her fists against it, and I wanted to open the door and hug her tight but forced myself to keep still.

"Elijah?"

My eyes snapped to Kristen standing in the door to my room, rubbing the sleep from her eyes.

"What's the matter?"

I shook my head. "Go back inside. It's nothing." The last thing I wanted was to see Kristen make that face that I saw on too many people. It was a face that said you were a horrible person for letting the *poor girl* scream like that. They didn't understand that sometimes, the best thing you could do for the poor girl was nothing.

She ignored me. "It doesn't sound like nothing."

"Kristen, I got this. Don't worry about it."

Linda gave me an exasperated look, and I sighed. "Okay, look. Anna's in the middle of a rage. It's like a temper tantrum on steroids. She gets pretty violent, so we're out here until she finds a way to regain control of herself."

"Do you want me to sing to her again?"

"No. That doesn't help now. She's like an overloaded circuit, and the breaker just blew. She needs nothing, absolute nothing. She has too much going on inside her head now and—"

Kristen poofed her fingers, adding an explosion sound effect.

"Yeah. Exactly."

I waited for the look. Any minute now, Kristen's eyes would go wide, and she'd suddenly remember plans to go shopping or get a haircut or do something with her friends—anything to escape. I watched her face carefully for the signs because yeah, I missed the sign of looming rage in Anna, but I wasn't going to miss this one.

Blue eyes met mine, a tiny frown between them. Kristen's hand came up and brushed along the welt Anna had put on my chin that still stung.

"You're bleeding."

Was I? I had no idea. I shrugged.

"Where do you keep Band-Aids?"

"I'll get them," Linda offered, putting down the box of movies.

I couldn't stand the waiting. "If you want to take off, it's fine."

Kristen's frown deepened. "No! Why? Do you want me out of your way?"

"No!" Crap, I didn't mean it that way. "I just…"

"Yeah, I know what you *just*, so stop it, okay?"

Linda came out of the main bathroom with a box of bandages. "Here, Elijah."

Obediently, I angled my face so she could dab at it with shit that made it sting even more than it already did before covering it with the adhesive strip. A loud thud from the other side of the door had all us jumping.

"What's she doing?" Kristen peered at the monitor.

"Kicking the door."

"Shouldn't we go in now?"

I shook my head. "Not while she's still enraged."

"I think she's slowing down." Linda pointed to the monitor. Sure enough, Anna moved away from the door and sank to her knees by her bed. She put a hand to her head, and I knew she'd have a bruise there by the time my parents got home. She rocked on her knees, face-planting on the bed over and over. "Repetitive behavior is part of the routine. It helps her feel like she's in control. She'll keep rocking until she exhausts herself." There was a long awkward silence, and then Linda patted my back.

"I'll go make her lunch. You call me if she amps up again, okay?"

I nodded. "Thanks, Linda."

A quick smile and then she disappeared downstairs.

I slid down to the carpeted floor, my back up against the wall. "You can go back to sleep if you want."

Kristen rolled her eyes. "What kind of friend would leave you here alone for a nap?"

Friend. That word shoved all kinds of thoughts around in my brain. When I thought of friends, I thought of Sam and Nick, not some girl. But Kristen wasn't *some girl*—not anymore. We'd sort of bonded over our music. We fought and argued and disagreed on every friggin' thing, and I wondered when I'd actually started to like her—really like *her*, not just the way she looked.

"Oh my God, it was rhetorical, you jerk. Don't fry your brain trying to find an answer."

I laughed. See? She made me laugh. I guess we really were friends now. Wow. "No, I just thought you hated me."

Her eyes popped wide. "Hated you? Seriously? Why would I sing in your band and put up with all that crap online and even deal with Sam's attitude if I hated you?"

Okay, when she put it like that, it was pretty lame, so I shrugged. "I don't know... It's just, well, you're always pissed off at me—"

"Am not. I only get pissed when you act like I'm nothing! Just some decoration for your band."

I squirmed and lowered my head. Yeah. I guess I was a dick, pushing all this online shit to its limits. "Kris, you are not *nothing,* and I'm sorry I made you feel like that."

She didn't say a word. I knew I'd blown whatever chance of hooking up with her I'd had a long time ago, but that was okay because now that I knew we were straight up friends, it would kind of wound me to lose her friendship. She shifted, and her hand touched my face, and the smell of leather tickled my nose. I looked at her hand, happy to see she was wearing the wristband I'd given her, and suddenly, it hit me like a kick to the stomach that we were something else. Not friends. More.

Holy God, I loved her. I fucking loved a girl I'd promised I'd never touch.

I could kiss her.

Right now.

All I had to do was lean forward…and we'd be kissing. And it would be fucking amazing because it was Kristen—who was BroadwayBaby17, my archnemesis and the girl who'd got half the food court at the mall to sing a Christmas carol for my sister. Kristen—who was my friend. The thought of kissing her made my stomach tighten and flip over because I wanted it, wanted *her*, so fucking much, everything else just faded away—my parents, my sister's screams on the other side of the door, Linda downstairs—it all just faded into background noise. I'd fantasized about getting my hands on her since the night of the *Cats* play, but I had made that stupid promise to Sam—

No.

No. That wasn't right.

I didn't make that promise only to Sam. I made it to *me*. Maybe I knew from the second I saw her that I'd want more from Kristen Cartwright than just a few fast gropes between sets at a show, more than a couple of flirty text messages back and forth for a week or two until she got bored and quit me. I'd wanted *this*.

Love.

Now that I had it, I wasn't letting go of it for anything.

Or *anyone*.

KRISTEN

Kristen Cartwright
@kristencartwright

Tweets	Following	Followers
6,953	**763**	**2,242**

@MadisonKellyLl

Loving the Rock Band War! My money's on

@kristencartwright Sorry, boys. #RockGirlzRule #KrisVsEli

@kristencartwright

@MadisonKellyLI Come to next show #BearRiverMall. We'll save you a ringside seat! #KrisVsEli bit.ly/BRqz878

@Ride_Out

@MadisonKellyLI @kristencartwright Challenge: accepted! #KrisVsEli The battle continues #BearRiverMall

@Rawr4Fems

Is @elijahhamilton just another boy with entitlement issues or a misogynist? #KrisVsEli #CatCall

@Paulie69

Meow for me @kristencartwright! #CatCall #KrisVsEli

@Paulie69

I'm making @kristencartwright meow & piss her pants! #CatCall #KrisVsEli tinyurl.com/kris673jg

@Paulie69

@kristencartwright Next time, I'll pull U to UR knees, bitch #CatCall #KrisVsEli

@Paulie69

I got somethin' 4 U @kristencartwright tinyurl.com/mlp909jg Lick it #CatCall #KrisVsEli

I watched a bewildering array of emotions cross Elijah's face as he stared at me. He'd apologized.

There was that.

Kiss me. I gave him the opening. I mean, oh my God, I did everything but send him a printed invitation. My hand tingled against his warm and scruffy cheek. But he never moved, and my heart sank a little bit lower. I dropped my hand, and that seemed to break him from his trance. He looked shocked to see me sitting there. Dark eyes went wide and then shut when his head fell back against the wall. He rubbed his face roughly, and I think I died a little more.

"Sorry," he muttered. He peered closely at the video monitor. "She's finally winding down."

"Yeah." Tears burned behind my eyes. "Um. That's good. So I should...um, I'm just gonna go." So I could fall to pieces in private.

Suddenly, he lunged, grabbing me by both arms. "No! Don't."

What, don't feel like the world just ended? Don't feel like curling into a tiny ball because for maybe five freakin' minutes I'd totally forgotten about Etta lying in a hospital bed with a hundred tubes and wires connected to her because the boy I was crazy about looked like he wanted to kiss me...but didn't?

"Don't what?" I demanded, shoving him off me.

"That," he said quietly, waving a hand at my face. "Don't cry. Especially not—" Abruptly, he clamped his lips together.

"What?" I demanded, flicking the stupid tears off my face.

"Never mind."

A snort escaped before I could think twice. "Yeah. Sure. What else is new? You know, I'm getting kind of tired of you always forgetting I'm not just another one of the guys."

He opened his mouth, closed it, and then opened it again, like he couldn't stop the words from falling out. "I didn't forget. I just have to…oh, fuck it." He dropped his head. "Kristen, I want to kiss you like I want to breathe, but I *can't*. I have to stay focused. The band, my sister, my parents—"

My brain latched on to his words. He wanted to kiss me. But he hadn't.

And he wouldn't.

"Yeah." I cleared my throat when my voice cracked. "I have to focus on Etta, too." I swallowed back tears and took a step away. "I…I think I'm just gonna go."

"Right." He turned and stopped with one hand on his sister's door.

My phone buzzed.

So did his.

I read the alert from Twitter. "Oh, God," I said, groaning.

Elijah's stunned eyes snapped to mine. "Did Madison fucking Kelly just tweet about us?"

"Yeah, she's apparently a fan." I waved a hand.

Elijah nodded slowly, lips moving as he reread the tweet. "*Loving the Rock Band War! My money's on @kristencartwright Sorry, boys. #RockGirlzRule #KrisVsEli.*"

Suddenly, Elijah came back to life.

"Wait, she's a fan, you said? You mean she tweeted you before?"

"Oh, yeah. I can't remember when."

"Oh my God." He swiped and tapped and held his phone out to me. "She has almost a hundred thousand followers," he said with a low whistle. "This is amazing." He clapped his hands to his head and turned in a circle. "We have to tweet her back, right now. Tweet her back."

"What do I say?"

"Favorite it. Retweet it. Then reply. Invite her to the mall events." His face lit up. "Maybe she'll come! Maybe she'll put us on the show."

His excitement spread to me, so I did exactly what he said. "Wait, wait. What about this." I tapped out a reply, reading it out loud as I did: "Come to next show #BearRiverMall. We'll save you a ringside seat! #KrisVsEli."

"Good, good, now shrink the link."

"I know." I waved him away but did what he said and sent the tweet. We watched our screens, Elijah holding his breath, waiting for some sign of life from the Internet. A moment later, another alert sounded, and he cheered.

"She favorited it!"

There it was. Madison Kelly. *Good Morning, Long Island*'s host herself. Just what Elijah wanted. I turned to go.

"Wait, I want to get in on this. Can't let that go unchallenged." He grinned at me, thumbs blurring over his keypad. The phone buzzed again, notifying me that the Ride Out account had retweeted and favorited the posts. But he wasn't done. A minute after that, another alert appeared in my feed.

> @Ride_Out
>
> @MadisonKellyLI @kristencartwright Challenge: accepted!
> #KrisVsEli The battle continues #BearRiverMall

Again, we waited and watched for more alerts, and they came by the dozen. The tweet was favorited and shared over forty times.

"This is fucking amazing," Elijah said. "We've never seen numbers or interest like this." He paced the small hallway in front of his sister's door. "Come on. We need to use this momentum."

I followed him back across the hall to his room where he booted up a laptop on the desk next to his bed, still messy from where I'd fallen asleep that morning. He logged on to the Beat and typed:

> **@Ride_Out:** So Madison Kelly from Good Morning, Long Island just tweeted about us. She's enjoying the Elijah and Kris rivalry. Whose team are you on?

"Elijah, Sam already hates me. Are you sure starting teams is a good idea?"

Elijah shook his head. "He doesn't hate you, Kris. He just likes to be the star, you know?"

Yeah. Yeah, I did know. It was the same issue I had with Leah Russo. I think it was the same issue Etta had with age. Sharing the stage meant you weren't the star, and if you weren't the star, that could only mean you were part of the background. Anonymous.

Forgotten.

"Yeah, I know, and that's why I think maybe you shouldn't keep trying to whip the whole Internet into taking sides."

Elijah shook his head. "Are you kidding? That's exactly what we should do. People love this kind of shit."

"Come on… I thought you wanted this to be all about the music, not gimmicks."

"Yeah, yeah." He waved me off impatiently. "That was before Madison Kelly tweeted us." His fingers flew across the keys like a man possessed.

Elijah pulled strings and conducted his virtual orchestra and never noticed when I turned and left his room.

———

It was sometime after I'd fallen asleep for the second time that day when my phone buzzed with an email from Mrs. Reynolds.

Hi, Kristen,

I'm so sorry to hear about Tisch, but I'm excited about your plan for a summer theater group. I think that's a fine idea and am happy to advise. In fact, I have a suggestion for you if you want to move on this right away. I've already licensed a series called Modern Day Shakespeare in the Park. It's a collection of scenes performed in today's language. Each performance includes two songs. The series is designed to be performed weekly over the course of a summer, but I think that might be a bit ambitious for middle school. I'm sending the list. Choose your favorites, and then we can discuss further.

Mrs. R.

Oh, I loved this idea. Shakespeare in modern language, plus musical numbers? I could have a blast with this. Revved up, I sent her a quick reply, asking if we could get started right away. A few minutes later, she replied, agreeing to run it by the administration so we could get kids signed up before the end of the term, plus get the space reserved.

It would be summer; nobody wanted to be in school during the summer, so I wasn't worried about that. What else would we need? Well. Costumes, for one thing. Shouldn't be a problem. The school had lots of things we could appropriate.

Scenes and sets. *That* could be a problem. But if we did lots of poster board and paint, maybe it would be fun.

That was critical. Fun. I wanted this to be fun for the kids who signed up. It would be hard work, yes…but fun like—

Singing in a rock band.

And just like that, my mind was back on my Guitar Hero for like the thirty-second time that day. Jeez, what was up with him? One minute, he acted like I was the best thing that ever happened to him, and the next, it was like he wanted to shove me headfirst off a rooftop. I just didn't get it.

I was so sure he liked me. From the night we met, when our eyes linked across the auditorium, I'd felt…I don't know—something that made me stand up a little taller, something that made my heart beat faster.

Something that made me want to lick my lips.

But did he feel it too? He *said* he wanted to kiss me. But it was pretty damn obvious he didn't like me that way, and that pissed me off. *Not special enough* again.

What was so wrong with me? I mean, all of my friends spent their time trying to fit in and be like everybody else. Conform. I was the only person I knew—besides Etta—willing to take a chance to stand out. To break away from the pack. That was pretty damn special, if you asked me. Elijah said rock was all about being defiant. I was the friggin' definition of defiant, and he still didn't care.

I put my phone on the table beside my bed and sank deeper onto my bed. He wanted me to sing? Well, all right then. I'd sing. I'd sing like it was my band, my show, my career.

The hell with Elijah Hamilton.

———————

"Kristen! You here?"

I opened my eyes and discovered it was after two o'clock and that I'd slept for a few hours. I got up, rubbed sleep from my eyes, and opened my door. "Yeah, Mom. In my room."

I heard her feet on the steps, and a minute later, she was in my room, looking like she'd been through hell.

I guess she had.

"How is she, Mom?"

Sighing, Mom sat on the edge of my bed and took my hand. "She's not bad, all things considered. It was a major stroke, yes. But the doctors are satisfied that they were able to treat her in time. They think much of the damage can be corrected with therapy. She can't walk, and she can't talk, but she will."

I pressed both hands to my face, tears spilling through the spaces in my fingers. "Oh, God, Mom, that's excellent news."

Her arms came around me, and I felt the sob in her chest. "Yeah. It is. I won't lie to you. It's not going to be easy. She can't be alone now. Ever. We'll have to do something with her place. She can't get up the stairs."

"Put the boys out there. They'll love it."

Mom's eyes went round. "That's…not a bad idea. We can probably convert the dining room into a space for her. We never use it."

We said nothing for a few minutes but clung to each other anyway. Mom adored Etta, as much as she teased her for her outlandish behavior. I knew she was as worried about her as Dad.

"How are Dad and Aunt Deb?"

"Holding on. I think everyone will be fine. I really do. They'll be home soon for showers, food, and fresh clothes. Then we'll go back to the hospital…and wait." She let me go and stood up, stretching her spine back until it popped. "That reminds me… Can you do me a favor and go out for me? I'll give you a list."

"Sure." I stood up, scraped my hair into a ponytail, and found my boots while Mom scribbled a short grocery list onto a sheet of paper she tore out of a notebook.

Twenty minutes later, I was rolling a cart up and down the aisles of our local Stop and Shop, feeling like I just going through the motions while someone operated my body with a remote control miles away.

I'd just reached the cold cut counter when I felt eyes on my back. I turned around and found two guys with baskets hung over their arms, studying me like I was one of the appetizers inside a glass case. Both were tall. One was skinny, and the other was wide, like a linebacker. The skinny one wore a Slipknot T-shirt. The linebacker wore baggy shorts with a sports jersey.

I turned away, ignoring them, and waited—not patiently—for my turn.

Finally, it was. I gave the white-coated worker an order for a pound of ham, a pound of turkey, and a pound of American cheese. Behind me, I heard one of the guys let out a low but very definite *meow*.

The deli counter worker heard it too, and shot them a look.

I wanted to evaporate.

"You know what? Don't worry about the cheese. Just do the ham and turkey, please," I said. "Fast," I added under my breath.

"Hey!" The bulky guy tried to get my attention.

I turned my back and locked eyes on the deli counter guy, begging him to help me.

"Hey." The skinny guy got in my face, blue eyes glued to my chest. "I wanna hear you meow for me."

So not gonna happen. "Back off, Tiny. I don't do requests."

Behind me, his husky friend let out a loud laugh. "Burn! Damn, Paulie, did you hear that? She don't do requests. Ha, ha, ha!"

Paulie's eyes left my chest long enough for me to worry about what I saw inside them. This was no behind-the-scenes type of nerd. This was a guy with real problems hearing the word *no*.

"Yeah, I heard her. And now I wanna hear her scream." He took a step toward me and dug in his pocket, and I swallowed hard, but he came out with his cell phone and not the switchblade I was expecting, and *Jesus God what the hell was I supposed to do now?*

My hand locked around the handle of my shopping basket. I should probably move it. Strangely, I couldn't seem to move at all. Paulie aimed his phone at me, and I just stood there.

Frozen.

"Meow...meeeeowwwww," he taunted. Shoppers stared and frowned, but nobody was doing anything.

"Here you go." The deli guy put two wrapped packages on the counter, but I was still frozen. Paulie grabbed them.

"Oh, look." He showed his big friend. "Kitty cat has some ham and some turkey." He read the labels on the packages.

I finally remembered how to move my limbs and held out a hand. "Give those to me."

"Oh, you want these?" He held the packages high over my head. "All you have to do is meow for me. Come on, pretty cat. Let me hear you hiss and scream."

"Leave her alone."

I looked up, surprised to find my only support come from an old lady, not the deli counter guy and not the meat counter guy across the aisle. Or any of the dozen other shoppers just watching.

Paulie lifted a blond brow and sneered at the woman. "Back off, Grandma. I'm just having fun."

"You're scaring this young lady. What kind of man are you?" she taunted him, lifting a bag of whole potatoes out of her cart.

He spun to face her. "I said, I'm just having fun. Now mind your own business."

"I am minding my own business. I'm making sure you leave this girl alone. I've already called the police. You still have time to get away."

Paulie's friend paled at this news. "Paulie, man. Come on. I don't want trouble. Let's just go."

"I am not going anyway until she fucking screams for me." And with that, Paulie grabbed a handful of my hair and forced my head back. At that point, I was ready to scream, meow, hiss, and hell, and use a litter box if he insisted, if it meant he'd stop pulling my hair.

But before I could do anything, something hit Paulie square in the face.

"Jesus, what the fuck!"

"Leave her alone."

Thunk.

Oh my God. It was a potato. The woman was throwing potatoes at him, one at a time, from the bag in her hand.

A uniformed security guard ran toward us—finally.

"What's going on here?" he demanded.

"These men are harassing this young lady. No one seemed willing to help her, so I did." the old woman said. Etta would love her. *Oh, God.*

"You two. Come with me." The security guard took hold of both men's elbows.

"Paulie! Run!" Tiny told his friend, and after a second or two of wrestling with the guard, broke free and ran for the exit, the guard on their heels. When they were out of sight, I began to shake and couldn't stop.

"It's okay now. It's okay." The woman's hands rubbed up and down my back. "Did you know them?"

I shook my head. "Never saw them before."

"But they seemed to know you."

Tears stung my eyes. "The Internet. They don't like that I'm singing in their favorite band."

The woman's eyebrows drew together. "This Internet and those social networks are going to get someone killed. My little granddaughter had to change schools because of the Internet. Can you imagine? She's just twelve years old."

Oh, I could. Too well.

The phone in my pocket vibrated. With dread balling up in my stomach, I pulled it out and read the messages. I opened my email app and tapped out a quick message to Mrs. Reynolds, informing her that we'd have to pull the plug on the whole summer theater program idea.

What if they came back? How could I protect the kids in my group when I couldn't even defend myself? That's when I let the tears flow.

At the mall that weekend, it was a packed house with people lining every empty inch of space around the catwalk erected for the fashion show.

I swallowed hard, trying to figure out the words to tell Elijah I was done. Out. Finished. Scared witless over what had happened at the grocery store the other day. I hadn't talked to him since Monday, when I fell asleep in his room and all but threw myself at him.

And he…well, he dropped the ball.

But when I poked my head out of the office the mall's manager was letting us use as a dressing room and saw hundreds of "Kris Vs. Eli" posters, I couldn't stop the tingle of excitement that raced up my spine. This was even better than opening night onstage. I tried to tell myself that had nothing to do with *us*… It was marketing and sales, the promise of drama. I even tried to tell myself Paulie and his big friend could be out there right now, but it didn't stop those tingles.

"Don't be nervous. I asked Brett for extra security." Elijah grinned at me in the mirror sitting on a desk where I'd just sat down to slick on another coat of lip gloss.

I turned to face him directly. I should have been nervous. "So… you know what happened at the grocery store." It wasn't a question. I could tell by the tone of his voice that he knew.

"Saw the tweets. Blocked and reported the asshole."

I waited for more… Maybe an apology or a promise that this would stop, that he'd do something besides make another freakin' hashtag out of the worst moments of my life. But *more* didn't happen.

I swallowed hard and looked at the door. I should just get up and walk out. Leave. Go back to the stage, my first love. Why was I still here? I shut my eyes and took a deep breath.

"Worried?" Elijah asked.

I opened my eyes and shook my head. "Excited," I admitted, hating myself for it. "Is it always like this?"

He shrugged. His hair was loose and flowing past his shoulders and shining under the fluorescent lights. He wore his trademark all-black outfit—black jeans, black boots, and black T-shirt that clung to his lean frame, showing off pecs. His wrist was still bare. I drew a fingertip slowly over the leather cuff now fastened to *my* wrist and cleared my throat. "Do you, um, want this back?"

Sam's eyes shot to us from across the room where he was adjusting his strings. Elijah tracked my finger and shook his head. "Definitely not. That's yours now. You're part of this."

Another tingle zipped down my back at his words, and I shook myself out of his spell. It was a leather wristband not an engagement ring. Jesus, he'd made it crystal clear that I was only a means to an end. "Kris." He nudged me with his shoulder. "How's Etta?"

I went still. *Damn it, damn it, damn it.* Just when I thought I had Elijah Hamilton all figured out, just when I thought he really *was* every bit the jerk he acts like, he goes and does something unspeakably sweet. "She's…she's marking time." My voice cracked.

Dark eyes stared into mine, full of concern and sympathy. "I'm really sorry." And then he smirked. "So how long are you gonna let her get away with that?"

I bit my lip and shrugged. It wasn't that easy, and we both knew it… Having to deal with family issues like—oh, jeez! "What about your parents? How did all their site visits go?"

A smile bloomed across Elijah's face, and my knees went weak. "Not so good. They didn't like a single place, so they're *reevaluating*." He made finger quotes.

I stared at him, eyes wide. "Oh my God. Elijah, that's amazing."

"Yeah, bro," Nick added from a folding chair in the corner, grinning and giving him a thumbs-up.

"Yeah. It is." Elijah held the smile for a long moment, and then it melted away. He lowered his voice just for me. "Um, listen, I'm—"

I flashed my stage smile and went full-out gush. "Oh my God, look at all these people! And those posters! This is bananas!"

I had to do something to stop the apology I was sure he was about to offer…and yeah, maybe to cover up my own stupidity for falling halfway in love with a guy who'd feed me to the wolves and sell tickets to the meal after he hashtagged it all over Twitter.

"Bananas?" Elijah smirked, angled his head, and studied me for a second or two before peeking outside the door. "Yeah. Uh, bigger turnout than I'd expected."

I wondered what you say to a rock band before a concert. Was "break a leg" appropriate? "Good show, everybody."

Sam rolled his eyes, but Nick held up a hand for a high five. "You too!"

Elijah shook my hand. "You sure you're okay? You don't have to do this if you'd rather be with Etta."

And there it was again. These unbearable glimpses of sweetness that made me want to wrap myself around him like a blanket.

"I'm good. I'm ready."

Intense dark eyes studied me, and then he smiled. "Good show, Broadway," he said softly, one finger stroking the back of my hand.

"Good show, Guitar Hero."

I turned and preceded him to the stage area, determined to get my head on right. Just sing and move on. All business. We were finally becoming a success. Mainstream news was here, and we were tonight's only music act—the headliners. I scanned the crowd, found Rachel standing near the barrier in front of center stage with a group of my drama club friends, and immediately felt calm. She was talking to a woman with long, dark hair—

Holy crap. It was Madison Kelly. She was here. With a camera guy.

Brett, the mall's event planner, was onstage, a mic in hand. "Ladies and gentlemen, welcome to our show. Today's show is being simulcast by 101.3 FM WLIS radio. We are proud to present the homegrown, hard rock sound of Ride Out!"

The crowd cheered and thrust their "Kris Vs. Eli" posters in the air. Blood pumped through my body, making me tingle in some places and go numb in others. I took my place just to the right of center stage, bouncing on my toes while Nick sat behind his drum kit, Sam checked the levels on his amp, and Elijah strutted to the mic stand, gracing fans with that smirk he must practice for hours in front of a mirror.

"Hello, Bear River!" he greeted them. "Are you ready to rock?" He thrust his fist in the air, and the crowd cheered. "Oh, that was pretty pathetic, you guys. I said: Are. You. Ready. To Roooooooock!" This time, he growled the last word in his trademark metal scream. The crowd reacted with so much energy, the building itself hummed.

Nick counted us off, and we started our first set, covers of rock hits by decade starting with the '70s and the Rolling Stones and ending with the '90s and Pearl Jam. In the second set, I got to kick things off with some Pat Benatar and Joan Jett and then some Bon Jovi. People danced, waved their hands in the air, and aimed hundreds of cell phones at us. They sang along, applauded, and shouted appreciation whenever Eli approached me, ready to banter. An hour later, I was sweating through my makeup when Elijah grabbed his mic out of its stand.

"This next song is not a cover. This is an original Ride Out song called 'Let You In.'" Wild cheering rang out across the crowd, and Elijah grinned, knowing some of these people really were here to see the band. "This time, we're performing it as a duet." He swept a hand toward me. "Kristen Cartwright, everybody!"

Elijah ran his hand over his strings, and the first chord ignited our audience, their energy spreading to the stage. He sang the first verse.

You're looking at me with those big, soft eyes
Everything in your heart is undisguised
I can see all of your hopes and dreams
Pinned on some words and a diamond ring

By the time we reached the chorus, I was feeding off their applause and cheers, the way they sang and danced with us, and even the things they shouted at us, swallowing it like manna.

"*Baby, let me in,*" I sang, adding my voice to Elijah's—soft and solid against raw and edgy. "*Inside my soul. Baby, let me in.*" I held the last note until the music faded and all you could hear was me and the audience.

When I lowered my mic, Elijah's intense eyes were shining. I lifted my eyebrows. *Not bad for a Broadway stage girl, huh, FretGuy?*

He smirked, knowing exactly what I was thinking.

We closed the show with my solo of "Going Under" and left the stage, the fans chanting, "More! More! More!" My body ached to get back out there.

Brett called over to us. "Guys, want to give them an encore?"

"Hell, yeah!" Sam punched the air with a fist, and we took the stage again, Elijah directing Nick and Sam on what to play.

"Kris, we're gonna howl," he said with a grin.

I smiled. "Seether?"

He nodded and leaned toward his mic, hands stretched out. When the crowd quieted down, he sang the intro: "*All I really want is something beautiful to say. All I really want is something beautiful to say.*"

The cheers rose again just as Nick came in on the drums and Sam added strings.

"Ah ooh. Ah ooh," I howled the backup part, and then Elijah sang the first verse. I picked up the second. We sang the bridge together, just like that first day in his garage. "*Say, can you help me right before the fall. Take what you can and leave me to the wolves.*"

And together, we delivered the chorus:

It's all so playful when you demonize
To spit out the hateful, you're willing and able
Your words are weapons of the terrified
You're nothing in my world.

That last line drilled right into my heart, and I almost choked. Resolute, I shoved it right back out. I may be *not that special,* but I was here, onstage, with a rock band, with a few hundred people dancing to the rhythm my voice set for them. I didn't care if I *ever* got accepted to a prestigious summer program or a conservatory.

I never, ever wanted to leave this stage.

———

"Hi, I'm Madison Kelly, Channel Twelve." The tall brunette shook everyone's hands. "That was an impressive show. Thanks for inviting me."

The four of us sat on stools lined up in front of the stage, facing Madison Kelly and her crew—a guy operating the camera and another guy holding the boom.

Elijah, always cool and in control, nodded and smiled. "No problem, Madison. We're glad you made it."

"We love you, Elijah!" a trio of girls shouted from across the mall. Elijah grinned and held up a hand.

"I love you, Kristen!" a deep voice countered. I laughed and waved as soon as I was sure it was *not* Paulie from the grocery store.

"Oh, yes! The infamous hashtag. So tell me, who's winning—
Team Elijah or Team Kristen?"

I looked at Elijah for help. What should I say? He sat, casual and
comfortable, head tilted to the side like being interviewed on the local
news happened every day. I watched him. Okay, I couldn't take my eyes
off him. When he was singing onstage, he had a…a *power*, I guess. It
was just part of him. Built in. Like some people could sketch and other
people can sing and still others can dance…Elijah *compelled*. There was
no other word for him.

And he was doing it right now.

A memory suddenly cued up in my mind. The night of my *Cats*
performance at the ice cream parlor. I'd watched him flirt with a fan
at the pickup window, and as soon as she'd walked away, he'd switched
off the power. Faded to the background. It struck me then that he was
acting, performing a part.

He was in *character*. Completely immersed in the role he was
playing.

Okay. If he could do it, then so could I. I was an actor, after
all. I took a deep breath and winked. "I am, obviously. These boys
would still be playing garages and coffee bars without me." I tossed
my hair back.

Madison grinned and turned her mic back to Elijah. "Elijah, any
rebuttal?"

He scoffed, lifting one shoulder. "Please, Broadway Baby here
hadn't even heard of Halestorm until she met me. Taught her everything she knows."

As if.

I opened my mouth to shoot back, but Madison beat me to it. "Okay, you two. Let's hear from the rest of the band. Sam, Nick, what's your take on the Kris versus Eli battle that's been waging for weeks?"

Nick smiled shyly and looked down. "Uh, well, I'll tell you this. The battle's just for stage. Off stage, you couldn't find two more professional or dedicated musicians."

Sam shrugged. "Hey, when do I get a hashtag? SamStrings. Or, wait, wait. How about SamStrums?"

Madison laughed, plainly impressed with us.

"Okay, next question. Elijah, you must have heard the buzz concerning the unfortunately phrased tweet you'd posted on the night of Kristen's performance in *Cats*. You said, 'I wanna hear her scream.' Since that night, that tweet has been shared and liked well over six *thousand* times. People call you a spoiled teen with entitlement issues and a misogynist who doesn't respect women. How do you respond to these reactions?"

Elijah pretended to think over the question carefully, scratching at his neck for good measure. "Well, Madison, I don't believe a bunch of anonymous people online can accurately judge me based only on something I said in less than a hundred and forty characters. Kristen knows me. I've given her no reason to distrust me."

Just one.

"Kristen, what about you?"

I jerk back to life.

"Elijah says you know him. Is he sexist and entitled?"

I looked at Elijah sideways. "Yeah. He can be."

"How so?"

"I object to some of the lyrics he writes."

"Yes." Madison checked her notes. "I read an entire exchange online about a line that featured the term 'pogo stick,' in which you expressed clear outrage. Did Elijah change those lyrics?"

I shook my head, afraid to look at him. "No."

Madison tilted her head. "Why not, Elijah? Kristen said the lyrics offended her, so why wouldn't you change them?"

"Because that's the reaction I wanted when I wrote the song."

Madison's eyebrows shot up, but she quickly recovered. "Okay then. So you're saying you intended to offend women with your music?"

Before Elijah could respond, Nick spoke up. "Ms. Kelly, you're making a mistake here."

Her jaw dropped, and I saw Elijah's hand twitch, but he quickly hid it. Nick continued. "You're assuming that all music is autobiographical."

"And it's not?"

"No. We've composed songs about bad breakups, about death, about two-timing girlfriends, and a few other things none of us have ever experienced personally. Bryan Adams sings about the summer of '69, but he would have been like nine or ten years old then—even if that song *was* about the year."

"It's not?"

Nick grinned. "No. It's not." But before Madison could ask the obvious follow-up question, he went on. "Some of the world's best art is good because it provokes. It makes you think about the conditions of the times, about hidden meanings."

"Yeah," Sam cut in. "Nobody believes 'Like a Virgin' was autobiographical for Madonna."

The guys all laughed, and Nick came to his point. "That's all we're trying to do here. Make audible art."

Holy hell. I had no idea Nick was so…so *deep*.

"Well," Madison said with a grin. "Your music certainly does provoke." She turned back to me. "So, Kristen, I have to ask you this… if Ride Out's music offends you, why are you here? Why put yourself through this?"

"Because these guys are incredibly gifted, and I want to learn from them."

"Even Elijah, whom the Rawr feminist blog calls a chauvinist-in-training?"

"Especially Elijah, because he is also patient and an incredibly insightful instructor."

Madison's eyes went wide. "Awww, then the rumors about the two of you are true? Should we be tweeting with a 'Kris *and* Eli' hashtag?"

Sam made a sound of annoyance, and Elijah's eyes snapped to his. "Madison," Elijah began. "I think I speak for all of us when I say we're committed to our music and taking Ride Out to the top. Kristen brings us a talent and a…fearlessness," he emphasized with a clenched fist, and something in my chest grew warm. "We respect her too much to risk losing her." He lifted a shoulder and shook hair off his face.

Madison gave her camera guy a signal, and he moved closer, framing only Elijah in his shot. "Elijah, will we hear lyrics with more romance, less violence, and less sexism, now that you've got your token female band member?"

Elijah's eyes narrowed to slits, and he angled his head, saying nothing. I shifted and looked to Nick and Sam. A flush was crawling up Nick's ears, and Sam was glaring daggers through Madison, but her back was to him. Finally, Elijah smiled. "I'll tell you this: we have some fans who've been with us since the beginning. Hard-core, loyal fans. And now that Kristen's joined our group, we're attracting new fans, just as loyal. When we perform original music, all of our fans will find something to love. That's a promise."

Madison's lips pressed together, her only sign of annoyance.

I, on the other hand, was amazed.

I had no idea Elijah could be so cool under pressure like this. She turned, gave me a look of sympathy, and said, "Kristen, I'm told tragedy has struck your family. Your grandmother, the stage actress Henrietta Cartwright, has suffered a stroke. How would she feel if she knew you were singing in a rock band?"

My mouth fell open. Etta already knows, so I was sure it was no big deal. I cleared my throat, remembered my part, and smiled wide. "Whose idea do you think it was?"

Madison laughed. "Your grandmother told you to sing in a rock band?"

"That's right." I relaxed a little. "When Elijah first approached me about joining Ride Out, I said no. I'm a stage performer, like my grandmother. I act, I dance, and I sing. But Etta suggested setting a few stretch goals could help me add breadth and depth to my talents."

"Stretch goals?" Madison echoed. "Well, yes, I suppose singing in a rock band is a stretch for a theater actor."

"Madison, I'm pretty sure I saw you rockin' out during our duets. Tell us." Elijah waved toward the camera. "Are you Team Elijah or Team Kristen?"

Madison turned toward the camera and laughed. "Oh, I'm Team Ride Out!" she answered smoothly. "This is Madison Kelly at Bear River Mall, rockin' out with Ride Out."

The guys all flashed rock fingers and cheesy grins at the camera, and then we were done.

"Thanks, Madison. That was really fun." I held out a hand.

She shook it and smiled wryly. "You guys are like total pros. Especially you, Elijah. Way to duck the question. Seriously, what does that pogo stick line really mean?"

Elijah just grinned and shrugged but said nothing.

"Okay, so we'll probably air this later tonight, starting with the six o'clock edition. For what it's worth, I'm totally Team Kristen."

"Aw, you wound me." Elijah pressed his hands to his heart.

"Good luck to you all. I had a great time and will definitely be following you online."

"Great! Maybe we'll see you at our next gig," Elijah said, pulling out a flier I'd never seen before. It bore the same logo engraved on the leather cuffs we all wore.

Elijah sure put a lot of effort into getting noticed. I wasn't sure why that hurt me.

But it did.

ELIJAH

Ride Out
@ride_out

3,744 FANS

BryceG: Okay, so @BroadwayBaby17 has a decent voice. But she's not metal, guys. Just put her in some rockin' leather pants, some studs, something hot.

SHARES: 288 LIKES: 497

"God, that was painful," Nick groaned once we were safely back inside the office.

"Chill, bro. It's exposure, and we need it." I fell into a chair, grabbed a bottle of water, and chugged it. "We didn't lose our shit. We didn't come across like unprofessionals. All that matters."

"Yeah, well, I'm with Nick," Sam said. He grabbed two more bottles and tossed one to Nick. "That chick was out for blood."

Kristen sat quietly in a corner, watching us debate Madison Kelly's interview. The office was small. There was a single metal desk in an L that had been cleaned of anything office-related. Someone had brought in a tabletop mirror that lit up and plugged it into a power strip on the side of the desk. A small plastic cooler sat on the floor under the desk.

"What was all that shit about inviting her to the show? Why didn't you tell us?"

Shit. "Oh, I, uh, kind of forgot."

Sam rolled his eyes. "Seriously?"

"Yeah." I tied an elastic around my hair. "I saw her tweet the Kris versus Eli hashtag, so Kristen and I pounced on it."

"Kristen and you," Sam said, a dark look on his face. "You guys hang out regularly now?" he asked, crossing his arms over his chest.

"Yeah, Sam, we do when we've both been up for thirty hours straight after sitting in a hospital." I stepped forward, ready to pound him into a fucking pancake.

Sam let out a long sigh and held up his hands. "Okay, I'm sorry. I forgot about Etta, Kristen. And your parents, Eli."

I nodded and waved a hand. I was too tired to keep fighting about this shit. Kristen didn't say anything. What the hell was up with her?

"Guys, now may not be a great time to bring this up, but have you looked at your phones?"

All eyes swung to Nick, who was scrolling feverishly through his phone. "I um…I think we're trending."

"No way." Sam grabbed his phone and so did I. "Aw, fuck. *We're* not trending. That stupid 'Kris versus Eli' hashtag is trending."

"Same thing, man," I reminded him.

"No. It's not. This should be about the music, not some battle of the sexes drama," he said, flinging his arms out wide.

I disagreed. "Whatever works."

"Eli, in case you forgot, Ride Out has three members—sorry, sorry!" He put up a hand before I could protest. "Four. It's not just the Eli and Kristen show."

"Fine, you want a hashtag too?" I started tapping on my screen. "How about hashtag SamVersusEli. Or better yet, hashtag SamLovesEli. People love a good bromance. Or, wait, wait, wait—I got it! Hashtag Sam'sEgo. 'Cause that's what this is really about."

"Fuck you, Hamilton."

Nick howled with laughter, but Kristen still said nothing. Sam turned his back on me, fluffing his hair in the mirror. I glanced at Kristen, not all that surprised to see her scrolling through her own phone.

"Kris, what's up? You okay?" I snagged another bottle of water and handed it to her.

She cracked the cap, sipped, and shrugged. "I guess. Just worried."

"About Etta?"

"About everything," she said, sighing. "My family's not happy about this," she admitted, waving a hand around our little room. I got it. She meant singing with us.

The tips of Sam's ears went red. "Why not?" he demanded. "They embarrassed or something?"

Kristen opened her mouth, but Sam shot to his feet.

"You know what? Forget it. I don't care." He pitched his water bottle into the trash and stormed out of the room, slamming the door behind him.

"Well," I said after a few moments. "We'd better go break down the gear and pack it all up."

Nick nodded, and we shuffled back to our instruments.

"Oh my God, it you! It's them! Ride Out! Please take a picture?" A girl bounced in front of me. I grinned and nodded, and that started the avalanche. We spent the next hour posing for selfies, signing stuff, and chatting with fans who lingered. It was amazing and awesome, and God—it was about friggin' time.

KRISTEN

Kristen Cartwright
@kristencartwright

Tweets	Following	Followers
6,959	**771**	**2,403**

@xxMakeKrisScreamxx

@kristencartwright Saw u at Smith Point Beach show but u didn't scream! When u gonna scream for us? #CatCall

---

@xxMakeKrisScreamxx

I tweet @ u every day but u ignore me. Scream for me! @kristencartwright #CatCall

@xxMakeKrisScreamxx

@kristencartwright Saw u at corner gas mart. Walked right by me. Bitch. Next time, I'll make u scream for me. #CatCall

@xxMakeKrisScreamxx

Bitch should get raped! Metal's for guys. Scream, bitch! @kristencartwright #CatCall

@Rosebud

Back off @xxMakeKrisScreamxx. #CatCall Threats aren't cool. Reported. Blocked.

@LIMusicScene

Is @Ride_Out planning to FIRE @kristencartwright? Find out here bit.ly/LIMS89ghlc #CatCall #KrisVsEli

"Is it true?" I quietly asked, my eyes pinned to my phone.

I was in Elijah's garage. I'd spent over an hour this morning blocking and reporting a whole new generation of jerks for inappropriate tweets. The Beat wasn't much better. Rape threats, and now I'd just read an article on a local music scene website claiming that Ride Out wanted to fire me. Elijah, to his credit, seemed outright stunned when I showed him the post.

It was the end of June.

It had been more than a month since Madison Kelly interviewed us, more than a month since Etta's stroke, and more than a month since our mall gig. Etta had been released from the hospital but not been able to come home.

Mom and Dad found a rehab center for her that was supposed to be amazing. I now totally understood why Elijah wanted to keep Anna out of a residence program. His parents still had Anna on various wait lists, and Elijah was holding out hope that the band would hit the charts before any of them had an opening.

Meanwhile, our numbers kept rising. We had more fans, more followers, and more online influence than ever, and that had begun opening a lot of doors. We'd been invited to play shows at a couple of bars along the beach and even at a music festival in Westbury. Elijah was trying to find us a manager and an agent and spent a lot of his time mixing demos for record companies.

He rolled his eyes when I showed him the latest blog posts posing as news.

"'Ride Out fires only female member.' Oh, hell, no. Come on, Kris. Don't you know how to tell the rumors from the facts by now?" He laughed and lifted the headphones again.

I gritted my teeth. "Oh. Rumor," I mimicked, adding in finger quotes for emphasis. "Elijah, there's a quote. From *you*."

"Kris, I never gave this blog an interview."

"Okay, so why aren't you pissed off that they quoted you without permission? Shouldn't you be doing something about this? They can say whatever the hell they want, and you're okay with that?"

"What are you getting so upset about? I told you it's not true."

He swiveled on his stool to study me, and that only pissed me off more. It was obvious, wasn't it?

Or it should have been.

"Look!" I practically threw my phone at Elijah. "Do you see what they're saying now? It's not the band anymore, Elijah." The latest group of tweets from some jerk calling himself @xxMakeKrisScreamxx on Twitter had seriously upset me. I hadn't stopped shaking since I saw them. "They're *following* me now, Elijah. This guy was in the same physical space as me, and I didn't even know. Do you not get how this is like a hundred times scarier than that jerk at the grocery store? There is a fan out there right now who hates me. He could be waiting for me so he could…so he could…"

Suddenly, I was crying and sobbing. I could be jumped. Beaten up. Raped. I didn't have fans—the *band* did. I had haters. I had challengers—morons and jerks who actually thought *they* would be the ones to make me scream. And Elijah? Instead of doing something about it, he was looking for a way to leverage this.

He shook his head and tried to hold me. "Kris, it's okay. Shh, shh, shh, it's okay. This is just talk. That's all."

I wrestled away from him, shaking my head. "Elijah, you have to pull the plug. I'm scared. Do you understand? I'm scared."

Frowning, he looked away. "Pull the plug on what? The Kris versus Eli hashtag? I haven't tweeted that since the grocery store incident. I can't control who else is still tweeting it." He lifted a shoulder like I'd just handed him a Pepsi instead of a Coke. What's the big deal? They're both cola, right?

I stared at him, trying to see, trying to understand why this didn't matter to him. Why *I* didn't matter to him.

"This is a Frankenstein monster now, Elijah. These assholes can say whatever they want! They threaten me. They say they'll make me scream if you can't. And now, they're following me. Jesus, I just told you I'm scared, and you say it's just talk?"

He stood up and rubbed his hands up and down my shoulders. "Okay, look. I get that it's scary, but it's harmless. It's just people venting because they think their little accounts on Twitter or the Beat actually get read. The key is not to get upset, not to react. The numbers are what's important."

I flung my arms up in the air. "Do you hear yourself? The numbers, the numbers! I'm so tired of hearing about these stupid numbers. These numbers don't mean anything unless they buy tickets. We played three shows last week alone—how many people came?"

He shook hair out of his eyes and shot back, "More than we had the week before, which was more than the week before that."

I sank onto a stool and buried my face in my hands. He didn't get it and never would. He was a guy. He didn't understand rape threats. "Elijah, I get scared when some jerk posts that I should be raped for daring to sing metal with you guys. Why don't you get that?"

He stared at my phone for a moment, and a muscle in his jaw twitched when he read the latest series of comments. He grabbed a stool and sat in front of me. "Kris, it's one guy. And he's obviously an asshole. If you want me to, I'll call him out on this, but it's probably not gonna help. He's a troll. He *wants* the fight. The only way trolls go away is when you ignore them."

My eyes popped. "Ignore him. You want me to ignore a rape

threat, pretend I'm not completely freaked out? Would you ignore it if this jerk threatened Anna?"

He looked at me sharply. "No. No, I wouldn't ignore that."

I bit my lip. Of course he couldn't ignore that. For Anna, Elijah was a white knight.

"Kris, Anna can't defend herself, so it's my job to do that for her."

"And me? I agreed to sing in your band. I agreed to this stupid online war. And you'll just watch these morons come after me?"

"Nobody's coming after you, Kris."

"They did once. They could again…"

"They won't. These guys are all a bunch of pimply wusses! The keyboard is the only real weapon they'll ever wield. In real life, they're faceless and gutless. Trust me. It's all just talk. It goes with the territory. The price of fame."

Trust him? I had just told him I was scared down to my bone marrow, and he wanted me to trust him. Inside me, something cracked, the something half in love with the soft side of Elijah Hamilton.

"Yeah, well, maybe if we were actually famous, it wouldn't be so terrifying. At least then, I'd have a security detail…maybe a hot bodyguard."

He lowered his head, holding my gaze. "I'll guard your body anytime."

I slapped his arm hard. "Will you be serious? I'm telling you, I'm afraid somebody's gonna leap out of a shrub and attack me out of some misplaced loyalty to you."

Elijah took my hands. "Okay, look. Maybe you're right. Maybe these people are taking this whole battle thing way too seriously. If you're scared, then we'll stop. No more posts except for appearance information."

"So no more battle of the sexes, no more make Kris scream?"

He held up his hand. "Swear to God."

"Okay." I sighed in relief. "You'd really do that?"

He leaned closer and repeated the vow. "I promise, Kris."

And just like that, I forgot why I was mad at him. I couldn't talk, couldn't breathe, couldn't even blink because I was afraid he'd let go. This was the part of him I adored. I clung to him for a long moment, and when his gaze drifted to my mouth, I wondered if—hoped—prayed—he'd finally kiss me.

And then, Etta's voice suddenly spoke inside my head. "Well, my *God*, darling, it's the twenty-*first* century. What on *earth* are you waiting for? You can kiss *him*."

I could. Yes. Yes, I could just lift my head and lean in and kiss Elijah Hamilton like it was a normal, ordinary occurrence.

Right. Like kissing Elijah Hamilton would ever be ordinary?

I'd watched him kiss that girl at the mall and was sure I'd memorized all the steps in his routine. He'd move in, grip my face between his hands, run his thumb along my jaw, and finally, glide his arm down around my body, pulling me against his own, all the while, peeking through his lashes to see if I enjoyed it.

I wasn't sure when I decided—even what made me decide. I just touched my lips to his and waited.

It took a second or two. But then there was a sudden, tiny squeak from him, and I felt the pulse in his wrist leap under my fingertips.

And then, his hands were in my hair, angling my head just the way he liked it, his tongue brushing against mine, so soft it might have been my imagination…except imaginary kisses were never so intense. He kissed me like I was a song he wrote, lips wrapped around every word until it hummed with hidden meaning and promise, and his hands held me the way they held his guitar—like the music would stop if he let me go.

It went on for a long time, and when we finally broke apart to breathe, I saw his eyes were all the way closed, and I smiled because this kiss was nothing like the one he'd given that mall girl.

"Whoa," he whispered, his hands still gripping me hard. "I've wanted to do that since the day I met you."

I blinked. "Yeah, right."

With a sigh, he dropped his hands and sat back…away from me. "I promised Nick and Sam I'd stay away from you. They were afraid there'd be drama, and you'd quit when I—"

Oh. When he dumped me. My face burst into flames, and I turned away.

"Kris, don't."

His voice was quiet and pleading. I spun around, studying him. He stood there, face naked—no smirk, no teasing glint in his eyes, not even a long look aimed at my chest. He'd dropped the act and removed the rock star costume.

There was only Elijah, and I liked it. Oh God, I really liked it.

"Kristen, I don't know how to be somebody's boyfriend. But I really want to try."

Try? Jesus, was I a pair of shoes at some department store now? The ridiculous urge to start talking like Yoda struck, but I managed to ignore it.

"I don't want *to try*, Elijah," I began, but hesitated when his shields came back up with a visible snap. A shiver ran down my back, and I quickly added, "I want us to work. I want you to put effort into us the way you do this band. I want you to want me—"

"I do want you."

"Not that way!" I flung up my hands and thought of my parents and how they shouldn't work but did. They were such different people but genuinely liked being together. I wanted what they had. Elijah and I…we really weren't all that different. I didn't know if that was a good thing or a bad one. I only knew that I wanted us to work. "I want you to want me around you, the way you want Anna. I want you to respect me."

"I do," he repeated. "Kris, if I didn't respect you, I would have made a move on you weeks ago."

"Oh, really." I shot him a glare.

"I've rewritten chunks of music because I respect the talent you bring to this group."

"Yeah, I know that but—"

"You don't believe me." His hand shot up, and his face went tight. "I get it. You don't trust me. Even after all these weeks, you still don't *see* me." He nodded, lips flattened into a line intended to mask the pain I knew I'd just caused him.

It was in his eyes.

I took a deep breath and tried again to explain. "Elijah. Sam and Nick are your best friends, right?"

He glanced questioningly at me and then nodded.

"So if *they* warned you to stay away from me, how can you be pissed at me for being a little scared to trust you? I mean, they know you better than I do."

He considered that for a long moment, dark eyes swimming with doubt. Finally, he smiled, revealing that dimple I adored so much. "Yeah. You're right." He stepped toward me, and my stomach flipped over. "So what do we do now?"

"Etta told me that not one of her four husbands ever worked hard enough to understand her."

He nodded slowly. "You want me to understand you? Is that like... even possible?"

I laughed once. "Maybe. I don't know how to do this either. I guess we start with...you know, being real." I held out my hand and waited for him to take it.

He did and suddenly, the tension was gone. His grin was real and so was mine.

"Okay. Real. I think I can do that." He tugged me to door that led to the kitchen. "I promised Mom I'd take Anna to the park. She likes to watch the birds. Come with us."

"Yeah," I said slowly. "That sounds perfect."

ELIJAH

Ride Out
@ride_out

4,209 FANS

Ride_On747: @elijahhamilton. Bro, heard what happened and it sucks. You rock. #fan4life

> **BryceG:** Way to go, @BroadwayBaby17. You busted up Ride Out? Go the fuck back to the stage and leave metal to us.

SHARES: 288 LIKES: 497

I pulled into a spot at the park and helped Anna off with her seat belt. She'd been singing "Ding dong, ding dong," in a soft high voice the entire drive here.

Kristen shook her head. "I should be offended that your sister looks at me and says 'ding dong,' but I'm not because it's pretty awesome," she finished with a little flair of her fingers that made me feel kind of goofy. Hell, I'd been feeling goofy ever since we kissed.

Holy hell, *we'd kissed*. Sam was going to kick my ass for this, and I honestly didn't give a shit. Kristen was mine now.

I grabbed the soft-sided cooler of snacks and drinks and took Anna's hand because I suddenly wanted to sit down and write a song. And not just any song either.

A freakin' sappy love song.

Puke.

Anna had other ideas. She wrestled free so she could walk ahead with her head down, still singing the ding-dongs.

"Anna, look at me. Look at Eli."

Her eyes found mine, held for a split second, and then looked away.

"If you're lost, what do you do?"

Her hand crept toward the pocket of her jeans where I'd already put the note with my name and number.

"Good. Let's go."

Obediently, Anna turned to walk along the path into the park. Kristen followed, but I stopped her. "Hold up a second."

She looked at me, confused, until I held out my hand. "Don't

293

laugh, but I've never actually held hands with a girl who wasn't my sister before."

A huge smile bloomed, and she took my hand. Together, we followed my sister down the path to the playground. Anna's favorite thing in the playground was the swings. She sat on one as soon as some kid got off. The playground wasn't all that crowded, which was good. Anna had issues with crowds. A few toddlers played in the sand, their parents hovering close by. A knot of older kids climbed over monkey bars, racing each other from bottom to top. At the cluster of picnic tables arranged under the shade of some trees, some older kids sat holding bottles of water, their heads bent over a cell phone. It was hot in the sun, and I scoped out a spot where I could open the cooler later.

"This is nice," Kristen said, leaning against the swing set's frame while I pushed Anna.

I lifted an eyebrow. "*Nice?* That all you got?"

"What's wrong with *nice?*"

Laughing, I held up both hands. "I've met Etta, and you are a lot like her. *Nice* is just such a boring word. I'm kind of surprised you'd settle for it. She wouldn't."

"Oh, I'm so sorry," she said, slapping a hand to her forehead. "How about, *this is stupendous!* Or, wait… I can do accents. *This is loco.* Oh, wait, wait, wait! *Ermahgerd, thers ers da berst dert erver.*"

I stared at her. "I have no idea what you just said."

"I said, this is the best date ever."

Date? Oh. Um. Sure.

I kept pushing Anna's swing.

"Elijah?"

"Hmm?"

"Is it…is this…" Kristen blew hair out of her eyes. "Are you gonna tell the guys?"

"Yeah."

"Sam's gonna be pissed, isn't he?"

It wasn't a question. I peeked over at her, arms wrapped around the metal pole that held up the swings, her eyes pinned to mine.

I shrugged. "As long as you don't quit the band, he'll get over it."

"Quit? Bet he'd love that."

"Nah," I said with a laugh. "He knows you're good, Kris. And he knows that all these new gigs we've been booking are all because of you."

Her cheeks went red, and I laughed.

"What?" she demanded, suddenly pissed.

I gave Anna's swing another push and just laughed again. "Nothing. It's just…you looked so shy for a second, and it was funny. *Shy* is so not a word I'd ever use to describe you."

She straightened up, folded her arms over her chest, and narrowed her eyes. "Just what words would you use to describe me?"

Oh, challenge accepted, baby. "Oh, let's see," I began, eyeballing her critically. "How about smart, unbelievably talented, confident, and loyal?"

Her mouth fell open.

"What?" I asked, giving Anna's swing yet another push.

"Um, nothing. It's just…well, I didn't expect words like that. I figured you'd go for sexy, hot, or something along those lines."

"You're all of that too." I let my eyes travel up and down her body.

No red boots today and I was weirdly upset by that. "Just not *only* that, you know?"

She launched herself into my arms, almost killing us when Anna's swing returned.

"Jesus, Kristen!"

"Shut up and kiss me."

Laughing, I pecked her on the nose, and she giggled, returning to her post by the support bar. A few more pushes, and when I glanced at her again, her forehead wrinkled, and I sighed theatrically.

"Stop worrying. Sam and Nick may be upset at first, but they'll get over it if they want to keep up this momentum—which I'm sure they do."

She shook her head. "No, it's not that. It's…I think I owe you an apology."

My eyebrows shot up. "For?"

"For being surprised by what you just said. For a long time, I thought the only thing you saw when you looked at me was a pair of boobs."

"They are pretty damn awesome."

"And then I thought the only thing you wanted me for was my voice."

"Also pretty damn awesome."

"But what you just said," she went on like I hadn't spoken. "About being loyal and confident and all that?" Suddenly, tears blurred her eyes, and she pressed both hands to her face. "It's just…sometimes, I think you don't see stuff like that or even care about it…and other times, you're… Well, you're more than what you seem, Elijah. You're a lot *more,* and I really like it. I like that side of you."

I swallowed. *Hell.* I liked the sound of that—of Kristen *liking* me instead of getting on my case about raunchy lyrics or whatever. I left Anna's swing to momentum so I could throw an arm around Kristen and pull her close. "Kris, for years, I've been putting on this act like I put on my shoes in the morning. You're the first person I ever wanted to see behind that act, you know? Sam and Nick don't even see me. Not really. But *you* do."

Blue eyes met mine, and she slowly nodded. "Yes. I do."

I lowered my head and kissed her again and again and again until Anna interrupted us.

"Eli. Swing."

"Whoops. Sorry, Anna." I gave the motionless swing a few pushes to get it restarted. Kristen grabbed the cooler and headed for a shady picnic table, scrolling through messages on her phone as she walked. She made a sound of disgust when she tossed the phone down.

"What?" I led Anna to a bench at the picnic table Kristen had snagged.

"Nothing." She whipped her hand around so I knew it was a hell of a lot more than nothing. "It's just these people never know when to give it a rest."

"What are they saying now?" I stuck a straw in a juice box for Anna.

She shrugged. "The usual. That I'm only singing with your band because I'm *desperate* to be with you," she said, pressing a fist to her heart theatrically. "Or you're only letting me sing in your band because you're still hoping to make me *scream.*"

Her mouth twisted into a sneer, and I wished I'd never tweeted that stupid comment. The phone in my pocket wouldn't stop vibrating. "Did you respond?" I tugged it out and scrolled through the alerts.

"Yeah. I tweeted that I'm done with the whole 'Kris versus Eli' thing and just want to enjoy a nice day in the park with you and your sister."

The phone vibrated again. For the first time, I felt a shiver of fear down my back. I'd tried to tell Kristen she was making too much out of this...taking it too seriously. But, Jesus, over two hundred and eighty likes on a single comment—and that was just on one site. Twitter was going nuclear now. What the fuck was wrong with people? How did they not get that this was just a little PR and marketing? With a sick feeling in my gut, I kept reading. Some asshat had tweeted that I deserved better than Kristen Cartwright. Someone like *her*. Yeah. Definitely not happening, despite the interesting picture that went with it. Another said I was a dick for challenging Kristen, for pushing her to deliver the kind of fury and aggression that rock was known for. Still others brought my parents into it, wanting to know who was raising me to be so sexist and misogynistic and entitled.

I put the phone away with a sigh. "Anna, are you hungry? Want a snack?"

Anna's head came up, so I took that as a yes. I took out a plastic container of grapes and sliced strawberries and put it on the table. Anna loved berries.

Our phones continued to vibrate. Kristen groaned, but before she could pick up her phone, I covered her hand. "Ignore them, Kris. I told you, this is all part of the package. It's not real. People talk because they *can*. Because these sites make them believe people actually give a shit about their opinions. All that matters is that they're talking about us, not what they say."

She didn't look convinced.

"Come on, don't you remember what happened with those red holiday cups at Starbucks? People were threatening boycotts and pickets and all kinds of retribution, and you know what happened? Sales went *up*."

She nodded and then flashed me a smile. "Okay. I guess I can—"

"Oh my God! Are you Elijah Hamilton? Are you from Ride Out?"

I whipped around and found a girl standing there, maybe fourteen. She wore shorts and a tank top with flip-flops, and she kept curling her long, dark ponytail around her finger. There were three more copies of her standing a little behind her. All four of them were fizzing with excitement, bouncing on their toes.

"Yeah, I am. And this is Kristen."

The first girl shot Kristen a look of malice. "Can I get a picture with you? Just you?"

Kristen rolled her eyes, but I obliged. "Sure." The girl whipped out her cell phone, glued herself to my side, smiled huge for the selfie, and sent Kristen another one of those disdainful looks.

"Thank you, Eli!" She pressed her lips to my cheek.

That opened the gates. The other three girls approached in a clump, so I repeated the pose, complete with rock-on fingers. They began to chatter, and one of them burst into tears, sobbing about the song she loved the most and how she'd viewed our last video post on YouTube over a hundred times. Anna didn't care for the intrusion and made her displeasure known, slamming her juice down with a loud thump.

"Eli." Her voice was tight.

That was my cue. I tossed the empty container back in the cooler and stood up. The first girl turned her malice on Anna. "Can you, like, chill out?" she said, curling her lip at my sister like she was a stain.

Before I could open my mouth, Kristen lost it. "Back off. She has special needs!"

I jerked like I'd just been kicked in the head. I whipped around, ready to argue, to jump straight down Kristen's throat for those words. *Nobody* labeled Anna. Anna was *my* sister—*my* responsibility. I got that Kristen thought she was helping, but Anna was nobody's fucking business but mine. The girl waved off Kristen's explanation before I could find the words through the red haze of my fury.

"Whatever she is, she can wait until we're done." She put her hand on my arm like I was some kind of Happy Meal toy to fight over.

I shook her off. "We're done." I took Anna's hand to lead her away.

"But I didn't get your autograph!"

"No. You didn't."

"Hey, that's not fair! I saw you at the mall back in April and then again in June at the beach and—"

"There they are!" a new voice shouted. "I love you, Eli!"

The cry sounded from the path. I spun around and found another group bearing down on us, cell phones and "Kris Versus Eli" posters clutched in their hands. Guys, girls, some young, some old…holy shit. A dozen. Two. It was a mob. An actual mob. My mouth went dry.

"Kristen, take Anna's hand. Get her to the car *now*."

Kristen, her face sheet white, took Anna's hand, but Anna fought her.

"No."

"Anna, go with Kristen."

"No. Eli."

"Elijah! Elijah!"

"Sign my poster!"

"Oh my God, I love you so much!"

"I can scream for you. Wanna hear me scream?"

Somebody shoved Kristen, and the space around Anna shrank. Anna put her hands over her ears and started to scream. I had to stop this. I had to do something.

"Back off!" I shouted in the deepest metal growl I could manage. The crowd froze. "I cannot sign anything or take pictures right now. I have to get my sister home because she's terrified."

"What's wrong with her?"

"Oh, is she like retarded or something?"

"It's okay! My brother has Down's syndrome. I can take care of her!"

Some guy flung his arm around Anna and raised his phone. My vision blurred around the edges, and my brain disconnected. Anna flailed, and the guy's phone went flying.

"Hey, my phone!" He chased after it. "She broke my fucking phone. You're paying for this." He thrust the phone in my face.

Suddenly, he was sprawled on the ground in front of me, blood spurting from his nose. I didn't remember moving and didn't remember hitting him. I was on autopilot. The only thought that registered was *Anna*. Everybody was shouting my name, shoving me, clawing at me, demanding I sign shit, but I couldn't find Anna. I couldn't see her. I couldn't even hear her shrieks.

"Anna! Anna!" I shouted.

I whipped my eyes left and right and up and down, but Anna was gone. Hands kept grabbing at me, but I'd had enough. Fists doubled, I barreled my way through the mob, shoving people off me, hitting those who didn't get the fuck out of my way, and ran back down the path...and straight into a pair of Suffolk County cops.

"It says here you're some kind of rock star." A cop in plain clothes tapped the file folder in his hand.

"Yeah, yeah, rock star. Can I get the hell out of here now? I have to find my sister." I sat back in the chair in the small, hot room, the handcuffs around my wrists clanking on the metal table.

The cop's eyes bored into mine. "Calm down."

"I can't! I have to find my sister. She's nonverbal and can get violent when she's scared."

"I understand that, but right now, you're the one I'm worried about. You're in some serious trouble. You understand this, right?"

"Look, officer. I was just spending a day at the playground with my sister and my girlfriend. Those people *attacked* us."

"It's detective. Detective Martin Katz." Katz flipped through more pages on his pad. "I got one guy with a broken nose, another with a black eye, and a girl with a chipped tooth. All say you hit them."

Did I? I couldn't remember. I shook my head violently because we were wasting time. Anna could be dead by now. "I was defending my sister. They wouldn't leave her alone. She was scared, and they wouldn't stop. Where is she? Did you find her?"

Katz waved an impatient hand. "We're working on it. Why did you hit those people?"

I cursed. "I just told you! They mobbed us. Do you understand how fucking scared my sister was?"

"Maybe you shouldn't take a kid like her to the park."

Waves of rage washed over me. "A kid like her." My body coiled. "What, you mean *defective*? You son of a bitch. She has every right to be in that park. Every fucking right. I have every fucking fight to be there too. Those people would not back off." His words replayed on infinite loop in my brain. *A kid like her.* I rattled my cuffs. "Maybe I should just keep her chained up in a dungeon. I'm done with you. Call my parents. Better yet, get me a lawyer." I waved him off and sat back.

Dick. Fucking asshole.

A muscle ticked in Katz's jaw, and he nodded. "Okay. If that's how you want it."

I lost all track of time, unsure how long I sat in that small, stinky room, or even how long it had been since the playground. There was a steady dull ache in my stomach that sharpened to knifepoint stabs every time I thought of that fucking asshole's arm around Anna. I'd told them! And Kristen told them that they were scaring her, but they didn't listen. They just kept coming and coming and coming—demanding I snap to their requests like a trained animal in a cage. Like they owned me.

Jesus. Where was she? Had Kristen been able to protect her? Oh, God. *Please.*

I stood and paced the cramped room, wishing I had my cell phone. I paced and cursed and tried to ignore the ball of pain in my gut, but it was all just blurring together, growing into some enormous beast that was about to claw—

The door opened with a bone-jarring screech, and my mother ran in.

"Elijah! Oh, God!" She crushed me in a hug I couldn't return because...handcuffs.

"Anna! Mom, I don't know where she is."

"Dad's got her, Eli. Dad's got her."

My knees buckled, and I fell back to the chair, hollow and beaten. I blinked up at Mom for a few seconds, and then the dam burst. I buried my face in my cuffed hands and sobbed for minutes, hours, days—who the hell cared? I'd failed. I'd told my parents over and over again that I could take care of Anna, and I...oh God, I fucking lost her.

When the sobs weakened and I became aware of Mom's arms holding me, I managed to find my voice. "Is she okay? Did they hurt her? What about Kristen?"

Mom lowered her eyes and twisted her fingers. "I don't know how or where Kristen is. The police found Anna by herself almost by the main road, half out of her mind with fear, holding the note you'd tucked into her pocket. She must have fallen. She'd hurt her knee. They...well, they had to tranquilize her." Her voice shook.

Another knife pierced straight through my soul. I nodded. "I need to see her. Can we go now?"

She shook her head. "No. They tell me you're under arrest for assault. You'll need to see the judge. We have to get you a lawyer." Her brown eyes closed, and it hit me then how exhausted she looked.

And then the true meaning of what she'd just said penetrated the haze of worry. "They? Who's *they*, Mom?" I didn't mean the *they* who put me under arrest. I meant the *they* who tranquilized my sister.

Her eyes snapped open, but she couldn't meet mine. She spread her hands and shook her head. "I know you didn't want this, Eli—"

"No." I swallowed down the lump in my throat, sour and greasy.

"I wish it could be different."

"No." Slowly, rhythmically, I shook my head, hands on my gut where the sour lump settled like a stone.

"I wish we didn't have to—"

"Mom, no!" I jumped to my feet. "She's your daughter. How could you let him—"

"Because she *is* my daughter!" Mom's palm slapped the table. "You have no idea, Eli. I know you think you do, but you really have no idea how it kills us both to watch her withdraw deeper and deeper into her shell, to wonder what you did or ate or drank that did this to her. You have no idea how many hours we've laid awake wondering who's going to take care of her when we get too old to do it ourselves. And you have no idea how much it rips our hearts open to know that she's better off away from us." Mom's chin wobbled, and she pressed both hands to her mouth as tears fell down her face.

I stared at her for a long time, wanting to hug her and promise everything would be fine, but also wanting to scream at the top of my lungs for putting Anna in a residence. The sour knot in my stomach put down roots, growing larger by the second. It was my fault. All of this. My fucking fault. We were there, right on the cusp of breaking out as musicians, every dream we ever had just inches from our grasp. I'd been recognized today. Recognized and begged for autographs and pictures. It was what I'd always wanted. Worked for. Planned for.

And it was all for nothing.

I sat on that sticky metal chair, rocking back and forth while my mother cried for her daughter—her heart—and then that whole sour knot of anxiety and guilt and shame rose up and out of me in a flood of vomit.

KRISTEN

Kristen Cartwright
@kristencartwright

Tweets	Following	Followers
6,963	**782**	**3,211**

@xxMakeKrisScreamxx

@kristencartwright Scream, bitch!

Oh my God, oh my God, oh my God. "It's okay, Anna. It's okay. It's time for ice cream, okay? Come with me." I'd tugged Elijah's sister away from the mob, but she was terrified. She kept pulling her hand free to run back to him. "In the car, Anna. In the car, so we can get Eli."

"Eli!" she kept shrieking.

People were watching. Staring. Following. The car was still too far away. I tightened my grip on Anna's hand and pulled her toward the lot.

"Kristen! Hey, Kristen!"

I whipped around, putting Anna behind me, and found four guys approaching us slowly, each wearing creepy grins, and a ripple of fear crawled up my spine.

"Hey, Kristen! Can I ask you something?" One guy stepped forward. He was tall and thin and wore cargo shorts with flip-flops, and had a ball cap low on his face.

My heart stopped.

It was *him*.

God in heaven, it was Paulie, from the grocery store.

I stepped back and shook my head. "No. I have to get this girl home."

"It'll only take a minute." He pulled a phone from his pocket. "I just need you to say one thing. *Paulie made me scream.*" He slung an arm around me, pressed close, aimed the phone, and said, "Ready? One, two, three. Go."

I shoved him off and hurried to Anna. "Anna, come with Kristen. Remember the ding-dong song? We can sing in the car."

"Hey! Come on, I said it'll only take a minute. What's the big deal?"

"The big deal is I said no."

Paulie lost his grin and charged. He grabbed me and pulled my hair. "Scream!" he said and snapped a picture.

I screamed. I also elbowed him in the gut, and when he dropped his phone, I smashed it under my foot. "I said no!" I told him again. When he opened his mouth to say something more disgusting, I kicked like a Rockette and got him in the teeth this time.

Anna cried, "Eli!"

I grabbed her hand again, but one of the guys had her. Anna, terrified beyond reason, bucked and twisted and slammed her head into the guy's nose. He let her go with a stream of curses, and Anna took off running toward the parking lot. I followed her, praying the pissed off guys would not follow and try to hurt her. Hurt us.

Where was Elijah? Was he really posing for pictures with those skanky girls? My God, this was a disaster. All we'd done was take a trip to the playground when—

Oh no. This was my fault. I'd tweeted where we were.

After I'd attacked Elijah for being reckless online, I'd drawn a map for a few thousand losers and hung a sign that said, "Come and get us!" I was cold and shivering despite the heat of the summer day. This was my fault. Entirely my fault. I'd rung the freakin' dinner bell. I ran faster. "Anna! Anna!"

A squeal of brakes paralyzed me. *No.*

No, please.

I forced myself to move, running past the parked cars to the playground's entrance, where I found Anna sobbing and clutching the note Elijah had put in her pocket. "Eli! Eli!" Two cops were trying to handcuff her.

"No! Leave her alone. She's autistic!" I ran to the first cop. "Anna! It's okay, Anna. They will help us find Eli." I tried to touch her, to soothe her, but Anna was lost to her fear. "Officer, please! Help my boyfriend! He's being attacked by a mob." I waved toward the playground. The officer nodded and took off running, shouting into his radio.

The remaining officer still wrestled with Anna, now in handcuffs and shrieking. "Where are her parents?" he asked me.

My knees buckled, and I dropped to the ground. I handed over my phone and gave the cop the Hamiltons' names.

It didn't take long...a few minutes, really. I looked up, and there was Elijah's father.

"Kristen! Kristen, what the hell happened?"

I shook my head slowly. "Uh...a mob. A bunch of people wanted autographs and pictures and then got pissed off because Anna got scared. They started pushing and shoving and grabbing at us, and Eli told me to get Anna out of here."

Eli's dad pressed his lips together and nodded. He turned back to the police officer and said something I couldn't hear. The police officer nodded a few times, and then I heard him say to Mr. Hamilton, "We've got your daughter but she's raging."

"She's severely autistic. Please. Just take her to Avalon Home. They're ready to admit her."

I wrapped my arms around my middle, struggling to hold myself together as the police officer climbed behind the wheel and drove off.

Mr. Hamilton followed right behind him in his own car, leaving me to explain to Elijah just how seriously deep I'd fucked up the one thing he'd asked me to do.

———————

I couldn't do it.

I could not look Elijah in the eye and see that look of total fury again, especially after what I'd caused to happen.

I was a coward…no better than those faceless, nameless thousands online, clinging to their little fictions and fantasies.

So I ran.

I wasn't at all sure how I got there, but I stopped at Etta's rehabilitation center, lungs wheezing and nose dripping. I couldn't escape into fiction and fantasy, and I knew that. But I needed to find a way to fix this, and if such a way existed, Etta would know it.

I stumbled into her room, sweating and still crying. She stared blankly at the TV bolted to the ceiling above her bed, tuned to some dumb-ass judge deciding who was right—the owner of a hair salon or the client who claimed the bright purple hair on her head was the fault of the salon who'd only cut her hair, not colored it.

"Etta," I said softly.

She turned her head toward the sound of my voice, hair flat and lacking its usual perfection, and when her eyes found mine, she smiled—an upward twitch of one side of her mouth. And then she took in my appearance.

Oh, I could imagine the things she was saying to herself.

Appearance was critical in Etta's eyes.

And I began to cry all over again because—just for a second, I forgot that Etta had her own problems and couldn't manage mine. She needed to get better. She needed to heal.

"Do you want me to leave so you can finish watching…your show?" I sniffled.

She tried to say something, but it came out garbled. I heard one word clearly.

"Off."

Thank God, because seriously, did anyone actually care who won this case? I aimed the remote at the TV, and it went dark. We stared at each other for a long moment, and I couldn't help but sneer at her flat hair and hospital-issued gown and bare face. Suddenly, I was furious with her.

"This is ridiculous, Etta! You know that, right? Okay, you've had a stroke. But you're not just anybody. You're *you*. Henrietta Cartwright!" I imitated her perfected delivery, right down to regal hand wave and cadence. "Are you seriously going to just lie there and fade to black without some kind of swan song?"

Blue eyes watched me pace her small room, but there were no more garbled words. They weren't clear words, but they were pissed words. "I'm not amused," she said.

Good, I was just getting started.

"You're not dead." My voice cracked on that final word. "The doctors said you're going to be fine. So stop feeling sorry for yourself and *move*."

Blue eyes flared indignantly at that.

"You could get up out of that bed, you know."

The eyes shut.

"Yes, I know what you're thinking. I can hear you, Etta. 'Kristen, *darling*, I know you mean *well*, but I've had a *stroke*, for God's sake, and I'm *paralyzed*.' And I know this is scary and painful and frustrating for you, I do, really. But it won't beat you, because you're Etta and there's literally nothing you can't do."

The lips twitched up again.

"Besides, you're not paralyzed. You're weak. And that means you can become strong again. It'll take some work, Etta. It'll be hard. But you can do it. You know how I know you can do it?"

One of her eyebrows twitched, and I almost cried because I knew she was trying to lift it in one of her trademark arches.

"Because you're Henrietta Cartwright. Nothing is ever too hard for you."

And I am not ready to say good-bye.

I moved to her side and wrapped myself around her in a gentle hug. She raised one hand and patted me awkwardly. When I pulled away, I saw tears in her eyes.

"Okay. First things first." I powered the bed controls so she could sit up higher. Then I searched the bag on the table beside the bed that Mom had packed for her and found her brush and comb. Gently, I brushed the fine white hair until it gleamed, using the comb to lightly tease the roots just the way she liked it. I stepped back, eyed her critically, and nodded. "There. Now you look more like you. Want to see?" I grabbed the hand mirror and showed her.

Etta angled her head from side to side, tried to smile, and then pushed the mirror aside with a whimper.

Did she hurt?

God, I hoped not, but I had no idea. I wished she could talk. Inspiration struck. I rummaged through my bag and pulled out my iPad, then swiped and tapped until I found a communication board app.

"Okay, Dad told me you pretty much have the stroke board mastered." I showed her the screen, and her eyebrows lifted again. "Talk to me." I had absolutely no idea what kind of damage the stroke did to her ability to understand language but figured there was no harm in trying. I held the tablet steady while she tapped the letters at the bottom of the board.

S

O

N

G

"What song?" I frowned when she pointed at me. What song did she want to hear? "'Fever'?" I asked with an eye roll.

She slapped my hand and tapped more letters. I waited patiently and fell into the chair beside her bed and laughed until my sides ached. She'd tapped out: "Don't be coy, darling."

Oh, yeah. Etta was still here. Now I had to find a way to tell her what had happened.

What I'd caused to happen.

My laughter suddenly changed back to tears. She squeezed my hand weakly, but it was enough to pry me out of my self-pity.

She lifted her hand and circled it slowly, and I knew she wanted to hear the whole story. I wiped the tears from my cheeks, took a deep breath, and told her all of it—how the online "Kris Versus Eli" hashtag had taken on a life of its own, with people betting on us, told her about the trolls making fun of us, told her about the new shows that we'd booked because of all the buzz, told her about the threats I'd been trying to ignore, and finally, I told her about the mob that attacked us.

"I can't do it, Etta. I can't face him again, and I damn well can't sing with his band anymore," I finally finished. "He did this…all of this so his parents wouldn't have to put Anna in a place like this." I waved my hands around her room. I closed my eyes, shivering, remembering Anna's screams when the crowd had closed in around us.

She was so quiet, I wondered if she'd fallen asleep. I glanced at her and found her staring at me, eyes full of reproach.

I sighed theatrically. "Oh, Etta! You don't understand!" Ignoring her next eyebrow climb, I hurried to explain. "It's *my* fault. I never should have tweeted where we were. I'd just yelled at Elijah for being stupid about the online accounts and then did something even worse. A mob of people just *swarmed* us like we were some…some door-buster sale on Black Friday."

She extended her hand to the iPad. I moved it within reach, holding it up for her so she could swipe at the screen until she found an app. She swiped, and I laughed halfheartedly.

"Instagram, Etta?" My mouth fell open and stayed that way when I saw the posts she was following. Shirtless men, men in kilts, men in chaps, men in uniform, men out of uniform. "Man candy? Oh my God, you look at *porn*?"

A distinct snort left her lips as she scrolled by all the muscles until she came to my name.

I pressed both hands to my open mouth when I saw images of me singing with Ride Out, videos of jams and concerts, snaps of me greeting a fan here and there. Most of them had been posted from Elijah's own account, but a lot were from other people—random strangers who legitimately liked us.

Whoa.

She watched me look at all the pictures and then tapped some letters on the communication app: *See it?*

"See what?"

She rolled her eyes in frustration and tried to sit up straighter. I rushed to adjust the bed, but she grabbed my hand and pressed it against my chest. I shook my head. "I don't understand, Etta."

She waved her hand under her eyes and then pointed to her drooping smile. She shut her eyes, defeated, and my heart ached for her. How this must be torturing her. Trapped in a bed, unable to move your own body without help, unable to speak, unable to simply *be* who you were.

After a moment, she took up the iPad again, tapping letters. It took her nearly three full minutes, and it clearly exhausted her, because when she was done, she let the tablet slide down on the bed next to her. I took it and read the message.

You looked happy. Don't give that up.

Days passed with no word from Elijah. He probably despised me for what had happened.

I hadn't been able to sleep. Most nights, I'd toss in my bed, worried for Etta. Tonight was no different. But if I were to be honest, Etta wasn't the only reason I couldn't sleep. I couldn't get those pictures on Instagram out of my mind. I didn't use Instagram. I spent most of my time on Facebook, Twitter, the Beat, and Tumblr.

My God, when did these networks develop their own personalities? Facebook's all about starting arguments, Twitter's worse than that stupid judge show on Etta's TV, and the Beat was like subjecting yourself to a public evisceration. Everybody on all these social sites seemed more into picking fights, or worse, finding things to take offense to and then punishing you for offending them. People posted hate and threats and any damn thing they wanted and called them *facts* and then got indignant if you dared to disagree. And yet, Etta, my seventy-something-year-old grandmother, had accounts on networks even I didn't use.

I pressed both hands to my stomach where I was pretty sure I was developing an Internet-related ulcer.

Judgy. Everybody was so freakin' judgy.

Your lyrics are so sexist.

My own voice echoed deep in my brain. Okay. Yeah. I admit it. I'd never have given Elijah Hamilton a chance if I'd known he was FretGuy99 from the Beat. And if I hadn't given him that chance, I'd never have gotten to sing in a band, never have met Anna, and never have gotten to discover the incredibly big heart Elijah had under his rock god image. I have *two* brothers and was certain neither of them loved me with that *I'd die for her* depth like Elijah loved Anna.

My chest panged when I thought of him. A dozen times, I wanted to text him, to call him. I deleted those messages unsent. I could still see his face the moment all hell broke loose. He'd hated me in that moment. He obviously realized it was *my* fault all those people had been there, *my* fault Anna had been in danger. Every time I thought about the ice-cold hatred in his eyes, my skin crawled in goose pimples.

It was only a few days until the county festival concert.

I couldn't go. Not now.

I rolled over, gave my pillow a punch, and willed myself to stop thinking about him.

Instead, I dreamed of crowds and strangers and stalkers and boys with intense eyes drilling me with laser-focused glares. When I woke up the next morning, my stomach pitched and rolled, and just the sight of food turned me green. I knew I had to face Elijah and try to apologize for what I'd done.

But I was a coward.

I wasn't like Etta, who could command any room she entered, no matter how she was feeling inside.

No.

No, that wasn't true.

I couldn't bear seeing him look at me like that again.

Did he actually believe I set up that park mob scene? He *knew* me. We'd hung out for weeks. He'd consoled me when Etta was first admitted. My God, I'd slept in his bed. How could he believe I was this monster who would knowingly, purposely post the whereabouts of his disabled sister so many Internet trolls delighted in making fun of?

I was the one who begged to pull the plug on the whole hashtag war. I wouldn't do this for publicity. And yet, he hadn't called, texted, or even tweeted me since. So yeah. I was pretty sure he hated me.

Tears dripped onto my pillow, and I forced myself out of bed.

I wouldn't do it. I would not sing in this show. Even if the entire conservatory admissions review board promised to attend, I just couldn't do it.

It would utterly destroy me to see that look again.

The alarm on my phone chimed, and I dragged myself out of bed to get dressed and do something with this day. It hit me then, a solid kick to the solar plexus, that I wasn't *me* anymore. I was a *thumbs-up*, a *star*, a *share*, a *comment*.

I was clickbait.

I was *something* only because they said I was, and I could be *nothing* as soon as they decided that's what I should be. Air backed up in my lungs, and the only thought in my head was Etta. Was this what it felt like for her? Trapped and suffocating under the inability to be who you are?

Or *were*.

God! I wrapped both arms around my middle and rocked, breath rasping through my parted lips halfway between gasp and sob. Enough. I wanted to go to the mall with Rachel and not have seventy-five strangers shout at me to scream for them. I wanted to perform the kind of music I enjoyed, write songs I liked, and produce shows I liked—not what a thousand faceless, self-proclaimed experts liked.

I leaped out of my bed, lunged for my laptop, and logged in to the Beat. I stared at the number of fans I had now, the number of comments, the number of shares, and for the first time since I'd joined the site, my stomach kinked in disgust. I opened my email app and sent Elijah a message.

I'm sorry.

Then I removed all of my accounts because I was the biggest coward to ever live. I ran to the bathroom, fell to my knees in front of the toilet, and decided this was the price you had to pay for fame.

ELIJAH

RAWR!
A BLOG BY WOMEN FOR WOMEN AND
THE MEN WHO RESPECT THEM.

If you haven't been living under a rock and have Internet access, there's no way you haven't heard about the drama that unfolded at a Long Island playground earlier this week. Sources confirm that the hard rock band Ride Out may be on the verge of breaking up before they've even broken out. After lead singers Elijah Hamilton and Kristen Cartwright were surrounded by an unruly mob that resulted in an arrest for Hamilton on charges of assault, Cartwright's entire social media presence was deleted. Hamilton, shown in cell phone video attacking a fan, is allegedly so incensed by this tweet posted by Cartwright on the day of the assault, he kicked her out of the band and refuses to take her calls. With the band headlining at the Suffolk Festival on Friday, the county hotline has been fielding phone calls by the dozen but still cannot confirm that Cartwright will take the stage.

@kristencartwright

Guys, no more #KrisVsEli. Just enjoying a perfect summer day at the playground with @elijahhamilton and his sister.

"I respect her musical talent," Hamilton has been quoted repeatedly as saying after criticism of this earlier tweet spread: "Wanna hear her scream. #CatCall" The band's blatant sexualized lyrics have kept them off the playlists at local high schools, but the viral popularity of the #KrisVsEli hashtag catapulted the group to home town fame. The band, formed four years ago when Hamilton and his friends met in eighth grade, only perpetuates the misogyny found throughout the hard rock genre, and Cartwright, blinded by promises of fame, turns an indifferent eye to it, defending Hamilton's brazen sexism, claiming, "It's all just an act." This blogger wonders why Cartwright wastes her considerable talents on a band that so clearly does not respect her, evident every time she sings, when the only thing Hamilton looks at it is her Barbie doll-proportioned chest.

Whether fact or fiction, the one thing we do know is the #KrisVsEli battle is now apparently very real, after Cartwright's tweet apparently attracted a mob that swarmed the pair during a playground outing with Hamilton's disabled sister. Witnesses claim several fans became unruly when Hamilton refused them autographs, which triggered a violent outburst from his sister. In the resulting chaos, Hamilton, his sister, and Cartwright became separated. Police found and returned thirteen-year-old Anna Hamilton, who suffers from profound autism as well as a genetic defect, to her parents' custody, who immediately enrolled her in a residence program. Cartwright and Hamilton have had no contact since that day. Does Hamilton blame Cartwright for what happened or did Cartwright finally see Hamilton for the sexist cliché he really is?

One thing's clear...whether you're a Ride Out fan or not, #KrisVsEli is dead, and we say, good riddance.

I stared at the screen in front of me, seeing the proof in vivid color but still not believing it.

"Eli. We should practice."

She *knew* me. She wouldn't do this. She fucking knew me, knew that I adored her singing voice, knew that I respected her, and knew I was fucking terrified of losing Anna.

But none of that changed a thing. She *had* done it.

I tapped the screen again and again, checking the Beat, Twitter, and Facebook, counting up all the fans and followers and likes and favorites. For so long, this was all that mattered to me.

"Elijah. Come on. Let's jam."

I logged in as myself this time, cycled through all the sites again, checking my friends lists.

Kristen had cut me off.

Deleted.

Gone with nothing more than a text.

I tossed my tablet to the table and dragged both hands through my hair, trying to ignore the searing pain of betrayal that sliced through my chest. How could she do this—now, so soon before the biggest gig of our existence?

I whipped my phone out of my pocket and texted her, but the phone remained stubbornly silent for minute after minute after minute after—

"Eli."

Nick's hand on my shoulder made me jerk in surprise. I looked up and saw Nick, Leah, and Sam staring at me. I'd forgotten they were there. "Guys. How—" I couldn't even say it. It was hard enough to think it. I surged to my feet. "I'm going over there."

"No." Nick's hand on my shoulder tightened. "You want to make everything worse? She's scared, Elijah. This online shit? It's not a game."

I laughed once. "Oh, *she's* scared. It wasn't *her* sister that a crowd terrified, was it? You don't see me deleting all *my* accounts because of it. I put the band first in everything." Maybe that was the reason for Kristen's sudden social withdrawal? Was she pissed off because I put the band ahead of her? I sank back to the stool and hung my head. I couldn't make my mind accept it.

Kristen *abandoned* us. Quitting the band was one thing. But after that kiss, I never expected her to turn away from *me*. "That fucking Rawr chick and her fucking blog! This is *her* fault. Calling me names, judging me, calling me out on shit that's all speculation and fiction. So I have a rep. Fuck, yeah, I do. So what? How could she think—" I broke off, shaking my head. Kristen should know who I am by now.

Better than anyone else. I never hid from her. I let her in and—I clenched my teeth together when the absurd irony struck me between the eyes. I should have followed the advice in my own song lyrics and not let *anyone* in. I thought I mattered. Just a little. I thought we were friends. I thought—fuck me, it doesn't matter what I thought. "She ghosted me, guys. I…I thought she knew *me*. But she…she ghosted me. This is bullshit."

"Yeah," Nick agreed quietly. "It is. But, Elijah, the show is this weekend, and we have to do it. With or without her."

He was right.

Black rage rose in me like a tsunami, and I wanted to jump up and smash every piece of equipment in my garage, every picture, every video, every fucking musical note that reminded me of Kristen. Fists clenched, I stood, shaking with the effort to control that urge until it passed. After a long moment, I slowly exhaled and managed to choke out, "Let's jam."

Leah moved to a stool near our soundboard. Nick and Sam took their places while I set up the camera. Nick counted us in, and before we played the first note, I cut them off when a new whim struck. "Hold up, guys. I want to play this." I grabbed my notebook from the table against the wall and showed it to Sam.

"Hey, isn't this Kristen's song?" He handed the book to Nick.

"Not anymore. Now it's ours."

"Eli, I—" Nick shook his head.

"You in or out?" I cut in.

They exchanged another look and finally nodded. "Okay. You

play it first solo. We'll chime in when we get the feel." Nick picked up his sticks.

I nodded and shut my eyes. I wouldn't be singing the original lyrics, the ones I'd written with Kristen. Oh, no, no, no. The song was mine now.

All mine.

I grabbed my bass, jacked in, and waited for my cue, the words clogging my throat while I searched for substitutions that tasted as sour and foul as Kristen's desertion.

It can't get worse; this is the way it hurts.
It can't get worse; this is the way it hurts.

Don't know how it all went wrong,
Thought what we had was so damn strong.
I showed you my heart, tore down my defenses,
They said I'm a jerk, said I'm offensive.

I braced for more pain, feeling like I was picking at scabs instead of strumming strings. Through a clenched jaw, I shoved out the next line with a bone-deep metal scream.

And you just turned away.

Fists clenched, I let the sound echo through me, afraid I'd explode if I didn't get the words out. Every last one. I attacked the chorus with a murderous aggression, but it didn't help release any of the tension that kept building inside me.

What can I say?
What can I do?
Everything I am means nothing much to you.
It can't get worse; this is the way it hurts.
I got nothing but my name,
Nothing but my songs,
Feelin' so much pain, but the words still come out wrong.
It can't get worse; this is the way it hurts.

You called me your friend, said you were sure,
Can't believe I was that insecure.
I fell fast and fell so hard,
I was yours, now I'm just scars.

I repeated the chorus, powering through the final notes, only dimly aware of Nick's drums and Sam's guitar behind me. When it was done, I paced the garage, sweat running down my face and panting like I'd run a marathon. A throat cleared behind me, and I looked over my shoulder to find my dad standing in the door to the kitchen, dressed in pajama pants and a T-shirt. He applauded slowly. "Wow. That was… uh…pretty intense."

You really don't know.

"Hey, Mr. Hamilton."

"Nick. Sam. You guys sound really great. All ready for the big show?"

"Yes, sir."

Nick took Leah's hand. "Mr. Hamilton, this is my girlfriend, Leah."

"Hi, Leah." Dad nodded with one of those tight-lipped smiles and scratched his neck. "Uh, so I was just passing by and wondered if you guys worked up a thirst? I got ice tea for you inside." He jerked a thumb toward the kitchen, then disappeared back inside when everyone accepted politely.

Sam took his guitar and propped it in a stand. "Hey," he turned and called back to me from the door. "You coming?"

I nodded. "Yeah, in a second." I lifted the bass off my shoulder and killed the camera. I glanced at my phone, sitting on the table where it had landed... It was still dark, a mocking *fuck you.* I joined everybody at the kitchen table, tall glasses of iced tea gripped in their hands. I took the last glass and chugged it. When I put the glass down, all three were staring at me.

"What?"

Nick shook his head. "It...feels weird. Not having Anna come out to *no, no, no* with us."

Another knife slashed through my gut.

"Hell, it's weird being able to jam when your parents are here," Sam added, shaking hair off his face.

"Yeah. Weird," I managed to agree.

"I keep waiting for them to come out and shush us."

I stared at my empty glass and watched the ice melt, wishing I could just evaporate along with it.

"How's it going, Eli?" Sam asked, jerking his chin toward the family room, where the TV played in the background. "Your parents getting along?"

I shook my head. "The house is empty. There's like…nothing to do." There was no way they could possibly know. But they both nodded like they did.

"That's good, though, right? Anna's safe, and your parents maybe won't keep fighting so much?"

I shrugged again. I wasn't hopeful. "Maybe." Sam was right, though. They were different. Not happier. Never that. But lighter somehow.

So was I, and that fucking pissed me off.

"Have you seen her since…"

I twisted the glass on the table, the screech it made sending a chill down my back. "Yeah. I visit her every day."

Nick drummed the table. "Yeah? Is she okay?"

Okay. What a bullshit word that was. People ask how you're doing, and you automatically say *okay. Yeah, I'm adequate, well enough, tolerable, thanks so much for asking.* Didn't anybody see how shooting for just *okay* was totally lowering the bar? A cop-out? A cheat? *Okay* is not the same thing as being *good, excellent,* or *awesome.* It's not even close. So why did I have to be okay because Anna was okay in her new home? *Because,* a tiny traitorous part of me forced me to admit, *she was okay.* I wanted to crack my skull apart and perform a self-lobotomy to remove that part.

"Fine." Yet another bullshit word. "She hasn't had any violent episodes since she got there. She sits and rocks. Maybe that means she's scared. Or maybe it means she's better than fine. I have no fucking idea."

"It hasn't been long, Elijah. She'll settle in."

I shook my head. "She shouldn't have to. I hate this, Sam. I hate it that we locked her up."

"I know, man. But at least the trolls online can't get at her now."

There was that. I nodded, appreciating the silver lining—even if it was just a cheap imitation.

I gulped down the last of my ice tea and then stared at Leah. "You're her friend. What the hell is up with her?"

Leah's eyes popped wide, and then she shook her head. She laughed halfheartedly and admitted with a tight expression, "Kristen and I have never been friends."

Oh.

"How come?"

Leah squirmed. "I don't know. It's not that I don't like her or anything… I mean, she's never done anything mean to me. Too competitive, I guess. We've been sharing the same stage since we were six years old, and it's just not big enough."

"Do you think I'm sexist?"

Next to Leah, Nick jerked like someone just stuck him with a knife. "Eli—"

"No, I need to know."

Leah shifted, hunched some more, drained her glass, and finally shrugged. "I don't know, Elijah. I don't know you well enough to tell. For what it's worth, I can tell you this: you guys have no idea what it's like for girls, always being scared."

"Scared?" I echoed. "What the hell are you talking about?"

Leah waved a hand at the cell phones on the table. "This. The Internet. I'm not on the Beat, but I've seen the stuff people post about Kristen, about you." She lowered her eyes, bit her lip, and shook her head. "It's scary. I mean really terrifying. You post some song cover that bombs, no big deal. People post some comments like *This sucks* or *OMG my ears are bleeding,* and it eventually goes away because you're guys. But when it's girls? Holy crap." She picked up her phone, tapped, and swiped. "Back in April, after the *Cats* show, some guy threatened me because I wouldn't meet him."

"What?" Nick snapped up straight. "Why the hell didn't you tell me?"

Leah looked at him sideways. "Not like you could have done anything about it."

Nick's eyes burned. "Oh, I—"

"Nick." I held up a hand. "Why are you telling us now?"

"Because I think I get why Kristen disappeared on you. The comments we get are personal and insulting and crude and even threatening. Nobody threatens to rape you when you post a song that sucks."

"And somebody did that to you?" Nick demanded.

Leah stared at him for a moment and then nodded once. He shoved back in his seat with a screech.

"Goddamn it."

"Can you imagine what Kristen's dealing with? First, it's all the hard-core Ride Out fans from the Beat upset because Sam's so publicly not onboard with her presence in the band, and then, the stupid 'Kris versus Eli' hashtag competition, and now this blog post that pretty much says the band's breaking up because of her?" Leah paused and rubbed a hand over her mouth. "Jesus, it's like you pinned a red sniper target to her chest."

She lifted her eyes to mine and nodded. "So, yeah. I do think you're being a bit sexist, Elijah. You got her into this, and all you're doing now is crying about her leaving you. Did it ever occur to you that she left to *save* you, save the band?"

No. It hadn't. I sat there for a long time, trying to process what Leah said.

Finally, Nick cleared his throat. "Maybe we should decide the set list for the show?" he suggested. I nodded again, grateful for the change of subject. I rose and got a notepad and pen, and we spent the next hour debating what songs to perform.

When the guys left that evening, I went back to the garage and viewed the video of our practice. That was the first time I'd sung "The Way It Hurts" because I'd always intended for it to be Kristen's song. But I liked it. It was raw and visceral and almost primal. It was everything hard rock was supposed to be.

It was everything Ride Out was supposed to be.

I kicked back, put my feet up, and sighed heavily. When did it all go to shit? Sam was right and who the fuck knows—maybe he'd been right all along... It was supposed to be about the *music*. Instead of writing kick-ass original songs, I'd been writing tweets and hashtags and comments that caused arguments. Kristen begged me to kill the online crap and showed me the shit these people said about her, but I still didn't listen. All I could see were the numbers. I thought those numbers meant we were close, that we'd get the bigger and better gigs, the record deal. I thought once we got the fans behind us, that the truth would be obvious—that Ride Out knew hard rock like *whoa.* I swallowed the bitter taste on my tongue and shook my head at my idiocy.

I'd once accused Kristen of being arrogant, but there was nobody more arrogant than me…believing the truth would be so fucking clear to our legions of fans. Let me tell you the truth about the truth.

It doesn't exist.

There is no truth!

It's a myth. A lie. There's only *perception,* and perception shifts with the goddamn tides, and it's all controlled by mouse clicks. I stupidly thought I could control perception, that by being patient and smart, I could control what people said about us, what people believed about us. I thought that by refusing to comment on some things, I'd compel them to focus on the things I *did* comment on, but in the absence of our version of the truth, they just substituted their own.

Oh my God, I am such an asshole.

It came to me then—the simple solution to unfuck everything. I posted the video, knowing damn well it was a stab in the dark:

> @Ride_Out
> Check it! New song The Way It Hurts written by
> @kristencartwright and @elijahhamilton. See it live at
> #CountyFest this weekend.

I added a link to the festival website and our own site. When it was done, I visited all of our social sites again. Our Facebook site had a ton of commentary on the playground incident, with most people of the opinion that if only I hadn't been such a dick and just given my autograph, I could have prevented the escalation that happened. Over on Twitter, they were making fun of Anna and her issues, with another raving asshole agreeing with Detective Jerk that I shouldn't take her to public places.

I accessed our account settings, and after I read all the stats I'd worked so fucking hard to collect, I deleted the account.

It felt so good, I went back to Facebook and then I went to the Beat and blasted them both off the Internet too.

I sat there, staring at the gaping blank spaces that used to make up my entire life and wondered if I had a hope of changing any damn thing at all.

KRISTEN

Kristen Cartwright
@kristencartwright

This account has been suspended.

@Rawr4Fems

What really happened in the playground? #KrisVsEli #CatCall

It was Friday and miserably hot, even for July. Today was the Suffolk Festival.

I would not be attending.

Instead, I'd gotten permission to use Mom's car and drove to Etta's convalescent home. It was just past breakfast time when I got there. I expected to find Etta staring at yet another inane TV show, her hair flat and eyes dull. Instead, I found her sitting up in bed, her hair neatly combed into a sleek bob, and a light amount of makeup on her face.

I scraped over the guest chair, sat down, and just smiled at her for a minute. "You look beautiful." I crossed my fingers behind my back and prayed God didn't shock me with a lightning bolt for what I was about to say. "It's about time you stopped feeling sorry for yourself."

Indignation flared in her eyes, and she took my wrist, gripped it hard, and slowly hauled herself up so she could very succinctly say, "Take me out of here."

I fought the urge to help her. "But I thought you liked it here. You have your TV shows and—"

She grabbed the remote beside her, flung it at the TV, and asked, "When. Do you. Sing?"

The joy and relief I'd felt a little while ago evaporated in the puff of air that got knocked out of me with that question. *Elijah.* God, I missed him. Worrying about Etta gave me something to focus on and obsess over instead of that devastated look on his face after we had almost gotten mauled by that insane mob.

"Oh, Etta." My face trembled. "I'm not singing anymore. Not with Elijah. He hates me. It's my fault they put his sister in a home."

A soft touch on my hair made me jerk. Etta smiled and pointed toward her iPad. I took it off the side table, woke it up, and tapped her comm app. She tapped one word.

Love.

I managed a weak smile. "I love you too."

She shook her head. "Not. Me. Him."

Him? "Elijah? Wait, you think I love him? No." I waved the suggestion away. But it was out there now, worming its way into my brain, taunting and teasing like the lyrics to a song you can't stop singing, and suddenly I knew it fit. It fit completely. "No," I repeated. "Oh, no, Etta. I can't love him." I lowered my head, and she stroked my hair while I tried to form a plan, something that could fix everything I had broken.

The iPad pinged with an alert. Despite the tears for my insane life, I laughed. Etta was more techy than I was. I tapped the notification and held the screen so she could see it. *You have one event today. Ride Out is performing at Suffolk Festival.* "A calendar alert? Are you seriously following concert schedules now?"

She refused to look guilty or even sheepish about getting caught. She just raised her eyebrows, unaware that only one rose, and inclined her head in a close imitation of that regal nod she'd perfected long before I was born. She tapped the link included in the notification, and it opened a YouTube video.

My shoulders dropped when the video played. Elijah had posted another jam session. It was my song.

Our song.

He'd…he'd rewritten it. Hardened it. Corrupted it into something manic and brilliant and twisted and bitter, full of growls and screams that compelled me to listen and then left me bruised after I did.

Abruptly, the music cut off. Etta had tapped the Stop button. "No, I'm okay. I need to hear it all, Etta." She wasn't convinced, so I explained. "We wrote this song together. He changed the words, though. He changed the mood, the tempo—everything." I couldn't pretend that didn't wound me all the way to the core.

She frowned but played the song all the way through. I paid close attention to the new lyrics and just kept shaking my head, unable to grasp what I'd heard with my own ears. He obviously despised me.

I sat numb for a long moment on the side of Etta's bed and then played it again. I watched Elijah closely as he screamed out the vicious lyrics and noted the clenched hands, the tight shoulders, and the closed posture. I saw the shine of tears in his eyes that he kept lowering so no one could see.

Elijah's version of our song was pure agony.

And I'd caused it.

My phone vibrated, and I hardly spared it a glance. What would be the point? It had been nothing but bad news on top of worse news. But I did look.

Leah.

I rolled my eyes. Could this day possibly get worse? What could Leah Russo possibly want?

Leah: Know u h8 me but thought u should know u really

338

broke E's heart. He thinks u ghosted him because u believe the Rawr post.

The Rawr post. What post was that? They'd started to blur together. I tapped out a reply. **Kristen:** Why are you telling me this?

Leah: Because I like him. He's a good guy. He's crazy for u. Nick bet me u 2 would be together by end of summer.

Holy crap.

Kristen: I almost got his sister killed. He can't even look at me.

Leah: No. He blames himself for that. Says he should have listened to u. Can u forgive him?

Kristen: I don't know if that's enough.

"More." Etta pointed to the alert on her tablet. I took it and scrolled through the links with a sigh. What more could these trolls possibly find to write about, to complain about? I tapped a link. It was to Rawr's latest blog post—was this the post Leah meant? "Oh my God!" I lifted my face to Etta's, a thick lump in my throat. "Why won't they just leave us alone, Etta?" I threw down the tablet. "I don't even know this woman. What business is it of hers if I want to sing in a heavy metal rock band?"

I jumped to my feet and paced around Etta's bed.

"This." I stabbed a finger toward the iPad. "This is total and complete crap. Look at this! She says boys like Elijah Hamilton and his friends only perpetuate 'the misogyny found throughout the hard rock genre, and Cartwright, blinded by promises of fame, turns an indifferent eye to it.' Seriously? She's never met me, never even asked me for an interview, and she thinks she knows what I think?" I dragged both hands through my hair, ready to tear it out. "I'm sick of this, Etta. Those boys work so damn hard on their lyrics and music, and yeah, maybe they take the whole dark sinister image stuff a bit far, but they're not the assholes she claims they are." I waved my hands and let them fall.

"You know what really twists me up over this? There's no mention of how Elijah cares for Anna, protects her, would die for her. Oh, no! He's just another chest-beating, woman-chasing jerk. Look! Look at this… She claims she cannot understand why I waste my considerable talents on a band who so clearly does not respect me, evident every time I sing when the only thing Elijah looks at it is my Barbie doll-proportioned chest. Ugh!" My hands curled into fists, and I deliberately turned my back on the iPad because the temptation to pitch it through the window was really freakin' strong.

I tried a few deep breaths and counted to ten, and when I was calmer, I turned back and found the iPad trembling in Etta's weakened grip. There was a deep vertical crease in her forehead as she read Rawr's post, and then she looked up at me. "Go. To. Him."

I couldn't help it. I laughed. "Oh, what happened to making them beg, making them come to me? I thought you knew all about men."

But Etta didn't laugh. She extended a shaky hand and managed to say, "Not a game now."

My laughter faded, and I nodded. It was never a game. Not to me. I glanced at the time and made a fast decision.

"Etta," I whispered, lifting my eyes to hers. "How would you like to go to a concert?"

ELIJAH

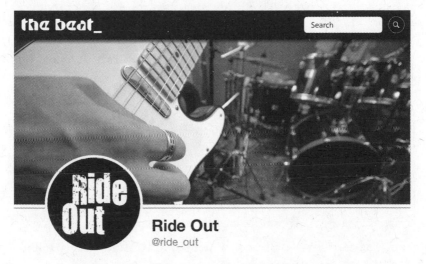

the beat_

Search 🔍

Ride Out
@ride_out

This account has been deleted by the owner.

BryceG: You guys need to cut Kristen NOW or I will. Girl's a band wrecker.

> **Ride_On747:** @BryceG: Hey it's not her fault.

> **BryceG:** @Ride_On747: U trippin'? She told the Internet where they'd be. Girl deserves what she gets.

> **Ride_On747:** Back off.

SHARES: 581 LIKES: 633

I'd spent hours in the garage, boxing up equipment and stacking it near the door so that it would be ready to be packed into Nick's mother's minivan. The garage smelled damp and humid, and even though my hair was pulled up, sweat poured down my back, and I hoped to God it wouldn't rain. I checked my lists time after time and was sure we had everything ready.

Except for one thing.

Kristen.

I still hadn't heard from her. That familiar urge to check my phone struck again, like a drug craving. I knew it was no good, knew it wasn't going to end any differently, knew all that and still couldn't stop myself from wanting to know. It was only by sheer force of stubborn, compulsive willpower that I didn't drive to her house and pound on the door, and with every day that went by, that craving got easier to bear. It was pretty fucking obvious that she *believed* all that shit Rawr wrote about me, and while I was sure I'd never get over the shock of that, at least I could be pissed off instead of hurt.

I liked *pissed off*. It was a hell of lot easier to be mad than sad. But right now, I had to be professional. We were close, so close I could taste it. We had fans, we had people who had followed us just for the music, and there was no reason not to expect a large crowd. I swallowed down the greasy knot that had been trying to choke me for days now and forced myself to focus.

I picked up the set list printouts. I'd deleted all of Kristen's solo songs, and as for the duets, I was pretty sure I'd be able to encourage the crowd to pick up her part.

"So you all ready?"

I glanced at the kitchen door and found Dad standing there with yet another cup of coffee clutched in his hands. That's what he did lately. Just roamed the house holding a bottomless cup of coffee, too damn stubborn to admit he missed her.

"Just about." I went back to my studying my lists, not really in a talking mood.

He nodded. "Good, good." He sipped and nodded some more. "Your mom's looking forward to it. She hasn't really ever listened to your band." He leaned against the doorframe and hooked one foot over the other.

My head snapped up to his. "You're coming?"

"Oh, yeah, sure. Wouldn't miss it—"

My eyes narrowed, and he abruptly stopped talking when he realized what he'd just said.

"Right. You both have all this time on your hands."

He straightened up. "That's not—"

"It is, Dad. We both know it."

"Jesus, Eli." He shoved off the wall. "You think this is easy for us? You think we like this?"

I stared him down. "Yeah. I do."

He held my gaze for a long moment, clenching his jaw so hard I could see the muscle ticking. He opened his mouth and shut it, like he knew he would just be wasting his breath. I hated him just then, and I was sure he knew that, so he turned and went back into the house, leaving me alone in the humid garage with absolutely no fucking reason to see this through. Jesus, they wouldn't even let me take Anna out of the facility without permission in triplicate.

I'd told Mom I wanted to check Anna out of jail and bring her to the show, but she'd completely flipped out on me. Said it wouldn't be possible for me to watch her and perform, and how could I even suggest such a thing after what happened at the playground?

I shifted and squirmed. Okay, she was right. Didn't mean I had to accept that.

Or give up trying.

I stuffed the set list printouts into the last box and fastened the lid, eyes falling on the ancient Mac sitting on the table. I powered it on and queued up that old footage of Anna singing "Brown Eyed Girl" with me. She'd loved it. Watching her face, the expressions of peace and joy as she sang, broke something inside me, and suddenly, I was throwing shit and punching the table, sweat dripping from my hair into my ears to mix with the tears.

"Hey, hey, hey! Eli, what the hell?"

Dad's arms banded around me from behind just the way we often restrained Anna. I struggled to free myself because the last thing I wanted was to be near him, but he only tightened his grip. "Let go."

"Uh-uh. Talk to me. Where's all this rage coming from?"

I felt rather than saw his reaction when he noticed the video of Anna playing on the screen.

"Oh."

I froze. "Oh? That's it? That's the only thing you can say?"

"I meant, I understand—"

"Bullshit, Dad!" I broke free, whipped around, and shoved him back a step. His eyes flared once, but he didn't retaliate. "You don't understand! You can't even admit you miss her. All you do is go on long walks with Mom and sit and watch TV, drinking gallons of coffee."

He stared at me, dark eyes blurred, and suddenly, he crumpled up and sank to the floor, sobbing like a two-year-old. "You're right," he choked out. "I don't miss her the way you do... She's my daughter not my sister, so it can't be the same. I go on those long walks to keep myself from grabbing the car keys and rushing out there to spring her loose. I drink all that coffee because I'm afraid to go to sleep at night in case she needs me, and I want to hear the phone if it rings. There's a piece of my heart beating outside my own body—that I'm supposed to protect and I can't. Don't you understand that? I *can't* and neither can you."

I shook my head. Pretty words but that's all they were. "Dad, I can't give up on her. It's not fair that I can talk and go to school and... and you know, have this normal life while—"

"It's not fair, Eli. It's not fair at all." Slowly, he climbed up off the floor, joints popping from the effort. "But it's not your problem."

My vision went red, and I advanced on him. "Fuck that."

345

Dad's hands shot up. "Listen to me. You are her brother, not her parent. Do you understand me? I'm her father, and I cannot take care of her anymore. Not with a house and a full-time job. You have none of those worries, and even if you did, it still would not be your responsibility."

I sucked in my cheek, glaring at him. "You didn't even let me try."

He shut his eyes, and it suddenly hit me he was so exhausted he was almost swaying on his feet. "Eli, I'm done arguing with you about this. You want to try? Fine, you do what you have to do. Have a good show."

He left me there, alone, his words echoing in the darkness.

I watched Anna's video over and over and over. "I will never give up, Anna. Not like he did."

Never.

"Okay, guys. This is it. You ready?" Nick asked me while we took our places behind the stage and waited for our introduction.

I peeked cautiously around the curtain, noting the guys in black T-shirts marked "Security," the crowd barriers, and—oh, God. "Channel Twelve is here," I reported, awed.

"Shit," Nick groaned, shutting his eyes for a second.

"Come on, guys. Walk in the park." Sam fluffed his hair and adjusted the leather cuff on his wrist.

My eyes fell to my own bare wrist. I'd given Kristen my cuff. Whatever. It was fine. Just another fucking blank space where she should be.

I scanned the crowd, a useless surge of hope forcing me to search for any glimpse of blond hair and cleavage. Of course there was no sign of her. But I saw so many people. Teens, parents with kids in strollers, a bunch of biker guys...pretty much everybody was holding a color print of the "Kris Versus Eli" battle poster, and against my will, a smile tugged my lips. Seemed that heavy metal had universal appeal. The smile melted when I wondered how many people in this audience were also in that ugly crowd at the playground. How many of them sent Kristen those online threats? I'd told her it was no big deal, part of the territory. She'd have to get used to it if she wanted to play with the boys.

What a fucking tool I was. *Am.*

I'd spent so long developing my rock god image, I wasn't exactly sure why it stunned me to realize that the perception I so carefully created was *reality* to fans, and that most people would never know there was a different side of me unless they took a really close look. Like Kristen had.

A loud "No" captured my attention. In the front row by stage right, a woman sat anxiously looking around at the people shooting her funny looks. At her feet, on the ground, a little girl sat. She was about ten years old, wearing baggy clothes. I took one look and knew, even before I noticed the hair hanging in her eyes or the way she rocked back and forth, shaking her head, that she was on the spectrum, and my heart clenched. I took another look at the crowd, my jaw tightening.

If they turned on her...Jesus. I caught the eye of the closest security dude and motioned him over. I asked him to have the crew keep an eye on her. "Don't make the mom anxious, though, okay?"

"No problem."

I ducked back behind the curtain. "Hey, Nick. Got any extra sticks you can give away?"

He frowned and shrugged. "Yeah, I guess." He checked his bag and took out a set of practice sticks. "Here."

"Thanks, bro."

I walked around the curtain and down the stage steps, ignoring the hoots from a bunch of teen girls who spotted me and slowly approached the little girl and her mom on the right. "Hi. I'm Elijah—"

"Oh, um. Yeah, I know who you are. You're, uh…you're why we're here."

It took me a minute to be able to talk. I smiled and nodded. "Thanks. Here. These are for her. If she's like my sister, the music speaks to her."

"Oh, it does." The woman covered her mouth with both hands and then took the drumsticks.

"She can beat on the ground if she wants. Or come onstage with us. Whatever you think will calm her."

The woman looked horrified. "Definitely no stage. Just sitting near music will help."

I nodded. "Does she respond to her name?"

The woman's eyes clouded, and she shrugged. "Sometimes. It's Maggie."

"Maggie," I repeated, but she didn't respond, and I knew better than to press her.

"Is your sister here?" Maggie's mother asked, and I shook my head.

"No," I admitted. "My parents refused to check her out of her residence program for today's gig."

"Residence? Which one?"

I didn't answer. Trust only went so far.

"Oh! I'm sorry. I didn't mean to—God, I'm an idiot. I didn't mean—"

"It's okay. I know what you meant, but I can't tell you. I can't risk the information going public."

"You're right. I'm so sorry."

A group of girls wearing sundresses decided to approach, and I took that as my cue to bounce. "Enjoy the concert."

She offered up the "Kris Versus Eli" poster. "Would you sign this for us?"

I grinned. "No problem." While I scrawled my name over my image, I casually asked, "Would you put your daughter in a residence if you could?"

"Thanks." She took the poster back like it was a soap bubble that might pop. "And yes. I would. Some people hope and pray to win a lottery, but me? I hope and pray I'll be able to keep her with me always. But I know that's not possible. This world doesn't understand these kids, and at some point, I'll have to provide her with her own world, one that—"

"Elijah! Elijah!" Chants started, and the girls surged forward.

I turned to go. "One that what?"

"One that's safe for her so I can stop worrying about what will happen to her when I'm gone." She angled her head and studied me. "For what it's worth, I don't believe the stuff they say about you. Anybody who loves his sister the way you do is not a jerk."

And there it was again. I managed a wink and an evil grin. "Shhh, I got an image to maintain."

"Elijah! Elijah!"

I turned and found a cameraman and reporter wearing a red suit and high heels jogging toward me, her heels tapping on the concrete. One of the security guys tried to hustle me back onstage, but I waved him off. I could handle this.

"How nervous are you about today's concert?" The reporter thrust her microphone under my nose, and my eyebrows rose.

"I'm excited and amped up but not nervous."

"The recent threats made against your family don't concern you?"

Ah. Now I knew what this was really about.

"Threats always worry me, but my family is safe right now."

"And what about Kristen Cartwright? Is it true she is no longer with Ride Out? Did you split because of the online battle or was it something more personal?"

Shit. What was this, a TMZ segment? I swallowed down my annoyance and neither confirmed nor denied. "Kristen had a family emergency that prevents her from singing with us today. Whenever she feels ready to pick up a mic again, Ride Out is happy—and lucky—to have her."

"Elijah, it's no secret you and Kristen have battled over creative differences as well as personal ones you so publicly debated on the music forum, the Beat. Where does that battle stand today?"

I opened my mouth, ready to deliver my standard response to every question just like this one that I'd been asked. And then, a flash of red from the corner of my eye caught my attention.

I swore I saw Kristen's red boots. She was here! The rock in my gut suddenly disintegrated, and I wanted to run, find her, tell her I was sorry, and never let her go, but when I searched the vicinity, the only red I saw was on a pair of sneakers belonging to some ten-year-old.

Kristen wasn't here, and she never would be again.

I took a deep breath and stared directly at the camera. "You want the truth?"

"Of course." The reporter revealed every perfectly capped tooth in her mouth, and I almost snorted.

"I messed up. If I'd listened to Kristen from day one instead of starting up that stupid Kris versus Eli hashtag, maybe we'd be having a different conversation."

"That's very direct, Elijah. But is it true?"

At this, I did snort. "Truth doesn't matter. Just perception." My new mantra.

The security guard took my elbow and led me back behind the stage just as the festival executive tapped the mic.

I took my position with Sam and Nick and waited for the executive to finish his speech thanking everybody and their uncle for coming and supporting local businesses. Finally, he said, "Put your hands together for your hometown heavy metal heroes, Ride Out!"

A deafening roar went up from the crowd, which I estimated to be about a thousand people. We took our places, grabbed our instruments, and readjusted our microphones one last time. The crowd's energy infused us, and I took a minute to let it spread to every cell in my body. Kristen may not be here, but half the school was. I recognized her friend Rachel and Nick's girl, Leah, standing in the front row. I leaned in and shouted, "Hello, Suffolk County! Are you ready to rock?"

The crowd roared its answer, and Sam counted us in to a cover of the '80s Bon Jovi classic "Wanted Dead or Alive" and strummed the guitar intro that had become iconic. I grabbed the mic and took a breath to deliver the first line of the song, and the crowd's cheer all but drowned me out. By the time I hit the chorus, they were singing along. The energy rose, the atmosphere sizzled, and everything faded out until it was just me, a guitar, and a microphone…

A crowd of adoring people shouting our names didn't hurt either.

From "Wanted Dead or Alive," we slid into current stuff like Thousand Foot Krutch's "Let the Sparks Fly" that got all those spectators counting to three with us, and Avenged Sevenfold's "Hail to the King." By the end of that one, some clowns at the front were striking their chests in some goofy salute before falling to one knee. I laughed and pointed.

We paused to chug some water, and just as Sam started the chords for Anna's favorite song "Brown Eyed Girl," a girl in the front row let out a shriek. It was Maggie. Her startled mom shot me a look of pure mortification, but I just waved it off. She couldn't help it, and I got that. But some witch sitting nearby flipped her hair over her shoulder and shouted at her.

"Oh my God, can you like control her or something so the rest of us can enjoy the show?"

Instant fury ignited, and I grabbed my mic. "Hey! I hear any more of that crap, and we're done up here." Security started moving toward the section I was glaring at.

"What? No way, I paid for these tickets. Kick *her* out for disrupting the show."

"She's fine. *You're* disrupting the show. I got no love for people like you who have no tolerance."

The chick just rolled her eyes and saluted me with one finger. I switched guitars, trading my bass for a Telecaster, and jumped off the stage. The witch thought I was coming to her and beamed bright and viciously at Maggie's mother. I elbowed her out of my way.

"Still got those sticks?"

Maggie's mom pulled the drumsticks from her bag and handed them to me. I put them in Maggie's hands.

Maggie never made eye contact, but she did stop shrieking. As soon as she noticed what was in her hands, she began rocking. I gently guided her hands to the chair in front of her, showing her how to beat the pattern I'd taught Anna.

"Sam, hand me the mic," I called. Sam took a mic from its stand and passed it to a security guard, who ran it down to me. I handed it to Maggie's mother. "Hold this for us, will you?"

I propped a leg on the chair Maggie was drumming and positioned my guitar. Into the mic, I said, "This next one goes out to my sister, Anna, and to Maggie."

I strummed the opening to "Brown Eyed Girl," Sam and Nick entered right on cue, and I sang the first lines directly to Maggie, who kept right on drumming the pattern I'd taught her. The audience loved it. Maggie's mother cried.

The bitch next to her stood with her arms crossed and a disgusted look on her face. By the time we got to the "la la la" part, Maggie was singing with us, as I'd figured she would because this song held magic. When the mean girl whipped around and pushed her way out of the row, a cheer erupted.

I grinned and shook the hair from my face.

Yep, magic.

When the song ended and the applause died down, I climbed back onstage. "Front row, I'm counting on you to help keep some space around Maggie. Just let her enjoy the music her way, okay?"

A big dude wearing motorcycle leathers thrust a fist in the air and moved closer to Maggie's mother. She looked up, up, up and then turned red. Whoa. Okay then. Like I said. Magic.

I figured now would be a good time to kick off the second half of the show.

This portion of our set list was all us—original Ride Out songs. The entire audience was standing, waving their hands, and singing along. A few shouts of "Kris! Kris!" rang out, but I ignored them...and the gaping wounds they slashed.

Finally, it was time for the last song—Kristen's song.

"The Way It Hurts."

I cued up the pain. I let it curl my hands into fists, and I let it force my lungs to constrict and my vision to blur. Nick counted us in, and Sam's fingers strummed the first chord, aggressive and raw. I opened my mouth and delivered the first line with a soft, heartbreaking tremor in my voice.

It can't get worse; this is the way it hurts.
It can't get worse; this is the way it hurts.

Don't know how it all went wrong,
Thought what we had was so damn strong.
I showed you my heart, tore down my defenses,
They said I'm a jerk, said I'm offensive,
And you just turned away.

You called me your friend, said you were sure,
Can't believe I was that insecure.
I fell fast and fell so hard,
I was yours, now I'm just scars.

The last line, I delivered with the aggressive and brutal metal growl I'd delivered during our practice in my garage, and the effect was instant. The audience went wild. When I hit the chorus, hundreds of hands went into the air, swaying to my sound.

What can I say?
What can I do?
Everything I am means nothing much to you.
It can't get worse; this is the way it hurts.
I got nothing but my name,
Nothing but my songs,

Feelin' so much pain, but the words still come out wrong.
It can't get worse; this is the way it hurts.

I paused here, shredding my notes in a riff that hadn't been in the original version. But I needed it. My heart was screaming for Kristen. I had to regroup. Focus on the pain. I bent the last note, extending it, and opened my mouth for the next line, when a deep growl stole the oxygen from the air.

Frantically, I looked around for the source, expecting it to be just reverb or feedback, but I saw…red boots.

I gasped, and my eyes damn near popped out of my skull.

Those red boots stepped up to the stage. I raised my eyes past them up the curve of sweet bare legs revealed in a short black dress, past the incredible rack that had starred in way too many of my fantasies, up to Kristen's face, her mouth open in the most chilling metal scream I'd ever heard. Goose bumps rose on every inch of my flesh, and my jaw dropped. She attacked the scream the way she did everything else— balls-to-the-wall, full out. It was brave, and it was so fucking muscular, I forgot to be mad, forgot she hated me, forgot everything except for the way that one sound held me captive.

She paused for a breath and sang the next line but changed the words.

You're wrong, and baby, I'm sorry.
But there's a whole other side to this story.
The hell with the fame, keep all the glory

Just don't turn away.
What else can I say?
What else can I scream?
The man that you are is everything to me
It can't get worse; this is the way it hurts.

She stepped toward me, blue eyes blurred, and all I wanted to do was drop the mic and grab her, hold her, and never let her go. It suddenly dawned on me that this was a concert, and there were fans who'd paid to hear me sing, and whoa, there was even a mic in front of me. I shoved the guitar behind my back, gripped the mic with both hands, and in a clear, strong voice, sang the next verse the way I'd first written it, with the words she'd called beautiful.

I watch you battle your way through the night,
Every little thing puttin' up a fight.
I'll be there next to you, just for you, for the rest of my life.

She smiled at me, took another step closer, and took my hand.

The world righted. Everything snapped into focus...the Beat, Twitter, the trolls, the crowd...lines and points, curves and edges, it was all clear as crystal now. Together, we finished it, voices lifted not in screams and growls but in harmony, Kristen filling in the downbeats as I sang the lead.

Baby, I'm yours
I'm yours
but this is too tough.
Yeah, things got rough
Why am I not enough?
I'm sorry I messed up.

What else can I say?
What else can I say?
What else can I do?
What else can I scream?
Everything I am means nothing much to you.
The man that you are is everything to me
It can't get worse; this is the way it hurts.
This is the way it hurts.

The last word floated and echoed, and then she was in my arms kissing me like I was a sip of water in a drought, and the crowd was on its feet, the applause so loud, it made my chest rattle. It didn't matter that she'd taken off, deleted me out her life. It didn't matter how many fans and followers and likes and shares we had, and it didn't matter that Sam would probably hate me for this.

All that mattered was her.

KRISTEN

Kristen Cartwright
@kristencartwright

This account has been suspended.

My heart was beating a rhythm against my ribs that rivaled Nick's percussion.

"You're here," Elijah murmured against my ear, holding me tighter.

"I'm so sorry!"

"Doesn't matter," he said and drew back to the swelling adoration of the crowd. He took my hand, raised it high, and bowed to the audience, now on its feet, aiming a thousand camera phones at us. For the first time in well, forever, I turned away from an audience and looked up into Elijah's eyes, burning with the intensity that had hooked me from the moment we met.

"I thought you hated me," I admitted. He looked blank, so I elaborated. "For what happened with Anna."

"No! God, no. It wasn't your fault. It was my fault. You tried to tell me over and over again, and I wouldn't listen. Then I saw that post on Rawr and thought you—"

"I didn't even know about that post until Leah texted me. When she showed it to me, I almost died. I never said any of those things, never felt that way, never believed them. I was so scared you saw that and hated me even more than you already did. I wanted to run away, but Etta convinced me that would be a huge mistake."

"I'm sorry, baby. I'm so sorry." His hands cradled my face, and he kissed me softly and then quickly pulled away with a frown. "So Etta's doing okay?"

I nodded and waved a hand toward stage left. "She's better. She's communicating now, and she promised me she won't give up. This was her idea." Etta managed a wave from her wheelchair. Mom, Dad, Gordon, and Dylan were all grinning and applauding behind her.

"It was a good idea." He shut his eyes, cursed, and shook his head and then grinned. "That scream. Oh my God, Kristen. Always knew you'd rock that." He grabbed a few bottles of water from the floor of the stage and handed one to me.

360

I slapped his arm and then lost my smile. "Anna?"

His eyes clouded, and he shook his head. "She's still in. I can barely look at my dad. But now…now, maybe, I think they were right." He chewed his lower lip and looked away, face full of self-hatred.

"You think you failed," I said on a gasp. "Is that what you think?"

Tears collected in the corner of his eyes, so I tugged Elijah behind the stage so we could talk.

"Eli, don't. Don't ever think that."

He laughed once, breaking my train of thought.

"What?"

"You called me Eli. Think that's the first time."

"Well, you call me Kris."

He lifted a brow. "Payback?"

"No, it's—oh, never mind that. Just listen to me." I slapped his chest, teasing him, but Elijah didn't laugh.

"I'm listening." He said it like a vow, all serious, and I froze for a second, and then I understood what he was saying. He hadn't listened to me before, but from now on, he would.

I took a deep breath, knowing this would hurt him. "Elijah, Anna is never going to college, she'll never get married, and she'll never have a life of her own." When he made a sound like I'd kicked him in the groin, I hurried to add, "It's *not* your fault. You're not responsible. You told me yourself it's a genetic thing. There is absolutely nothing you can ever do to change her."

"I know. But that's not it." The mask he wore fell, and for the first time, I saw the truth in his eyes. "I…God, Kris. I don't want her to forget me." He gripped his head and sank into one of the folding chairs that lined the backstage area. "When she was born…before we knew… Dad sat me down for a man to squirt talk, you know?" He managed half a laugh. "He said, 'Eli, you're a big brother now. That's an important job. You ready for it?' I nodded, all solemn—like I had any idea what he was talking about—and he told me that baby Anna was tiny and fragile and needed a bodyguard."

Elijah's intense eyes crinkled at the corners when he grinned. "*That*, I totally understood." He took a worn bandanna from his pocket, mopped his face, and let the smile fade. "I took my job seriously, Kris. For the last thirteen years, I worked my ass off to make sure nothing scared her, nothing hurt her, nothing touched her." He shoved the bandanna back in his pocket and stood up. "This one time…I messed up. She fell, hit her head. Six stitches, right here." He ran one long finger along his hairline, near the temple, where beads of sweat had collected. "For a long time, I thought that's what caused her problems. I hated myself for that. Swore I'd never slack off again."

Oh, God. The playground. He'd never get past that. My heart gave a tight squeeze. "Elijah, I am so—"

He put up a hand. "No. It's not your fault. It's not," he repeated, taking my hand when I frowned. "Kris, the truth is, my parents are right. Anna's growing up. She's getting stronger, and her episodes more frequent." He spread his hands. "And none of us are pros." He shut his eyes. "She needs more, Kris. More than just us." He opened his bottle, poured some water over his head, and shook the wet hair from his eyes. "I keep telling myself she's better off there. But underneath that,

I'm all… Aw, fuck. I actually *want* her to have some sort of a giant meltdown so they kick her out."

He finally lifted his eyes to mine. "Tell me I'm not really that big of a selfish douche bag."

"For which part?" I laughed.

But when it was obvious he wasn't seeing the humor, I nudged him. "Come on, Elijah. You're giving her a world that's *hers* instead of forcing her to adapt to ours. That's pretty damn unselfish if you asked me."

He still didn't look convinced, so I tried again. "Besides, you have a connection with Anna nobody else does. Music. All you have to do is sing, Elijah. She'll remember."

He stared at me for a long moment and then smiled. "Yeah," he agreed. "Yeah." He tapped his bottle to mine and swallowed some water. "I was a real dick to you, and I'm not sure why you stuck around as long as you did, but I'm so glad you did."

My mouth went dry. "Really? You haven't figured it out yet? I thought you were smart."

He shot me a look that was all smirk, and if my mouth hadn't already dried up, I'd have drooled. "Figured what out?" he asked.

"You know." I lowered my eyes, suddenly afraid to say it out loud.

"I wanna hear you say it. Don't make me tweet it." He smirked.

A laugh burst out of me, and I rubbed my hands over the stubble on his cheeks. "I love you, Guitar Hero."

"Love you right back, Broadway," he whispered and kissed me. The cheers still coming from the crowd provided our very own soundtrack.

ELIJAH

> **The Beat:** *account deleted*
> **Facebook:** *account deactivated*
> **Twitter:** *account suspended*

"Uh, guys? Sorry to interrupt but…" Nick poked his head around the stage. "There's somebody here who wants to talk to us—*all* of us." He jerked his chin at Kristen.

She met my eyes, and I just shrugged. I had no damn clue. I took her hand and followed Nick back around to the front of the stage where the crowd had already left, probably filling their bellies with popcorn, cotton candy, and funnel cake before waiting on yet another insanely long line for one more ride on the Ferris wheel.

Two dudes sat on empty seats by center stage, dressed in khakis and ball caps bearing a logo that—

Holy shit.

I knew that logo. It was Island Sound, a record label.

Kristen squeezed the hand I nearly forgot she was holding, and immediately, I found my center. I nodded amiably. Sam's face was red, and Nick's knees bounced to a rhythm only he could hear, but judging by the tempo, it was either bounce or he was gonna launch into orbit.

Dude One held out a hand. "So this is Ride Out?" he asked with a grin. "I'm Bryce Morton, and this is Cameron Finnley."

Bryce handed us each a business card bearing the Island Sound logo—a map of Long Island bent into an eighth note—that listed him as a producer.

Holy hell.

"Cam and I have been following your tweets since the first CatCall hashtag. The whole Eli Versus Kris thing was a stroke of brilliance."

Cameron spoke up. "Marketing genius aside, you guys are way more than just talk. You back it up with solid talent. Based on the reaction we just heard, you've got the potential to top the charts. That's where we come in." Cameron looked back at Bryce, who leaned forward, smiling for a moment before asking us the one question I'd wanted to hear for half my life.

"Assuming your parents go for it, how would you guys like to cut an album with us?"

"Hell, yeah!" Sam pumped a fist in the air before I could call for a conference.

"Me, too." Nick held up a hand for a high five.

"Elijah?"

I held up a hand, wishing I could freeze this moment and put it under glass to preserve it forever.

This was it.

I was a rock star.

The one thing I'd wanted more than anything I'd ever wanted before. Or the one thing I *needed*—the one thing that was going to solve every problem. Money, providing trained caregivers to Anna, taking the pressure off my parents—everything. And here it was, extended on fancy-ass business cards, and I was just sitting there, stunned because it suddenly wasn't the *only* thing. Did I *need* this or did I *want* it? Those were now two very different questions.

"Elijah. Bro, come on." Sam slapped my arm.

"Give us a minute." I stood up, held out my hand to Kristen, and jerked my head at the guys. All of us walked a few feet away, aware of the eyes drilling into our backs.

"Holy shit, Eli. This is it." Nick mock-punched my arm.

"Yeah. It is. I just want to make sure we all still want it. There's still a year of school left. You know our parents are gonna give us grief over that."

Sam cursed. "Yeah. True."

"Yeah, but you heard that tall dude. He said they'd have to get our parents approval too."

I rubbed both hands over my face hoping to get the blood pumping because this still felt like a dream. "The truth is, if we do this, we'll have to work harder than we ever did before. It won't be just jam sessions in my garage on Saturday mornings. It'll be every day. There won't be time for things like football. Or drama club," I added, turning to Kristen. Her blue eyes were bright and her face flushed and she looked so beautiful, and I knew I could do this—*would* do this—no matter

what her answer was, and that really fucking scared me. I just got her...
and now, I could lose her.

"Kris, no pressure. You already know what my answer will be, but
I need to know what you want to do."

"I get a vote?"

Beside me, Sam shifted and shoved his hands in the pockets of his
jeans. "Okay, look. I was a total ass to you."

Kristen waited a minute and then rolled her hands. "And?"

"And I'm sorry for it."

"And?"

Sam cursed and shot his eyes toward heaven. "And I was wrong.
You got some wicked pipes, and we would not be standing here, having
this discussion, if it wasn't for you. So this happens for us only if you're
part of us."

Kristen chewed her lower lip, eyes darting back to the record
label guys. "You guys know I did this just for something to put on my
conservatory applications, right?"

Nick scratched the back of his neck, a shadow crossing over his
face. He looked away. "Yeah. But that was before."

He left it at that. Before Anna went away. Before Etta had a stroke.
Before everything went wrong.

Kristen nodded.

I squeezed her hand. "If you still want to do that, we need to know
now so we can tell them."

She took a deep breath and nodded, eyes filling up with tears. "I
still really want to do that."

And then she pulled her hand free.

I studied her for a long moment, blood pounding in my ears. I watched her chewing her lip, the tears falling down her face, and knew her gut was probably churning right now, just like mine. But it wasn't just the gut. It was the heart too. I loved this girl, and I think maybe I'd loved her since I heard the first note she ever sang. When that heart seemed to twist behind my ribs, it was because I held the power to make her biggest dream happen—like she'd just done for me. If I loved her, didn't I *have* to give her that? Didn't I owe her that much?

I turned and walked back to center stage, where we'd left Cameron and Bryce. I cleared my throat and looked directly at them. "You guys just made a dream come true for us. But it's a no."

Sam made a choking sound. Nick's hand came down to my shoulder and squeezed.

"I'm really sorry." I spoke to the record label guys, but I was apologizing to everyone. "I can't do this without Kristen, and she wants to do the college thing. A conservatory." I thought the words would get stuck in my throat.

But they came out easy.

Because this was *right*. Kristen may not have been with us when we started Ride Out. But she was one of us now. So we'd wait…as long as it took, we'd wait until *all* of us were ready for the next step.

Bryce and Cameron exchanged a glance. "When you're ready, make sure you talk to us before you deal with any other label, okay?"

I laughed and shook their hands. "Deal."

I looked at Kristen, standing a bit away from us, tears rolling down her cheeks. Her family surrounded her, all wearing identical looks of extreme pride—except one of her brothers. He looked at her like she was nuts. I laughed and walked over to her, and she put a hand on my face.

"You said no?"

I shut my eyes and nodded.

"But this is what you always wanted."

I nodded again. "Yeah. But now there's something I want even more."

A throat cleared. "We'll just give you a moment." Kristen's dad smiled tightly and began pushing Etta's wheelchair over the rutted ground. They'd made it to the fence around the stage when Etta stuck her hand in the air, and Kristen and I both burst into rib-cracking laughs.

Rock on, her hand said.

We would.

EPILOGUE

"So, Elijah. You're notoriously private and haven't granted an interview since that county festival back when you were seventeen. Does this sudden reversal on sharing your personal life have anything to do with being back on Long Island, just an hour's drive away from the Tony Awards, where odds are, Kristen Cartwright will take home an award? Does it hurt, knowing she's a success without you?"

I flash my trademark smirk while Savannah Roberts, the current NBC daytime darling, crosses her very nice legs and sits back, waiting for me to confirm or deny, and I have to suppress an eye roll because it's so obvious that Savannah is new at her job.

I'm not.

We're sitting in my studio…one of many additions to the house I'd made when the money started flowing. Nick, Sam, and I are sitting on the old stools I'd saved from our days in my parents' garage. Across the room is Frank, our manager, and all of Savannah's people—makeup artist, producer, sound guy, lighting guy, and assistant. Sitting on a low table in front of us is our Grammy for Best New Artist.

The Grammy, plus the release of our third album, means we have to do some press. I'd learned years back that people make up their own shit to fill in the gaps in our narrative, and I'm fine with that so long as they leave Anna out of it. I'd agreed to this interview because Savannah's people had promised to keep questions about Anna off the table, which was apparently the green light to double her assault on Kristen. And her first volley is a hard one to let go by.

If I say yes, people would assume I mean it hurts. If I say no, people would assume that I agree with the rest of the statement…that Kristen's a success despite her association with us…or worse, that she's the reason we'd won a Grammy.

I sit back, tilt my head, and share our version of the truth—one Sam, Nick, Kristen, and I had planned ahead of time, knowing this question would come up. "Savannah, I know I speak for Sam and Nick on this… We're excited and pretty damn proud of Kristen. Nobody's worked harder than she has, and it's awesome to see her rewarded."

"Oh, aren't you sweet?" Savannah smiles, and I wonder if the camera would pick up the lipstick on her teeth. "Does this mean you'll be attending the Tony Awards?"

"You'll just have to tune in later and see." I wink. Another thing I'd learned is never to reveal my plans. People can't swarm around you if they don't know where you'll be. The phony smile plastered to her face doesn't waver, but her eyes flash.

Keep diggin', baby.

She flips over a note card and shoots me a calculating look. "Let's talk about your music, Elijah. Ride Out's at the top of the charts, your first two albums have gone gold, your third was just released and is already predicted to go multiplatinum, *and* you've got a Grammy in your hands. Are the rumors true that Ride Out's creative genius is all Kristen?"

Savannah Roberts doesn't know jack about our music or about Kristen or even about me. I catch Nick's eye, silently asking permission to mess with this chick. He nods, a tiny lowering of his chin. *Go ahead, bro.*

"Savannah, here's the thing. Everything that happened to me, to us, to my family—it all goes into the stories we tell in the songs we write."

Savannah checks one of her cards. "Yes, your family. I understand your sister is on the spectrum?"

I freeze. Anna is off-limits.

We'd agreed.

I glance at Frank, our manager, and when he shakes his head, I make a mental note to make sure Savannah Roberts is never welcomed back. "She is. It's sad that we still know so little about curing autism. That's why the band established a charity in my sister's name."

"Anna's Song."

I feed her the PR line. "That's right. Music has a beneficial effect on kids like Anna, and we wanted to help fund more research into its use. Anna's one of the reasons why so many of our songs have such a strong and brash percussive element. She responds well to rhythm."

"That's incredible, Elijah." She turns to my bandmates and laughs. "Sam and Nick, do you contribute anything? Does it bother you that Elijah's written nearly every song on three albums?"

Whoa, what? First, Kristen's the genius, and now it's *me*? I fight the urge to glance in Sam and Nick's direction because if I do, it might be seen as agreement with her thinly veiled suggestion that they do not contribute.

"Uh, well, they say I'm the heartbeat of the band," Nick says, tapping a beat on his thighs.

Sam laughs. "Right, and *they* also say I play a mean guitar."

Savannah laughs for the camera. "Who are *they*? Your fans?"

I shake my head and pull the ship back on course. "Critics, mostly, but the fans are pretty vocal too. Seriously, Savannah, Sam's got a sharp ear for tone. I may draft some lyrics to a new song, and we'll try it out in the booth, and it'll just lie there lifeless. He can carve away the blocks and smooth out the protrusions until what's left is pure and perfect." Before she can interrupt with another lame-ass question, I give Nick some props. "And Nick understands the way music moves through time. Good drummers can do that…distill the sound down to beats and fill them with the right mood. But truly excellent drummers like Nick can do that with every part of a song. Both of them are geniuses."

"I love you, man!" Nick mugs for the camera, and Sam and I both laugh.

Savannah sees through the maneuver. "Still it must be hard with all of you so talented not to bruise egos," she adds sweetly.

"What egos?" I revel in the frustration she's trying so hard to hide. "Look, we just all do whatever needs doing. Sam had an idea that became 'Let You In,' from when he went through a painful breakup. Nick wrote 'Pretty Sly' when he saw this girl trying to snare a guy at an airport."

"And you wrote 'The Way It Hurts' with Kristen Cartwright."

Before I can respond, she's swiping the tablet on the table in front of us. "Kristen, are you there? Can you hear us?"

The tablet flickers, and a moment later, Kristen's stage smile lights up the screen. "Yes, I'm here. Hello, Savannah."

"Thanks for joining us. It must be pretty exciting. First a Grammy, and now, you're up for a Tony."

"I won't lie, it feels pretty amazing. Our single, 'The Way It Hurts,' was just released, and that was a special moment for all of us, but for me…and for Eli…it was *the* moment."

"*The* moment? Does this mean the rumors about the two of you breaking up and then reuniting over that song are true?"

I laugh. Savannah has obviously done her research but had reached the wrong conclusions.

"Not exactly. We never broke up over the song. We broke up because of Twitter." Kristen wrinkles her nose. She *still* hasn't returned to social networking.

"Twitter?" Savannah echoes.

"No," I cut in. "It was because of Rawr."

"Roar? What's Roar?" Savannah asks, but we don't answer the question. I wave a hand. Like so many things on the Internet, Rawr is gone now and good riddance.

"Doesn't matter. The important thing is we not only got past those challenges, we used them to write an even better version of the song."

"Oh, yes. There are now four versions of that song, is that right?"

"Fourth time's the charm," Kristen says from the tiny speakers.

"Millions of fans agree, if we go by the download stats," Nick adds.

"Yes, let's talk about the album." Savannah shifts gears neatly. "Is it true you said no to Island Sound when you were all just seventeen years old?"

Kristen laughs. "Not exactly. *I* said no. The boys said yes."

Savannah's polite smile curves a bit more deeply when she smells blood in the water. "The boys recorded without you?"

"Not exactly," I repeat Kristen's words. "We'd agreed from the beginning that any success we achieved had to be all or none, so when Kristen said she wanted to pursue conservatory study and then Broadway, we turned down the deal."

"So you did say no?"

"But Island Sound wouldn't accept that," Sam confirms. "They offered to record Ride Out first and then Ride Out featuring Kristen Cartwright later, whenever Kristen was ready." He waves his hand over an imaginary marquee.

"And that was fine with me since singing metal is a lot harder than it sounds. That's also why 'The Way It Hurts' wasn't included on the debut album," Kristen finishes. "It was *our* song, and we agreed to hold it back until I had time to record."

"It's your song, Kris. It was always for you." I meet Kris's eyes, and she smiles.

"And now it's a number one single." Savannah holds up the CD case. "Congratulations to you all, and break a leg tonight, Kristen."

At that, the producer stops the action, and the lights and camera are shut down. An assistant scurries over, disconnects the mics clipped to our collars, and that's that. Savannah and her entourage exit without a word. When the last of the equipment is packed away and the crew is finally out of my house, I fall to the sofa. "Hell, Frank. What was that chick's problem?"

"I'm on it." Frank had his phone to his ear and strode out after Savannah and her crew.

I rip the elastic out of my hair. "Jeez, that was painful."

Sam shakes his head. "No, bro. You were clutch." He clenches a fist.

"Yeah, you were great!" the tablet squeaks.

"Hey, Broadway. I miss you." I smile at my girl.

Kristen grins back. "Hey, Guitar Hero. When will you be here?"

"I'll be there tonight."

"Sam, Nick, you guys are coming too, right?"

Sam's face splits into an evil grin. His long blond hair is tied up in a man bun that nearly broke Twitter the first time he wore it in public. "Wouldn't miss it, Yoko."

Kristen giggles and flips him off. "Okay, see you later. Eli, give Anna a hug for me."

The screen flickers again, and she's gone.

"When's the car coming?" Nick asks, dragging his T-shirt over his head and heading for the bathroom.

"Six. We've got some time." I pull my suit out of a closet and toss it over a chair. "You guys get dressed. I'll be back in a bit."

On the patio at the back of the house, I find my sister. Anna sits in the special hot tub I had built for her. Sienna, one of her aides, is in the water with her. Linda, one of the first aides she'd ever had, is on the bench beside them. I'd wanted to move, but Anna likes this house, so with my parents' blessing, I brought in contractors because I figured Anna might like the house even more if it liked her back. She's got the hot tub, I've got a soundproof recording studio, Dad's got a new greenhouse, and Mom's got lots of help.

I watch her for a long moment. She's all grown up now—so beautiful with her dark hair and blue eyes and musical genius. Oh, we'd have ripped the charts apart if—

If. My heart squeezes behind my ribs, and I shake it off.

"Anna banana."

"Eli." She looks up and then away. At nineteen, Anna is still prone to outbursts of violent temper. She spent a few years in the residence, and at the time, it was good for her. Maybe even the best thing. But she lives at home again with around-the-clock professional caregivers who Linda helped us hire so my parents can have something that used to be a luxury to them: permission to be Nathan and Stephanie once in a while.

"How's she been today?" I ask Sienna, the aide in the pool with her. Sienna's about my age but insists on calling me Mr. Hamilton.

"Today's been a good day, Mr. Hamilton. She's been calm and extra verbal. She answered questions."

Whoa. That's definitely a good day. I crouch down and try to draw her eye. "Anna, how does the water feel?"

She looks at her hands in the water and holds them up. "Water's warm, Eli."

And then she looks up, flashes that heartbreaking smile, and I'm gone. I stare at the water, and a slow smile forms. I take a cautious look around. "Sienna, where are my parents?"

"Um, Mr. Hamilton is in the front yard, trimming hedges, and Mrs. Hamilton is out."

Out. Out where? The hell with it...doesn't matter. Grinning wide, I take the important stuff out of my pockets, kick off my shoes, and climb down into the tub. Linda rolls her eyes.

"Eli." Anna smiles at me. "Sing."

"Yes, ma'am. What should we sing? La la?" "Brown Eyed Girl" is still her favorite.

But not today. Anna shakes her head. "Kris."

My heart stutters and then takes off racing. Kris's song. Does she know about the Tony Awards? Is this Anna's way of acknowledging that? "Sienna, do you know the words to 'Carol of the Bells'?"

She shrugs. "I think so."

"How about you, Linda?"

"No, not really."

"Okay. I'll sing the lead, and you guys come in with ding-dongs when I give you the sign, okay?"

"Ding-dongs?" Sienna looks at Linda who just shakes her head.

"Don't worry. Just follow Anna."

I take a deep breath and sing the first verse and then give the ladies a signal to join in.

"Elijah!"

Busted. I shut my eyes, cursing silently. I look up and find Mom's furious face looking down at us.

"How many times—"

"Steph, leave the kids alone. They're having fun." Dad walks over to us, a few clippings stuck to his hair. "In fact, I think I'll join them." And fully dressed, Dad steps into the hot tub, picking up the ding-dong part Anna adores.

I start the song all over again, Anna's clear high voice ringing out over the yard, overpowering the flat and slightly off-key voices of her backup group. Mom watches us for a few beats and then flings up her hands. "Oh, fine!" she says, and steps into the tub with a giggle. We can spend the next twenty minutes serenading our neighbors with Christmas carols in June before the limo arrives to take me to the city, to my girl.

But for now…there's time. I watch my sister, rocking back and forth, singing *ding-dong* in perfect pitch, while Dad tugs Mom onto his lap, which makes her giggle again. We start the song again when Nick and Sam climb in with us.

I catch their eye. Sam presses a noisy kiss to my cheek, and Nick just shakes his head. I ease back, settle into the warmth of the water, content, and yeah, even happy, but it's *not* because we're big-time famous rock stars.

It's because we're still *us*.

Okay, but being big-time famous rock stars is pretty cool too.

ACKNOWLEDGMENTS

If you ask authors where they get their ideas, you'll hear them tell you that ideas are everywhere. You just have to open yourself up to them.

That's exactly how this story was born. I have an active social media presence, and because I write issue-driven novels, I find it extremely hard to remain silent and uninvolved whenever I witness injustice. Social media gives equal weight to every voice, and it also amplifies and boosts the signal of those who'd otherwise never be heard. Sometimes, this is a good thing. But when the voice shouting the loudest urges violence and hatred, I feel compelled to shout just as loud against it.

It was during such a Twitter firestorm when this idea was born. My eternal gratitude to Kimberly Sabatini, an awesome author (*Touching the Surface*) who patiently exchanged emails with me while I debated this idea's merits. I've never met Kimberly in person but count her as a true friend…one of the many benefits of social media when it's done right. When it's done wrong, the result is what you read in this book. Social media shouldn't be used to harass and threaten and mock and bully but to educate, to share, to enlighten, and to encourage.

Okay, enough preaching.

I owe all the thanks in the world to Evan Gregory, my agent, and to Aubrey Poole, my first editor, who believed in me enough to take a risk. Good luck to you in your future endeavors! Thank you also to Annette, my new editor, and everyone at Sourcebooks Fire—a more creative and enthusiastic team can't possibly exist. Did you *see* this artwork? I'm amazed and proud to work with you all. Thank you!

Thank you to my incredibly talented writing pals of the LIRW, CTRWA, and YARWA chapters of RWA, who provide so much inspiration and support. I think I'd still be writing fan fiction if I hadn't found you. (Don't ask.) Special thanks to Leslie Anne Bard, whose loan of dictation software after a newly diagnosed autoimmune disease prevented me from touching a keyboard for months helped me get this manuscript delivered only few months late.

Thank you to Shaun, Dale, and John, the members of Seether, for trusting me with your lyrics. "Words as Weapons" is a personal favorite of mine and *had* to be part of this story, and I'm so grateful to you for its use.

Thank you to my sons, Rob and Chris, who continue to kick my butt whenever I question my abilities—in other words, every day—and my husband, Fred, for a few hundred little things but also for patiently listening to every single song lyric in this story sung karaoke style without once bleeding from the eardrums.

Finally, thank you to my readers and book bloggers (especially Alyssa, the Eater of Books) and fans who look for me at signings and conventions or send me tweets and emails and never, ever download bootleg copies of books (right?). You remind me why I continue doing work that fills me with equal shots of anxiety and pride—because my words matter to *you*.

Rock on.

ABOUT THE AUTHOR

Powered by way too much chocolate, award-winning author Patty Blount loves to write and has written everything from technical manuals to poetry (and now, song lyrics!). A 2015 CLMP Firecracker Award winner as well as Rita finalist, Patty writes issue-based novels for teens and is currently working on a romantic thriller. Her editor claims she writes her best work when she's mad, so if you happen to upset Patty and don't have any chocolate on hand to throw at her, prepare to be the subject of an upcoming novel. Patty lives on Long Island with her family in a house that sadly doesn't have anywhere near enough bookshelves…or chocolate.

No Monday in history has ever sucked more than this one.

I'm kind of an expert on sucky days. It's been thirty-two of them since the party in the woods that started the battle I fight every day. I step onto the bus to school, wearing my armor and pretending nothing's wrong, nothing happened, nothing changed when it's pretty obvious nothing will ever be the same again. Alyssa Martin, a girl I've known since first grade, smirks and stretches her leg across the empty seat next to hers.

I approach slowly, hoping nobody can see my knees knocking. A couple of weeks ago during a school newspaper staff meeting, Alyssa vowed her support, and today I'm pond scum.

"Find a seat!" Mrs. Gannon, the bus driver, shouts.

I meet Alyssa's eyes, silently beg her for sympathy—even a little pity. She raises a middle finger. It's a show of loyalty to someone who doesn't deserve it, a challenge to see how far I'll go. My dad keeps telling me to stand up to all of Zac's defenders, but it's the entire bus—the entire *school*—versus me.

I gulp hard, and the bus lurches forward. I try to grab a seat back but lose my balance and topple into the seat Alyssa's blocking with her leg. She lets out a screech of pain.

"Bitch," she sneers. "You nearly broke my leg."

I'm about to apologize when I notice the people sitting around us stare with wide eyes and hands over their open mouths. When my eyes meet theirs, they turn away, but nobody *does* anything.

This is weird.

Alyssa folds herself against the window and shoves earbuds into her ears and ignores me for the duration of the ride.

The rest of the trip passes without incident—except for two girls whispering over a video playing on a phone they both clutch in their hands. One of them murmurs, "Six hundred and eighteen hits," and shoots me a dirty look.

I know exactly what she means and don't want to think about it. I look away. As soon as the bus stops, I'm off. On my way to my locker, most people just ignore me, although a few still think they've come up with a clever new insult. An elbow or the occasional extended foot still needs dodging, but it's really not that bad. I can deal. I can do this. I can make it through school unless I see—

"Woof! Woof!"

My feet root themselves to the floor, and the breath clogs in my lungs. And I know without turning who barked at me. I force myself to keep walking instead of running for home, running for the next town. I want to turn to look at him, look him dead in the eye, and twist my face into something that shows contempt instead of the terror that too often wins whenever I hear his name so he sees—so he *knows*—he didn't beat me. But that doesn't happen. A foot appears from nowhere, and I can't dodge it in time. I fall to my hands and knees, and two more familiar faces step out of the crowd to laugh down at me.

"Hear you like it on your knees," Kyle Moran shouts, and everybody laughs. At least Matt Roberts helps me up, but when Kyle smacks his head, he takes off before I can thank him. They're two of *his* best buds. Nausea boils inside me, and I scramble back to my feet. I grab my backpack, pray that the school's expensive digital camera tucked inside it isn't damaged, and duck into the girls' bathroom, locking myself into a stall.

When my hands are steady, eyes are dry, stomach's no longer threatening to send back breakfast, I open the stall.

Miranda and Lindsay, my two best friends, stand in front of the mirrors.

Make that *former* best friends.

We stare at one another through the mirrors. Lindsay leans against a sink but doesn't say anything. Miranda runs a hand down her smooth blond hair, pretends I'm not there, and talks to Lindsay. "So I've decided to have a party and invite Zac and the rest of the lacrosse team. It's going to be epic."

No. Not him. The blood freezes in my veins. "Miranda. Don't. Please."

Miranda's hand freezes on her hair. "Don't, please?" She shakes her head in disgust. "You know, he could get kicked off the lacrosse team because of you."

"Good!" I scream, suddenly furious.

Miranda whips back around to face me, hair blurring like a fan blade. At the sink, Lindsay's jaw drops. "God! I can't believe you! Did you do all of this, say all this just to get back at me?"

My jaw drops. "What? Of course not. I—"

"You *know* I like him. If you didn't want me to go out with him, all you had to do was say so—"

"Miranda, this isn't about you. Trust me, Zac is—"

"Oh my God, listen to yourself. He breaks up with you, and you fall apart and then—"

"That is *not* what happened. I broke up with him! I was upset that night because of Kristie, and you know it."

She spins around, arms flung high. "Kristie! Seriously? You played him. You wanted everybody to feel sorry for you, so you turned on the tears and got Zac to—"

"Me? Are you insane? He—"

"Oh, don't even." Miranda holds up a hand. "I know exactly what happened. I was there. I know what you said. I figured you were lying, and now there's no doubt."

Lindsay nods and tosses her bag over her shoulder, and they stalk to the door. At the door, Miranda fires off one more shot. "You're a lying slut, and I'll make sure the whole school knows it."

The door slams behind them, echoing off the lavatory stalls. I'm standing in the center of the room, wondering what's holding me up because I can't feel my feet…or my hands. I raise them to make sure I still have hands, and before my eyes, they shake. But I don't feel that either. All I feel is pressure in my chest like someone just plunged my head underwater and I tried to breathe. My mouth goes dry, but I can't swallow. The pressure builds and grows and knocks down walls and won't let up. I press my hands to my chest and rub, but it doesn't help. Oh, God, it doesn't help. My heart lurches into overdrive like it's trying to stage a prison break. I fall to the cold bathroom floor, gasping, choking for breath, but I can't get any. I can't find any. There's no air left to breathe. I'm the lit match in front of a pair of lips puckered up, ready to blow.

Minutes pass, but they feel like centuries. I fumble for my phone—my mom's phone since she made me switch with her—and call her.

"Grace, what's wrong?"

"Can't breathe, Mom. Hurts," I push out the words on gasps of air.

"Okay, honey, I want you to take a breath and hold it. One, two, three, and let it out."

I follow her instructions, surprised I have any breath in my lungs to hold for three seconds. The next breath is easier.

"Keep going. Deep breath, hold it, let it out."

It takes me a few tries, but finally I can breathe without the barrier. "Oh, God."

"Better?"

"Yeah. It doesn't hurt now."

"Want me to take you home?"

Oh, *home*. Where there are no laughing classmates pointing at me, whispering behind their hands. Where there are no ex-friends calling me a bitch or a liar. Where I could curl up, throw a blanket over my head, and pretend nothing happened. *Yes, take me home. Take me home right now as fast as you can.*

I want to say that. But when I glance in the mirror over the row of sinks, something makes me say, "No. I have to stay."

"Grace—"

"Mom, I have to stay."

There's a loud sigh. "Oh, honey. You don't have to be brave."

Brave.

The word hangs in the air for a moment and then falls away, almost like even it knows it has no business being used to describe me. I'm not brave. I'm scared. I'm so freakin' scared, I can't see straight, and I can't see straight because I'm too scared to look very far. I'm a train wreck. All I'm doing is trying to hold on to what I have left. Only I'm not sure what that is. When I say nothing, she laughs too loudly. "Well, you're wearing your father's favorite outfit, so just pretend it's a superhero costume."

That makes me laugh. I glance down at my favorite boots—black leather covered in metal studs. My ass-kicking boots. Ever since Dad married Kristie, Mom lets me get away with anything that pisses him off, and wow does he hate how I dress.

"Grace, if you feel the pressure in your chest again, take a deep breath, hold it, and count. Concentrating on counting helps keep your mind from spiraling into panic."

"Yeah. Okay." But I'm not at all convinced. "I missed most of first period."

"Skip it. Don't worry about getting in trouble. Where are you now?"

"Bathroom."

"Why don't you go to the library? Relax and regroup, you know?"

Regroup. Sure. Okay. "Yeah. I'll do that."

"If you need me to get you, I'll come. Okay?"

I meet my own gaze in the mirror, disgusted to see them fill with tears. Jeez, you'd think I'd be empty by now. "Thanks, Mom." I end the call, tuck the phone in my pocket, and head for the library.

The library is my favorite spot in the whole school. Two floors of books, rows of computers, soft chairs to slouch in. I head for the nonfiction section and find the 770s. This is where the photography books live—my stack. I run a finger along the spines and find the first book I ever opened on the subject—*A History of Photography*.

I pull the book off its shelf, curl up with it in a chair near a window, and flip open the back cover. My signature is scrawled on the checkout card so many times now that we're old friends. I know how this book smells—a little like cut grass. How it feels—the pages are thick and glossy. And even where every one of its scars lives—the coffee ring on page 213 and the dog-eared corner in chapter 11. This is the book that said, "Grace, you *are* a photographer."

I flip through the pages, reread the section on high-key technique—I love how that sounds. *High-key.* So professional. It's really just great big fields of bright white filled with a splash of color or sometimes only shadow. I took hundreds of pictures this way—of Miranda, of Lindsay, of me. I practiced adjusting aperture settings and shutter speeds and overexposing backgrounds. It's cool how even the simplest subjects look calm and cheerful. It's like the extra light forces us to see the beauty and the flaws we never noticed.

I unzip my backpack and take out the school's digital camera. It's assigned to me—official student newspaper photographer. I scroll through the images stored on the card—selfies I shot over the last few weeks. Why can't everybody see what I see? My eyes don't sparkle. My lips don't curve anymore. Why don't they *see*?

I shove the camera back in my bag. With a sigh, I close the book, and a slip of paper floats to the floor. I pick it up, unfold it, and my stomach twists when I read the words printed on it. A noise startles me, and I look up to see Tyler Embery standing at one of the computers. Did he slip this paper into my favorite book? He's had a painfully obvious crush on me forever. Every time he gets within five feet of me, his face flushes and sweat beads at his hairline. Tyler volunteers at the library during his free periods and always flags me over to give me the latest issue of *Shutterbug* that he sets aside for me as soon as it arrives. He grabs something off the desk and walks over to me. I smile, thankful there's still one person left in this world that doesn't think Zac McMahon is the second coming of Christ. But Tyler's not holding a magazine. He's holding his phone.

"Six-eighty-three." There's no blush, no sweat—only disgust.

I jerk like he just punched me. I guess in a way he has. He turns, heads to the magazine rack, and places this month's issue, in its clear plastic cover, face out, in a subtle *fuck you* only I'd notice. I stuff the paper into my backpack and hurry to the exit just as the bell rings.

I make it to the end of the day. At dismissal I make damn sure I'm early for the bus ride home so I can snag an empty row. I plug in my earbuds to drown out the taunts. *It's not so bad*, I tell myself repeatedly, the taste of tears at the back of my throat familiar now. I don't believe me.

Once safely back in my house, I let my shoulders sag and take my first easy breath of the day. The house is empty and eerie, and I wonder how to fill the hours until Mom gets home. Thirty-two days ago I'd have been hanging out after school with Miranda and Lindsay or shopping at the mall or trying to find the perfect action photo at one of the games. In my room, I stare at the mirror over my dresser, where dozens of photos are taped—photos of me with my friends, me with my dad, me at dance class. I'm not welcome at any of these places, by any of these people anymore. I don't have a damn thing because Zac McMahon took it all. I think about Mom killing all of my online accounts and switching phones *just until things settle.* But now that the video of me that Zac posted on Facebook has 683 Likes, it's pretty clear that waiting for *things to settle* is a fantasy.

I rip all the pictures off the mirror, tear them into tiny pieces, and swipe them into the trash bin next to my desk. Then I pull out the slip of paper I found in the photography book, and after a few minutes of staring at it, I dial the number with shaking hands.

"Rape Crisis Hotline, this is Diane. Let me help you."